Heat Wave

A Novel

Jill Marie Landis

BALLANTINE BOOKS • NEW YORK

Heat Wave is a work of fiction. Names, characters, places, and incidents are the products of the author's imagination or are used fictitiously. Any resemblance to actual events, locales, or persons, living or dead, is entirely coincidental.

2005 Ballantine Books Mass Market Edition

Published in the United States by Ballantine Books, an imprint of The Random House Publishing Group, a division of Random House, Inc., New York.

Ballantine and colophon are registered trademarks of Random House, Inc.

Originally published in hardcover in the United States by Ballantine Books, an imprint of The Random House Publishing Group, a division of Random House, Inc., in 2004.

This book contains an excerpt from the forthcoming book *Heartbreak Hotel* by Jill Marie Landis. This excerpt has been set for this edition only and may not reflect the final content of the forthcoming edition.

ISBN 0-345-45325-5

Printed in the United States of America

Ballantine Books website address: www.ballantinebooks.com

OPM 9 8 7 6 5 4 3 2 1

TO ANN CARROLL,

TO HER MOM, JANET,

AND TO PAUL EDHOLM . . . AGAIN.

AND JIM SCHMITT
. . . HE KNOWS WHY.

TO MEL MONTGOMERY
FOR EMERGENCY HELP.

TO STEVE,
WHO PUTS UP WITH MY WHINING.

Heat Wave

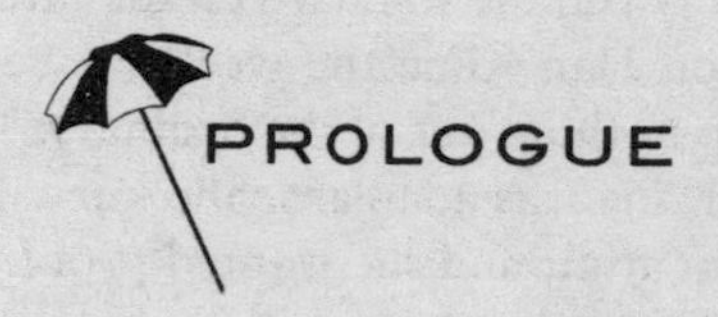

PROLOGUE

LONG BEACH, CALIFORNIA

Sometimes it paid not to answer the phone.

When the call for help came, Kat Vargas had just kicked off her shoes and sat down to eat a take-out Chinese chicken salad.

She slid wooden chopsticks out of their paper wrapper as she glanced at the caller I.D. It was Sandi Kline, a new client who suspected her husband was having an affair.

Kat picked up the phone, remembering the hollow sound of the woman's heart-wrenching sobs the day Sandi had first walked into the office.

Kat was no stranger to betrayal.

"Hi, Sandi." She tucked the phone between her ear and shoulder. Starving, she was tempted to take a bite of salad but spared Sandi having to hear her crunch a mouthful of cabbage.

"I found them!" The other woman's breathing was rapid and shallow, rasping over the line. "I followed him to the Seal Beach Inn and Gardens. They're in there right now. Together."

Kat's adrenaline spiked. She pictured the neat, old building built around a courtyard on a quiet residential street. The place was the quintessential bed-and-breakfast with lace curtains at every window. Trailing vines loaded with hanging cup of gold blossoms and morning glories clung to the exterior walls.

She'd already run the standard credit card checks and surveillance on Dan Kline the weekend before, but so far, turned up nothing out of the ordinary.

But Sandi Kline was adamant. She knew her husband was having an affair and she wanted proof. She wanted him to pay. She wanted more than half of everything they owned, and if what Sandi said was true, half was a considerable amount.

"Are you sure it's him?" Kat picked a slivered almond off the top of the salad and popped it into her mouth. "You definitely saw your husband go into the motel with someone?"

"No, but I saw him walk into the office alone, then he came out and went into the room. She must have gone in ahead of him. He's in there with her right now."

"Where are you?"

"Parked across the street from the inn."

"Look, Sandi. Go home. I'll drive over there and handle this." Kat glanced through the half-open mini-blinds, watched the rain streak the windowpane. "You don't have a birthday or anniversary coming up, do you? Maybe he's checking the place out, planning to surprise you with a getaway."

"Fat chance. The asshole is cheating on me. I *know* he's with another woman."

In Kat's experience there was always "another" someone. Another woman. Another man. She was convinced happy endings were only for romance novels and that ninety percent of the population shouldn't even bother getting married.

No "other woman" would suddenly be appearing in her life again. Once was more than enough.

"Please, Kat. Meet me here." Sandi Kline's voice broke.

Kat set the Styrofoam take-out box on her coffee table. Mrs. Kline had done her own legwork, but it would take a level head to get good pictures. Juicy photos always helped when lawyers started tossing deals on the table.

Kat shoved her salad aside, her appetite curbed by the rush of catching a wayward husband in the act. It might be raining cats and dogs out, but Sandi was her client and this was her job.

Besides, she was an insomniac by design anyway. Staying up all hours on surveillance helped keep her from facing her own nightmares. Still, she had already been on the job nearly twenty-four hours and was looking forward to unwinding with a new martial arts movie tonight—but Sandi's tears got to her.

She wasn't fond of driving around in the rain, not with the streets as slick as snot on a doorknob. But the woman's pitiful pleas had clamped on to Kat's heartstrings, inspiring her more than the thrill of the hunt or the hefty retainer Sandi was paying.

"Where are you exactly?" she wanted to know.

"I'm on the corner of Electric and Fifth. In the gold Mercedes station wagon."

"You go on home. I can be there in ten minutes and I'll get photos."

"I'll wait. He might come out before you get here."

Rain always reminded Kat of the worst night of her life. Tonight was no different. The wet streets glistened in the beams of her headlights. She drove carefully, slower than usual as she headed to Seal Beach. She forced herself to focus on the case and not the head-on collision she'd been involved in on Kauai five years ago.

That was old news. She ought to have let it go by now, but the ache hung on despite the fact she'd left her old life behind and thrown herself into her work.

Once she reached Seal Beach, she edged her red Honda CRV to the curb behind Sandi Kline's Mercedes station wagon and cut the engine. The woman stepped out of her car and rushed over to hover beside Kat's door. Kat rolled down the window.

"They're still in there," Sandi whispered, clutching the lapels of a long trench coat together.

"Why don't you go home and let me take it from here?" Kat glanced over at the B&B. "It could be hours before he comes out. Trust me to get photos. You don't need to do this to yourself." She shivered inside her hooded navy sweatshirt and pants.

"I want to confront him. Come with me."

Kat shook her head. "I'm a P.I., not a marriage counselor."

Sandi's fingers trembled uncontrollably as she tried to wipe her wet bangs off her forehead. Her wedding band with its huge solitaire diamond glistened beneath the glow of the nearby street lamp. Mascara smeared her cheeks, mingled with the rain, and her tears.

"I'll pay you double," Sandi tempted.

"I don't need the money." Not *that* badly anyway.

Sandi was a good fifty pounds overweight, her face puffy but still somewhat attractive. She wore her thin, dark brown hair short, framing her heavy cheeks, but her clear blue eyes, though bleak, were her best feature. She hugged her coat close, haunting the curb beside Kat's car. Rain blew through the open window, dampened the sleeve of Kat's sweatshirt.

"You don't realize what this is doing to me. How much this hurts. You can't imagine what I'm going through," Sandi said.

Kat clamped her jaw tight, tempted to tell Mrs. Kline that she knew exactly how much betrayal hurt. She didn't have to imagine what Sandi Kline was going through.

Which is why, against her better judgment, emotion won out and she gave in.

Camera in hand, she stepped out of her car and hit the alarm button. Her heartbeat accelerated as she anticipated seeing Creep Kline's face when they caught him red-handed.

She and Sandi fell silent as they diagonally crossed the intersection to stand in front of the narrow door that faced the street. Low light filtered through the shade behind the lace curtains at the window.

Kat hoped to God that Dan Kline was inside, that in Sandi's zeal to prove he was cheating, she hadn't mistaken some other poor bastard for her husband.

Then, without warning, Sandi Kline started beating on the door.

When no one answered, she intensified her pounding.

"Dan? Dan, you bastard! I know you're in there. Open this door!"

Another moment passed. A handful of frantic heartbeats.

Beside her, Sandi's breathing became labored. They heard a man's voice behind the door before it opened far enough to reveal a tall, good-looking guy with light blond hair. He was wrapped in a stark white terry-cloth robe. Six feet, bare-footed, medium build, an excellent specimen of manhood.

Sandi had given Kat a photograph of Dan Kline.

This was not Dan Kline.

Kat quickly reached for her client's arm. "Let's go, Sandi. Obviously you've made a mistake."

With surprising strength, Sandi shook her off. "I *know* I saw him go in this room. I know it."

"Then you're mistaken." Kat grabbed Sandi's elbow. The woman was becoming more distraught by the moment.

"I don't understand. I *saw* Dan go in there." Sandi stared at the silent man holding the door partially open. He didn't seem at all upset by the disturbance. In fact, a half smile, half smirk slowly hiked one corner of his lips. He glanced over his shoulder into the semi-dark room.

"This might be the perfect time to tell her, you think?" He stepped back, opening the door to reveal Dan Kline.

Dan was seated on the edge of a queen-sized bed, the sheet and nothing more draped around his hips, elbows propped on his knees, head supported by his hands.

The situation was immediately clear to Kat, but Sandi's gaze shot back and forth between her husband and the other man as if riveted by the final round of a tennis match.

Suddenly, Sandi shoved her hand into the deep pocket of her oversized coat and pulled out a handgun.

"Shit!" The blond man immediately raised his hands and reeled back. Sandi took aim at her husband.

Kat acted instinctively. Years of Tae Kwon Do training and discipline kicked in. She raised her arm and swung it in a downward arc, attempting to knock the gun out of Sandi's hand, but the woman lunged to the side and fired off a round.

The shot went wild. The sound of breaking glass fused with the echo of the gunshot reverberating in the small room.

Dan Kline bolted to his feet and ran toward them. Kat easily knocked Sandi off balance just as Dan reached his wife.

Sandi was still waving the gun around with a berserk look in her eyes. Kat raised her arm, and in that split second when she realized she was looking down the barrel of Sandi's gun, one thought streaked through her mind.

Not now. Not like this. I want—

Suddenly, Kat's left hand was on fire. The pain drove her to her knees. Nude, Dan Kline threw himself on Sandi and they hit the ground.

Kat's hand hurt like hell, but even through the intense pain, she knew she'd recover. This wasn't the worst thing that had ever happened to her. Not by a long shot.

But it had been one hell of a wake-up call.

Twelve hours later she was back in her apartment, sitting on the sofa with her bandaged hand cradled in her lap. Last night's Chinese chicken salad lay limp and ugly in the Styrofoam carton in the middle of the coffee table.

Her former partner, Jake Montgomery, was pacing around the room, driving her stark raving mad. He stopped long enough to close the lid on the salad carton and carry it to the overflowing rubbish can in the kitchen.

When he came back, he didn't sit. He loomed over her, shaking his head.

"Get up and show me what to pack for you, Vargas. You're coming home with me."

She refused to look at him. "You're making way too big a deal out of this, Jake."

"You were almost killed. That *is* a big deal."

"I was shot in the *hand*. It's practically a flesh wound."

"That's not the point. You were very, very lucky."

When his genuine concern got to her, she had to wipe her eyes. "I'm fine. And I'm not going to your place. Besides, you're leaving on vacation in four days."

"Exactly. That's why it's perfect timing. Carly's been

on me to find somebody to house-sit. You'll have the whole place to yourself for six weeks."

She glanced around her compact one-bedroom duplex apartment. The kitchen was just large enough to hold a stove and refrigerator. The bed barely fit in the back room. She wasn't the greatest housekeeper in the world—there was stuff piled everywhere.

"What in the hell would I do with a whole house?" *Besides mess it up.*

"Relax, for one. You rarely take a day off. You've been living on adrenaline and caffeine for so long that you're addicted to them."

"I don't need caffeine detox. I've got a business to run. By myself, thanks to you."

Fine partner he turned out to be. A year ago he'd split up their business, married, and moved to Twilight Cove, a small town sandwiched between Oceano and Pismo Beach up the coast.

He ignored her last comment altogether.

"While you were in surgery I called a friend who recently retired from Alexander and Perry. His name is Arnie Tate, and he'll be happy to step in and run things until you get back."

"Aren't you just the busy bee?" It was exactly like Jake to want to look out for her, to even go as far as to call in reinforcements. He'd started out at Alexander and Perry years ago. It was still one of the best investigative firms in the business.

He walked over to the other end of the sofa and sat down. The fact that he looked worn-out only added to her guilt. She hadn't called him last night, the hospital had—since he was listed as her emergency contact.

It was a sorry statement on her life that her only emergency contact lived three hours away.

"You've got to get a life, Kat. You're a twenty-nine-year-old workaholic."

"My life is just the way I want it." She'd designed it to be hurt-free, which meant that she stayed out of serious relationships by keeping busy. "Besides, you're one to talk. You wouldn't be bugging me about this if you hadn't changed your tune and fallen in love with Carly. Now you're born-again married!"

She needed a pain pill. Her hand hurt, almost as much as it hurt that Jake had found someone to love. Before he left the firm, they hadn't just been partners, they'd been kindred spirits who'd sworn off relationships.

He'd gone through a bitter divorce. She'd never married, but she'd been engaged once.

After years of waiting for the right guy to come along, convinced she was the oldest living virgin on Kauai, she'd finally given a man her trust, her love, and her virginity. His betrayal had hurt so deeply, the consequences so unbearable, that her life had been forever altered.

Unlike her, Jake had taken a chance again. He'd not only married, but adopted his wife's eight-year-old son. He had made a commitment to his new family. He had a life outside of private investigation. He'd found love and contentment.

Her job was all she had. It was all she wanted, at least that's what she'd thought until last night.

Most of the time she tried not to feel anything. Feeling brought back memories and memories were nothing but land mines buried in a field of pain. If she'd been *thinking* when she talked to Sandi Kline instead of feeling sorry for the woman, she'd have remembered that. She'd broken a cardinal rule when she put herself in Sandi's place and let her emotions take over.

In that stark, desperate moment when she thought her life *might* be over, she realized she wanted more. More time. More than being alone. She wanted more out of life, period.

"Kat?"

Finally she looked at Jake. It was odd seeing him in her apartment. She'd never had anyone over before.

"I'm not leaving you here alone." His tone was gentler, but firm.

"What am I supposed to do for six weeks in a place like Twilight Cove?" The idea of all that downtime was terrifying.

"There's a great view from the house. You can read. Watch movies. Stroll through town. Walk on the beach. Swim. Hike. If you give the place half a chance, you might like it. Maybe you'll meet somebody interesting. All you have to do is water Carly's garden and potted plants, pick up the mail. Make the place look lived in."

He stared at the chaos in her cluttered living room. "Shoot, we'll even keep the cleaning lady coming in."

"You can get a ten-year-old to water the plants and pick up the mail." She held up her bandaged hand. "I have to go to physical therapy sessions."

"You can do that in Twilight. If there's no therapist in town, you can drive over to San Luis Obispo. It's only a few minutes away." He noticed her stack of martial arts videos and CDs on the table beside the sofa. "You still watch these?" Jake picked up one of her old favorites, *Return of the Dragon*.

"Sure. It's fun to critique all the ridiculous stuff in them."

Jake glanced at his watch. "We've really got to get going if we want to miss the traffic."

"You're kidding, aren't you?"

There was no missing the L.A. traffic, day or night, but Jake looked perfectly serious.

"You're welcome to leave anytime you want," she encouraged.

He didn't budge. "You're either going with me or I'm calling your family and telling them what happened."

"Like hell you will." He was scaring her now. The last thing she needed was her mom and pop or her sisters—all of them happily married with more kids than she could count—descending on her from Kauai toting "local" foods and bossing her around. Smothering her. Feeling sorry for her again.

"I'll do whatever I have to do to get you to slow down and think about what you really want out of life. There's more to it than work, kung fu videos, and the occasional one-night stand."

"Get *out,* Jake. I mean it."

It wouldn't have simultaneously pissed her off and terrified her half as much if she hadn't been thinking the exact same thing since the shooting last night.

"I'm not butting out this time," he assured her. "You can come home with me now, or so help me, I'm calling your folks and telling them what happened."

ONE

TWILIGHT COVE, CALIFORNIA
FIVE DAYS LATER . . .

Another night. The same old nightmare.

The sorrowful sound of wind chimes. The roar of the surf. The tang of salt on the air. Dense, gray sheets of rain. The shimmering pavement. Tall stalks of sugarcane bowed by the storm, slick with moisture.

Her vision blinded by tears, she tries to blink against the light, to comprehend the blazing glare of headlights aimed straight toward her. The impact. The screech of metal on metal.

The never-ending scream that fills the silence afterward.

Kat awoke tangled in twisted sheets, sweaty, alone.

She shoved back the covers with her good hand, stepped out of bed, and walked through puddles of morning sunlight streaming through the windows. The unfamiliar house was cool and silent.

It had been a bad idea to agree to house-sit. She could feel it in her bones. She'd be better off in Long Beach working one-handed. At least her mind would be occupied.

The minute Jake had driven off with Carly and Christopher and their mutt, she started wondering how in the hell she ever let him convince her to take six weeks off. The peace and quiet were already driving her nuts.

She should have known her nightmares would come with her.

She paused by the window. In the distance, the Pacific sparkled like a polished aquamarine. The summer sun worked diligently to burn off the thin layer of morning haze that hovered over the tranquil California coastline.

Poised on a sandstone bluff a couple of miles away, the seasonal resort of Twilight Cove was a tourist stop for summer sojourners searching for old California with its golden, sun-drenched beaches and small-town atmosphere.

Downstairs, she found the damp chill of the night air still lingered in the shadows though it was already late morning. The cozy Craftsman-style house Jake was refurbishing had absorbed his family's happiness. Photos of Jake, Carly, and Chris were on display in every room. Carly's stunning oil paintings, works that included ghostly white figures set against vibrant local landscapes, adorned the walls.

Kat picked up a framed photo of Chris in a baseball uniform and rubbed her thumb over the glass. It was still hard for her to believe that Jake, of all people, had a kid. Though she'd never told him so, she envied his newfound happiness, his pride in Christopher, the love he'd found with Carly.

She set the photo down. Beside it was one of Carly and Chris walking along the beach at Twilight Cove. The love in Carly's eyes was there for all the world to see, hopeful, fragile—as love always is—and yet constant.

Kat teased Jake, but deep down she was happy for

him. He had a family now. Something she had once wanted.

She crossed the open, casual living-dining room, thinking it was just too damned ironic that Jake, who'd sworn off romance, had wound up married again and living on an out-of-the-way road named Lover's Lane.

She tried to flex her injured hand and winced. Getting along with a bulky bandage was a chore, but she'd already regained some mobility in her thumb and fingers.

Every time she looked at her left hand, she was reminded of just how far betrayal could drive a perfectly normal person to commit an irrational act.

It was also a brutal reminder of what happened whenever her feelings got in the way. Whenever she thought with her heart, her head stopped working and she wound up hurt.

The sun was already above the top of the eastern hills behind the house. She couldn't wait to make a pot of coffee and stretch out in one of the teak lounges on the back deck, lift her face to the sun, and make up some of the sleep she'd lost last night, but just as she reached the kitchen, the front doorbell rang.

She glanced down at the crumpled knit shorts and tank top she'd slept in, then up at the clock on the wall. It was later than she thought—already noon.

Jake's nearest neighbors were beyond shouting distance. The place was totally isolated.

Insistent, the bell chimed again.

She hesitated. Even with a bum hand, she was confident that she could defend herself. Still, she was wary. She'd definitely seen too many movies about fugitives stumbling across isolated homes in the middle of nowhere, heard too many news stories about home-invasion robberies.

And right now she *really* wished she hadn't stayed up

all night to finish Edward Cain's novel *An Even Dozen,* the serial murder thriller that everyone was talking about.

Her purse was on a chair drawn up beneath the dining table, and as she passed it on her way to the front door, she slipped out her .380 automatic.

Get a grip, Vargas. You're not in L.A. County. It's probably just a Girl Scout selling cookies, someone out to save your soul, or the Avon lady.

Lord knows you could use a makeover.

Nearing the front door, she glanced out the picture window and spotted a Toyota Land Cruiser in the driveway. Black, newer model, parked parallel to the house. At this angle, she couldn't see the license plate.

The stained-glass window set in the front door gave her a mottled glimpse of a tall, dark-haired man hovering on the other side. His image was blurred by rippling red, yellow, and green glass. He was alone.

Kat took a deep breath, refusing to let the incident in Seal Beach infect her courage. She cracked the door open, kept the automatic out of sight. Her attention was immediately absorbed by the man standing on the opposite side of the threshold.

Khaki shorts, black polo shirt open at the throat. Over six feet, wide shoulders. His blue eyes stared directly into hers. His lashes were thick, his brow smooth, his jaw strong. His hair was just as black as hers, close-cropped.

She'd never laid eyes on him in her life, but he was smiling as if actually *happy* to see her.

He was mind-numbingly handsome. Definitely the kind of man she'd sworn off of a long, long time ago. Her mind was going blank.

She opened her mouth to ask what he wanted but all she managed was a very weak, embarrassing, "H-hi."

Great. He'd reduced her vocabulary to a fractured syllable.

"Hi." Impossible as it seemed, his smile intensified. "Are you Kat Vargas?"

She tried to focus, cleared her throat, and attempted not to stare. "Who wants to know?"

"I'm Ty Chandler. You're a private investigator."

"I know."

"I mean, I'm *looking* for a private investigator."

"Oh, I get it." She relaxed and laughed. "Jake put you up to this."

She could imagine Jake and Carly playing Cupid. Especially after the "Don't you want somebody to love? You better find somebody to love" speech Jake gave her on the drive up.

The man shook his head. "No, actually. Selma Gibbs at the Plaza Diner suggested I look him up, then she remembered he was going out of town. She said another P.I. was house-sitting for him."

Kat knew Selma Gibbs. They'd met two nights ago when the Montgomerys took her to the diner where Carly used to work.

As she stared up at Ty Chandler, she figured the bad news was that he probably had a wife who was cheating on him, which meant either his wife was nuts, or that he was no prize in the husband department.

The usual rush hit her. It was the same when any prospective client called. She was curious to learn the details, but she could just hear Jake telling her to send the guy on his way, reminding her that she was supposed to be relaxing and sorting things out, deciding what she was going to do with the rest of her life.

"Sorry. I'm on vacation. You'll have to find somebody else. I'm sure there are some fine private investigators in San Luis Obispo." She kept her tone cool, firm, and waited for him to leave, but he didn't look discouraged. In fact, he didn't look deterred in the least.

"Selma had nothing but good things to say about Jake Montgomery," he said. "I hoped you'd be willing to help. Can I just come in and explain? It won't take long."

He was very charming. Certainly friendly enough. And he looked perfectly harmless. But then again, so had Ted Bundy.

"Sorry."

He sighed. Frustration and disappointment were etched across his face, but he didn't budge. He obviously wasn't going to give up easily. She admired that in a person.

"Look, Ms. Vargas, I'm desperate. I've been searching for somebody on my own, but I keep running into dead ends." He shoved his hands into the pockets of his khakis and shrugged. "Just hear me out before you turn me down."

Surely Selma wouldn't have sent a total stranger to her door, let alone a serial murderer.

When she didn't answer, his gaze shifted out to the sea and then slowly back to meet her eyes. "If you can't take the case, is there anyone you'd recommend?"

Spending a few minutes listening to his story would give her something to do other than roam through the house wondering how to stay sane while being suffocated by peace and quiet.

What would it hurt to hear him out? Maybe give him some advice?

She opened the door a bit wider and with a wave of her hand indicated the two wooden rockers side by side on the expansive covered porch.

"You can have a seat out there."

His eyes widened when he caught a glimpse of her gun.

"Don't worry. I've never shot anyone who didn't deserve it." She set the handgun on the table by the phone and joined him outside. By the time she crossed the porch, he'd chosen one of the rockers. She leaned against the low porch wall.

Kat couldn't help but notice that his gaze swept the length of her bare legs before it slowly traveled up to meet her eyes.

"So, exactly who are you looking for, and why do you think you need to hire a P.I.?"

He stopped rocking, leaned forward, and rested his elbows on his knees. "You might as well sit down. This'll take a few minutes."

TWO

Ty Chandler had expected someone . . . well, someone larger and definitely sturdier. A female version of Columbo. Maybe Janet Reno. Certainly not this petite, exotic, and undeniably sensual young woman in a wafer-thin white tank top and wrinkled plaid shorts. The top of her head barely came to his chin.

He waited as Kat Vargas gave him another slow once-over, maybe, finally, deciding he wasn't a serial killer, and slipped into the empty rocker beside him.

Her shoulder-length, jet black hair glistened and moved every time she did. A slight smattering of golden freckles dusted the bridge of her button nose. But it was her eyes that arrested him most. They sparkled with an unspoken challenge, as if daring him not to even think about getting close.

He watched, unable to look away as she crossed her shapely legs and gingerly rested her bandaged hand in her lap. Selma Gibbs had explained that Kat was in town to house-sit and recoup from an injury, but if Selma knew any of the details, she hadn't shared them.

From the moment the lovely Ms. Vargas opened the door, her expression had remained guarded. There was an edge to her ready stance, a studied distance broken now and then by a glimpse of curiosity and a flash of warmth in her eyes.

His business had honed his people skills until he thought he could read most of them like a book, but Kat Vargas wasn't giving anything away. He wondered if she was naturally wary, or if her experience as a P.I. had made her that way.

She remained silent, patiently waiting for him to begin. Ty shifted, glanced out at the ocean, trying to decide where to start.

He hadn't driven up Lover's Lane since high school and he'd forgotten the magnificent view that stretched on and on from up here. Between the shore and the horizon, the deep blue-green ocean was dappled with frothy whitecaps. He caught himself wondering if the albacore were running.

He wasn't exactly sure where to begin or how much Kat Vargas really needed to know before he could convince her to help. He started at the beginning.

"Until a few months ago, I lived in Alaska. I moved up there right after high school and stayed for nineteen years. Eventually I established my own fishing and hunting camp and grew the business. Three months ago, my mom, who still lived here in Twilight, called and told me she was dying."

He felt the pain of that phone call again, the shock of the cold reality in his mom's voice. Barbara Chandler, assertive, a born leader who was always larger than life, was mortal after all.

"The prognosis was six weeks. She only lasted three, which in many ways was a blessing." He looked out at the ocean again. "Once Mom learned her illness was terminal, she refused more treatment and began to put her affairs in order."

It was just like Barbara Chandler to want to be in control right up to the end. She directed while he sorted her personal belongings into boxes and told him to deliver them to close friends, thrift shops, and the local women's shelters.

She even had a real estate agent waiting in the wings to sell the house. She'd taken charge of everything, not because she wanted to spare him, but more than likely because she didn't trust him to do it the way she wanted it done.

Though Kat Vargas sat patiently, listening intently, he could see that she hadn't relaxed. She struck him as someone who, like him, didn't ordinarily like to sit still, let alone wait around for anything or anyone.

"What about your dad?" she asked.

"He died when I was fifteen." There was nothing more he wanted to tell her about his dad. Thom Chandler had checked out of their lives a long time before he died.

"Both my parents are still living—in Hawaii." She spoke softly, almost as if thinking out loud.

Hawaii. That explained her striking, exotic look. Her golden-brown skin, the slight almond shape of her eyes.

"You're lucky, then, to have them both." He saw a flash of unspoken questions in her eyes—questions of someone who has never lost a parent.

How did you get through it?

What will I do when it happens?

What will life be without them?

But her concern had barely blossomed before he watched her hide it. Besides, he hadn't come to philosophize. He'd come seeking help.

"My mom was very driven. Always in control. She'd been active around Twilight Cove all her life. President of the P.T.A., head of the Booster Club when I was in high school. She served on the boards for town beautification and the Twilight Historical Society for years."

There had been standing room only at her memorial. She had lots of friends and associates, but she had never really communicated with him very well. She was better at giving orders than listening. Better at running organizations than holding a family together.

"One day, weak as she was, she insisted on going to the park to sit in the sun. She wanted to watch people doing ordinary, everyday things—all the things she'd never be able to do again. She wanted to watch the kids playing in the park."

He'd bundled her up and taken her to Plaza Park on the bluff above Twilight Cove. The sun was shining, the air crystal clear after three days of rain. He'd never forget that day.

He bought ice-cream cones neither of them finished.

With a gesture unlike her, she took his hand and told him the secret she'd kept from him for nineteen years. It wasn't the kind of last-breath, deathbed revelation of feature films—nothing as dramatic as that. Just a few words softly spoken on a sunny afternoon. Words that altered his life forever. Words that left his world totally shaken.

"You're a father, you know." Her voice was rough and dry. She'd worn a jewel-toned kaftan, her baldness concealed beneath a garish, orange knit turban. Gulls screamed as they soared and dove overhead.

"You're a father, you know."

"What did you say, Mom?" He had wondered if the medication was affecting her mind.

"You have a child out in the world somewhere. Amy's child. And yours."

Kat Vargas had grown very still. Ty focused on the present, on the attractive young woman beside him.

"My mom confessed that my high school sweetheart had been pregnant with my child when we broke up. Her name was Amy Simmons. She was from the other side of town and she ran with a fast crowd, while I hung with the jocks. We dated our junior and senior years, but my mom never liked her."

They'd lost their virginity to each other in the back of his Volkswagen van the night of the homecoming game. Back then, he thought they'd be together forever.

"During our senior year, Amy got into alcohol and drugs. I was a seventeen-year-old kid, in love, scared, confused. I couldn't fight Amy's addiction for her, so I broke up with her, hoping that might shake her up enough to make her stop.

"She ran away with a girlfriend before graduation and moved down to Southern California, where they met someone who took them to River Ridge, a compound in the Angeles National Forest. It was a phony drug rehab. They promised success using New Age techniques."

Ty shoved his hand through his hair with a sigh. Kat listened intently, showing no reaction.

"I went after her, but she refused to come back. My mom was so glad it was over. I got in my van and headed north and didn't stop driving until I ended up in Alaska.

"Later, I tried to contact Amy through her parents, but they had moved and I never heard from them again."

He'd lost Amy, and for a while lost himself in the wilderness. Then he'd picked up the pieces.

"I worked odd jobs, construction on log homes, a guide for outback tours. Eventually I started Kamp Kodiak, a fishing and hunting camp. I worked my ass off turning it into a lucrative business. Amy was out of my life for good, until my mom told me about our child."

"How old?" Kat's smooth, even voice startled him out of his revery.

"I just turned thirty-seven."

Her lips instantly curved into a half smile. She shook her head and rolled her eyes.

"Not *you*. How old is your kid?"

"Nineteen."

"Boy or girl?"

"I have no idea. All I know is that Mrs. Simmons told Mom about the pregnancy right after I left town. When I'd gone after Amy, she wasn't showing yet. I had no idea."

"So your mom knew all the time?"

"Yeah. She knew."

"Why did she wait all these years to tell you? Why would she keep her own grandchild a secret?"

"Believe me, I've asked myself that a million times. She knew I'd do whatever it took to be with Amy. That I'd always be connected to her through our child. My mother wanted to spare me the heartache of ending up stuck with way more than I could handle."

Kat Vargas leaned toward him. Rested her elbow on the arm of her chair, propped her chin in her hand. "Could you have handled it?"

"I'd have damn well tried. I'd have done something. It was my *kid*, for Christ's sake."

Satisfied with his answer, Kat leaned back. She could see that he was emotionally drained. He rested his head against the chair and slowly set the rocker in motion.

That he was an outdoors man was evident in his rugged good looks, his deep tan, the not unattractive creases at the corners of his eyes that came from squinting against the sunlight.

He filled the rocker, made it seem insubstantial for a

man of his height and build. His gaze slid past her as he focused on the ocean once again, staring out to sea with such longing that she had a feeling it was the way he'd look at a woman he hungered for.

She contented herself with studying the breadth of his shoulders, the way his polo shirt clung to his well-defined upper arms like a second skin.

Jake had told her to get out and meet someone interesting. Ty Chandler was that, but he was exactly the kind of guy she wasn't looking for. Justin Parker had been handsome, too. Way too handsome. Her former fiancé was the kind of guy women openly admired.

She wasn't going down that road again.

Her injured hand began to ache. She lightly rubbed the bandage, working her wrist back and forth. Chandler suddenly stopped rocking, walked over, and leaned against the low porch wall.

When he noticed the brass wind chimes lying on the railing, he picked them up and they clattered against one another. It only took him an instant to locate the empty hook in the ceiling above his head.

"Want me to hang this for you?"

"Please don't!" Kat realized she had overreacted and softened her tone. "No, thanks. They were driving me crazy so I took them down."

He set the wind chimes on the rail, went back to the rocker, and sat down. Leaning forward, he planted his elbows on his knees again and threaded his fingers together and stared into her eyes.

"So, do you think you can help me?"

"You're not looking for one of those little dimpled cherubs on a Pampers commercial, you know. You're going to end up with a nineteen-year-old, somebody with baggage—and from what you've told me about the mother, probably plenty of it.

"Mom was on drugs and alcohol. The kid could have severe physical and/or learning disabilities. Maybe even followed in her mom's footsteps." She tapped her bare foot, speculating. "You don't even know if your old girlfriend kept the kid or not. Maybe she gave the baby up for adoption. Maybe even made a little drug money that way."

She saw him blanch. "I'm sorry for having to be so blunt, but you need to know you might be opening a real can of worms."

"I've thought of that," he admitted.

"All of it?"

He nodded, even more solemn. "I know it'll be an adjustment."

"To say the least."

"Hey, I've been fortunate in my life. I hate to think there is a child of mine out in the world somewhere who needs me or what I can give him . . . or her. I just hope it's not too late."

Their eyes met and Kat found herself having to look away from the raw emotion on his face.

She doubted a man like Ty Chandler had been living like a monk since his breakup with a high school sweetheart. "How does your wife feel about all of this? What about your kids?"

He stopped rocking. "I was married for a while after moving to Alaska, but it only lasted five years. Victoria got sick of Alaska and of me devoting so much time to the business. I wanted to build a life, start a family. She wanted to move home to the East Coast and go back to college."

He leaned on the arm of the chair and continued. "The Chandlers have a long history here in Twilight. We go back generations. I'm the last of the line. I want to find my child, whatever that might mean, and share our history."

"I've seen these things go bad," she warned, compelled to be totally honest. "Reunions like this aren't the same as the ones shown on *Oprah* or *Montel.* Not everyone ends up happily reunited." She had seen searches like this end in heartache. She hated getting caught up in anything that had to do with kids.

Parental abductions, guardianship and custody battles—those were the cases she'd handed over to Jake when they'd been working together in Long Beach. She made it her policy to stay away from anything to do with children because she didn't have the heart for it.

Give her a cheating husband to track down and she was happy, but long-lost kids? She didn't need to witness that kind of heartache. It hit too close to home.

"So, will you help me?"

Say no and send him on his way.

When she realized he was getting to her, Kat reminded herself that he didn't specifically need *her.* There were countless P.I.s out there who would be happy to take his money. He could probably even find his child himself if he had the patience and knew where to look.

"You can do this yourself," she suggested. "You can hook up with a service on the Internet, run a search, and eventually track down Amy Simmons, if not her child, maybe in a matter of hours."

Ty shook his head. "I bought a book on how to find anyone anyplace, and it's not as easy as it sounds. I have Amy's parents' last known address, but that was a dead end. I can't devote round-the-clock time to this because the new owner of Kamp Kodiak has asked me to stay on until the end of the year and help make the transition as smooth as possible. I built up a lot of repeat visitors and he doesn't want to lose them."

"So where do you live now?"

"I moved back here for good. I'm hoping that Amy's child . . . that our child . . . is somewhere in California. I run the Kamp Kodiak website and guest registration from here, but I've already had to make three trips back to Alaska in the past couple of months. So," he shrugged, "I'm anxious as hell, but the search has been slow going. It's definitely not as simple as it looks in the book."

"Hey, that's why I make the big bucks."

"Really?"

When she laughed, he realized she was joking and finally smiled again. It was such a slow, steady smile that it warmed her in places she hadn't been warm in a long, long time.

Ty Chandler spelled trouble. She felt it in her bones. More specifically, she felt it in her heart—a heart that, despite her best efforts not to notice, was letting her know that it hadn't turned to stone after all.

Maybe it was her imagination, but whenever Ty Chandler looked at her, she thought he might be a little more than interested in something other than her investigative skills.

She'd have to be blind not to be aware of his good looks, but it was his story and his desire to find his child that moved her most—but the worst thing she could do was take his case based on an emotional reaction to his story.

She rubbed the bandage on her hand, reminded of what happened the night she let herself feel sorry for Sandi Kline.

She held up her injured hand, waved it back and forth in front of him.

"I'd have to use the Internet, and I can't type right now."

His smile intensified into the eye-crinkling, heart-stirring kind of smile that made a few lucky actors major box office material.

"No problem. I took first place in the Twilight High typing contest."

Maybe it was the beautiful June day, or the fact that the sun was shining and the birds were singing. Maybe her brain wasn't used to all this pure, smog-free air. Maybe it was the thought of all the peace and quiet that really scared the hell out of her. Or the echo of Jake's words—*"You need more in your life than work, kung fu videos, and one-night stands."*

She wished Ty Chandler's eyes weren't shining with as much unrelenting hope as they were warmth.

"You're not lying about the typing, arc you?"

He shook his head. "Nope. Besides, if I'm part of the search, I won't havc to keep bugging you about how it's going."

"You're absolutely *sure* you want to do this?" She might very well be asking herself the same thing about having to work with him.

"I've never been more sure of anything in my whole life."

She wished she could say the same.

"So when do we get started?" He was up and out of the chair and raring to go.

"Started?"

"Searching."

"Did I *say* I was taking the case?"

"You haven't said you wouldn't."

She couldn't help but laugh. "I just got up. I need a shower and a cup of coffee in the worst way."

"But you will take the case?"

"Against my better judgment."

No doubt women weren't in the habit of turning him down.

She looked at her left hand again, a painful reminder of the last time she let her emotions get wrapped up with a client's needs and wants. But she was a big girl, and when it came to protecting her heart, she could be tough as nails if she had to.

"I call all the shots," she warned.

"Right. You're the boss."

"Before we do anything, I'll go over my retainer fee."

"Great." He actually looked thrilled to be spending his money.

Jake was going to throw a fit when he found out she'd taken on a client.

"How about I go get some coffee started?" Ty suggested. "How do you like it?"

"Strong and hot." She didn't realize how that must have sounded to him until she looked up and caught him smiling.

"I think I can handle that." He stepped aside to let her pass.

That's just what I'm afraid of.

As she walked into the house, she hoped he hadn't noticed her blush.

THREE

True to his word, Ty had the coffee ready by the time she'd showered and changed into a knit, sleeveless shift. He'd dug up a bagel somewhere and toasted it for her, too.

She led him straight to Jake's office, a small alcove off the living room, where Ty pulled up a chair for himself so he could use the keyboard.

When she sat down beside him, they were so close their bare knees touched. His skin was warm, and such intimacy, even innocent, was disconcerting. She took a deep breath, forced herself to concentrate on the monitor.

She outlined her standard fee and had him type up an abbreviated contract that would work until she could have Arnie Tate send one up from her office.

Then Ty reached into his front pocket, pulled out a folded piece of feminine ivory stationary, and handed it to her. She caught a slightly floral scent and noted his mother's name and address embossed at the top of the page. Inside was a brief note with an address printed in bold, precise manuscript lettering.

"That's Amy's folks' last address," he told her. "I found it in the top drawer of my mother's desk. She'd left it right where I couldn't miss it."

"One more thing she kept from you." Kat watched his mouth harden. She was glad she wouldn't be meeting Barbara Chandler.

"Yeah. Another piece of the puzzle. I guess she wanted all of my attention and thought this should wait until she was gone."

Kat kept her opinion of his mother to herself and couldn't blame him for staying in Alaska for so long.

"I checked the directory for Carson City, Nevada, but they weren't listed," he volunteered.

She reached over and fumbled with the bagel, trying to tear off a piece one-handed.

"Let me help." Ty reached across her, his biceps brushing her breast, and tore the bagel into chunks that she could manage. She inhaled his clean, masculine scent, blushed, and leaned back. It had been way too long since she'd gone out with anyone.

If he noticed her discomfort, he didn't let on.

"That should help," he said.

"Thanks." She stared at the bagel and tried to collect her thoughts.

Get a grip, Vargas.

Do your job. Find his kid. Don't make a production out of this.

"So where do we start?" He rubbed his palms together and then flexed his fingers.

"Directory assistance."

Ty laughed. "Directory assistance? I hired a P.I. for directory assistance? *I've* already tried that."

"This isn't brain surgery. You just need time, patience, and access to the right websites. Let's try directories for surrounding counties."

She told him what to type and enter as they negotiated a maze of multiple cross-reference directories, and after twenty minutes, they came up with a listing for Diane and Marvin Simmons in Yerington, Nevada. It was in the same county as Carson City, but farther east.

Intending to leave him alone while he made the call, she got up. He grabbed her good hand, gave it a gentle tug, and in a hush requested, "Stay."

She sat down, finished up the bagel and coffee while he connected with the Simmonses for the first time in years.

She tried to imagine herself having to track down Justin's parents and speaking to them again. Worse yet, actually talking to Justin—but that part of her life was over. Finished. All *pau,* as they say in Hawaiian. The tie between them was broken.

Ty's tension was visible in the way he sat hunched over and turned away from the computer with his elbows resting on his knees. Obviously, the Simmonses were more than willing to talk, but she could tell that whatever it was they were saying had upset him. When he continued to stare at the floor, she knew the news wasn't good.

He finally raised his head. As he listened, his expression went from one of sorrow to anger. She turned her attention to the wide window above the desk. A red-tailed hawk circled over the nearby arroyo where some hapless creature on the ground was about to become lunch.

Ty hung up; his eyes were bleak, his mouth set in a hard, determined line.

"Bad news?" She wiped her fingers on a paper napkin and waited for him to explain.

"Amy's dead." His voice sounded thick. He had trouble swallowing and cleared his throat. "She died eight years ago."

No stranger to hurt, she wanted to reach out but she

was out of practice. Tentatively, she touched the back of his arm, hoping to communicate her sympathy.

"I'm sorry," she said softly.

"So am I." He turned toward the window. She followed his gaze. There was no sign of the hawk.

Young love, first love. Old memories with the power to fuel fantasies and what-ifs that last for a lifetime.

Ty's first love was forever gone. There would be no chance of a reunion, no communication with Amy, if and when he found their child.

"Did they know anything about the child?" She tried to draw him out of his dark mood.

He nodded, looking into a shaft of sunlight streaming through the window. She let him have his moment. Finally, he shot up and started pacing back and forth.

"Amy had the baby at River Ridge. All the Simmonses know for certain is that she gave birth to a girl, sometime in September of eighty-four. She named the baby Sunny. The first they'd heard of the birth of their granddaughter was eleven years later, when one of her friends called to tell them that Amy had OD'd."

He shoved his hands in his pockets, stopped pacing, and stared down at Kat without really seeing her.

"What happened to the little girl?" She'd been picturing a boy child, one who looked just like Ty with striking dark blue eyes and dark hair.

"The residents of River Ridge were busted for drug dealing by the authorities shortly before Amy died."

Ty finally sat down heavily in the chair beside her. "When the place was raided, the children were placed in various foster homes in L.A. County. The Simmonses tried to trace Sunny, but by the time they got word, she was already lost in the system. Their case got bogged down and they didn't have the money to pursue it."

"They didn't think to contact you?"

"They called my mother." His hand fisted on his knee. "I can't *believe* she didn't help them. She always fought for worthy causes, raised money to save old buildings, and solicited funds for civic beautification. She had no love for Amy, but I can't believe she turned her back on her own grandchild." His eyes were dark with anger, shadowed by guilt. He shook his head, mumbled a curse and added, "I thought I had my mother all figured out. What a joke. I never really knew her at all."

Kat took a deep breath, hoping to get him to calm down enough to relate the rest of his conversation with the Simmonses.

"Do they know if Sunny was ever adopted?" She doubted his daughter ever had a chance at a real home life. Adoptive parents wanted infants, babies with no past, no memory of their birth mothers or previous lives to overcome. They certainly didn't want an eleven-year-old raised by druggies in a communal situation.

"The Simmonses have no idea what happened to her."

It might be better if he stopped looking, because at this point, there was no telling what he'd find, but the hope and determination in his eyes stopped her from saying so. Besides, she would try to move heaven and earth if it were her own daughter she was looking for, no matter what she might find.

Unwanted emotion welled up inside her and threatened to spill over. Her eyes smarted with tears. She quickly looked away and grabbed her coffee mug.

"Hey." Finally, she was in control again. "It's not over till it's over."

He looked at her, but he wasn't smiling anymore. "So what's next?"

"Sunny's last name would help."

"They had no idea. We could try Simmons, or Chandler."

"Did the Simmonses indicate whether or not Sunny was a nickname?"

"No. That's all they know."

He was a bundle of nervous energy. When he wasn't using the keyboard, he was checking out every pen in the holder or lining up paperclips.

"Do you ever sit still?"

"Not if I can help it."

"Somehow I figured that out."

"Your investigative skills are astounding."

"You're stuck in here for now, so let's get to it. If you really want to find your daughter, you're going to have to settle down and help."

He stared at her intently, then nodded. "Just tell me what to do."

They ran birth and death records for Sunny Simmons but came up empty-handed. She had him send off an email to reunionnetwork.com, a website that connected adoptees and their birth parents.

He sobered even more when she had him bring up the Social Security death index.

Two hours flew by and by the time they checked out ancestry.com, her stomach was growling and her butt was numb.

"I can't sit here anymore." Ty shoved away from the desk just as she was about to suggest they take a break. He gave her a half smile.

"Okay, let's stop." It was almost four.

He leaned back, stared at the screen saver.

"Is there really any hope, Kat, or am I just kidding myself and wasting your time?"

She had hoped this would be an easy find, that all they'd have to do was make a couple of calls and Ty would find his daughter. It worked that way sometimes, but not often enough.

"We can go other routes. Misdemeanor criminal records." She watched him blanch. "Filings of civil cases. Marriage licenses." She had planned to call Jake later, just to check in and tell him everything was going fine.

She decided to run the details of Ty's case by him, hoping he might have some other ideas. She looked at Ty and said, "I'm beat. Let's call it a day."

His eyes filled with concern. "Are you all right?"

"Just tired of sitting. We've covered a lot of ground."

They both stood. She walked him to the front door, and when they stepped outside, the breeze off the ocean rejuvenated her almost immediately.

"I probably should go back and see if there are any new reservations posted," he said. "What time should I pick you up?"

"What are you talking about?"

"I'm fixing you dinner."

"I don't recall you *asking* me to dinner."

He shrugged. "You need to eat."

"I make it a habit never to go out with clients."

"I didn't say anything about it becoming a habit. I'd just like to show you around town and make you dinner."

"A tour of Twilight Cove takes all of five minutes. Besides, you're too late. Jake and Carly already did that."

"Are you calling Twilight small?"

She found bickering with him immensely enjoyable. "Is it even on a map?"

"Depends on which map you're looking at. I'll pick you up at six thirty."

"Hold it right there, Mr. Chandler."

He paused on the top step. The breeze coming up the canyon ruffled his dark hair. "I don't give up easily, *Ms. Vargas.*"

"I *don't* go out with clients."

"Are you telling me you don't meet with clients to discuss a case?"

She hesitated. "We've already discussed it. Call me tomorrow. Jake's number is in the book."

He threw her the kind of smile that no doubt brought weaker, less determined women to their knees.

"Okay. Well, I guess I'll have to share all the fresh fish I was going to barbeque with my neighbor."

Her mind flashed on Jake's refrigerator. There was nothing in it but a collection of condiments and the few start-up supplies that Carly left her; a carton of watery nonfat milk, some fruit, a couple of yogurts, a sadly dried-out baked chicken, and half a loaf of bread.

Had he tried to tempt her with dinner at a fancy restaurant, a bouquet of flowers, or a box of candy, none of them would have worked like his offer of barbequed fresh fish.

At heart she was still an island girl raised on fresh *ahi,* mahimahi, *ulua, ono.* And she was the only one of her father's daughters who truly loved fishing. She adored spending hours bobbing on the open water waiting for a strike, motoring miles out to sea, following the birds to schools of fish.

It wouldn't hurt to ask.

"What kind of fish?"

"I caught a thirty-pound yellowfin tuna yesterday afternoon. It's been on ice since. I'm headed home to filet it."

He shoved his hands in his pockets and sounded quite proud of himself.

Kat sighed. She *was* here for a little R&R, and Jake had advised her to get out, to meet people, to give the local guys a chance.

The offer of fresh yellowfin tempted her into spending

time alone with Ty as much as the thought of getting to know him better.

"Okay. I give up. Pick me up at six-thirty."

She ignored the flash of victory in his eyes, but not the spike in her heartbeat when he smiled.

FOUR

Dinner. That's it. Dinner and polite conversation.

Kat made that her mantra before she opened the front door to Ty again a couple of hours later.

He offered her what looked like a folded map. "You look great."

"Thanks. What's this?" She noticed the warmth of his hand when their fingertips met.

"A map of Twilight. Just to prove it's on one. Thought you might need it. It lists the stores and shops in town, and historic sites, too."

"Thanks." She was surprised by his thoughtfulness. He was making himself way too easy to like.

He drove through Twilight, down Cabrillo Road where the shops were full and lines of tourists waiting for tables spilled out of crowded eateries. Through quiet residential neighborhoods they passed all manner and style of homes, from nondescript stucco boxes to Craftsman, California ranch, Tudor, and even a few Victorians.

As he pointed out the town's most prominent features—the Plaza Park on the bluff, his favorite ice-cream parlor, a shuttered, turn-of-the-century hotel on the coast road—there was a hint of pride in his tone, as if he'd founded the place himself.

When Ty turned down a narrow dirt road with a

handful of older cottages built on lots covered with sand and succulent ground cover, she fought a tinge of uneasiness.

The houses thinned until there was only one left standing alone on the point against the panoramic view of the Pacific. The view was as spectacular as the one from Lover's Lane and the area was just as isolated. She felt more than a twinge of uneasiness.

Could I have read him wrong? Trusted him because he seemed like a nice guy? Why is he stopping out here?

"Don't you think it's a little early in the game to bring me to a make-out spot, Chandler?" Kat tried to keep her tone light, but she was dead serious.

Ty frowned, puzzled for a second, then threw back his head and laughed. "Sorry to disappoint you, Ms. Vargas, but this is where I *live.*"

Blushing again, she turned her face to the window as he pulled into a driveway beside a two-story wood-shingled cottage with a bay window on the first floor and a small deck off the room upstairs. The house faced the spectacular view.

Like the handful of other homes situated along the road, this one was on the edge of the point and had been buffeted by the wind, baked by the sun, beaten by years of salt air and sea spray that drifted up from the rocks below the cliff. Like a wizened old man it remained proud, almost defiant, though a bit faded and worse for wear.

The peeling wood trim needed a new coat of white paint. Here and there some of the shingles were cracked or missing, but Kat loved it at first sight, from the old mast in use as a flagpole in the overgrown flower garden, to the faded red front door at the end of the crooked stone walk.

A white picket fence surrounded the yard. The roofline sagged like the back of an old nag. A dilapidated garage stood off to one side.

She hit the car door handle before she realized Ty was already headed around to open the door for her. He stood back while she stepped out and took in the setting.

"My great-great-*great*-grandfather built this place in the eighteen-forties."

"It's really charming." Eager to see the inside, Kat was astounded by how much she liked the feel of the place.

She tried to ignore the warm touch of his hand on her waist as he opened the gate and let her lead the way up the flagstone path. The front door was a rustic footnote to all of the rest. A small brass porthole had been set into its weathered planks.

The door was unlocked, reminding her of the way things were when she was growing up on Kauai. She stepped inside and found herself surrounded by wood-paneled walls covered with photos and memorabilia of Twilight Cove.

Old shop signs, framed topographical maps of the California coastline, wooden pulleys and thick rope, nautical clocks and barometers were on display beside cork carvings of ships at sea. A bare-breasted mermaid that once proudly adorned the prow of a ship now hung on the wall above a wide-screen television.

"You could give tours. It's like a museum in here." Kat turned full circle. It would take hours to see everything.

"Not likely." Ty shrugged. "It's just old family memorabilia. My great-great-great-grandfather settled Twilight and named the town. The story goes that he was on the run from the law back East, and when he got to California he jumped ship. He married the daughter of a wealthy Spanish landowner, and through that marriage acquired quite a bit of land along the coast. He'd been the ship's chandler, so he took Chandler as his name. We've no idea what our real family name was. He took it to his grave."

She walked to a side table covered with various-shaped jars filled with colored beach glass, and her thoughts drifted back to Kauai. Her mom had kept glass containers of all shapes and sizes full of beach glass that she'd collected on the windowsill in the kitchen, where their muted colors were highlighted by sunlight. She once had her own collection, but she'd left it behind with everything else when she moved to Long Beach.

She picked up a small jar, studied the bits of frosted color inside. "Did you collect these?"

"My grandmother did. Sometimes I can't resist picking a piece up myself when I see a good one."

"Some of the best places to hunt for beach glass on Kauai are secret."

She'd half expected a few awkward silences, some moments when they'd be ill at ease, but there were no such lapses. He told story after story about the town, reverently relating his family history. It was impossible not to notice his pride, and yet he wasn't in the least boastful.

She sipped wine and watched him put together a crisp green salad, garlic bread, and sliced red and gold bell peppers to grill along with the yellowfin.

She found herself more relaxed than she'd been in a long while. His voice was as smooth and warm as good brandy. His eyes were constantly straying to her lips, his gaze colliding and locking with hers.

Her heartbeat was erratic by the time she held the

door for him and he carried the dishes out to the brick patio lined with terra-cotta pots filled with geraniums, impatiens, petunias, and rosemary.

The only drawback to the perfect setting was the tinkle of an old glass wind chime hanging in the branches of a dwarf lemon tree nearby.

The house was situated so that the sea and a showy, smog-tinted sunset took center stage. As if he'd choreographed the moment, Ty poured two glasses of wine in time for a toast as the blazing sun kissed the horizon. They watched until it sank out of sight, leaving behind a sky stained bright pink and hot orange.

In the glow of twilight, Ty lit the hurricane lamp in the center of the table while she took a sip of wine and closed her eyes. The sun was still shining in Hawaii. In three hours' time, it would set again in the islands.

"Are you all right?" His concern sounded genuine.

She opened her eyes. He had leaned closer. She finally found her voice.

"I'm fine. How about some of that yellowfin?"

He filled her plate, made certain she had everything she needed, waited until she took the first bite. The fish was fresh, firm, grilled to perfection. Pure ecstacy.

"Fabulous." She sighed and quickly forked another piece. "You really caught this yourself?"

He nodded, took another sip of wine. "I just bought my own boat. Keep it moored over at Gull Harbor a few miles down the road. I try to go at least twice a week."

"I used to go fishing with my dad off Kauai." She stopped abruptly. She'd made it a rule never to talk about her past.

"What's wrong?"

Kat shook her head. "Nothing."

He didn't need to know her story. Like him, she'd lost

her first love. Hers wasn't such a pretty tale, either, but it was no one's business but her own.

"You haven't told me very much about yourself," he noted.

"There's not much to tell."

"You know all about me and *way* more than anyone ever needed to know about my family."

"You didn't need much prompting." She couldn't help but laugh when he feigned offense.

"Are you saying I talk too much?"

She lifted her wineglass for a refill. He obliged, then thoughtfully tore off a piece of buttered baguette for her and set it on the edge of her plate.

"I can't help but wonder what happened to your hand." He picked up his fork again.

"I ended up between an irate wife with a gun and her cheating husband." She shrugged it off. "That's what comes of getting involved with clients."

"Rest assured I have no intention of shooting you."

Kat laughed. "Mrs. Kline didn't, either. She was aiming for her husband at the time."

"Ouch. A woman scorned, huh?"

"Right."

His smile faded. "Are you often in danger?"

Kat shook her head. "Not unless you count the stress of freeway driving or sitting hunched over a keyboard too long, which is eighty percent of what I do. But there are occasions when I have to go into some iffy areas to interview someone or serve court docs to somewhat less than desirable characters."

"Do you go armed?" He pretended to check her out. "Did you bring your gun along tonight?"

"No, but don't get any ideas. I hold a black belt in Tae Kwon Do."

* * *

Ty had been getting more than ideas since the moment Kat opened her door tonight and he caught a hint of her perfume. The exotic scent held just enough spice to tease and tempt and remind him how long it had been since he'd been with a woman.

He had no idea what to expect of Kat Vargas, but he admired the blend of bravado and wariness in her eyes, and he'd yet to discover why she remained so guarded.

She hadn't hidden her appreciation of the old cottage, though, which meant more to him than he would have guessed.

Sharing dinner and conversation tonight only whetted his appetite, and made him want to know her better.

Every time he looked at the bandage on her hand, his stomach knotted, yet she appeared nonchalant about the injury, treating it as if it were no big deal. He hoped what she'd said earlier was true—that she wasn't often in harm's way.

He could count the women he'd been as physically attracted to on one hand. Amy had been first and foremost. Certainly Victoria's looks had caught his eye long before she'd captured his heart. By the time they parted ways and divorced, it was without hard feelings. In fact, there had been very little emotion left between them at all after they realized they had entirely different goals and very little in common outside of sex.

A few years later he'd ended up sharing a small cabin in the outback with a former flight attendant for a few months until she, like Vic, decided life in the land of the midnight sun was driving her stark raving mad. After that there weren't a hell of a lot of opportunities for a guy living in Alaska to meet eligible women.

He wasn't fool enough to think that he'd ever burn

with the kind of teenage infatuation and intensity he had at seventeen, but there was something about Kat Vargas that ignited his imagination, made him want to get to know her better, to spend more time with her. It wasn't in the least difficult to fantasize about making love to her.

He finished and pushed his empty plate aside, for the moment content just to watch her. From the way she attacked the yellowfin, he figured she was bound and determined to polish off every bite.

"How long have you lived in California?" He figured she was honest enough to tell him to back off if she didn't want to answer even the most general question.

"Around five years." She swallowed another bite, then reached for her wineglass.

"Do you ever go back to visit?"

"A few times, but not for over a year now. I've got a business to run, you know. Did you come back home to see your mom very often?"

"Not at first. After I married Victoria, we came down for Christmas a few times, but she and my mom didn't get along."

"You said your mom never liked Amy, either."

"After I married Vic, it was pretty obvious I'd probably never choose anyone who could live up to my mom's standards." He shifted in his chair, leaned back to study Kat against the flickering lamplight.

"You must be pretty angry about what your mom did, keeping you from your child."

"Things are what they are. I'd rather put my energy into finding my daughter."

As if some unseen hand had flipped a switch, the sound of crickets suddenly filled the night air. The thunder of the surf kept time to the slow and steady beat of his heart.

A backdrop of stars dusted the night sky. A sliver of moon was doing its best to make up for its size. He drank in the loveliness of the beautiful woman beside him, tempted to reach over and run his fingertips across the back of her wrist just to see if her skin was as soft as it looked.

He smiled to himself when he recalled she'd mentioned her black belt and let the temptation pass.

"Have you ever been married, Kat?"

"No." Blunt and to the point.

Obviously, that was a forbidden subject, so he asked, "How did you end up here when you could be living in paradise?"

When Kat's lovely mouth tightened and she frowned, he wished he hadn't asked.

She fell in love with Justin Parker the first time she laid eyes on him. Two minutes after they were introduced, he asked her out. She was a few months shy of her twenty-fourth birthday.

Within two weeks she was no longer a virgin. He had moved into her place in Kapa'a, she was in love, and walking on air.

He traveled a lot, naturally. He'd been a pro surfer since his early teens, and though the celebrity shine on his surfing star had tarnished a bit, he still had plenty of contacts.

He was counting on his name selling surfboards as well as a line of board shorts and beachwear. All he needed was a backer.

She got used to driving him to the Lihue airport, dropping a lei around his neck, and kissing him good-bye. He never failed to bring a new wind chime back for her from wherever he went.

Life couldn't get any better. Justin was bound to find an investor. He promised her a big wedding as soon as his business was off the ground.

She had no idea that his promises were all lies.

What he found on a trip to L.A. wasn't a backer, but supermodel Tara Roman, or Tara found him, at a cocktail party hosted by Justin's sports agent.

Kat shook off the memories, preferring to keep her past to herself. It was bad enough that she'd had to live it.

Why couldn't Ty just be content knowing she was Kat Vargas, P.I., owner of a well-established firm? Enthusiastic. Dependable. Reliable. Honest. Thorough. Successful. *Finito. Pau.* End of story.

She looked at the distant first star. He was still waiting for an answer, wanting to know why she had left paradise.

She gazed at him over the rim of her wineglass. What would he say if she told him that one man's paradise was another man's hell?

"I left because I needed a change and the job market was better over here."

He didn't need to know the gory details or that she couldn't stand being surrounded by memories or the scent of jasmine on the night air, or views of haunting mists hovering around the emerald mountaintops. She couldn't stand being reminded of Justin or the accident, or how she'd been naive enough to believe that people never lied when they said "I love you."

She was still haunted by nightmares. Even now the sound of wind chimes, no matter how faint, would revive old memories capable of wounding her all over again.

But mostly she left Hawaii because here, in California, no one ever looked at her with pity in their eyes. Here she wasn't suffocated by her family wanting to help and not knowing how.

The warmth of Ty's hand suddenly penetrated hers when he reached across the table, covered her hand with his.

"I'm sorry, Kat."

She took a deep breath, savored the human contact, the heat of his palm before she slipped her hand out from beneath his, finished off the rest of her wine, forced a smile. "Don't worry about it. The reasons I left were too many to count. Besides, that was a long time ago."

Long enough now that you should be over it, Vargas.

Ty got up and began to clear the table.

"Let me help," she offered. He waved her away.

"Relax. I'll be right back."

She got up and walked across the sandy yard, past the edge of the patio, to stand and look over the bluff.

A high tide had carved the beach into a mere sliver of milk-white sand glistening in the moonlight. An old wooden stairway hugged the cliff, zigzagging its way down to the beach.

Without actually turning, she knew when Ty had crossed the yard, knew the minute he drew near. She half expected him to touch her hand, knowing that despite the fact that she wanted to take things slowly, she was anticipating his touch.

But he didn't touch her again. Instead he locked his arms behind his back and stood beside her, much like a seafaring man on the deck of his ship. The sound of the sea surrounded them as together they stared out at the dark, churning water.

She was the first to break the stillness.

"How many steps are there in that old stairway?" It was too dark to tell but it seemed to go on forever.

"It seems like a thousand when you're climbing them under the heat of the sun. A Chandler built the original stairway."

She imagined a man who looked like Ty hand-sawing every piece of wood, climbing up and down the cliff-face to nail them into place. "That must have taken a lot of time and patience."

"Chandlers are as stubborn as hell."

He was obviously proud of the family trait. She heard it in his warm, deep voice as it wrapped itself around her. Their shoulders brushed.

"I'm sure all the work was worth it," he added. "It gave the house access to the beach."

"A thousand steps aren't very many when they're taking you home," she said softly.

She doesn't know the hurt shows.

Ty heard it in her voice and saw it in her eyes, even in the glow of lamplight when he'd asked why she'd left paradise. She tried hard to hide it beneath a no-nonsense exterior, but a couple of times tonight she'd looked so sad and vulnerable that he'd been tempted to wrap his arms around her and hold her close.

Somewhere between knocking on her front door this morning and standing here now, he had decided Kat Vargas was worth getting to know better. He wanted to find out all about her, and discover who or what had put the sorrow in her eyes. If she was interested in him in return, she hadn't shown the slightest indication.

He watched the wind off the water brush loose strands of her shoulder-length hair across her face, watched her lift her hand and sweep the strands back into place.

Her every move was filled with grace and sensuality, down to the merest flick of her wrist.

"Are you a dancer?"

"What makes you ask?"

"You're very graceful."

"I dance hula."

"Really?"

"Crazy, huh?"

"I'd love to see you dance sometime. Keep your eyes on the hands, not on the hips. Right? Isn't that what they say?"

She laughed. "Yes. That's what they say. I worked my way through college dancing in a Polynesian review. I don't dance much anymore, but it's something that never leaves you."

Standing beside her, listening to the steady rhythm of the sea hitting the rocks was comforting in its constancy. For the first time since his mother had told him about his child, the anxiety and impatience building inside him had taken a backseat to a tense, visceral need, stoked by the lovely Ms. Kat Vargas, P.I.

"I'm glad you've taken my case, Kat."

"Don't remind me you're a client," she said softly.

"Right. You don't fraternize with clients."

"You're finally getting it."

He laughed and then, together, they turned toward the sound of a car on the road out front.

"Probably some kids parking."

"Don't get any ideas, Chandler," she teased.

"Don't worry. I value my *cajones* too much to try anything with you. I have the feeling you'd either karate the hell out of me or plug me with a bullet."

"Finally. You're getting the message."

They were both laughing when the back screen door banged and he heard a familiar voice call out, "Hey, Chandler? Arrgh, matey! Prepare to be boarded!"

Ty tried not to groan. He and Kat turned and watched a man in a bright Hawaiian shirt, faded threadbare jeans, and flip-flops pause outside the door and look around the patio.

"I brought grog!" He waved a bottle of wine over his head.

"Who *is* that?" Kat whispered.

"An old friend, but I'm taking him off the list as of this minute. His name's Ron Johnson. Everyone calls him R.J."

"Does he always talk like a pirate?"

"No, thank God."

"Chandler? Where are you?" R.J. walked over to the patio table, checked out the wineglasses, and stared out into the darkness beyond the halo light from the hurricane lamp.

Ty put his hand on Kat's waist to help guide her across the uneven ground in the darkness. The innocent physical connection seemed natural. As if she'd been made for him to touch.

"Over here," he called to R.J. "Nice of you to drop by unannounced, *buddy.*"

R.J. set the wine bottle on the table and waited for them to cross the yard. "Since when do I need to call first?" He let go a deep laugh.

As Ty and Kat stepped into the light, Ty introduced them, and Kat tried not to notice that R.J. was checking her out.

"Shoot. I didn't know you were entertaining or I'd have crashed the party sooner." He continued to stare at Kat.

"We just finished—"

R.J. cut Ty off with a wave. "Please, no details."

"Have a seat," Ty invited.

With a flourish, R.J. held out a chair for Kat and then sat down beside her.

"Don't try anything," Ty warned. "The lady has a black belt *and* a gun."

The first thing Ron noticed when he met Kat Vargas was the thorough once-over she gave him. She was totally composed as she smiled and offered him a handshake, but her smile never really reached her eyes. If he'd interrupted anything intimate, it sure as hell didn't show.

"You afraid I'll shanghai her?" he asked Ty.

"No. I just thought I'd warn you. Kat's a P.I.," Ty explained.

"That's it, then."

"That's what?" Kat Vargas asked him.

"The way you keep sizing me up."

Ty laughed but the lady didn't. Instead she said, "Old habits die hard." Then she smiled and took a sip of the wine he'd offered.

"I hired her to help me find my daughter." Ty shifted, moving closer to Kat.

"Daughter?" The last R.J. had heard, Ty knew that Amy had been pregnant with his child but knew none of the details.

"We've already tracked down the Simmonses. They told me Amy had a girl and that she named her Sunny." Ty glanced at the petite P.I. beside him. "We haven't gotten any leads yet, but we're working on it."

We. Ty already looked like a goner, so R.J. focused on Kat. He hoped the woman wasn't leading his buddy on a wild-goose chase.

"You really think you can find her?" he asked Kat.

"I'm sure as hell trying."

He noticed her left hand was bandaged, also that she had the body of an athlete. Gorgeous eyes with dark, slender brows, thick lashes. There was a golden glow to her skin. And she had a plump mouth, the kind that could put a lot of ideas about kissing her in a man's head.

He wondered how long Ty would be able to resist. He doubted it would be very long before the poor sucker fell for her.

Back when they were kids, Ty had won all the trophies and made the local headlines every football season. Chandler was the one all the girls had been after in high school, but once he fell for Amy, he never played around.

Unfortunately, by the time they were seniors, Amy had been too messed up to know a good thing when she had it.

As for himself, he'd lived with the same woman for ten years without ever getting around to asking her to marry him. Then one day she up and left him for a guy with three kids and—more's the pity—he hadn't really cared. If he had a soul mate out there somewhere, he'd yet to meet her. Then again, he wasn't looking very hard.

Women were great, but having one in his own life on a permanent basis wasn't a necessity, at least it never had been.

Ty, on the other hand, was the settling type. He always talked about how he'd do this or that if he had kids, but despite being married for a while and living with some gal after that, Ty still hadn't ever gotten the family he'd always wanted.

Ever since Ty's bitch of a mother told him Amy had left town pregnant, Ty had been chomping at the bit to find his long-lost kid. Now he'd somehow hooked up with a P.I. who looked more like a sexy aerobics instructor than a private dick.

It appeared both Kat and Ty were trying not to notice that they were attracted to each other. One thing he knew for certain was that it wouldn't be long before his buddy was in a free fall without a parachute.

Kat noticed Ty didn't feel the least bad about outrageously hinting that R.J. ought to take off a few minutes later. She wasn't the least bit sorry to see him go, either.

She realized Ty had noticed when he asked, "You didn't think much of R.J., did you?"

"What makes you say that?"

"You're not very good at hiding your feelings."

She leaned back. "I think I'm pretty good at it."

"*Did* you like him?"

"I don't even know him," she hedged.

"Would you *want* to get to know him?"

"Where's this going exactly?"

"Most people really take to the guy. He's been my best friend since we were in the Pee Wee League together."

"It shouldn't matter to you what I think."

"It does."

She hadn't warmed to R.J., but not because of anything he'd said or done. It was just that he reminded her of Justin—outgoing, the life of the party. Justin was on every minute, always making deals, chatting people up, working the room. He used his considerable charm and golden-boy image to get ahead.

"He reminds me of somebody," she admitted.

"Someone you don't like."

"Somebody I loved once." The moment she said it she wished she hadn't.

Ty was silent for so long that she hoped maybe he hadn't heard. But he had.

"You've had to listen to me going on about my life all day. You want to talk about it?"

She laughed at that. *Talk about it?* She'd been trying to wipe out the memories for years. She never talked about what happened in Hawaii. *Never.*

"Nope."

"I didn't think so. But if you ever change your mind, Kat—"

"Don't worry, I won't."

Kat was subdued on the way back to the house on Lover's Lane as Ty hummed along to a Jimmy Buffett CD.

"*Living' on sponge cake, watchin' the sun bake . . .*"

When they reached her place, Ty killed the motor but didn't make a move to get out. In the confines of the car the warmth she saw in his eyes made her catch her breath.

"What time should we start in the morning?" he asked.

"I have physical therapy. How about afternoon? Say around two?"

"*Two?*" His impatience was showing.

She was braced for an argument, but after a moment's hesitation, he nodded in agreement.

"Okay. I've got a conference call and some other loose ends I should clear up first."

She could tell there was more he wanted to say. "What is it?"

He fiddled with the gearshift. "Do you *really* think we'll find her?"

"We won't if you spend all your time asking me that." She couldn't look away from the intensity in his eyes. "This really does mean a lot to you, doesn't it, Ty?"

"She's my daughter. It worries me that she might need

help." He sighed. "And it haunts me to think that she probably doesn't even know I exist."

In that split second she realized that if she wasn't careful she'd end up trying to move heaven and earth to find Sunny for him. But she was pragmatic enough to know that sometimes things just didn't work out.

Her pop liked to say, "Honey, sometimes God says no."

"I'll do my damnedest, Ty, but I can't make you any guarantees."

"That's all I can ask."

He got out, walked around the car, and opened the door. Then he took her hand to help her out; perhaps he held it a little longer than necessary, but it didn't feel wrong.

There was an infinitesimal second when she could have stepped around him and started walking for the door, but she didn't, couldn't, move. He reached out and cupped her jaw, bent his head, and kissed her, softly, gently, before he let go and stepped back.

"Thanks for coming over for dinner."

The simple, brief exchange was so soul stirring that she was too stunned to say a word. Instead, she merely nodded, pulled herself together, and started walking toward the house.

When they reached the front porch she had the feeling he might try to kiss her again and realized she was holding her breath, waiting, but he didn't even try.

Instead, he shoved his hands in his pockets and said, "I'll see you tomorrow, Kat."

She told him good night, and as she watched him walk away, she decided that her earlier impression of Ty Chandler had been way off the mark.

He was certainly handsome. He was polite, low-key, and considerate. He was interested in her and actually *listened* to what she had to say. He knew who he was and what he wanted, but he wasn't in the least obnoxious about getting it, just determined.

He was the kind of guy who would quietly lay siege to a woman's heart until he captured it.

But he wasn't really harmless at all. He was possibly the most dangerous man she'd met in a long, long time.

FIVE

For the first time in forever Kat went to bed at a decent hour, slept through the night, and awoke to the sound of birdsong, refreshed and looking forward to the new day.

She pulled on shorts and a tank top and gave her hair a quick combing before she went to physical therapy in Twilight Cove, then took time to walk along the beach.

She'd forgotten the tranquillity that came from being on the water and savored the walk in the ocean air, the sound of the surf, and the sand between her toes.

She didn't have to remind herself that this kind of peace was a fragile and fleeting thing.

After she got back to the house she showered, wrapped herself in a batik *pareau*—a long rectangular swath of colorful cloth splashed in varied hues of aqua and green—and tried to keep her thoughts on a smooth, even keel and off of Ty Chandler.

She turned on *CNN Headline News* for background noise and wondered how long it had taken Jake to change gears and slip into the laid-back rhythm of Twilight Cove. Then she remembered he'd had Carly and Chris to help him adjust.

She polished off a Cup o' Noodles and hurried into the office to pick up yesterday's notes. Added to the Simmonses' address on Barbara Chandler's stationery was the name Sunny, along with the month and year of the girl's birth. Not much to go on.

It was almost one in the afternoon. Two in New Mexico. She found the number of Jake's vacation rental and punched it into the phone.

Carly, Jake's wife, answered almost immediately.

"Hi, Carly, it's Kat."

"How's everything going? Are you finding things all right?" Carly sounded upbeat and happy. But then, both Jake and Carly always sounded that way now that they'd found each other.

"Everything's great," she assured Carly. "Actually, I've taken on a case."

"In *Twilight*?" Carly's shock registered over the line. "You're kidding. I thought you were going to relax."

"It's not complicated. Just a missing-person search. I have a couple of questions for Jake, though, if he's not busy."

"Sure. I'll get him. You take care of yourself, okay, Kat?"

"Thanks." Kat tapped the end of a pen on the notepad in front of her. Jake's wife was not only beautiful, but a talented artist and a great mom, too.

Suddenly Jake was on the line. "What's up, Vargas? Couldn't stand to just veg out?"

Kat laughed. It was good to hear his voice. She imagined him sitting by the phone, kicked back, lounging on the sofa.

"That's about it. Actually, I'm helping a guy search for a daughter he didn't even know he had until a few months ago. She's nineteen now. We've got her month and year of birth, no day. A first name. Mother's last name."

"Ever adopted?"

"No idea."

There was momentary silence on the other end of the line and then, "You've tried all the preliminaries?"

"Do frogs fart in a pond?"

"Okay. How about Social Security?"

"Nothing under the names we tried."

"Whoa. Did you just say *we*? What's up?"

"Okay, so the guy is typing for me."

"What's wrong with one-handed hunt and peck?"

"Shut up, Montgomery."

"Did you say the girl is nineteen now?"

"Right. Ended up in foster care when she was around eleven years old."

"How about the mom?"

"She was caught up in drugs and some phony rehab compound in the Angeles National Forest when the baby was born."

"River Ridge?"

"You've heard of it?"

"It was in all the papers. The DEA was pretty proud of that one."

"Well, Mom's out of the picture. Deceased." She heard voices in the background—Jake's son, Chris, talking to Carly—a reminder that Jake was on a family vacation.

"Jake, if you're busy—"

"What about the welfare rolls? With her background, you might find a lead there."

"You have a way in?"

"I've got a contact in Sacramento. Hang on. I think the password he gave me is in one of the files I brought with me."

She started doodling waves on the notepad while Jake retrieved the information. He was back in seconds.

"Here you go." He recited the information. She jotted it down and thanked him.

"Remember, you didn't get that from me, okay, Kat?"

"I know. If I tell anyone, you'll have to kill me."

"Hey, Vargas?"

"What?"

"Take it easy, okay? You're supposed to be relaxing."

"This *is* relaxing. You told me to get out more."

"So who's the client?"

"A guy named Ty Chandler."

"Never heard of him. Is he a good guy?"

"So far, so good. But he is a client." She didn't tell Jake that for a moment last night she caught herself wishing Ty was a date.

"Give him a chance, if he's interested. Don't be a hermit."

She hung up on him without saying good-bye. It was an old joke between them, seeing which one could hang up on the other first. She knew Jake would be laughing on the other end.

Ty knocked promptly at two and Kat called out for him to let himself in. He watched the news broadcast for a couple of seconds before he found the remote, turned off the television, and walked into the home office.

He had his back to the door but he knew the minute Kat stepped into the room. He turned and saw her framed in the open doorway, her gaze warm yet uncertain.

He'd just gone through three major life quakes; his mother's death, his move to California, and hearing the news that he had a child. The last thing he needed right now was the challenge of a new relationship, but Kat Vargas was too hard to resist.

She looked like summer in a pair of baggy white linen

pants and a short, red Hawaiian print top. Like a model in a Roxy ad in *Surfer* magazine.

"Hey, you look great." He could see that his compliment took her by surprise when she had to glance down to see what she was wearing.

"Thanks." She crossed the room, and when he pulled out the chair beside him, she slipped into it, smelling like soap and coconut shampoo.

His impatience to start the search again was all that kept him from being distracted by her nearness.

"Okay, what are we doing?" He rubbed his hands together.

She read off the numbers she wanted him to enter, explained how they were going to search the California welfare rolls.

"So now I'm a hacker? Can we get arrested?"

"Not unless you go around broadcasting this."

"What'll you give me not to tell?" He caught himself staring at her lips, thinking about last night. He hadn't meant to kiss her, he simply hadn't been able to resist.

She broke the stare and mumbled, "You should be afraid of what I'd do to you if you did."

At first they had trouble accessing the site, then suddenly, bingo, they were in.

"This is it. I just know it." He reached out, touched the back of her hand where she'd rested it on the desk. "Thanks for calling your partner on this, Kat."

She finally turned his way again. Her gaze probed his face. Her smile had dimmed.

"What's wrong?" he asked.

"I don't want you to get your hopes up too high. This could be a dead end. In fact, it's a real long shot."

"It's better than nothing."

When they entered the scant information they had, they came up with countless hits. There were so many listings for young women born in September of eighty-four that he was overwhelmed.

"It's going to take days to go through this county by county."

She leaned toward the monitor. "We'll start with the most obvious—L.A."

"Which probably has the most listings of all."

An hour and a half later, he straightened, rubbed his palm against the back of his neck, and let go a sigh.

When Kat stretched, arching her back and unconsciously emphasizing her breasts, he looked away.

"Are you tired?" Her hand grazed his sleeve, drawing his attention back.

It took him a minute to collect his thoughts. He was tired of sitting, but wanted to keep going.

"We can't stop now." Seeing all those names had only heightened his urgency.

"How about we take a break, have some iced tea or a soda?"

He opted for iced tea.

She was headed for the kitchen when his cell phone rang.

Kat listened as Ty responded to the call with quick, sure answers. His strong hands gripped the phone as he sat perfectly still, listening.

When he hung up she asked,"Trouble in River City?"

He shoved the phone back into his pocket. "I've got to do some quick damage control. An A-list reservation got canceled for the week after next by mistake."

"Oops."

"A *real* oops. I hate to go." He glanced down at the monitor, regret all over his face.

"You take off. I'll print these out and look them over."

"Call me if you find anything. I'll try to get back as fast as I can."

He looked so torn about whether to leave or not that she had to warn him, "I will, but don't count on it, okay?"

After he left, she tried to ignore a moment of disappointment and poured herself a Diet Pepsi. She juggled the cell phone and the printout and went out to the back deck.

She sat down and started circling possibilities, but in a few minutes found herself daydreaming about Ty and realizing she was looking forward to talking to him again.

When he didn't call, she devoted her attention to scanning the list until her eyes were tired. She was about to toss the printout aside when an entry caught her eye a third of the way down the page. A Social Security number was listed for a Sunny Simone at an address in Hollywood.

Sunny Simone. Almost Sunny Simmons.

Kat pictured a blue-eyed, dark-haired ingenue with Ty's smile waiting tables in a beat-up coffee shop on Hollywood Boulevard, hoping to be discovered by a talent agent.

That would be the *good* news.

Hollywood Boulevard was a haven for pushers, pimps, prostitutes, and panhandlers. Sunny Simone sounded like a stage name on a porn video.

She circled the listing, got up, and paced the deck.

Sunny Simone. Sunny Simmons.

She walked back inside, got a pencil and notepad ready, picked up the phone, and punched in 411.

A generic, computerized voice came over the line. "What city and state?"

"Hollywood, California."

"What listing?"

"Sunny Simone."

Within seconds a real live human came on the line. "I have no listing for Sunny Simone. Do you have a street address?"

Kat gave him the address. Still nothing. She tried Sunny Simmons, with no luck, thanked the operator, and hung up. Knowing what the possibilities would mean to Ty, she found it hard to focus on the bucolic scene around her.

If she left now, she could be in L.A. in four hours at the most. She could run by the Hollywood address, see if Sunny Simone was the girl they were looking for. She hated to have Ty get his hopes up for nothing.

Sometimes it was better to have a third party make the first contact anyway. If Sunny Simone wasn't his daughter, then they'd be back to square one.

It felt great to have a plan. Her adrenaline was pumping as she mentally ticked off a list of what to throw in an overnight bag. She'd spend the night at her place in Long Beach and check in with Jake's retired buddy, Arnie, who was handling her open cases.

Suddenly, the house phone rang. She walked inside in time to hear the answering machine pick up. Jake's recorded voice urged the caller to leave a message after the beep.

"Kat? Are you there? It's me, Ty. Pick up, okay?"

She hovered beside the phone, torn by indecision.

"Kat, listen, now something *else* has come up and—"

Perfect. She picked up the receiver.

"Hey, Ty. What's up?"

"How's it going?"

Unexpectedly, she caught herself smiling at the sound of his voice. "Fine."

"You find anything?"

"Not much."

"Listen, there's been a real glitch. One of the equipment suppliers has filed bankruptcy and I have to find another outfit to handle our orders ASAP."

"Are you going to Alaska?" If so, she might have time to slip down to L.A. and get back without him being the wiser.

"No need for that, but this is going to take me a lot longer than I expected. It looks like I'll be tied up for the rest of the day. I just wanted to call and tell you I have no idea when I can get back over there."

Handsome and considerate. This guy is too good to be true.

She stalled, glanced down at the answering machine, imagining him in his quaint house on the point, remembering the feel of his lips upon hers.

"Listen, Ty, something's come up for me, too. I . . . have to go down to Long Beach on business and while I'm there I thought I'd stop in and let my doctor take a look at my hand."

"You haven't reinjured it, have you?"

"It's fine. Just a quick turnaround. I'll be back tomorrow evening at the latest."

There was a pause on the other end of the line and then he asked, "This is kind of sudden, isn't it?"

When she hesitated a moment too long, he read her like a book.

"You have a lead, don't you?"

His suspicion was so right on that it took her a second to recover.

"What?" she hedged.

"You found something and you're driving down to check it out."

There was no way she could outright lie.

"Listen, Ty, this may be a dead end. There are hundreds of names on that printout. It's something kind of close. And I *do* need to go down to Long Beach." Okay, so that part was a stretch. "I just didn't want you to get your hopes up."

"Any higher, you mean?"

"There's no telling what I'll find. Besides, if it *is* her, it's not such a bad idea to have a go-between. Did you ever think she might not want you popping into her life? That she might have a life of her own and a sudden appearance by a father she never knew might just screw it up?"

"What do you think she's got going, Kat? You found her name on the welfare roles. At the very least, I'm a meal ticket. That might be my kid out there and she might need me."

"She might not."

"Maybe not. You're right, but when you find her, I want to be there. Promise me you won't go to L.A. until I can go with you."

"Ty—"

"Hey, you work for me, remember? Promise, or I'll blow this company thing off and pick you up right now. You'll have to live with the guilt of all those unhappy A-list campers sleeping out in the open without tents this summer."

"Now, that would be a real tragedy."

"Yeah. It would be."

She tried to find the will to protest, but there was not only insistence in his voice, there was hope and a rock-solid determination. She knew he'd keep badgering her until she agreed.

It was his hope that won her over. That and the anticipation of spending time alone with him on the drive south.

"Okay, I'll wait."

"I'll get on this and stay on it all night if I have to so that we can take off for L.A. bright and early tomorrow morning."

"I'm not ever very bright when it's early. Today was an exception."

She wondered if she'd be lucky enough to sleep through the night again. Maybe there was something to fresh air and peaceful surroundings—or maybe it was just being around Ty.

"Kat?"

"Yes?"

"Thanks."

"Don't thank me yet. There's no telling what we'll find."

SIX

SAN FERNANDO VALLEY
LOS ANGELES, CALIFORNIA

It was hard to hide three hundred people out in the open—even in the dark. Big crowds added to the winnings, but they drew a lot of police attention.

With too many people around—along with too much booze and drugs—the danger quotient went up and so did the chances of an accident or a bust, or both.

The risk was high, but one she had to take, now more than ever, so she didn't think about the crowd. She couldn't let her mind go there at all. There was too much at stake.

It didn't matter that she was one of the only females involved tonight. She was good at what she did and she knew it. This was a level playing field, where a girl could challenge the big boys and make as much as she wanted to.

It wasn't might or brawn that counted here, but split-second timing, experience, and guts.

Guts or stupidity, depending on your point of view.

Her right hand rested on the gearshift, her foot on the accelerator. She revved the engine, kept her eye on the starter, her left hand on the wheel. When her heart started whooshing in her ears, she began to take slow, deep breaths.

Acres of parking lot were jammed with cars. Deep bass thumps pounded out of boom boxes—tribal, primal, frenetic. In the distance the night sky was stained gray by city lights. The air was filled with fine dust that had yet to settle.

A mix of nitrous oxide and gasoline exhaust was the perfume of the night.

Someone wolf-whistled, shrill and high. She blocked the sound, shifted around in the low-slung leather seat.

She stroked her left hand over the steering-wheel cover. This wasn't her car—she could never afford anything like this, not now anyway. But guys begged her to race their rods for them. They wanted the bragging rights.

Not just anyone could entice Sunny Simone behind the wheel of his car. The choice was up to her. It had to be the right car and the right night.

She revved the engine again. Cut her eyes to the Asian driver in the Rice Rocket beside her. They'd competed before. He was real good, too. But he wasn't hungry. His dad had a huge bankroll.

He wasn't desperate.

She was.

She concentrated on the starter. Refused to let the crowd down. They were chanting her name now. A low, steady repetition that picked up the pace until it kept time with her heartbeat.

Sunny. Sunny. Sunny.

She couldn't see the starter's eyes, but instinctively she knew when he was going to give the signal. She hit the accelerator at the exact instant he waved his arms.

SEVEN

L.A. was L.A.; smoggy and crowded.

The heart of the city beat with an underlying Latin tempo. Wanna-be stars, panhandlers, and illegals selling bags of oranges and crates of strawberries shared the corners of palm-lined boulevards with the rich and famous.

Ty drove all the way with his stomach in knots, wondering what they'd find, if and when they found Sunny at all.

"You think I'm crazy for wanting this?" he asked Kat.

"No. Not crazy. I understand completely."

"But you don't sound very sure."

"Legally, she doesn't have to have anything to do with you if she doesn't want to. She might tell you to take a leap."

"I know, and I appreciate your honesty, but I have to find her. She's family. She's mine."

The idea that they might not find her today was bringing him down, so he concentrated on the city as he drove. He hadn't been to Southern California for years and the changes were dramatic. Hollywood was nothing like it had been portrayed in the movies.

Tinseltown had spilled over into Burbank, Studio City, and Culver City, where the major studios were located.

The industry had moved and left behind Mann's Chinese Theatre and its footprints of the stars preserved in cement.

Now tourists, mimes and clowns, pimps, hookers, and panhandlers—not to mention a cluster of transvestites outside the Frederick's Lingerie Museum—all mingled on the Walk of Fame stars on Hollywood Boulevard.

Growing up in Twilight Cove and living in Alaska hadn't helped Ty hone his city driving skills. Thankfully, Kat navigated with a Thomas Guide in her lap as they wound their way along Hollywood Boulevard to Franklin Avenue.

Ty made a right, and out of nowhere a low, black BMW came at them, headed across double-double center lines. As he hit the brakes, Kat drove both her feet into the floorboard and threw her hands up over her face. The map book flew off her lap and slammed into the dash. Ty honked and swore as he swerved, avoiding a collision.

He immediately pulled into the parking lot outside a 7-Eleven convenience store and cut the engine. Kat's face was already drained of color and she was staring straight ahead, shaking violently. It had been a close call, but not that close.

"Kat?" He reached for her shoulder, but she rocked away from his touch. When she bumped against the passenger door, she seemed to snap out of it.

"Are you all right?" he asked.

She opened her mouth to answer, but nothing came out.

He asked again if she was all right. It was obvious she wasn't, but he had no idea what to do.

Slowly she began to nod her head yes.

"I'm okay," she whispered. Then in a stronger voice, echoed, "I'm okay. Really."

"No you're not."

She bent to retrieve the map book from the floor. She laid it in her lap and then rested her bandaged hand atop it.

"Yes." She nodded again, as if to assure herself more than him. "Yes, I am. I'm fine. Let's go."

"I'm sorry, Kat, but that guy came out of nowhere."

"I know. It wasn't your fault. I'm just a little . . . I was in a pretty bad accident a few years ago. It left me a little . . . a little . . . shaken up." She took a deep breath, making a real effort to smile, but failed miserably.

He glanced at the traffic whizzing by on the crowded street. The BMW was long gone.

"Let's go. I'm okay," she urged.

"You're sure?"

"Just drive."

He took it slow as they pulled into traffic again. When they hit Fair Avenue, they started looking for Sunny's address. It was two o'clock and he was starving. It had been his idea not to stop for lunch. Now it was too late and he regretted it.

"There it is." Kat's voice cut the silence she'd maintained since the near-miss and startled him so that he had to slam on the breaks again to keep from rear-ending a Volvo wagon in front of them.

But this time Kat didn't flinch. Instead, she let go a shaky laugh. "Now I know why you preferred the wide-open spaces. You drive like crap."

He pulled in behind a Harley chopper parked alongside the curb in front of a classic California courtyard apartment comprised of a two-story building built around a central garden.

Giant bird of paradise plants filled each corner of the

garden. Groupings of old metal lawn chairs, once painted in bright rainbow hues, were rusted and peeling. Two faded pink plastic flamingos guarded an empty, lopsided birdbath.

Ty released a long, deep sigh but it didn't help calm him. He wished he could jog a mile or two and let off some steam, but inhaling all the smog would probably kill him.

Before he could step out, Kat reached over and touched his hand.

"It'll be okay," she assured him. "Either way. If we haven't found her, we'll keep looking."

He closed his hand over hers and gave it a squeeze. She reacted by blushing, and he pulled away.

All business again, she grabbed her straw bag, slipped the leather straps over her shoulder. Noting the protective way she tucked the bag under her arm, he didn't have to ask if she was carrying her handgun.

She turned to him. "Ready?"

"Ready as I'll ever be." When he glanced out the window at the apartment building, nausea and anticipation hit him. Again he wished he'd pulled over for a quick bite. At least then there would be something besides acid churning in his stomach.

"Number six? Right?" He knew the apartment number like he knew his phone number but he just had to ask to make this more than surreal.

"Right. Six."

"Well. Okay, then." When he reached for the car handle, his damn hand shook. He desperately wanted this, but it was such a shot in the dark. "Let's go."

EIGHT

As they walked along the narrow sidewalk, Kat pressed her bag into her side, thankful for her .380.

The place was run-down, which didn't necessarily mean trouble, but after what happened to her in an upscale, pricey neighborhood like Seal Beach—in the company of an upstanding, wealthy housewife—she wasn't taking any chances.

Fate was like lightning. It could strike anywhere, anytime.

She let Ty lead the way as they passed the birdbath. Not only were the faded flamingos beside it, but a beheaded statue of St. Francis. The saint's cement head smiled up beatifically from where it lay in the dirt.

Kat glanced at Ty. His tension was infectious. Still shaken by the close call with the Beemer, she took a deep breath and forced herself to relax as Ty knocked on the arched, solid oak door, a reminder of California's Spanish heritage that certainly wasn't standard issue on houses anymore.

An elderly woman with bleached blond hair wound in a bun and held in place by a chopstick opened the door.

"Hi. I'm Happy!" she chirped.

"That's great." Ty cleared his throat. "Does Sunny Simone live here?"

"Donny Leon? I've never heard of Donny Leon." The woman craned her neck and looked up, her blue eyes focused on Ty. "You're a big one, aren'tcha?"

"Sunny. Sunny Simone," Kat raised her voice and leaned close to the woman. "Do you know her?"

"She doesn't live here."

"Do you know her? Do you know where she lives?"

"Sure. I know what gives," the woman shouted back. "They never get married anymore. Wear those tight clothes and let their belly buttons hang out. Bunch of tarts, if you ask me. Hussies."

"Do you know *anyone* named Sunny? She's nineteen."

"Try across the walk. They got a bunch of 'em in there."

"Which apartment?" Ty asked.

"Nine."

They crossed the courtyard. Kat waited while Ty knocked. She was thinking about how much she liked all the doors when the one he'd knocked on was partially opened by a thin young woman with limp, dishwater brown hair and green eyes that were far too big for her face.

A beaded black choker was clamped around her slender neck, a long-sleeved black knit top and black jeans covered most of the rest of her. She looked like a candidate for an anorexia clinic. Sure enough, her bejeweled belly button floated in the middle of a concave abdomen.

"Yeah?" Clinging to the edge of the door, the girl stared at Ty for a second, then at Kat.

Apparently, Ty had suddenly been rendered mute, so Kat made direct eye contact with the girl and donned her best P.I., no-nonsense persona.

"We're looking for Sunny Simone."

"If that idiot Gomez sent you about the rent—"

"No one sent us. We're here on a personal matter. It's about Sunny's mother."

"Sunny doesn't have a mother."

Pay dirt. "So you're not Sunny Simone?"

Miss Anorexia slowly shook her head. "Not *even.* If you tell me what you want, maybe—"

Suddenly the door swung open to reveal another girl. She, too, wore black jeans and a tight tank top, which showed off her well-defined arms, one of which was tattooed with a thin, barbed-wire design around her biceps. The tattoo showed off the kind of sleek muscle definition Kat envied.

Her hair was long, a vibrant chestnut streaked with red highlights. Her eyes, heavily outlined with black liner, were as blue as a smog-free summer sky. She was a few inches taller than Kat, long and lean, and altogether stunning.

She had Ty's coloring, and *maybe* a hint of his features, but Kat realized she might be seeing what she wanted to see, hoping for Ty's sake that this was Sunny.

Kat sensed from the way Ty had stiffened when the girl first appeared that he recognized something in her, perhaps something that reminded him of Amy.

"*I'm* Sunny." She gave them a quick once-over. "What's this about my mother?"

Kat, distracted by a repetitive squeak, turned in time to see the old woman with bleached hair pulling a collapsible aluminum shopping basket down the walk. She waved and called out to Kat, "Flea market today!"

Kat focused on Sunny again. "Can we come in for a minute?"

Sunny Simone sized them both up in a quick glance, nodded, and stepped back. As they cleared the door, they heard a wail from a back room, a child's cry. The thin, mousey-brown-haired girl took off down the hall. She wasn't over fifteen.

The apartment was small and cluttered, but all the furniture appeared to be expensive and fairly new. One wall was occupied by a big-screen television tuned to *One Life to Live*. The TV was surrounded by the latest in home entertainment equipment.

Kat tried to ignore the cries of the fussy child in the background and concentrate on the exchange between Ty and Sunny Simone instead.

Sunny didn't ask them to sit down. "Are you police?"

Ty shook his head, found his tongue. "No. My name is Ty Chandler. I'm from a little town up the coast. Twilight Cove."

"So?" If Sunny had heard of the place, she didn't let on.

"Was your mother Amy Simmons?" he asked.

"Why?"

"If she was, then I'm your dad."

Kat winced. *Nice going, Ty. Real finesse. Why not just hit the kid over the head with a two-by-four?* She couldn't keep her heart from going out to him as she watched him flounder.

The girl's expression barely changed.

"You're shittin' me. I don't have a dad."

"You do now, if Amy Simmons was your mother. Were you born at a place called River Ridge?"

"Yeah. I lived there until they busted up the place. My mom died."

"And you ended up in foster care—"

"But not for long."

"Were you adopted?"

"Fat chance. I was eleven. I hung around a few years, then I ran away."

"How old were you?"

"It's none of your business."

Ty glanced around the cluttered room, met Kat's eyes for an instant. He looked like someone had sucker-punched him.

At that point the younger girl walked back into the room with a green-eyed toddler on her hip. She crossed the living room and went into the kitchen.

They heard her open the refrigerator. Glass bottles and jars clinked together before she walked back into the living room and sat down on a low-slung leather couch littered with tabloid newspapers, clothing, crumpled fast-food bags.

She set a cold jar of baby carrots on the smeared glass-and-chrome coffee table, plopped the wide-eyed, curly-headed little girl down beside her.

The toddler lost her balance and let out a whine while the teenager paused to twist the top off the jar. Then the teen righted the little girl and fished a plastic spoon out of the mess on the table.

With tearstains on her cheeks, the toddler goo-gooed and smiled triumphantly at Kat through spiked lashes. Kat looked away.

It was obvious from the items in the room, the expensive watches and clothes the girls wore, that they had income other than welfare. Sunny could be into anything—dealing drugs, turning tricks, fencing stolen property.

Kat had the urge to scoop up the toddler and see that she was put in foster care.

Nothing gave her the right to play God, but sometimes she was convinced He was on vacation most of the time. Her mom believed God had a plan for everyone, but Kat had decided long ago if that was true, He was sorely in need of a good assistant.

The little girl was whining, but she didn't appear to be

mistreated or neglected. Poor housekeeping skills weren't a crime—if they were, Kat knew that she'd have been locked up long ago. Besides, the baby could land in an even worse situation.

Calling the authorities wouldn't help, not without concrete proof that anything illegal was going on. Kat reminded herself not to get involved. Ty had hired her to find Sunny. Case closed.

When her gaze strayed of its own volition to the toddler again, she noticed the child was no longer fussing. Kat had to force herself to look away this time.

"What'd you say your name was?" Sunny asked Ty.

"Ty Chandler. And this is Kat Vargas. Listen, Sunny, I'd like to talk to you, get better acquainted. I'd hoped you'd agree to come up and visit Twilight Cove—"

"You gotta be kidding me, man. I don't even know who you are or even if you're telling me the truth."

"She's got a point there," Kat mumbled, earning herself sharp glares from both Ty and the girl. As far as Ty knew, Amy could have lied to her parents about Ty being Sunny's father.

"Why now?" Sunny threw her head back, flipping her long hair over her shoulder. "It's a little late to start playing Dad, don't you think? If you were so hot to be a father, why'd you wait so long?"

"I didn't even know you existed until a few months ago."

"How come my mom never even mentioned your name? How come she never told you about me?"

"I was in Alaska."

"No phone service up that far?" Sunny's lip curled.

Ty shoved his hand through his hair and glanced over at Kat. She knew how important this moment was to him. If she were in his place she'd say whatever she had to say, go to the end of the earth and back to win her daughter over.

"Look." Kat stepped up to Sunny, as if speaking confidentially, woman to woman. "It's complicated. Mr. Chandler and your mom split when they were in high school. He took off for Alaska and never heard about you until three months ago. Now he's offering you a chance to be part of his life, if you want to, in a nice, cozy little town up the coast."

"And I'm supposed to just walk out on my *own* life to be the kid he never knew he had?"

Ty cleared his throat. "That's up to you. We could start slow. Maybe go out for something to eat. Have lunch and talk. Set up a time for you to come up and visit."

"How do I know you're really my father?"

"I knew it the minute you came to the door. Your eyes are exactly like my grandmother's. The rest of you is all Amy. But if you want a paternity test, I'll pay for one." He took a deep breath and backed off a bit.

"Why don't I give you some time to think all this over? We're heading back up the coast tomorrow, but we can pick you up on our way, if you'd like to come visit for a few days. It's your move." He looked adrift on a sea of regret and uncertainty, but he was excited by all the possibilities. "Have you got a piece of paper?"

Sunny ripped a corner off of a Burger King bag and handed it to him. Kat reached inside her purse and rooted around for a pen. He jotted down his address and cell number.

As he handed the scrap back to Sunny and the pen to Kat, the door opened. Three men in their twenties slouched in. The first one in was Hispanic with dark eyes and hair. He was heavyset, with what looked like a permanent scowl. He headed straight for one of two black leather recliners in the room, the pricy kind from Sharper Image, tricked out with a massage unit. He swiped the television remote off the coffee table and switched off the soap. A black-and-white SciFi classic filled the screen.

The second man was shorter than the Hispanic. He could have been the boy next door. Spiked brown hair, blue eyes, pants that hung off his hips, a thick wallet chain, and a tight white T-shirt. James Dean of the new millennium. He wandered into the kitchen without a word to anyone.

The oldest, last one in, was a blond with fair, angelic coloring, a hard edge to his mouth, and suspicion in his eyes. His hair was long, blond, knotted with dreadlocks gone bad. He walked directly over to Sunny and immediately squared off with Ty. Kat casually hung her good hand over the open edge of her purse.

"What's up with this?" Dreadlocks wanted to know.

Sunny shoved the tattered piece of paper with Ty's address into the pocket of her Levi's.

"This guy claims he's my dad."

"You gotta be shittin' me."

"Yeah, that's what I thought, but he knew all about my mom, Jamie."

"So? That doesn't mean he's your father."

"Look, buddy—" When Ty took a step in Jamie's direction, Kat laid her bandaged hand on his forearm. He immediately froze, but didn't step back.

"Listen, Sunny," Kat said softly, trying to cut through a mounting layer of testosterone. "Why don't you think things over and give Mr. Chandler a call if you change your mind?"

"Change your mind about what?" Jamie's cold eyes narrowed. His fingers bit into Sunny's arm but she easily shook him off.

Kat waited to see if Sunny had the situation under control, not the least bit worried about stepping in if Jamie started to bully the girl. Beside Kat, Ty remained tense.

But Sunny didn't look afraid of Jamie. In fact, she shot him a glance that clearly warned him to back off, and he did.

Relieved, Kat looped her arm through Ty's elbow in an attempt to steer him toward the door.

"Say good-bye, Ty," she murmured. "*Now.*"

At first she was afraid he wasn't going to budge, but then he slowly nodded.

"Call me, Sunny," he said. "I'd like a chance to get to know you. That's really all I came to say."

Kat's heart ached for him as they walked out the door. Sunny hadn't even said good-bye.

NINE

Ty Chandler's address was burning a hole in Sunny's pocket. If he was the real deal, then he just might be the answer to her prayers.

Not that she needed or wanted a dad anymore. Those days were behind her. But now she might have somewhere to run to, somewhere to get away and think about things.

Right now, anyplace was better than here.

It wouldn't be easy to leave. No doubt about it. Callie and Jamie, Butch and Leaf were her family—all the family she'd ever known—and like real family, they wanted her to stick around. More than that, they *needed* her. She was the one who brought in the most money, and lately there was never enough.

She hadn't ever dreamed of leaving. There had never been a glimmer of hope before.

But getting away, even for a while, wouldn't be easy.

She glanced at Callie, who was still sitting on the couch with French Fry on her lap. She couldn't even tell Callie what she was planning. If Jamie found out, he would put such a guilt trip on her that she probably wouldn't have the nerve to leave.

Who'd have ever thought her *dad* would magically show up at the door when she most needed help?

As soon as Chandler left, Sunny stepped away from Jamie, pretending not to give a damn about what just happened—a real challenge, considering all the possibilities and questions running through her mind.

She'd watched Ty Chandler and the woman closely, wondered how they were connected, if they were screwing each other. If so, it didn't show.

She wondered how he'd found out about her.

Chandler had acted real intense. As if he actually *cared* whether or not she wanted to talk to him.

Go figure.

"So, what'd he want? Why did he ask you to call him?" Jamie scratched his matted dreadlocks.

She tried not to notice the grease stains beneath his nails or the smell of automotive fluids that permeated his clothes. He wasn't much taller than she, certainly nowhere near as tall or muscular as Dodge had been, but Dodge wasn't here anymore.

"Don't ever look back, Sunny. It's a waste of fucking time."

Her mom hadn't taught her much of anything else. What kind of a guy was Chandler, if he'd been mixed up with her mom? Amy Simmons had been a real piece of work, certainly no model mother. Far from it.

Sunny caught Callie's eye and tossed her a warning glance that as good as said, *If you give Jamie any details, I'll have to hurt you.* The fourteen-year-old was feeding the baby again, scraping sick-colored orange goo from French Fry's chin with a plastic spoon.

"Sunny? What's up?" Jamie was waiting for an answer. No way in hell was she telling him that Ty Chandler had asked her to visit him.

Sunny shrugged, looked Jamie straight in the eye. "He said he'd like to get to know me, that kinda thing. Said if I ever wanted to talk, I could call him, you know? But I told him I didn't need him hanging around."

The lie slipped from her tongue so easily, she sounded so sincere, that she amazed herself.

Callie finished feeding French Fry, wiped her up with a paper napkin, and tossed it on the coffee table beside the empty carrot jar. The toddler started waving her hands and talking gibberish.

Across the room, Butch dropped the television remote onto the chair he'd just vacated, belched, and then reminded Jamie that it was time to get going. Jamie turned to Sunny.

"You ready? We need to get on the road. Fontana tonight."

"Yeah. Let me get my jacket."

God, I'm tired, she thought. The routine was wearing on her, getting her down. Especially without Dodge.

Ty looked so tired and dejected when they left Sunny's apartment that Kat had driven with him straight to Long Beach, fed him, and then taken him home. She'd never asked a man over before. Jake certainly didn't count—and besides, she hadn't exactly *invited* Jake over, he'd barged in after driving her car home from the hospital.

She regretted having Ty there the minute they walked through the door and everything seemed to move to a more intimate level. They were alone in her house, where she slept, showered, ate, hung out.

Bad idea. Bad, bad idea, Vargas.

She'd broken another cardinal rule tonight by taking pity on him, but he didn't seem in any condition to be left alone at a motel.

He sank into her sofa and didn't move. She left him staring into space while she went to collect a blanket and pillow. When she returned, she tossed them at him to see if he was dead or just comatose.

He snagged them both without looking up.

She asked, "What are you thinking?"

He shook his head. "I was just thinking what a dolt I must have sounded like today. I don't even remember what I said." He groaned and punched the pillow. "I didn't ask if she was in school or if she had some kind of a job. I just assumed she would want to pick up and go back to Twilight with me."

He shoved the bedding on the floor and dropped his head to the back of the sofa with a groan. "You think there are any self-help books for this kind of thing?"

"Maybe. We can always check out the late-night *Jerry Springer* episode descriptions in the television guide." She walked into the kitchen for a bottle of wine.

"I can't get over how beautiful she is. Do you think she's pretty?"

Kat paused with her hand on the refrigerator handle and stared blankly at the faux brick linoleum floor.

"Actually, she's stunning." After a pause she asked, "Does she look like her mother?"

"Yeah. Only much prettier. She looks a little like my grandma, too. I knew she was mine the minute I saw her."

Kat sighed and wondered why it somehow mattered that Sunny looked exactly like Amy, that she'd forever remind Ty of his first love.

"Want a glass of wine?"

"Sure," he said.

She had to dust a second glass, not easy with one hand wrapped like something out of Abbott and Costello's *Meet the Mummy.*

Back in the living room, she noted he hadn't moved.

The pillow and blanket were in a heap on the floor at his feet.

Melancholy didn't suit him and she doubted he'd wallow in it very long. He was an outdoors man, used to action, but there was nothing he could do to change Sunny's mind.

"What would you do right now if you were in Alaska?"

He looked up, leaned forward, and picked up the wineglass she'd set on the coffee table. "What do you mean?"

"To let off steam in the land of the Kodiak. What would you do?"

He shrugged. "Go hiking. Roll up a tent and a backpack and take off. Camp out alone for a few days to clear my head."

"So why not do that when you get back to Twilight Cove?"

Finally. Half a smile. "I'll probably go fishing instead."

"Good idea, as long as you remember to share."

"You bet." He raised the glass, silently toasted, and took a drink. "Thanks, Kat. For everything."

"Don't thank me. Maybe I haven't done you any favors."

"Maybe she'll call."

"You really think so?"

He shrugged again. "A guy can always hope."

She turned on the television. Knowing how bad he felt was breaking down all her defenses. She found herself wanting to sit beside him and give him something else to think about.

Ty finished his wine and watched Kat sit at her desk and start to flip through the *Pennysaver* throwaway ads and Have-You-Seen-Me? missing-kids postcards. Bulk mail. The stuff of future archaeological digs in mountains of landfill.

"Thanks for letting me stay here. Otherwise I'd be moping around by myself."

"No problem. Always room for another moper on my sofa." She smiled but didn't look up as she paused for the briefest of seconds before she continued sorting. "Friends don't let friends mope alone."

He tried not to laugh and wondered if she ever took her own advice. She was definitely uncomfortable being alone with him. The difference in her was obvious.

Earlier, at Sunny's apartment, she'd been confident and poised. She'd stood up for him more than once. But now she was having a hard time settling down, as if she didn't know what to do with herself.

"Was private investigating something you always wanted to do, Kat?"

She dumped the last of the junk mail and sat back, started twirling the stem of the wineglass between her thumb and forefinger, swirling wine up the sides.

"I'd never thought about it in my life. I was desperate for a job and Jake Montgomery's ad sounded interesting. He hired me to answer the phone, run errands, that kind of thing. I found out I was an adrenaline junkie and really got into it. I worked on getting the requirements for a license out of the way and a little over two years later, we were partners."

"Now you're on your own."

"Yes." Her eyes filled with shadows again.

"Were you in love with him?"

"Who?" She set her wine down.

"Montgomery. Were you ever in love with him?"

Her hair gently swayed against her shoulders as she shook her head. "No. We were just friends."

His gaze touched her all over, moved to her bandaged

hand, and his insides involuntarily clenched. She looked so sensual, even in the casual way she sat there with her bare foot tucked under her and her head propped on her hand.

She was easy in her skin, a woman confident in herself and her looks, one who wouldn't really care if anyone thought she was beautiful, even though she definitely was stunning.

"Kat?"

She looked pensive, almost wary when she finally met his eyes.

"Come over here. Please."

After a moment's hesitation, she got up and walked across the room to sit beside him. She didn't say a word when he reached for her bare foot, but she tensed up until he began to massage her arch.

"You've done this before, haven't you?" She leaned back, let him rest her foot on his knee. Her feet were small, but they fit her. Her toes were tapered, neatly polished a deep red.

"I've been told I'm good at it."

"You mean I'm not the first? That's no way to make a girl feel special."

"Somehow I get the distinct impression you don't let anyone treat you special." He paused, cradled her foot in his hands.

At first she didn't say a word. Didn't respond other than to stare into his eyes.

"What makes you say that?"

"You're a beautiful woman, and yet there's no man in your life—"

"Are you sure?"

He looked around the room, at her cluttered desk, her pile of videos, the clothes hanging on an exercycle in the corner. From where he sat he could see into the efficiency kitchen.

"My guess is that you hole up here with your stack of movies and eat take-out meals alone and dress on the run because you push yourself to work constantly. I saw your calendar in the kitchen. Tae Kwon Do and office hours. Not much else there. You told me yourself that you'd never been married but didn't say why. You're house-sitting alone—"

She cut him off. "None of that adds up to proof of anything."

"Let's just say, if you were mine, I'd never let you go off house-sitting alone for six weeks. Especially after you'd just been shot."

She dropped her eyes, stared at her bandage. "No, I don't suppose you would."

"Who was he?"

"Who was who?"

"The guy who broke your heart."

"That's none of your business."

"You're right, it's not, but I'm asking anyway."

In many ways she was as stubborn as he. He didn't think she'd answer, but when she did, her voice was so low and hesitant that he had to strain to hear.

"His name's Justin Parker—"

"The pro surfer?" He was impressed. He used to surf when he lived in Twilight, and had kept up with the sport.

She nodded.

"I read a big article about him in *Sports Illustrated* a few years back," he recalled.

"He's great at P.R., but not so great at being faithful."

"He's a real good-looking guy."

"He knows. We were engaged until I found out he was cheating on me." She shrugged, grew silent.

He knew damned well there was a whole lot more to the story—he could see the pain in her eyes.

It suddenly dawned on him that R.J. looked a little like Justin Parker. Not as much of a pretty boy, but he had the fair-haired, handsome, water sportsman look. But R.J. wasn't a player.

"I don't play around, Kat."

She instantly came back from wherever her thoughts had taken her.

"Oh, really? And why is it you think I need to know that?"

"I like you. A lot."

"Your feelings are raw right now. You've got things all jumbled together. Just because I'm the one who helped you find your daughter you're transferring—"

"It's more than that and I think you know it. I've known it since I first laid eyes on you."

His right hand moved to her ankle. He ran his fingers up her calf, kneaded it. Her muscles were firm, yet supple and feminine. He heard her breath catch and tried to distract her.

"How long have you been kickboxing?"

"*Not* kickboxing. *Not* karate. Tae Kwon Do."

"Whatever." When his hand reached her thigh, he grazed the skin beneath the hem of her shorts with his fingertips.

"I've been at it long enough to know that I could easily render you senseless right now."

"There are plenty of other ways you could render me senseless." He leaned closer, his gaze trained on her mouth, wanting to kiss her in the worst way, wondering if she'd let him.

He shifted positions and wound up sitting closer. She'd fallen silent, as if contemplating what he'd said.

He moved in to steal a kiss, half expecting her to balk,

but she didn't. He found himself staring into her eyes when their mouths met, realized she'd parted her lips. She leaned back against the arm of the sofa as the kiss deepened. He thought he heard her moan.

His hand grazed her knit top where it covered her breast.

Her hand landed on his shoulder and there was a second when things could have gone either way before she gently pushed him back and ended the kiss. In one swift move, she stood up.

"It's been a real long day, Chandler. I'm gonna hit the sack. You need some time to cool off." Before he knew it, she was halfway across the living room, turning off the television.

"Are you sure you want to leave me out here all alone?"

The cushions on the sofa were deep and soft—a backache waiting to happen. Kat crossed her arms, pretending to think it over.

"You're just lucky that you made it through the door tonight in the first place."

In her bedroom, Kat was trembling as she peeled off her clothes and shrugged into an oversized tank top. Her legs were still shaking when she slipped into bed.

She left the light on and leaned back against the headboard, with her knees to her chest, her chin on her knees, and thought about the man in the living room.

Tempted by Ty, she'd let her guard down, and realized—almost too late—that her body reacted to his in a way it hadn't responded to a man in a long, long time. She knew exactly what might have happened if she hadn't been terrified into calling a halt to his kiss.

Not only had his kiss moved her, but he'd asked her some simple, straightforward questions, and for the first time in years, she'd opened up and actually talked about Justin.

Why now? Why with Ty Chandler?

She'd dated men since Justin. Not often and not many, but she had dated. She'd even gone to bed with a handful. They'd all been one-night stands, nothing more, few and far between.

She didn't need a man in her life, at least she was fairly convinced of that by now—but more to the point, what she *really* didn't need was to be hurt the way she'd been hurt before.

Hurt, hell. *Shattered* was a better word.

It might have been different if she'd had some experience before Justin Parker blew into her life. The pain might not have cut so deep, might not have driven her to be so reckless if she hadn't believed that Justin was the man she'd been waiting for all her life.

Her girlfriends used to tease her about being the oldest living virgin on Kauai.

She'd fallen in love with Justin's good looks as much as with the notion that he was a celebrity in the surfing world.

It never dawned on her that he might only want her because she was "local," with dark hair, eyes, and coloring. It helped Justin to be seen around the islands with a "Hawaiian babe" on his arm. Being with her gave him entrée to places where haoles weren't welcome.

It never occurred to her that he would move in with her, ask her to marry him, and still sleep with other women. She'd been so trusting, so blinded by love, that it hadn't occurred to her at all.

She'd let desire get in the way of her common sense once. She wasn't about to let it happen again.

Feeling in control again, Kat reached over and turned

out the light, then wadded up her pillow and lay there in the dark with her eyes wide-open.

After dredging up the past, she was afraid to fall asleep.

A crack of light appeared beneath her door and she heard Ty moving around in the bathroom. Then the light went out again and she heard him walk back through the kitchen to the living room.

He probably wasn't going to get any sleep tonight, either.

She tried to forget about his admission of being attracted to her from the moment they met. What bothered her more was that the feeling was mutual.

She shouldn't have let him kiss her again tonight. She never would have dared if she'd only known how quickly his kiss, his touch, would turn her on.

TEN

Early evening, the sky is a dull pewter, hanging close to the ground, hiding the mountaintops. Fierce rain squalls roll one after the other, over Kauai.

Torrents of runoff water carry rust-red dirt down hill-sides, along rivers and streams, to the sea, where it clouds the reef. Rain slicks the highway, turns it into a shimmering asphalt ribbon.

She runs out of the apartment, jumps into her Mazda. The windshield wipers fight a losing battle against the rain.

Sugarcane grows tall on both sides of the Kapa'a by-pass road, a lush corridor of swaying green stalks. She speeds along, mindless of the storm, negotiating another curve as she wipes tears from her eyes.

The pickup truck suddenly appears out of nowhere. Maybe it's the buildup of water on the windshield, maybe it's the waving cane or her tears that distract her. Whatever.

All she knows is that one minute she's driving, and the next, a Nissan pickup on oversized tires materializes directly in front of the hood of her car.

Metal grinds against metal. Glass shatters. Tires scream and fail to grip the wet road.

The gray sky, the rain, the glistening cane stalks—

everything turns inside out and disappears. Her world explodes and goes black. She sees nothing. Feels nothing.

Inside her, a scream starts to build. A scream that has no end.

Ty was still awake when the sound of Kat's scream tore through him, set his teeth on edge, and started his heart pounding.

He bolted off the sofa. His feet tangled in the blanket and he almost went down when he hit his shin against the low coffee table. Cursing, he negotiated the dark interior of Kat's apartment, guided by the sound of her screams.

His heart pounded triple time as multiple scenarios flashed through his mind—Kat tripping in the darkness, a burglar slipping in through the back door, a rapist cutting the window screen.

He found her alone, tangled in the bedsheet, thrashing against an unseen threat. He knelt on her bed, pulled her into his arms.

"Kat! Kat, you're dreaming." He tried to calm her, not to frighten her any more than she was already.

"No! No, please, no!" She shoved at him. Tried to push him away.

Afraid she'd do damage to her injured hand, he grabbed her wrists, held her still.

"Kat. Wake up."

She calmed, crying but no longer flailing around. He switched on a lamp on the nightstand. When he turned, he found her staring at him as if she had no recollection of who he was or what he was doing there.

He gently cupped her cheek.

"Kat, it's me, Ty. You're all right. You're in your own room."

Her eyes were wide but no longer wild. Her lips trembled. Tears glistened on her cheeks. He thumbed them off, pulled her against his chest, and held her tight.

She didn't protest as he shifted around to lean against the headboard and hold her close. She shuddered and sniffed, wiped her eyes. But she didn't pull out of his embrace.

"I'm suh . . . sorry," she mumbled, sniffing again.

"Hey, it's okay. It's okay." He was just glad he was there, that maybe he could help.

He rubbed his hand down her back over and over again. Her skin was clammy. The white tank top she slept in exposed her firm, shapely legs. When he noticed she only had a minuscule silk thong beneath it, he almost broke out in a cold sweat himself.

He glanced around the room. The windows were open, but bars protected the screens. Nothing appeared to be out of place.

"What happened?"

"Nightmare."

"You want to talk about it?" It had to have been one hell of a whopper to make her scream like that.

Her head moved against his chest. "No," she whispered.

"Has this ever happened before?"

"All the time. *Almost* all the time. I don't sleep much."

He remembered seeing stacks of videos in the living room, here and at Montgomery's, imagined her driving herself to exhaustion during the day, then sitting alone night after night, afraid to fall asleep.

He was amazed that someone so together, seemingly so confident, could be so terrified by a dream. He wondered what terrible images her mind conjured.

Her tremors had subsided, but she continued to cling. He had no idea how she made it through these episodes alone. Then he recalled how frightened she'd been this afternoon after the BMW had nearly collided with them.

"I was in a pretty bad accident a few years ago. It left me a little . . . shaken up."

Shaken up, hell, he thought. Maybe what happened earlier today had brought it all back.

"Do you dream about the accident?"

"It never goes away," she whispered.

"Did it happen here, or on Kauai?"

Again, she hesitated at first. "Kauai."

He didn't know anything about nightmares or the psyche, but instinct told him the worst thing she could do was keep it all bottled up inside.

"Was anyone killed?"

She let go a deep breath. "A teenager in the other car. He'd just graduated from high school. The kids caravan in June. Some play chicken. Stupid, when their whole lives are ahead of them."

"Is that why you left the island?"

He felt her nod yes against his chest. He let her be, and didn't ask any more as she lay there in his arms, occasionally wiping away silent tears. The heat of her skin aroused him. He kissed the crown of her head, gently, wanting nothing more than to hold and comfort her despite what she was doing to him inside and out.

He skimmed his hand up and down her arm, lightly stroking her skin, petting her, calming her, until her breathing slowly returned to normal.

He thought perhaps she'd fallen asleep, when she suddenly pressed her open palm against his bare ribs and slid her arms around him. Then she tilted her head and looked into his eyes.

"Kiss me, Ty," she demanded, offering him her plump mouth.

He knew her urge was primal, a grasp at consolation,

or perhaps a lifeline. A way to numb her mind. To prove to herself she had survived another nightmare as well as the wreck that caused them.

She needed what he could give her tonight as much as—maybe more than—he needed what she was offering after the day he'd had.

Solace. A few brief moments of blissful oblivion, a time out from the state of things, from the upheavals in his life. Physical release. Contact with another being at the highest level.

"Are you sure?" His fingertips skimmed across one of her taught nipples.

"Don't make me beg, Chandler."

He kissed her. Gave her what she wanted. Took what he wanted. She met him halfway, scooted onto her knees so that she could kiss him deeply. She tasted sweet as honey, warm as velvet. Her lips were as soft as he'd known they would be, her skin smooth as silk.

The kiss went on and on until, breathless, she pulled back.

"Help me." She tried to pull off her tank top with one hand. He obliged, quick and sure. Then she slipped out of her thong and was naked beside him. He reached for the lamp. She stopped him.

"Leave it on. Please."

He pulled off his shorts, then his briefs. Tossed them on the floor, and remembered. "I don't have a cond—"

"The bathroom cupboard. Third shelf, beside the Band-Aids."

He thought she might come to her senses while he was gone, but when he came back, she was holding the sheet across her breasts, watching the door, waiting. He walked into the room, naked, fully aroused. He paused, waited for her to change her mind.

He slipped into bed beside her, took her in his arms, stroked her back, let her make the next move.

"Kiss me again," she ordered.

She was easy to please. He kissed her deeply, slowly, until she moaned. He ran his hands down her tight abdomen to the soft flesh between her thighs, found her wet, slick and ready.

He kissed her breasts, teased her nipples with his teeth until she cried out and came against his hand. When she'd recovered, when she was breathing even and deep, she guided him with a gentle nudge until he was lying on his back. She leaned over him, kissed him, ran her tongue over his lips and down his throat until he shivered.

The torture was exquisite. She took her time, running her fingers down his ribs, kissing him everywhere, licking him. She knelt between his thighs, took him in her hands.

He held his breath, watched when she took him into her mouth, teased him with her tongue. When he couldn't take it anymore, he closed his eyes.

In the next breath she was on her knees, over him, drawing him deep inside her.

It was as good as he knew it would be. He held her hips. She used her body to stroke him. Slowly at first, she tortured him until his tension and desire spiraled. Only then did she begin to quicken her movements.

He thrust in return, filling her. He wanted to give her everything and more. To take away her fears, her pain, whatever it was that haunted her nights and put shadows beneath her eyes.

They came together, let go, rode wave after wave of pleasure until she lay draped around him with her cheek pressed to his heart, until her breathing slowed and settled into a normal rhythm.

Five, ten, fifteen minutes went by. Carefully, so as not to disturb her, he turned out the light, wrapped an arm around her waist, and let her sleep.

Kat woke before Ty. The sun was already up. She slipped out of his arms and into the shower and had coffee made by the time he came out of her room. His dark hair was spiked in clumps, his eyes barely open. But he was smiling.

Embarrassed, she turned and took two coffee mugs out of the cupboard. She never spent the night with men. Never. Not since Justin.

Now she didn't know what to say or do, but she prided herself on being honest and up front, and this was no time to change.

"Listen, Ty." She turned, saw him leaning against the doorjamb, watching her. She tugged on the knot of the bright Tahitian *pareau* she'd tied around her, making certain it was secure above her breasts.

"I'm sorry about last night—"

He was across the small room in two long strides. She took a step back, came up against the tile counter. He had her in his embrace before she could get another word out.

"I'm not sorry." He lifted her chin, met her eyes, searched her face with such intensity that she feared he could see into her soul and read her deepest, darkest secrets.

"Is this where you try to give me the brush-off?"

"No. This is where I apologize for your having seen me like that."

It was the reason she lived alone, the reason she never let anyone in. The nightmares were as real as life when they hit her. Her memory just wouldn't let go of the details. Her greatest weakness was her night terrors, her shame of what they'd done to her, what the accident had done to her.

"And I wanted to thank you for . . . for caring. Last night was . . ." Her face was on fire. "It was wonderful of you to . . ."

"Last night was pretty damn great for me, too, Kat."

"But—"

"Why don't we just take this one step at a time?"

"It's just that I—"

"You're *not* brushing me off, Kat, until you hear me out."

He braced his arms on the countertop, pinning her between them. Her heart started pounding when her body instinctively responded to his nearness.

"Okay. So, talk," she whispered, tempted to kiss him. Afraid once she started she wouldn't be able to stop.

"So, let's just stay calm and see where this goes, all right? Let's give it a chance."

He was scaring the hell out of her now. He didn't know he was asking for a lot more than a chance. He was asking her to open up to feelings she'd denied for so long that they had probably atrophied by now. He was asking her to tear down the walls around her heart, leave it open and vulnerable, and see what happened.

Damn it, Jake. You got me into this.

But she couldn't blame Jake for last night. He'd wanted her to date, to get out and test the waters. She's the one who wanted Ty Chandler in her bed last night. This was all her doing.

"Kat?"

"What?"

"I like being with you. How about we just take this one day at a time?"

One day at a time wouldn't sound very dangerous if

there weren't hearts at stake. And hers had already taken a beating.

She thought of last night and marveled that they'd come this far already. Maybe it was time. Maybe it was worth investing a few days, a few weeks even. She wasn't going to be in Twilight Cove forever.

"One day at a time sounds do-able," she confessed. "Okay." She hoped she hadn't lost her mind. What really scared her was that she might lose control of her heart.

ELEVEN

One-day-at-a-time ended as soon as they got back to Twilight and the new owner of Kamp Kodiak called needing Ty to hold his hand. Ty dropped her off at Jake's and was on a plane headed for Alaska by evening.

She settled into the damn peace and quiet of the big house on Lover's Lane again, and her nightmares had settled in, too.

If she fell sleep, she awoke screaming, listening to the echo of her own voice until it faded into the walls. Drenched in sweat, she'd jump out of bed, and turn to Jackie Chan.

When Jackie, Bruce Lee, and Chuck Norris failed, there was always channel surfing.

Mind-numbing infomercials were her new best friends. It was noon on her fifth day back when she realized she was dialing a 1-800 number to order a rotisserie. She never cooked.

Get your ass up, Vargas, and move it. You're going completely nuts.

Refusing to live in a vegetative state any longer, she dug out her running shorts and shoes. Her hand might still be bandaged, but there was nothing wrong with her feet. She drove down the hill to town, pulled into the public lot near Plaza Park, slipped her cell phone into the pocket of her nylon running shorts, closed the velcro pocket, and took off.

She circled the park, then ran down the long flight of stairs to the cove below.

The sun was so bright she was squinting behind her sunglasses as she stretched and watched the surfers shred short rides on knee-high waves before she took off again.

Beyond the breakers, sailboats bobbed at anchor, but there were no signs of any fishing boats out to sea.

When her thoughts drifted to Ty again, she became irritated with herself. Maybe time in Alaska had brought him to his senses and he realized he'd spoken in the heat of the moment. Maybe she wouldn't hear from him again at all. The case was closed. She'd found Sunny. He didn't need her anymore. She'd go back to the way things were before they met. She didn't need him.

Things would end just the way she always ended them—nice and neat. No strings attached. No getting in too deep. No making another terrible mistake.

You wouldn't be feeling this way if you were working.

As she made her way through the soft sand at the edge of the water, she was convinced that it was the peace and quiet, the homey small-town atmosphere that made her feel so isolated, so alone. It was much easier to lose herself in L.A., lose herself in the crowds and fast-paced city life.

Avoiding a piece of driftwood, she headed toward the north end of the cove where tourists explored the rocky point and tide pools exposed by the low tide. Careful not to misstep, she climbed up onto the rocks and rounded the point. Finding herself on another small stretch of cove, she started running again.

Sunlight glittered on the wet sand, a bright spot that drew her attention. She made a U-turn and doubled back, bent over to retrieve a piece of green beach glass.

The outgoing tide had churned up the sand. Between the foam that slid in and out on the tide, she collected more glass, frosted bits of milky white, murky green, amber, even a couple of pieces of rare cobalt blue.

She watched them glitter in the palm of her hand, then she shoved them into her pocket and started running again.

She reached the end of the second beach and stopped to take her pulse. She raised her arms high overhead, then stretched her calves. Her cell phone rang.

"Vargas Investigations."

"Hey, you look great. How was the run?" Ty's voice sent her heart into overdrive. She kicked the toe of her shoe into the sand and twisted it back and forth.

"How do you know I'm running? Where are you?" She glanced around, half expecting to see him down the beach.

"Look up," he said.

It wasn't until then that she realized she was directly below the point where his house was located. She saw him standing on the edge of the bluff, waving his arm over his head.

"I just got back. I'm sorry I didn't call. Things were hectic."

"I'm sorry I didn't call. I got tied up. You know how it is. Time got away from me."

Justin's words. Justin's excuses over and over. She'd fallen for that already.

"Kat?"

"What?"

"Are you all right?"

Walk away. Hang up and run.

That's the easy way. The safe way. Get out before it's too late.

She made the mistake of looking at the point again.

He was standing on the edge of the bluff, waving his arm over his head. She bit her lips together to keep from smiling.

"Kat, can you hear me?"

"I'm here."

"I'm not Parker, Kat. I'm not the one who broke your heart."

"I know." He already knew her so well he'd known what she was thinking.

"Give me a chance to prove it. Are you hungry?"

A portly man wearing a straw hat and Bermuda shorts with the whitest legs she'd ever seen strolled by and said hello. She was too far away to make out Ty's features, but she heard the smile in his voice.

She *was* hungry. "Fish?"

"R.J. just dropped some by."

"Maybe I'll reconsider, because of the fish. What time?" A bead of sweat slid down her temple. She swiped at it, calculated how long it would take her to drive back to Jake's, shower, and change. Way more than the promise of a fish dinner had her anxious to see him again.

"Now."

She laughed. "I'm sweating like a *pua'a*."

"A what-a?"

"A pig. I need to shower and change."

"I've got plenty of hot water. There ought to be something around here you can wear. If worse comes to worst, I'll yank down a curtain and you can tie it around yourself like that Hawaiian thing you look so damn hot in."

An image flashed through her mind, the heat in his eyes. It set off an instantaneous ache she couldn't deny. Besides, she'd never worn a curtain. Scarlett O'Hara had always been one of her idols.

"I'll run back to town and get my car. Then I'll be right there."

The man has an outdoor shower.

Just when she thought things couldn't get any better, he led her around the corner of thc patio, and there, hidden behind an overgrown schefflera plant and a fuchsia bougainvillea, was a cabana-style shower. Completely private, with hot-and-cold running water, it was open to the sky. She hadn't showered outdoors since she'd moved to California.

"Take your time," he told her. "There's plenty of hot water." He started to walk away.

"Ty, wait." She reached into her pocket, pulled out the beach glass, and held out her hand. "For your collection."

She dropped the pieces into his palm. There were six of them of every color—white, blue, soft green, amber. Ty stared at them a for a second, then met her eyes.

"This means you thought of me at least six times, you know."

"I guess it does." The notion that she'd thought of him almost all the time he'd been gone scared the hell out of her.

"I missed you, Kat."

But you were too busy to call. It was the first thought that popped into her mind. She shut it down, refusing to compare him to Justin. He'd given her no reason not to trust him.

"I missed you, too." The words came easier than she thought they would and she realized she meant them. She *had* missed him.

Ty left her alone while he went to put marinade on the fish.

As she stepped into the shower and stripped off her

jogging clothes, she asked herself what there *wasn't* to like about him. He was easy-going, loved the outdoors. He appreciated life and had chosen to do what he loved up in Alaska, working at something that gave him satisfaction, not a job he hated just so he could buy bigger toys.

And he could cook.

In many ways, Ty reminded her of her dad—constantly on the move, but at the same time taking things easy. He made enjoying life look simple.

She was rinsing shampoo out of her hair when there came a quick knock from outside. She wiped her eyes, opened them in time to watch the wooden door swing open and Ty step in. When he stripped off his shorts, she got a pretty good idea of what he was there for.

"Do you mind?" He reached around her for the soap.

She answered with a slow smile.

His hands were slick with soap when he touched her. He circled her nipples, pressed his palms against them. Warm water sluiced down her back. She wrapped her arms around his neck. His soapy hands slid around her, down her spine, over her hips. He cupped her behind, started to lift her to him. Slippery with soap, she laughed when she slid out of his grip. He moved beneath the shower spray, lifted her again, held on tight.

She gasped when he slipped inside her, filled her. They moved beneath the water, connected, complete. Terrifying that it felt so right, so natural, so soon.

Kat urged him on without words, moved against him, took him farther inside her until she could take no more, and finally, she was ready for release, ready to let go.

He came with her, and when it was over they were both breathless.

She slid down his legs until they were separate entities again. Her toes hit the wet brick, her feet were finally on the ground, but she was still halfway between the earth and the sky, floating amid the stardust of release.

She wasn't sure where she was or what she was doing anymore, and for this one moment, she tried not to care.

He grabbed her chin, tilted her face to his, gave her such a loud, smacking kiss that she giggled.

"I put some clothes on the bed that might work for you. Upstairs, first door on the left. Help yourself to whatever you need in the bathroom. I'll finish up here and meet you inside."

Reaching out of the stream of water, he handed her a huge, fresh bath towel and then reached for the soap. Tempted to offer to help, she stopped herself. She could get way too used to this. All of it.

She wrapped herself in the towel, scooped up her running clothes, and hurried across the patio to the back door.

Ty was still dripping, wearing a towel slung low around his hips, when he walked through the back door and into the kitchen.

He stopped at the sink, filled a glass with water, swallowed it in four long gulps. He set down the glass and braced his hands against the edge of the tile countertop.

The ceiling above him creaked beneath Kat's steps and then he heard the hair dryer go on. He liked knowing she was up there, in his house. He'd missed her like crazy in Alaska, so much so that he begrudged every minute of his time away from her and had worked like a dog to get things accomplished so that he could get back.

He was falling fast, but she made it so damn easy. He wanted her physically, and more than that, he wanted to be with her. But it was impossible to tell what she was feeling or thinking. He had no idea how to go about getting her to trust him.

Before he could think things through, the doorbell rang.

He made sure the knot in the towel was tight, then called Kat's name, hoping she was dressed. He walked to the archway between the living and dining rooms and stared at the front door. Upstairs, the hair dryer was still running.

The bell rang again. He crossed the room, looked through the porthole to see who was there, and nearly had a heart attack when he realized Sunny was on the other side, looking back at him.

She's here. She's home.

And I'm wrapped in a damn bath towel, dripping on the hardwood floor.

He opened the door. Both of their mouths fell open at once when she realized he was half-naked and he realized she was holding the toddler he'd seen at the Hollywood apartment.

"Hi." Sunny recovered first. "You said I could come visit. Here we are."

"So I see." He couldn't help staring at the toddler as the little girl coyly laid her head on Sunny's shoulder and tried to shove all the fingers of one hand in her mouth. With her other hand, she clutched a small, plush skunk to her chest. Her hair was strawberry blond, her eyes huge, and curious. She was wearing new denim overalls and a bright red knit shirt beneath an open pink sweatshirt.

Sunny, on the other hand, was wearing a black spandex skirt that barely covered what ought to be covered, and a thin, dark purple top that showed off her midriff and pierced belly button. Her eyes were outlined with black liner, her vibrant hair looked as if she didn't own a brush. A huge plastic purse with disposable diapers sticking up over the top dangled from her left shoulder.

"This is French Fry," Sunny said, jiggling the little girl up and down.

Ty thought maybe he had gotten water in his ears. "Did you say Francine or Frenchie?"

Sunny rolled her eyes. "*French Fry.* Her real name's Alice. And by the way, you're her grandpa." With that she stepped past him and walked into the house.

"Watch the water." Afraid she'd slip, he saw his caution fell on deaf ears. She was already in the middle of the room looking around at the flotsam and jetsam displayed on the walls.

"Is this an antiques shop or something?"

"No. Just a family collection of odds and ends."

Family that she is a part of now.

His gaze shot to the toddler, who hadn't taken her eyes off him yet. Sunny was family, and so, it seemed, was . . . French Fry?

Sunny's gaze drifted to the stairs. Ty's followed, and there was Kat, standing in the middle of the staircase wearing his faded "My Girlfriend Said She'd Leave Me If I Go Fishing Again" T-shirt, and what appeared to be nothing else.

Though the T-shirt came to her knees and Sunny's spandex skirt was far more revealing, Kat looked undeniably tousled and sexy. She was eyeing the toddler in Sunny's arms.

"Kat, you remember Sunny," he fumbled.

"Of course." Kat half smiled and stayed right where she was.

Ty felt like an idiot clutching the towel, grinning from ear to ear, but he couldn't stop.

Kat didn't move. He noticed her hand had tightened around the handrail. She looked as shocked as he felt.

"Looks like you can call me Grampa," he joked as he ran his hand through his hair. He'd remember this moment for as long as he lived.

"I . . . I'll be right back." Kat hesitated a second longer, looked at him, then Sunny, then Alice before she turned and hurried back up the stairs.

Sunny was standing awkwardly in the middle of the room. He glanced out the open front door. "Did you bring a bag?"

She indicated the huge striped vinyl purse over her arm with a shrug. "This is it."

He closed the door. When he walked up beside Sunny, the child in her arms smiled at him and then tentatively offered him her stuffed skunk. His heart melted into a puddle of mush.

"That's Stinko," Sunny said.

"Hi, Stinko." He had no idea what else to say. It had been enough of a shock to find out about Sunny, let alone have her show up without warning with a child of her own.

He looked at the baby again and murmured, "Alice."

"For Alice in Wonderland."

"How old is she?"

"Seventeen months."

He thought of that day in the apartment and how he'd assumed the child belonged to the other girl.

"I had no idea she was yours."

Sunny shrugged. "Why would you? I didn't say anything because I figured it was none of your business."

"You're right." He wondered if the other shoe was about to drop. "What about her father?"

"What about him?"

"Where is he? Did he come with you?"

"He's . . . out of the picture."

Her eyes had grown bright, her expression closed. He

could tell by her tone she didn't want to talk about Alice's father and he decided on the spot that this wasn't the time to question her. She was barely through the door and still sizing up the situation herself. He figured the best thing to do would be to back off, to take it slow.

Besides, he was so damn glad to have her here, in the house built by her great-great-great-great-grandfather, that he only wanted her to feel welcome.

Kat came downstairs again, this time wearing the yellow nylon shorts he'd left out for her. She hesitated by the armchair near the stairs and finally walked over to stand next to him. He took her hand, squeezed it, and when she met his eyes, he felt relieved when she smiled.

"Why don't you go up and get dressed? We'll be fine." Though she continued to smile, he sensed a new tension about her.

"I'll be right back." He headed for the stairs, but not before he turned to look at Sunny and the baby again.

It appeared his "easy" life had just gotten a bit more complicated.

TWELVE

Sunny's jitters gradually dissolved when she realized Ty Chandler was as nervous and shook up as she. He and his gal pal had obviously been into something hot and heavy before she got here. No need to wonder about their relationship now. From the looks of it, she'd caught them in the act.

On the way up from L.A., she'd worried that Chandler might balk when he found out about French Fry and hoped he really wanted both of them here. From the look on his face, though, he'd seemed shocked but excited about the baby. He wasn't going to send her on her way, at least not tonight.

He'd practically tripped all over himself welcoming her, but the woman, Kat, had barely cracked a smile. After she gave French Fry a cool once-over, it was obvious that she was trying not to even look at her.

Kat Vargas just might be a problem she hadn't counted on.

She thought that Chandler was going to stand there all night clutching his bath towel until Kat suggested maybe he ought to get dressed. Like something out of an old *Father Knows Best* episode, he actually *excused* himself before he went upstairs.

She hated to admit it and hoped she wasn't getting

weird or something for noticing, but her dad was a real hottie. At least she wouldn't be embarrassed to be seen with him, *if* they ever went anywhere together.

At least he wasn't a complete nerd.

The way Kat was still eyeing Alice gave her the creeps. She started to wonder if Kat Vargas hated all little kids in general, or just French Fry.

Sunny sat Alice in the middle of the living room floor near an old recliner that should have been hauled away a long time ago. She sat down on it, leaned forward, draped her arms over her knees and started to wind one of French Fry's curls around her index finger.

"Ty was just going to fix dinner." Kat lingered, standing a few feet away as an awkward silence blossomed and thrived in the room.

Sunny thought maybe the woman was uncomfortable and embarrassed about almost getting caught screwing Chandler.

Before she could comment, Kat asked, "Are you hungry?"

Sunny had been starving since the last bus stop in San Luis Obispo. They had to transfer and wait for a shuttle that only ran every two hours and it was just lucky they'd gotten there when they had, or she would've had to spend the night in the Greyhound station with a fussy toddler.

From what she'd seen of Twilight Cove, it wasn't much of a town. When the bus let them off at the park, she caught a cab and had to pop for the fare to get all the way out here, which used up almost all the cash she'd brought with her. She had five dollars left to her name.

She looked around again, thankful that they had a roof over their heads tonight and someone to worry about them for a change instead of her having to worry about everyone else.

Her relief was tempered by the fact that every time she thought of French Fry, her heart ached.

Kat Vargas was waiting for an answer.

"I could eat."

"Ty was just about to cook some fish. We could start a salad for him." Kat turned around and headed out of the room.

Sunny decided that something was up with Kat Vargas, but she wasn't going to make waves yet. She picked up French Fry, who gurgled in approval, and followed Kat. The house wasn't particularly large, but the rooms were bright and airy.

The jury was still out on whether or not she liked the place. It was so crammed full of old stuff. Most of it looked like junk other people had thrown out, but all of it had something to do with either the beach or Twilight Cove. There were vintage photos of streets, wood and metal business signs. It was crowded, but definitely not boring.

The television in the living room looked new and it wasn't a postage stamp, either. Chandler obviously had some money. And no matter how old or run-down they were, homes by the beach didn't come cheap.

When they reached the kitchen and Kat still hadn't said anything, Sunny scooted French Fry up on her hip again, then straightened the strap of the baby's overalls. "I'm really sorry about interrupting whatever it was you two had going on."

Sunny expected Kat to flush with embarrassment, or make some lame excuse. Instead Kat met her gaze head-on.

"We were finished, actually." Kat fumbled with a wooden salad bowl as she set it down near a cutting board on the counter, then she opened the refrigerator and pulled out celery, tomatoes, green onions, and a bag of mini carrots.

Sunny couldn't help but admire her honesty. "I'll do that if you want me to," she offered, figuring the task couldn't be easy one-handed. "Would you hold Alice?"

For a second Kat didn't say a word. She slowly went pale, and as she did, her expression hardened. Sunny thought that for a minute she was going to walk out of the room.

"I . . ." Kat Vargas seemed to be at a loss for words.

Maybe she'd never been around kids before. She looked more terrified than anything else.

Before things got any more strained, Ty came breezing through the kitchen door, and some of the color rushed back into Kat's cheeks.

"I can make the salad," Sunny told him, then indicated the baby with a nod. "But somebody's got to watch her."

Kat turned around and started trying to rinse a head of lettuce with one hand. If Ty noticed the woman's discomfort, he didn't let on. Instead, he suggested cheerfully, "Why don't you go in the living room and sit down, and we'll call you when it's ready?"

"Great." More than great. The pale, strained look on Ms. Vargas's face was freaking her out.

As soon as Sunny left the room, Kat tried to pull herself together. She had no idea that the girl's request for her to hold Alice was going to send her into such an emotional tailspin. Her hands had instantly gone clammy and she hadn't been able to think of a single thing to say in response.

It had been forever since she'd been around children. Her sisters had a houseful between them all, but she hadn't been home to visit for so long that the memories of taking care of them, of laughing and playing with them, were fading.

Seeing Sunny standing there in Ty's living room, holding her daughter tight in her arms, had slammed home a reminder of everything Kat once dreamed of, everything she'd ever wanted. Not to mention the memories she'd fought so hard to bury inside.

Hopefully Ty had been so preoccupied with Sunny's appearance that he hadn't noticed. She helped herself to a glass of wine but didn't feel settled even after she took a couple of sips and carefully set the glass down.

Ty was in the middle of chopping a tomato when he suddenly stopped, wiped his hands, and surprised her by taking her into his arms.

The thrill she'd experienced when he'd called and she'd learned that he was home from Alaska came rushing back, reminding her that she had been far more excited by the sight of him on the bluff, by the sound of his voice, than she wanted to admit.

Their lovemaking had not only been satisfying but exciting, so thrilling that it had left her wanting more. The stark realization that he could move her in so many ways really scared the daylights out of her.

Now, as if he knew just what she needed, he kissed her again, moved his lips and tongue against hers in a heated kiss. When he lifted his head, he kept his arms locked around her.

"I didn't want you to feel neglected," he said softly, his dark blue eyes full of desire.

She glanced toward the door to the living room and kept her voice low. "Sunny already guessed what we were up to before."

"We're consenting adults. Besides, with the life she's led there probably isn't much she hasn't seen or heard."

His expression darkened and Kat knew that he wished things had been different for his daughter.

"I know you're thrilled, Ty." She knew how much it meant to him to have Sunny show up, and was happy for him.

"I still can't believe it."

She wondered if he had any idea what he was in for. There was no way of knowing what Sunny must have endured in her young life. No telling what her life in Los Angeles had been like, but it couldn't have been easy growing up virtually alone.

Kat wanted to believe that things were going to go smoothly for Ty and Sunny, that this was just the beginning for them both. She hoped it wasn't too late for Ty and his daughter to bond with each other, to become family on some level, but she'd been a P.I. too long to shake off all doubt once it took hold.

The fact that Ty knew nothing about Sunny except what they'd learned from Amy's parents didn't help.

"What's got you so quiet?" He bumped his hips against her, nudged her suggestively.

She shrugged. He deserved a straight answer.

"I wish I could shake the feeling that there might be more to Sunny showing up here out of the blue than meets the eye."

"You've been a P.I. too long."

"That's what I keep telling myself."

He turned back to the cutting board and started to dice another tomato. "Right now I'm just glad she's here."

She watched the easy way he handled himself, admired his well-defined shoulders and arms, the way his back moved beneath his shirt.

It was hard to believe that he was not only a father, but a grandfather, too. In a heartbeat he'd gone from attractive single man to attractive single man with a family.

Though her body reacted to his nearness, her mind was racing. She couldn't shake the memory of the apartment where they'd found Sunny. The girl's companions had looked like hard-as-nails street kids and the place was filled with things that none of them appeared to be able to afford, but there could be a logical explanation that didn't involve anything illegal.

Still, Sunny's life as a young single mother couldn't have been easy and Ty had offered her a way out. Maybe all she was after was a new beginning, a chance to start life over with her own father in the picture.

There was nothing in the world wrong with that.

Kat walked over to Ty, stood on tiptoe, and kissed him on the cheek.

"I'll try to put my suspicions on hold. After all, she's come this far."

"Right." He kissed her again, a kiss filled with such promise that it made her knees weak. She leaned into him, pressed him up against the kitchen counter.

When the kiss ended he whispered against her mouth, "You'd better step back, or I'll be after more than a kiss. Or maybe you're willing to go for it again already, Ms. Vargas?"

"A very empty threat with your daughter and granddaughter in the next room."

"Want to try me?"

"You're a real tough guy, you know, Chandler?"

He pulled her up against him, wrapped his arms around her, and slid his hand over her breast, kneading it through the fabric of the borrowed shirt. Her nipple became a tight bud. He grasped it between his thumb and forefinger and she moaned, even as she tried to push away.

Finally, he let her go, but not before he kissed her thoroughly and left her warm and wet.

He smiled, and then acting as if he wasn't in the least aroused, he asked, "Would you go ask Sunny to come help carry things outside while I finish this up?"

Kat collected herself before she went into the other room and found Sunny juggling Alice on her knees.

"Would you like to join us?"

"Sure." As Sunny walked by, Alice reached both arms toward Kat. "I think she likes you. Want to hold her?" Sunny offered.

Kat froze, and as she fought down a wave of unexpected emotion, she quickly shook her head and tried to smile. She succeeded, but weakly.

"She . . . she doesn't really know me yet."

Sunny stared at her for a minute before moving into the kitchen. Kat took a deep breath and forced herself to calm down by doing what she did best—thinking like a P.I.

She asked herself, who walked out of their lives without so much as a change of underwear—except people on the run?

They helped carry things to the table on the patio and Ty sat beside Kat when he brought out the last of the meal. She looked across the table—at Sunny with her multitude of ear pierces and the stark barbed-wire tattoo that stood out on her arm, at Alice contentedly picking hunks of butter off of her dinner roll and smearing it around her mouth like a makeup artist on speed. Ty was carrying on a nearly one-sided conversation, pointing out landmarks along the coastline as Sunny ate ravenously, nodding now and then.

All of a sudden, a thunderous sound ripped through the air. Sunny, already halfway through her albacore, dropped her fork. It clattered against her plate and bounced onto the checkered tablecloth.

"What the *fuck* was that?" she cried.

Kat bit her lips to keep from laughing when Ty winced.

"What *was* it?" Sunny looked over her shoulder as if expecting a tidal wave to wash up over the bluff.

"Sonic boom." Kat indicated due north with her fork. "Vandenberg Air Force Base isn't far away." She turned to Ty and couldn't risk teasing, "Would you please pass the rolls, *Gramps*?"

Hand in hand, Kat and Ty walked down the narrow stone path through the garden to where she'd parked her Honda. She opened her car door and tossed in her jogging clothes, then placed the albacore fillet that he'd given her on the seat before she turned to him again.

"I'll get your things back to you soon," she promised.

"No hurry. It's probably going to be a little hectic around here from now on."

"To say the least." She reminded herself that no matter how hard Sunny looked or how suddenly she'd appeared, she was little more than a child. From what she'd seen tonight, though, Sunny was doing a good job with Alice.

"Thanks for dinner, Ty," she added. "It was delicious."

He snagged her wrist, drew her close, and skimmed his hand up beneath the hem of her shirt and cupped her breast. She tipped her head back, welcomed his kiss.

He held her until she relaxed in his embrace and gave him more. It was a long, slow, sweet exchange. When they parted, he continued to hold her within the circle of his embrace.

"Don't use Sunny's appearance as an excuse to start

building those walls again. Her being here doesn't change a thing between us."

He knew her so well already. Oddly, she felt safe in his arms, but she warned herself against feeling too secure. He gently placed his hand beneath her chin and then he was kissing her again. In half a heartbeat, she was kissing him back. When the kiss ended, she was amazed at the depth of her feelings, not to mention frightened by them. She hoped the darkness masked the turmoil that surely showed on her face.

She wanted to trust him so badly, wanted to believe in this fragile beginning more than she'd wanted to believe in anything in a long time.

Across the overgrown front garden, golden light spilled out of nearly every window of the old Chandler house. Ty followed her gaze, turned to look at his house.

She knew he was surely thinking about Sunny, and his little granddaughter, too. How could he not?

Standing in the dark, caressed by the sound of the crashing waves and the mist off the sea, her old insecurities surfaced. Now that Ty had his daughter to focus on and some major issues to settle, this was the perfect time to break things off if she wanted.

So get in the car and go, Vargas.

Before she could decide what to do, she felt Ty's warm hand cupped around her breast. Her knees nearly went weak as he rubbed his thumb across her nipple. His touch was hot, captivating. It made her yearn for something she hadn't dared to dream of in a long time. But those same feelings made her fear for her heart.

Before Kat's self-control melted as fast as an ice-cream sundae in the sun, Alice let out a howl that carried across the yard.

Ty immediately turned toward the house.

"Go on in, Ty. They need you."

I don't need anybody.

It was a hollow thought. One she had forced herself to believe in. Now it was in danger of becoming a lie because of Ty Chandler.

He kissed her good-bye then whispered against her mouth, "I'll call you tomorrow."

She watched him sprint up the crooked stone path, back to his daughter and her child, easily negotiating every tilt and angle of the familiar walkway, even in the dark.

Silhouetted in the open doorway, he paused on the threshold long enough to raise his hand and wave good-bye before he went inside.

"See you, Ty." Her whisper was quickly swallowed by the sound of the sea.

THIRTEEN

The next morning, French Fry woke Sunny demanding juice.

Sunny hauled her downstairs, trying not to wake Ty, only to find him in the kitchen squeezing fresh orange juice. The minute she stumbled through the door, he told her to sit down at the table.

"How'd you sleep?"

He was certainly perky for a man who'd crawled around in the attic until he found the pieces of an old crib and then made up a bed for her in the front bedroom upstairs. She and Alice fell sound asleep on the guest bed while he sat in the middle of the room assembling the crib.

"I didn't know what you like for breakfast, or what she can eat, but I've got lots of cereal and some frozen waffles. Maybe those aren't the best for her." He stared at French Fry, concern all over his face.

"Have you got any Cocoa Puffs?"

"Cocoa Puffs?"

He stared at her as if she were speaking a foreign language, and from the looks of all the sugarless cereals he had lined up on the counter, he would never think of buying any Cocoa Puffs.

Sunny shrugged. "They're her favorite, but she might eat waffles."

He fixed waffles, then watched her feed French Fry. He kept reaching over, offering her a paper towel to wipe the baby's hands and continually mopping the sticky syrup off the table, which was both frustrating and endearing.

More than anything, she wanted him to become acquainted with Alice, so she offered, "Will you hold her while I eat?"

"Sure." Though he instantly agreed, his tone sounded hesitant.

She handed the baby over, and after a couple of awkward moments, he started to bounce French Fry on his knee, pretending to understand her gibberish.

Sunny fixed herself a bowl of his dry-as-dust natural rice puffs. She sat down at the table, and when she looked over at him, Ty was watching her as if he'd never seen anyone eat before.

"I still can't believe you're here," he said softly.

She looked down at the puffs floating in skim milk, pushed a few under with her spoon, and watched them rise to the surface again.

"Yeah. Me, either."

"You're welcome to stay as long as you want. Consider this your home."

She was afraid for a minute that she was going to cry. He seemed like a good guy and sounded like he really meant it. She wondered if he'd be so eager to have her here if he knew everything about her.

Finally she managed to whisper, "Thanks."

"So what made you change your mind and come up here?"

What would he think if she told him she was desperate? That she was afraid her life back in L.A. was about to take a turn for the worse and that she didn't want Alice involved? That she'd do anything she had to in order to keep Alice safe?

She swallowed, thought about it for another second, and hoping to avoid having to answer all kinds of questions, she said, "I was kinda shocked when you showed up out of the blue like that. Then, the more I thought about it, the more I figured it wouldn't hurt to get to know you, to give you a chance to know Alice."

He studied her carefully until Alice reached for a spoon and started banging it on the table. Gently he pried it out of her hand and passed her a paper napkin instead. She immediately shoved the napkin into her mouth.

Sunny took the napkin away and handed Alice an empty plastic cup.

"What did you do in L.A.?" He was jiggling the baby on his knee again. "Aside from taking care of Alice," he added.

She hesitated. "Nothing really." Uncomfortable with where the conversation might be headed, she changed the subject. "How'd you find me, anyway?" She put the last bite of cereal in her mouth.

"I hired Kat. She's a private investigator."

Sunny almost choked on her rice puffs.

A P.I.? She wondered exactly how much Kat Vargas had found out about her. She was pretty sure her own record was still clean, but Jamie had racked up a few misdemeanors. Obviously whatever Chandler knew hadn't soured him on the idea of inviting her into his life.

Apparently, he hadn't noticed that she'd fallen silent. He continued to bounce Alice on his knee.

"We found your name on the welfare roles," he admitted.

Again, she felt her cheeks heat up. All the cash she

made racing wasn't traceable, so it had been easy to qualify for welfare. It wasn't much money compared to what she made street racing, but these days she needed all the money she could get.

Chandler shifted and stood Alice on his thighs. "You're going to need some diapers for the baby, some clothes and things while you're here."

He sounded so hopeful that she didn't want to burst his bubble by telling him she wasn't sure exactly how long she'd be around. Sooner or later she had to go back to L.A. She wasn't sure about anything right now. Not him, not the situation here or the one back in Hollywood.

"I didn't have a chance to pack. I left kinda sudden."

Alice started squirming to get down but he had a firm grip on her. "Are you in some kind of trouble, Sunny?"

"No." She shook her head. So far it was the truth. She wasn't in real trouble. Not yet anyway. "I . . . I just didn't want any of my roommates to start asking a lot of questions or to talk me out of leaving. We've been together a long time."

"Since River Ridge?"

"Yeah." She glanced around the kitchen. Thinking about the others back in Hollywood made her gut twist. Without her they wouldn't be bringing in half as much on race nights. The least she could do was take back all she could save.

"I'd like to get a job right away," she said suddenly. "You know of any?"

"What about school? Have you graduated from high school? If so, you could live here and go to college. Or you can get your GED."

Go to school? He had to be freaking kidding. She'd been in public schools a total of three years and they'd been a joke.

"I'd rather work," she hedged.

"You'll need time to settle in."

She didn't need time, she needed cash, but she doubted she'd make very much in a town like Twilight Cove. She tried to imagine working nine to five, flipping burgers, or dipping ice cream for five bucks an hour, and didn't know whether to laugh or cry. Maybe she should have thought things through before she left L.A. But she was here now, and for the time being she had to make the best of it.

Her life had never even been close to a *Happy Days* rerun and it was way too late to dream of that for herself now. She was flat broke, and although Ty Chandler sounded like he was willing to take them in on a permanent basis, she didn't know him well enough to commit to anything. Besides, she had commitments of her own back in L.A.

It was nice sitting in the cozy kitchen, surrounded by so many old things, comfortable things. Each and every one of them had probably meant something to whoever picked them out a long time ago. She wondered how many Chandlers had lived in the old house, amazed to think that they had been related to her.

Then she wondered if her mother had ever been here as a girl. How long had Chandler known her mom?

She tried to imagine her mom as a teenager, hoping that for some part of Amy's life she had been not only drug-free, but happy.

"Do you have any pictures of my mom?"

He stopped jiggling French Fry and stared at her. "Pictures?"

"You know. From when you two were together?"

He looked thoughtful and then said, "Maybe. Come to think of it, there was a boxful of old photos someplace around here. I'll look for them."

She nodded, knowing already that he was the type who wouldn't forget.

The sound of the sea soothed her deep down inside, surprising her. Oddly enough, she felt content here already, and yet, even as she savored the moment, she reminded herself that she couldn't turn her back on the situation in L.A.

This wasn't the real world, not hers anyway, but it might be a perfect place for French Fry.

While Chandler amused Alice, Sunny washed the dishes. Then he asked if she wanted to take a walk around outside, to go see the garden and the beach. She would have liked that, but she turned him down, telling him that he was welcome to take Alice out if he'd like.

The sooner he bonded with the baby, the better, but he looked uncertain. "Will she go with me?"

Sunny looked at the way French Fry was nestled against Chandler's chest, twisting a button on his shirt. "She'll go. Just make sure she doesn't fall when you put her down. Sometimes she gets going too fast and takes a header."

"I appreciate you trusting me."

"Is there some reason I shouldn't? You're not some pervert, are you?" She meant it as a joke, but from the look on his face, he obviously didn't think it was very funny.

"Why do you call her French Fry?"

"When she was born, her legs were so skinny that Dodge thought they looked like two little fries hanging out of her diaper. Everybody calls her French Fry now."

"Dodge?"

"Her dad."

"Does he still see her?"

"No." Sunny didn't want him thinking ill of Dodge. "But you didn't see me for nineteen years, either."

"I tried to explain the circumstances."

"Right. And there are circumstances in this case, too." Her eyes suddenly flooded with tears, and as she quickly swiped them away with the back of her hand, she said, "He's . . . he's dead, and I don't want to talk about it." Saying little was easier than going into everything that had gone wrong.

"I'm sorry, Sunny."

"Yeah. Me, too." She got up to pour herself another cup of black coffee and started looking for a sugar bowl but didn't see one. Chandler picked up Alice and said that he was going to take her for a walk outside.

Sunny took her coffee into the living room to hang out on the sofa. An hour later, she still hadn't moved. It was the most relaxing morning she'd had in months.

At first it was actually hard to loaf, but eventually she was able to lounge on the sofa like a total slacker, flipping the TV channels, watching whatever she wanted without Jamie or Butch grabbing the remote. Leaf never bothered her. He was a pushover, like Callie.

She reached for the remote again, noticed that a wet ring had formed on the *Outdoor Trails* magazine beneath her cold coffee mug. She pressed the remote and watched the channel logos at the bottom of the screen flick by: ESPN, HGTV, SCIFI, DIS, HBO, HBO2, HLN, EYEWITNESS NEWS.

She stopped to watch a breaking news story filmed from a news chopper high over a major freeway—a car chase in progress—held her breath until she remembered this was a local channel, not a broadcast from L.A., then started to breathe again.

Flipping to Cartoon Network, she glanced out the front window and watched as Ty walked French Fry around the wildflower garden.

He seemed perfectly content to stop at every flower

and let the baby touch and smell them. He shortened his steps to match hers, took her hand when she teetered, squatted so that he could talk to her at eye level.

Sunny could tell by the way French Fry gazed up at Chandler that she already adored him. The kid loved all the guys—Jamie, Butch, Leaf, and the others—even though none of them ever doted on her the way Dodge had. Jamie had no time for her. Butch and Leaf would play with her for a while but soon got tired of her cute baby tricks.

Callie was the only one who truly loved French Fry enough to help care for her night and day, the only one besides Dodge that she'd ever really trusted the baby with—until now.

She hoped Callie was getting along all right. She hated leaving her behind with the guys, but she knew they'd look after her. There was just no way in hell she'd wanted to show up at Chandler's door with both French Fry *and* Callie in tow.

She glanced outside again, watched as Ty lifted French Fry up onto his shoulders. It was pretty clear he was already getting hooked on the kid.

Good. Good for French Fry.

She fought off an intense wave of sadness, reminding herself as she watched Ty carefully center the kid on his shoulders that this was exactly what she had hoped for. Every time the sound of French Fry's sweet baby giggle floated in through the window, it was followed by Ty's deep, masculine laugh.

What would it have been like to grow up here, in this funky beach house, with a real dad? Without a mom who was stoned twenty-four hours a day?

Her mom had slept with everyone, *everyone* at River Ridge. Everybody thought the place was some kind of a New Age religious retreat and rehab facility, but that was just a front for what really went on. It was about drugs and sex. And money.

They used to act like one big happy family—but drugs, alcohol, and the threat of getting busted can do funny things to your mind, not to mention your nerves. It wasn't all bliss behind the big wooden gates of the private estate high above L.A.

She had no idea what it would be like to have a dad and a mom all to herself, but she wanted things to be better for French Fry.

In a few minutes she got hooked on a Turner Classic showing of Jane Fonda and Robert Redford in *Barefoot in the Park*. Some old guy with an accent was wearing a silk scarf and getting everyone drunk on ouzo when Chandler walked through the front door.

When she looked up into French Fry's smiling face, she saw Dodge's eyes looking back. She wanted to scoop her up and hug her, love and kiss her, inhale the precious baby scent and feel her soft skin. She longed to tell French Fry that this was all going to work out for the best, but her eyes betrayed her and stung with tears. She turned back to the television until she was in control.

She loved Alice. She really, really did. She loved Alice way more than her own mom had ever loved *her.* She loved Alice enough to want a perfect world for her.

But, damn it, she was only nineteen herself.

Life wasn't supposed to be this hard.

Ty stopped beside the sofa where Sunny had stretched out, her long, bare legs crossed at the ankles, her hands stacked beneath her head as she lay there engrossed in an old film.

She seemed like a miracle to him, a combination of Amy and him rolled into one. There was so much he didn't know about her life, so much he wanted to know, but he refused to bombard her with questions. He wanted to savor every minute, to let things happen gradually.

She looked away from the television and smiled up at them. Alice leaned over his arm, stretching her hands out toward Sunny.

"I hope you have some diapers left." He held Alice out at arm's length. His nose wrinkled at the smell of a soiled diaper.

"Stinky, huh?"

"Right."

"I guess you don't want to volunteer to change her."

He shook his head. "I think that's something I'll have to work up to, but I'll watch."

He stepped aside as his daughter—he was amazed every time he thought of Sunny as his daughter—gracefully got off the sofa and headed for the stairs.

He followed her up to the small guest room at the front of the house where he'd set up the crib he found in the attic last night. The room wasn't spacious, but it was light and airy. There was an old dresser painted mint-green that they could share.

Sunny was swift and efficient as she changed Alice's diaper. He noticed there were only a handful left in the big vinyl bag she'd been toting when she arrived. He made a mental note to drive them into Twilight to pick up some necessities. It was quickly becoming apparent that taking care of a toddler was a round-the-clock job.

"Who was the girl feeding Alice the day I was there?" He'd taken it for granted the other girl was the baby's mother.

"That was Callie." She made certain the tabs on the diaper were tight and then lifted Alice to her shoulder. "She was a runaway. One of the guys found her on the street and brought her home. I don't actually remember if it was Butch or Leaf."

What kind of a world is it, he wondered, *where kids are left on the streets to be picked up and taken in like lost kittens or puppies?* He shuddered to think of what Sunny might have already endured in her young life.

"What now?" He watched her redress Alice in her overalls.

"She's due for a nap."

"I'll run into Twilight for some diapers later."

A sudden, awkward silence filled the small room.

"I've only got five dollars left." Sunny spoke so softly that he could tell she was ashamed, but she didn't flinch or look away.

"I'll take care of it."

"I'm sorry."

"Hey, don't mention it. The way I see it, I owe you for nineteen missing years."

"I don't want you thinking that you owe me anything." She shifted Alice to her shoulder again. At the small window overlooking the ocean, the simple white cotton cafe curtains his grandmother had made billowed and luffed in the breeze.

"All I meant was that I want to help in any way I can."

It was a moment before she gave him a slow half smile and said, "Okay."

In that brief second he saw something in her eyes that told him she wanted to believe him, but experience had taught her to be wary, or worse, not to hope at all.

As Sunny turned and walked out of the room, Alice smiled at him over Sunny's shoulder. His heart had never felt so full.

Ty left Sunny sitting on the floor with Alice lying on an old quilt his great-grandmother had made. The toddler was chewing on the skunk's tail, fighting to keep her eyes open.

He walked out the front door, down the uneven flagstone walk, and kept going until he came to the edge of the bluff. He paused at the top of the stairway to the cove and pulled his cell phone out of his pocket.

The morning was long gone, the hours flown, but not a moment had passed that he hadn't thought of Kat and wanted to talk to her.

As he waited for the call to connect, he scanned the ocean and the sky. It was a perfect day for fishing. Clear, no wind, not a cloud in the sky, but he wouldn't be going anywhere near his boat for a while.

He paced the edge of the bluff, and when Kat didn't answer, he left a message and then tried her cell. Again, she didn't pick up, so he dialed R.J., who answered on the second ring.

"Hey, R.J., it's me." He stopped pacing, kicked a pebble over the edge of the cliff, watched two pelicans soar over the water and dive for fish.

"The albacore are still running."

"Count me out for a while."

"What's up? Business in Alaska?"

"My daughter Sunny's here. She showed up yesterday afternoon."

"At your place? Are you kidding? That's great, man."

"Yeah. She's here and so is my granddaughter. She's a year and a half already."

"Your *what*?" R.J. started laughing. "You're in for it now, old buddy."

"They're great. I can't wait for you to meet them."

"Are they here for a while?"

"I'm not sure. I think she's just testing the water, but she said she wants to get a job."

"Wish I could help her out, but I've already got two kids alternately working the sunset cruises."

Sunny's working for R.J. would have been a perfect solution. He trusted Ron more than anyone else in the world and it would be easy working the tour cruises, greeting guests, passing around appetizers, and helping people climb aboard.

"She'll find something. I still know a lot of people in this town." Ty pictured the tattoo on Sunny's upper arm, her minuscule skirt, and wondered if he was being way too optimistic.

"If I hear of anybody needing summer help, I'll let you know," R.J. volunteered. "I'll ask at the Sail On Inn."

"Great." The small dockside eatery at Gull Harbor would be a good place for Sunny to start. R.J.'s sailboat was moored nearby. "Sorry about the fishing."

"No problem. Hey, congratulations, and good luck with the kid. Or I should say *kids*?"

Ty hung up on R.J.'s laughter and then punched in Kat's number again. Still no answer, so he decided to go inside and see how things were coming along before he went upstairs to surf the Amazon listing of how-to books on his laptop.

Surely somebody had written one entitled *How to Raise a Teen Daughter You've Never Met Before Who Also Happens to Be a Mother.*

FOURTEEN

After a couple of cups of strong coffee and a long walk that morning, Kat checked her messages and saw that Ty had called. Although she wanted to talk to him for her own peace of mind, she also wanted to wait until she had time to run a cursory background check on Sunny. No matter how hard she tried, she just couldn't shake the feeling that there might be something behind the way the girl had shown up out of the blue.

One-handed, she typed slowly, hunting and pecking the keys, and then she made a couple of calls to contacts at the Department of Motor Vehicles and the L.A.P.D.

The good news was that the background check hadn't turned up anything. No police record. Sunny had a couple of old speeding tickets, but no misdemeanors or felonies. No car was registered in her name.

Kat ran the plate numbers she'd seen on a customized bright yellow Honda Civic parked outside Sunny's apartment.

The souped-up Civic was registered to Jamie Hatcher, who had a string of excessive speed tickets. She thought, with a car like that it was no wonder, but there was nothing else.

She was about to call Ty when the phone suddenly

started ringing and the caller I.D. displayed his cell number.

She took a deep breath, answered, and savored the warmth that oozed through her the minute she heard him say hello.

"How's it going over there?" she asked.

"Pretty smooth. We actually had a nice talk this morning. She says she came up here to give us a chance to get to know each other and she even wants to work part-time already. She never graduated from high school. That's pretty much all I know at this point."

"Hey, it's a start." Since nothing had turned up during her search, she decided not to tell him that she'd done a background check on Sunny. She was happy that he had been right and her own misgivings had been groundless.

"They both need clothes. Sunny needs things to wear to work. The outfit she showed up in won't cut it."

"The teen-hooker look doesn't quite work in Twilight."

"Exactly. I have no idea what she needs. I'm afraid that if it was up to me, I'd wrap her from neck to toe in sackcloth."

She pictured Sunny in her tight mini, cropped top, and heavy eyeliner, and then remembered the way the girl had looked standing in the middle of Ty's living room clutching Alice in her arms. Maybe Sunny hadn't led the life of Miss Teen America, but she was just a kid, and doing the best she could from the looks of it. Kat had to give the girl the benefit of the doubt.

"What if *I* take her shopping?" The minute she volunteered she knew he had her so infatuated that she wasn't thinking straight.

"That would be great, Kat. After the way Alice smelled this morning, running out of diapers and clean clothes isn't an option." He sounded so relieved that Kat had to laugh.

"How about I pick her up after lunch?"

"I owe you *big* for this one."

She closed her eyes, pictured him walking into the outdoor shower, tall, broad-shouldered, his dark hair glistening in the sunlight, his muscular chest shimmering with water droplets as he moved toward her, soap in hand, a smile on his lips and heat in his eyes.

"Don't worry," she assured him. "I'll think of some way to make you pay."

By the time she pulled up in the driveway and stepped out of her car, Ty and Sunny were already outside waiting on her. Sunny was carrying Alice in her arms. When the toddler, who was chewing on Stinko's ear, smiled a sweet, shy half smile and buried her head against Sunny's neck, Kat's heartbeat faltered. She turned her gaze on Ty and took a deep breath.

He gave her a quick kiss and whispered hello. She couldn't help but blush in embarrassment. She felt Sunny watching them closely. It was another moment before she realized that Sunny intended to take the baby shopping. She had the cheap diaper bag slung over her shoulder and the child on her hip, ready to go. Alice was carrying a plastic leftovers container lid. She stuck it into her mouth and start chewing on it.

Kat turned to Ty. "Will you watch her until we get back?"

He looked at Alice, then Sunny, and then Kat. "By *myself*? How long will you be gone?"

"As long as it takes."

Sunny laughed. "You passed Diaper Changing 101 earlier," she reminded him. "She'll be all right until we get back. Maybe she'll take another nap."

When Ty looked as if he was going to refuse, Kat came up with the perfect excuse. "I can't take her anywhere without a car seat."

Thankfully, Sunny backed her up. "It's against the law."

"Okay, but don't be gone long." He sounded less than confident.

"You scared, Chandler?" Sunny handed Alice to him and hung the diaper bag over his arm. "Big guy like you?"

He ignored her as he dug into his back pocket for his wallet, juggling Alice as he took out some cash and a credit card. He handed them to Kat and told her to buy whatever they needed.

Then he fished around in his front pocket and pulled out a piece of paper. "Would you stop by the bookstore and pick these up for me? Get some picture books, too."

Kat stared at the paper in her hand.

Pick out books and clothes for a toddler. She tried to focus on the book list.

The American Academy of Pediatrics's *Caring for Your Baby and Young Child, Birth to Age Five.*

The Baby Book: Everything You Need to Know About Your Baby from Birth to Age Two.

How to Talk So Kids Will Listen and Listen So Kids Will Talk.

He followed them over to the car. Kat started the ignition and glanced over at Sunny, who was waving bye-bye to Alice. Ty walked around to Kat's side of the car and bent down to kiss her again. When Alice grabbed a handful of Kat's hair and gave it a tug, the toddler's hand grazed her cheek.

Kat closed her eyes for a second, then gently tugged her hair out of Alice's grasp.

Ty was saying something. She tried to concentrate.

"Drive carefully," he added.

"Okay," she managed, trying to forget the way Alice's soft hand felt against her cheek.

He was waving Alice's arm up and down, repeating, "Bye-bye, bye-bye," over and over.

The little girl started fussing when she realized Sunny was actually leaving. She alternately whined and chewed on the stuffed skunk's sopping-wet ear. Sunny waved but didn't look back as they pulled away.

Kat drove through Twilight and up the canyon road that wound its way inland. Never one for idle chitchat, she was perfectly content with the girl's silence. If Sunny wanted to talk, that was up to her.

Finally Sunny shifted in her seat, adjusted the seat belt on her shoulder, and out of the blue asked, "Do you love him?"

Kat hit the turn signal and passed a slow-going tourist in front of them.

"So, are you in love with Chandler?" Sunny asked again, as if Kat hadn't heard.

"He's a wonderful man."

"Somebody your age would probably think he's hot."

"I like him a lot." *If I didn't I wouldn't be here.* "I make it a habit not to fall in love."

Sunny drew her knee up, turned to face Kat. "Not ever?"

"Not anymore." It frightened her to think that her resolve might be slipping because of Ty.

"Weird. How do you stop yourself?"

How do I stop myself?

"I just do."

"You think he's in love with you?"

"We just met last week."

"What'll you do if he falls for you?"

What will I do?

"I'll figure that out if and when it comes to that."

"I fell in love with French Fry's dad when I was seven. We grew up together at River Ridge."

"Where is he now?"

There was a long, uncertain pause before Sunny said softly, "Dead."

There was no hint of sadness in Sunny's voice, just a cool, blank matter-of-factness that hit Kat too close to home, reminding her of herself and the way she guarded her emotions.

"I'm sorry," Kat said, glancing over at the girl. Sunny was staring straight ahead, trying real hard to act as if she didn't care, but her eyes were suspiciously bright.

Sunny's tears got to Kat. "Things can't be easy for you, raising a child alone."

"That's the way it goes."

"Ty said you mentioned job hunting."

"Yeah. I'd like to get something right away."

"Have you worked before?"

"Sure, but I don't plan on going back to what I was doing in L.A."

"Which was?"

"This and that. In a place like Twilight, there probably aren't many choices, though."

Kat surprised herself when she advised, "Don't sell the place short. There are good things to be said for living in a small town."

" 'Where everybody knows your name'?" Sunny folded her arms, shifted her legs, and then tugged on the hem of her miniskirt.

"Something like that."

Twilight Cove was just a bit bigger than the town she was born on on Kauai. The trouble with a small town was that it was impossible to bury your past there.

In Kapa'a, it took thirty extra minutes just to go to the

post office because she would run into so many folks she knew.

Folks who knew everything about her, yet they never mentioned the accident because they didn't have to—their expressions said it all.

Sunny turned on the stereo, tuned it to a hip-hop station. "I'm used to L.A. Have you lived here long?"

Kat reached over and turned down the volume a notch. "I don't live here. I'm from Long Beach. I'm just house-sitting for a friend while my hand heals."

"What happened?"

"I got shot."

"No *kidding*? Did it hurt?"

"Like hell."

"How'd it happen?"

"Accident."

"Did you shoot yourself?"

Kat glanced over at Sunny to see if she was kidding. Behind all the mascara and eyeliner, she really was a stunning girl.

"I'm a private investigator. I was on a case."

"Chandler told me that he hired you to look for me."

Kat took the off-ramp for the mall she'd seen from the highway.

"We met when he came to me for help."

"It didn't take you very long to find me."

Kat pulled the car into a parking space and killed the engine. Sunny was watching her closely.

"If you know where to look," Kat met her stare, "you can find out just about anything."

Ty called her cell every twenty minutes. Kat heard Alice crying in the background and assured him that they were shopping as fast as they could.

Sunny chose very little for herself in the way of clothes,

shoes, and undergarments. Instead, she spent most of their time and Ty's money in the toddler department.

Kat had convinced herself the outing would be no problem, and it wasn't, not until they entered the area of the store where they were suddenly surrounded by pastel clothes, plush animals, mobiles, and moms with kids in strollers.

She might as well have opened up a vein.

"You all right?" Sunny was at her elbow, her arms piled high with soft knit pieces for Alice in a rainbow of pastel colors.

Kat cleared her throat and rubbed her hand across her eyes.

"I'm fine. Why?"

"You look kinda pale."

Kat shook her head and tried to sound convincing. "I'm okay. I was up late last night, is all."

"How many of these should I get?"

Kat focused on the little outfits and cleared her throat.

"Ty said, whatever you need."

"You think this is too much?"

Kat thought it a conservative amount of items draped over Sunny's arm. She shook her head. "No. In fact, since there's a buy one, get one half off sale, I think you should pick out some more. And be sure she has some socks and sweaters, too."

Luckily, between all of Kat's sisters, she had so many nieces and nephews that she knew what it took to keep them all clean and dressed.

She waited while Sunny chose what she wanted, then helped her at the checkout desk.

When they finally drove up to the house, Ty was waiting at the end of the walk. Kat parked and got out. She couldn't help but laugh when she saw him, and when she glanced over at Sunny, she saw that the girl was fighting a smile.

The front of his navy polo shirt was smeared with baby food, his hair was spiked in all directions. Alice started howling the minute she saw Sunny in the car and Ty couldn't hand her over fast enough.

Once Sunny had taken Alice inside, Ty leaned against Kat's car, let go an exhausted sigh, and grabbed her hand.

"I don't see how anybody can actually do that all day long."

"Sometimes you get what you wish for," she reminded him.

"And I wouldn't trade a minute of it. Stay for dinner?" He started to pull her close, but she reached for his other hand and held them both tight. Then she shook her head. "I'm beat. I think I need a quiet night at home."

She desperately needed time alone. Time to think.

"I'll take a rain check, if that's okay."

"You sure?"

"I'm sure."

He wouldn't let her leave until he kissed her.

"I don't think I'd be very good company anyway. I'm pretty beat, too," he admitted.

She left as soon as he unloaded everything, but once she got back to the house at Lover's Lane, all she could think of was Ty. She found herself wondering how things were going at the old Chandler house and wishing that it didn't matter as much as it did.

FIFTEEN

Justin is in California for three weeks. They speak almost every day at first, less often as the days pass. He makes some great mainland contacts. Things are looking good for his new line of surf gear.

There's a knock at the apartment door. Her sister Kainani—the family gossip—shows up after work carrying the latest issue of People *magazine.*

Nani reads every issue cover to cover, justifies paying over a hundred dollars she can barely afford for the subscription by passing it on to her sisters when she is through.

Nani has the magazine rolled up in her hand. Nervous and edgy, she heads straight for the refrigerator.

"You got iced tea?" Nani opens the refrigerator, scans the shelves, forages.

"Have a soda. What's up?" Kat easily slips in and out of the pidgin English they use when they are together. She knows by the look on her sister's face this is no casual visit. Nani is on a mission.

"Got the new People.*" Nani holds up the magazine. Julia is on the cover again.*

"I see." Kat sees, but doesn't know what this has to do with the price of taro.

"Okay. Well, I just look through already an' . . ."

Nani swallows, her eyes huge. She flips the magazine open to a dog-eared page and thrusts it at Kat.

"And?"

"Look yourself."

Kat stares down at the "Star Tracks" section featuring photos of celebs at play. There is Justin with his arm draped around a tall, lanky blond model with a megawatt smile. Ken and Barbie.

Stunned, Kat reads the caption.

"Seen about Tinseltown, Justin Parker, Hawaii's former golden-boy surf champion, and Tara Roman, hot new Model for Revlon . . ."

They still call it Tinseltown?

She hands the magazine back to Nani. "It's just a promo shot."

She prays the tremor in her voice doesn't work its way down to her hand before her sister takes the magazine back.

Nani taps the photo with the tip of a long acrylic nail coated in hot magenta. "Looks like the real thing to me."

By now Kat's heart is lodged in her throat. Nani isn't buying it and neither is she. When she looks at the photo, the edges of her heart turn brittle. Her chest feels so tight, she can't breathe, but she fakes a smile and tries to hold on. Her sister starts to fill the awkward silence with inane chatter about the family; she hangs around, waiting for Kat to crack.

All her wind chimes—Justin gives them to her from all over to keep her company while he is gone—dangle from the ceiling of the small lanai outside their kitchen. Their song becomes the sound of heartache.

So does the laughter of children that floats in through the front slider. She watched them earlier, five black-

haired, brown-skinned local kids scrambling over the rocky shoreline, playing tag with the tide.

Finally, finally *Nani leaves. Shaking harder than a Tahitian dancer's hips, Kat dials Justin's hotel room. His voice mail picks up, as it has for the last week.*

Now that she knows he's playing her for a fool, she cringes when she thinks of all the cheery, encouraging messages she's left him.

"I saw you in the People *magazine. Call me. Now." It's all she says this time.*

He calls back when he knows she'll be at work. Leaves her a lame message about how things happen when we least expect them to, how he's sorry, but his life has taken a new direction.

His tone has changed. He is suddenly a stranger. She doesn't know him at all.

The man she's dreamed of, the man who has all her love, her trust, her adoration, is suddenly a stranger.

Kat forced herself to wake up. She blinked, tried to focus and figure out where she was. Her mouth tasted like the inside of a dryer filter full of lint. She finally realized she was on the couch in Jake's living room and it was the middle of the night.

She went to the kitchen and pulled a Diet Pepsi out of the fridge, popped the top, and drank half of it at the kitchen sink, hoping the caffeine would kick in quickly.

Since this whole house-sitting, get-out-and-test-the-waters gig was Jake's idea, she felt like calling and waking him up.

Granted, he couldn't have predicted her meeting a guy like Ty Chandler.

She'd managed to fend Ty off for three days, turning down invitations to go out, to join him at home, to jog on the beach.

Time alone had helped her face the truth—he was great in bed, fabulous with a bar of soap, one heck of a cook, and fun to be with, but she was scared to death of caring too soon—about Ty and about his kids.

She even thought about taking the coward's way out and finding someone else to house-sit. She could run home to Long Beach and go back to living her life without worrying about her heart.

As she stood there staring out at the night through the kitchen window, the house around her echoed with emptiness.

SIXTEEN

The sun was shining the morning Ty carried Alice out to her car seat with all its latest safety features. The diaper bag was full of snacks, juice, and Huggies. Alice and Sunny were both wearing new outfits.

He thought Sunny's tight knit top too revealing, but Kat had obviously okayed it, so he took the advice of one of his how-to books and decided to choose his battles. So far there hadn't been any.

"Does Kat live close by?" Sunny wanted to know as he hustled them to the car.

"Fairly, but I want to stop by the flower stand first." It wasn't every guy who tried to impress a girl with flowers and two kids in tow. That ought to count for something, he thought.

Kat had come up with one excuse after another not to see him for the past three days but he wasn't about to let her slip out of his life. Not without a fight.

He glanced over his shoulder at Alice in the backseat. "Are you sure she's buckled in tight?"

"I checked three times already," Sunny assured him.

He put the Land Cruiser in gear and headed away from the point.

He might have been missing Kat but he hadn't been idle since Sunny arrived. He'd fielded emails from Kamp

Kodiak and helped Sunny find a summer job. And with Alice around, life had already begun to center on meals and changes, naps and playtime.

Within minutes, Sunny was holding the bouquet of orchids he'd picked out as they wound their way up Lover's Lane. A calm settled over him as soon as he saw Kat's bright red CRV parked on the circular gravel drive and knew she was home. He pulled in and parked behind it.

He left Sunny and Alice in the car and went to the door.

Kat finally opened after he knocked twice, looking like she'd been dragged behind a runaway horse. She had bedhead, her hair flat on one side and sticking straight out on the other. Her eyes were puffy and bloodshot.

"What's wrong?" He stepped inside and closed the door behind him, set the flowers on a side table and pulled her into his arms.

As he held her close, he glanced around the room. The television was on, the sound turned low. A tangled quilt hung off one end of the sofa, a rumpled bed pillow was shoved up against the other.

"Did you sleep down here?"

"Actually, I was trying to stay awake down here."

She slipped out of his arms and tugged on the hem of her wrinkled tank top with her good hand, rubbing one of her bare feet over the other.

"Nightmares again?"

She nodded. Her shoulders were rigid, her expression blank as she walked over to the sofa and sat down. He followed, tried to take her in his arms again.

"Don't. Please, Ty. I don't want to fall apart. Not now."

He ached for her, wished he knew how to take the pain away.

"I'll make you a pot of coffee." It sounded hollow, useless, but it was all he could think of.

She smiled weakly. "That would be great."

He was across the room when he heard her say, "You brought flowers."

He turned around, saw that she hadn't left the sofa. He went back and picked up the bouquet, handed it to her, and watched her turn back the cellophane paper so that she could touch the petals of the lavender and white blooms and stroke their velvety surface with her fingertip.

When she turned to him again there were tears in her eyes.

"Thank you," she said softly.

"I didn't mean to make you cry."

She nodded. "I know. It's just that . . . no one's given me flowers for a long time."

"Hey," he smiled, tried to lighten the mood, "I'll bet I'm the first *grandfather* you ever had trying to win your heart."

"Is that what you're trying to do? Win my heart?"

He reached for her, ran his hand down her cheek. "Win it, Kat. Not break it."

Her gaze traced his face, locked with his before she lowered her lashes and touched the orchids again.

"How about that coffee?" she whispered.

He left her then, walked to the kitchen, and started opening cupboards and drawers until he found the coffee and the basket liners. When he looked up, he found her watching from the doorway.

He was across the room in a heartbeat, drawing her into his arms, holding her close, rubbing her back, comforting her the way he'd learned to comfort Alice when she was fussy.

"I wish you wouldn't do that." Kat's voice sounded thick and rusty, and though she protested, she slowly relaxed and made no attempt to pull away.

He found himself wishing he'd driven up alone.

"I left the girls outside."

She drew back slightly, visibly tried to pull herself together as she ran her hand over her hair.

"Oh, Ty. Have them come in."

"You must really be desperate for company." He gave her arm a slight squeeze before he let her go. "Sit down. I'll get your coffee when I get back."

"I'm all right, really."

He took her by the arm and led her to the dining room table, where he deposited her in a chair.

Sunny and Alice were already out of the car. Alice was squatting in the driveway, inspecting rocks with Stinko lying on the ground beside her. Sunny was staring out at the ocean.

She looked so much like a combination of his grandmother and Amy that he was continually caught off guard. Just now the breeze lifted her chestnut hair off her shoulders, exposing the pale skin at the nape of her neck.

Framed against the expansive horizon, she seemed much younger, and far more vulnerable than she acted.

She was only a kid, really. A kid with a child of her own.

She turned to Alice, took hold of her hand to keep her from running down the steep hillside. Then Sunny picked Alice up and brushed the little girl's hair back off her cheek and kissed her on the forehead.

He waited a few seconds before calling, "Kat says to come on in."

Sunny waved to let him know she heard and he lingered until she caught up, and then he headed back to the house. Kat was still sitting at the dining table, with her chin resting on her hand.

"I hate to say it, but you look like hell."

"Gee, thanks." Kat futilely tried to fluff her hair with one hand.

"Way to go, Chandler." Sunny walked in right behind him, obviously having heard his comment.

She turned to Kat. "You really do look like hell, though. What happened?"

"Bad night."

"I've had a few of those myself." Sunny put Alice on the floor beside a dining room chair. Alice started slapping it with both hands. Ty walked into the kitchen, leaving Kat and Sunny in awkward silence while he poured coffee.

"Want a cup?" he asked after Sunny wandered into the kitchen.

"No, thanks. Can I go out on the deck?"

"Ask Kat."

Sunny turned toward the dining room. "Is it all right?"

Kat nodded. "Sure, why not." Ty watched her try to muster a smile.

After Sunny left the room, Kat concentrated on her coffee as Alice threaded her way through table legs and chairs with Stinko in hand.

"How's the job search going?" Kat blew on the coffee before she took a sip.

"We walked all over town, picked up some applications. I talked to Selma at the diner. She said summer was too hectic for her to train someone with no experience and suggested Sunny try again in October."

"That's too bad. Selma seems like the motherly type."

He nodded. "She suggested Mermaids, the shell and trinket shop next door to the diner. It turns out the owner needed someone for the two-to-seven shift, five days a week. He hired Sunny on the spot."

Alice suddenly ran out from under the table, headed for the living room. Ty took off after her. She dropped Stinko, squealed, and grabbed the television remote.

When he turned around, he found Kat watching them.

"What about a baby-sitter while Sunny's at work?"

"Are you volunteering?"

She looked into his eyes, her expression bleak. "Sorry."

"I plan on watching her for now." He thought he could manage a few hours in the afternoons while Sunny worked, but he didn't want to lose any of the precious time he had left with Kat. The fact that it was only a month before the Montgomerys came back was never far from his mind. "I was hoping you'd volunteer to come and keep the babysitter company."

He glanced over and saw that Alice was holding the remote to her ear like a cell phone and talking gibberish into it.

"I think she's gifted." The child continually amazed him.

"I hate to break it to you," Kat was finally smiling, "but she's probably just imitating Sunny."

Alice had moved to the arm of the sofa, still occupied with the remote. He sat down on the chair beside Kat's and leaned closer.

The instant their lips met, all rational thought drifted away. Kat's fingers, warm and tender, curled around his wrist.

Suddenly they heard Sunny walk in behind them. *"Damn it!"*

She bolted into the living room. Ty glanced over at

Alice, who had taken the batteries out of the remote and was about to shove one into her mouth. He shot to his feet and so did Kat.

As Sunny grabbed the thin triple-A battery, Alice started wailing. Sunny snatched her up onto her hip and tossed the remote on the coffee table, where it landed with a clatter.

"You're okay, baby. It's okay," Sunny murmured to Alice before she turned on Ty.

"Will you *really* watch her while I'm at work? Or are you going to be too busy screwing your girlfriend?"

He was as upset as she was over what could have happened. "I'm sorry, Sunny. I just looked away for a minute. I had no idea—"

"Yeah? Well, maybe you'd better go through those books you're so into again." She flashed a furious look at Kat, as if it were all her fault. "We'll wait outside."

Sunny turned her back and stalked out with Alice screaming in her arms. When Ty turned around, Kat's cheeks were on fire.

He tried to calm down but it was hard to shake the image of Alice with the battery up to her lips.

Finally, he took a deep breath and let it out.

"At least our little Chandler family house call has put some color in your cheeks." Levity didn't help much, though Kat did smile. He walked back to the dining table and took her hand. "It's hard to think straight around you."

"Is that a compliment?"

"Go out with me tonight, Kat."

"It looks like you've got enough going on—"

"Don't turn me down. I'm going nuts. I want to be with you."

"You do look pretty desperate." Finally, she smiled. "How about tomorrow?"

"No more excuses. Besides, it has to be tonight. Sunny starts work tomorrow and then, hopefully, we'll be spending time together at my place. Tonight I want to take you out on a real date. Dinner, candlelight. The whole nine yards."

She debated with herself for so long he was sure she was going to turn him down.

"I'm not taking no for an answer," he warned. "I'll go get the girls and we'll all camp out in the living room until you accept."

She laughed and raised both hands in surrender. "Okay, I'll go."

He didn't like leaving her alone with the haunted look that never left her eyes, not even when she smiled.

"Are you *sure* you're going to be all right by yourself?" He picked Stinko up off the floor, hesitant to go.

"I'll be fine."

He didn't believe a word of it.

SEVENTEEN

The restaurant was off the main drag in San Luis Obispo, a small mom and pop place run by Hawaiian transplants from Kona who had been living on the mainland for thirty years.

The minute Kat walked through the door, she felt at home. The walls were covered with bamboo and woven *lauhala* mats. Palm leaf fans beat an uneven rhythm as they circulated the air. Dim light filtered through blue glass float balls that once buoyed Japanese fishing nets.

There were Hawaii travel posters on the wall, waiters decked out in gaudy aloha shirts. Best of all, the soft, lilting sound of Hawaiian slack-key guitar floated on the air.

Ty ushered her in, obviously pleased with himself.

"Surprise," he said softly, resting his hand at her waist as they walked to the hostess stand.

"How did you find this place?"

"Actually, R.J. recommended it." He took her hand, led her to a private table in back.

"I think my first impression of R.J. is mellowing. Tell him *mahalo*." Standing in the midst of what might have been an intimate local eatery in the islands, the Hawaiian word for thank you slipped naturally from her lips.

Dinner was intimate and fun. Their host and hostess, Albert and Lou Kaku were eager to please when they found out she was Hawaiian. Kat savored shredded *kalua* pork, potato macaroni salad, sticky white rice, and fresh poi flown in from the Hanalei Poi factory on Kauai. She ate until she was sure she was going to burst.

The low hum of conversation from other tables ebbed and flowed around them. In a situation like this, Justin would have been distracted, seated where he could watch the door, waiting for someone important to stroll in, smiling at the other diners, and hoping someone would recognize him.

But Ty focused on her and her alone. He had a way of looking at her that made her go hot all over. Not only that, but he made her feel special, that he truly cared for her.

She wished she wasn't so afraid to believe it. She looked over and found him watching her toy with the paper umbrella that decorated her mai tai.

"Is Sunny ready for her first day on the job?" she asked.

"I think so. She calmed down and apologized after we got home this morning."

"She was just scared for Alice. We all were." She had been ready to fly over the couch herself to grab the battery out of the toddler's hand. "She's a good mother, Ty."

"Considering all she must have been through, she's a *great* mother. She still hasn't opened up about her past, though."

"Does Sunny ever talk about Alice's dad?"

He shook his head. "Just the name Dodge."

"Last or first?"

"First. She's made it pretty clear she doesn't want to talk about him."

"Dodge," she said, thinking out loud.

"She did say he was named after his dad's favorite car."

"Good thing the guy wasn't into Oldsmobiles."

Ty laughed.

Kat twirled the paper umbrella.

"Did she mention his age?"

"Are you on the job, Vargas?"

She laughed. "Just curious."

"Sometimes I wonder if there might not be someone out there from his family—parents, aunts, or uncles—somebody who might want to be part of Alice's life."

"Someone like you?"

"I guess."

"Sometimes the past is best left in the past," she said softly. Yet she couldn't stop thinking about what he'd just said.

Dodge. Deceased. No other information. Not much to go on. She could start by searching for Alice's birth records, but she didn't even know if Sunny had named her Alice Simone, Alice Simmons, or given her Dodge's last name.

It helped to have something for her brain to latch on to, something to focus on other than all the what-ifs that had been driving her crazy lately.

She studied Ty in the shifting candlelight. The soft, soothing sound of Don Ho singing "I'll Remember You" filled the room. She tried not to concentrate on the lyrics, afraid the melancholy tune would melt her heart and break down the last of her defenses.

"I will remember you, long after this endless summer is through. . . ."

Kat picked up her tumbler, swirled the remnants of ice before she set it down.

"You're a thousand miles away." He reached for her hand. "What are you thinking about?"

"I'm thinking we should have another mai tai."

They had another mai tai. The blending of rums and fruit juices warmed his blood, but not as much as being with Kat did.

Kat rubbed the back of his hand with her fingertips. Her words drifted softly to him over the exotic music.

"Now I want to know what *you're* thinking."

Ty looked into her eyes. Kat was more to him now than just a lovely dinner companion, more than someone he wanted to date for a few weeks this summer.

"I'm thinking that you're the most beautiful woman in the room."

Kat looked around. It was late. The place was almost deserted. "I'm one of the *only* women in the room."

He leaned close, kissed her. "I mean it, Kat. Don't brush the compliment aside."

She lowered her lashes. "Thanks, Ty. Really. It's just that I'm not used to this."

"This what? Appreciation?"

"Attention. Kindness, I guess."

"Is it that hard to take?"

She shook her head. "No. The trouble is, I could get used to it."

"Then why fight it?"

Kat murmured, "I wish I could give you what you want, Ty."

"What do you think that is?"

"It's been so long, I'm not sure."

"Then give me what you can."

"Take me home," she whispered, leaning close, her eyes rich with promise.

* * *

When they reached his car, he slipped his hand beneath her chin, tilted her face up to his, and gently kissed her.

She leaned into him. Her breasts, soft, tantalizing, flattened against his chest. He heard her sigh. She tasted, delved, explored his mouth. Ty pressed her up against the car, wondering why in the hell they were standing out in a dark parking lot like two sixteen-year-olds when they both had empty beds at home. Then he remembered he couldn't count his place—not with Sunny and Alice in the house.

When her hands slipped beneath his shirt and began to massage the small of his back, he didn't care about a bed. He wanted her then and there.

"Quick. Get in the car," he murmured against her lips, his hands all over her before he reached around her and fumbled for the door handle.

"I guess it is getting late," she whispered as she grabbed the button above his fly.

He glanced around the parking lot. Except for a couple of cars parked across the lot, the place was practically deserted.

"How about the backseat?" he suggested.

"You're kidding."

"I've never been more serious in my life." For good measure, he rubbed against her, let her feel exactly how serious he was, and then he closed the front passenger door and reached for the backdoor handle. Kat glanced over her shoulder.

"Are you sure?"

"I want you, Kat. I haven't thought of anything but making love to you for days. Say no and we'll leave, or climb in the backseat. I'm ready to do it on the hood of the car."

She looked around the deserted lot. "What about the security guard?"

"What security guard? This isn't L.A."

"The restaurant staff—"

"They're busy cleaning up so they can get out of here. The closest car is a quarter of a block away."

Even in the dim light, he could see that she was tempted. He kissed her again, long, slow, and deep, until she moaned and cupped his arousal.

Breathless, she whispered against his lips, "Okay, but I can see the headline now. 'Naked P.I. Arrested in Parking Lot.' "

"You don't have to get naked and we're not going to get arrested."

"Because this isn't L.A."

"Right."

She slipped past him and climbed up into the car. He climbed in after her.

"I must have been more agile at sixteen," he mumbled, slipping his hand up her skirt, tangling his fingers into her thong and tugging it down to her thighs.

With an urgency that matched his own, she leaned over and unzipped his fly. "You were probably shorter."

"Not down there."

He caught the flash of her smile a heartbeat before she took him into her mouth, surprising him, thrilling him, arousing him until all he could think about was Kat, Kat's lips, Kat's tongue, Kat's eyes, her mouth, her body, her smile—and the way she made him feel.

She brought him to the brink of climax more than once, then withdrew and let him teeter on the edge. She kicked off her sandals. He drew off her flimsy scrap of silk that barely passed for an undergarment.

The street lamps outside radiated fading rainbow smudges on the steamed windows. Kat moved up and over him, climbed on his lap. Warm and wet, she took him inside, rode him until he grabbed her hips and captured her, gently eased her down until he was sheathed deep inside. So far inside that she let go a low, throaty moan before she covered his mouth with hers.

She raised her hips, drew herself up the length of his penis, plunged again, kneeling over him. Other than the sound of the leather upholstery creaking beneath him, Ty was oblivious to everything, to the night, the fact that his knees were shoved up against the back of the driver's seat. His entire consciousness was centered on Kat.

Her need, as great as his own, communicated itself through her every move, her every touch, her every sigh.

He wished she could let herself love him, trust him as deeply as she craved this intimacy they shared. Their bodies were so attuned to each other that they moved as one.

If only she could trust enough to give him her heart the way she gladly gave her body. If only she'd let him bring her heart and soul to life so that she could really live again.

He unbuttoned the linen sheath she wore. She wasn't wearing a bra. He exposed her breasts, found her nipple, sucked it into his mouth. She cried out with pleasure, threw her head back, and rode him harder. Driving him over the edge, Kat buried her fingers in his shoulders as they came together.

Replete, she collapsed, still straddling him. He hadn't the urge to move. He wanted to stay inside her, enveloped by her.

It was Kat who drew back first, to stare into his eyes.

"That was a great idea," she whispered, kissing him again. Then, with the grace of a dancer, she swung her leg over him, twisted around to sit beside him, and began searching for her thong on the floor of the car with her toes.

He reached down and scooped it up for her. Before she buttoned up her dress, he ran his hand over the smooth ivory skin of her breast.

"I don't want you to leave when the Montgomerys come back."

She went perfectly still, her hands paralyzed on a button.

He leaned into her, whispered against her temple, "I mean it, Kat. I wish you'd think about staying in Twilight."

"Impossible." She didn't mean to voice the thought aloud, but it was the first thing that came to her mind.

"Anything's possible." Ty ran both hands through his hair and then zipped his fly. "Who'd have thought I'd have my daughter with me already?"

"I have a business in Long Beach. I just can't walk out on it." His life was nice and tidy now. He had Sunny and Alice here, his own long-distance business seemed to be running fine, but she'd worked long and hard to establish her agency, and life had showed her more than once that there were no guarantees.

"Look, Kat." He could feel her shutting down. Even if she was thinking over what he'd suggested, she'd fallen silent. "Just think about it, all right? That's all I'm asking."

Think about it.

Didn't he realize that all she'd done for the past few days was think about him and wonder what in the hell she was going to do when Jake got back?

EIGHTEEN

Two freaking hours to go.

Sunny had no clue how she'd lasted almost the whole week at Mermaids.

If it weren't for Alice, she'd have walked out of town and never looked back. Chandler put her on a small allowance and told her that she could keep all the money she earned, but that he expected her to contribute by helping out with chores.

She turned her back to the store surveillance camera, pulled a fresh stick of gum out of her jeans pocket, quickly slipped it out of its foil wrapper, and popped it in her mouth.

Earl Stanley, her boss and the owner of the shop, didn't allow gum chewing on the job. On her first day at work, he'd given her the list of rules that he expected his employees to abide by.

He hated chewing gum, not because it was a dirty habit, but because he claimed teenagers never properly disposed of it.

He freaked whenever he found a gum wad stuck beneath the countertop or the one, hard wooden bar stool he had in back of the counter, in the off chance any of the clerks ever had time to sit down.

Earl never worked the register—he acted as if dealing

with tourists was beneath him—but he hung out all day in the tiny back room, hovering in the doorway, overseeing everything.

Floor to ceiling, Mermaids was crammed full of tacky tourist ware. Anything with a mermaid on it was jammed into the eighteen-by-sixty-foot space. There were mermaids made of sand dollars, mermaids with seashells strategically covering their breasts, mermaids under glass snowballs, mermaid Christmas ornaments, mermaid place mats, mugs, silver spoons, charms, key rings, woven mermaid throws.

You name it, Earl had it.

Though she hated Earl and the shop, the job gave her the opportunity to get out of the house and leave Chandler and French Fry alone together. She'd finally decided on a plan, and if things were going to work out, she had to be certain the baby and Chandler really took to each other. Chandler was already *obsessed* with raising Alice right. He absolutely doted on her.

Kat Vargas seemed to be getting used to having Alice around. She and Ty went jogging on the beach together in the afternoons and they'd started renting old movies to watch at night while he baby-sat.

Chandler had been in a great mood all week, but something about the way Kat acted around Alice made the hair on the back of Sunny's neck stand up. And knowing Kat was a private investigator only made things worse.

Chandler had been taking care of French Fry from one in the afternoon until seven at night. At first he'd been anxious about doing everything right, but now he actually seemed to enjoy it.

He used his time in the mornings to work on the computer and make phone calls when French Fry was napping.

His expensive how-to-raise-a-kid books were all over the house. As far as she was concerned, no one needed a book to tell them how to raise a kid. You fed them, changed them, kept them from harm, hugged and kissed them a lot. Big freaking deal.

Chandler was constantly making a major case of everything, worrying about whether or not Alice was "on target" for her age, taking notes, comparing her to what the books said she should be doing by now.

Because Alice did some things ahead of schedule, he was convinced she was exceptional in every way. He bragged that she was, without a doubt, the smartest kid on the planet.

I could have told him that. She gets it from me.

Me and Dodge.

Dodge had always run the show. Butch, Leaf, even Jamie couldn't touch Dodge's mind. He had a knack for business and had been on the way to making a real name for himself. Unfortunately, he was a legend now.

"Do you have any of these in green?"

Sunny raised a brow, looked down her nose at a stout woman with overprocessed red hair and freckles showing her a ceramic mermaid spoon holder.

"Excuse me?" She entertained herself by making customers ask everything twice.

"Do you have this in green? My kitchen is all done in green and it just has to match."

"My kitchen is all done in green."

Give me a freaking break.

Sunny popped her gum. Loudly. "Sorry, ma'am. Those only come in hot pink and neon yellow." Leave it to Earl to stock only the tackiest colors.

Disappointed, the woman set the spoon holder down beside the cash register and walked away. Sunny picked it up and put it on the go-back pile and then glanced over toward the corner where a dumb, pimply-faced junior high geek hovered over the mermaid pocketknife collection.

She'd noticed him when he walked in fifteen minutes ago. Who wouldn't? He was wearing a baggy sweatshirt on one of the hottest days yet. Who in the hell but a shoplifter wears a heavy, hooded sweatshirt with pockets on a summer day?

He'd been fingering the knives with mermaids on the handle. Hold it up and the mermaid's tits were covered. Turn it upside down and they were bare. To each his own.

She snapped her gum and watched him slip the knife into his sweatshirt pocket. She went to help a woman take an ornament off the fake Christmas tree in the front window. The tree had been there so long the dust on the branches gave the impression of fake gray snow.

The minute the geek in the sweatshirt crossed the threshold, Earl came tearing out of the back room, grabbed the kid by his hood, and dragged him back into the store.

Earl had owned the place for thirty years and probably hadn't bought himself any new clothes in all that time. Dressed in plaid polyester pants and a yellow shirt with a pleated shirtfront, a white belt, and matching loafers, he was totally retro—though not by design. He was completely clueless. His thick, oversized horn-rimmed glasses magnified his eyes to twice their size, giving him a fishy look.

"Give it up, young man!" Earl shoved the kid against the counter, no doubt having seen one too many episodes of *NYPD Blue*. Andy Sipowitz made taking down perps look easy. Earl was doing his part to stop crime.

The kid was shaking and sweating. Sunny was sure he was either going to burst into tears or throw up. Earl held out his hand and waited. The kid reached into his pocket and out came the mermaid knife, flashing bare tits. The kid's face was red as a cherry when he dropped the knife into Earl's palm.

Earl read the kid the riot act then tossed him out the door, onto the street.

"If I ever see you in this store again, I won't hesitate to call the police!" Earl wagged his finger, making sure everyone in the vicinity had overheard.

Sunny was ringing up a cash sale for two eleven-year-olds who had selected shells from the fill-a-bag-for-a-buck box. She looked up and saw Earl bearing down on her looking like a Rat Pack fugitive long overdue for a cocktail.

"You *watched* him pocket this knife, didn't you, Miss Simone?" He waved the knife under her nose. "Don't try to deny it. I saw you on the monitor. You were looking right at that young cretin when he slipped this into his sweatshirt, and you didn't say a thing."

"I wasn't really paying attention."

He rose up onto the toes of his white patent-leather shoes.

"You most certainly were, too."

She shrugged. "He's just a kid."

"That knife cost five ninety-five plus tax."

A good three inches taller than Earl, she leaned over the counter until they were nose to nose and popped her gum.

"What did you pay for it, Earl? Fifty cents? A buck? *He's just a kid.*"

"He's a thief, and you were aiding and abetting."

"Give me a break," she mumbled.

Earl was sweating profusely. His bald spot gleamed beneath the flourescent lights. "You're fired."

"You've got to be kidding."

"You're through at the end of your shift."

She stepped out from behind the cash register. "You think I'm going to finish out my shift? Get real."

"If you want your full week's pay, you will."

"Give me what you owe me up to this minute 'cause I'm outta here."

A small crowd waiting for help had gathered near the cash register. Earl fumed, finally stalked off to the back room, and came out with her check. She glanced at the piddling amount. It didn't come close to what she needed every month. She shoved the check in her back pocket.

Not enough to cover a third of the bills piling up in L.A.

Sunny took the gum out of her mouth and, right in front of Earl, stuck it under the countertop before she walked out.

July crowds jammed the street. Sunny took a deep breath and reveled in her newfound freedom. Pulling the scrunchy out of her hair, she shook it free, and when she glanced up, noticed a halfway decent-looking guy window-shopping two stores down.

It was too early to go back to Chandler's, though she was missing French Fry like crazy. Working all these hours at Mermaids meant she'd been away from her baby more than ever before, but if Chandler and Alice were going to bond, they needed time alone together.

The guy looking in the shop window wasn't her type, but she started toward him. When he looked up, he immediately spotted her. He was young and tan, somewhere close to her age, but maybe a bit younger. He smiled shyly.

She shoved her hands in her back pockets. The move drew her tank top tight across her breasts.

He was drawn to her like a fly to sticky paper. Men were so easy.

"Hi." He had a quick, open smile. "You here on vacation?"

"Just moved here. How about you?"

"I live in Canyon Club, the new development."

"The one on the golf course? Behind the gates?" She'd passed by it on the way to the mall with Kat.

"That's the one."

"Sweet." She couldn't care less where he was from. She was so tired of hanging around Chandler's watching him watch French Fry do her amazing baby tricks or sitting through old kung fu movies that she was willing to put up with this kid for a couple hours of freedom.

He was so mesmerized by her breasts that he couldn't speak.

"Got plans?" she asked.

"I've got some beer. I was gonna take it down to the cove. You thirsty?"

"That depends on what kind of beer."

"Pacifico?"

Perfecto. A couple hours of freedom and a couple of free beers was just what she needed.

NINETEEN

Kat watched Ty walk to his front door and stare through the screen as a Volvo cruised past the house. It stopped at the end of the point, made a U-turn, and headed back toward the highway.

"The pizza's getting cold." He paced across the room. "Where in the hell is she? She's an hour late."

"Good thing you missed her formative years," Kat teased.

He tried to smile. His gaze found Alice, safe and sound on a comforter spread out on the floor. She was rolling around with Stinko in her hands, chewing on the skunk's tail.

"I should let her drive my car to work instead of taking the shuttle. She'd be home sooner."

Even Kat took the shuttle around town whenever she found a good parking space and wasn't willing to vie for another. The Twilight Cove shuttle was efficient, inexpensive, and usually packed with tourists. It stopped at the end of Ty's road and then went on, all the way to nearby Gull Harbor.

"Ty, relax. Why don't we go ahead and eat? Maybe she went to the diner with someone after work."

"She should have called."

Kat got up from the sofa, walked to his side, and rubbed his shoulder.

"She's not a child. Besides, she's been on her own for years. She probably has no idea you're worried about her. Why don't we just go ahead and eat and save her some pizza?"

They ate, then curled up on the couch together to watch television. At least, Kat watched and Ty pretended to. At ten, when there was still no word from Sunny, Kat wrapped the extra pizza in Saran Wrap and stuck it in the refrigerator. Ty changed Alice and got her settled on the comforter, where she promptly fell asleep.

When Kat walked back into the living room and sat down beside Ty again, she reached for his hand, wondering if he even knew she was there.

After a few minutes, he let go a frustrated sigh, glanced at his watch, and then got to his feet.

"Would you mind staying with Alice for a few minutes while I go into town and look for Sunny?"

Alice was still asleep on her stomach on the comforter, sucking her thumb, her fist curled against her lips.

"How about I go look?"

"I don't want to sit here worrying about both of you."

His concern made her uncomfortable. She wasn't used to anyone caring this much outside of her family.

"I spend a lot of late nights out on surveillance."

"Don't remind me. I'd rather go myself, if you'll stay with Alice."

It was obvious how badly he wanted to go himself. There was nothing she could do outside of flat-out refusing to stay. Besides, she couldn't ignore the worry in his eyes.

She glanced over at Alice, who was blissfully asleep. "Okay, I'll stay."

He grabbed his keys and was out the door before she could change her mind. Kat got off the sofa and began to pace. It was ten-thirty, not too late for a nineteen-year-old to be out, but very late for someone due home at seven-twenty.

Kat went into the kitchen, got herself a glass of water, walked back out, flexing her injured hand. Therapy was going well. Her bandage was off, and though not as bad as she'd expected, the scar was definitely noticeable.

A constant reminder to keep her wits about her.

Standing over the coffee table, she reached for one of Ty's baby books, flipped through the pages, and quickly set it back down after it fell open to a series of photographs depicting all the stages of fetal development.

Alice's toys were scattered over the living room floor. Kat started picking them up and dumping them into a plastic toy bin. She gathered up a tiny knit shirt with enamel snaps and eyelet trim, one that Sunny chose on their shopping trip. She folded it carefully, and then pulled a little pink tennis shoe out from under a side table.

She was cool, calm, in control—until she glanced down at the sweet shoe cupped in the palm of her hand. A little yellow duck decorated the toe. The shoe was so little, so precious and feminine. When her eyes unexpectedly smarted with tears, she dropped the shoe like a hot rock.

This is exactly why you're better off alone.

First you feel a little niggle here and there, then you start to care. You open up some more, give away a little more of yourself, and pretty soon, you're up to your ass in heartache.

She picked up the remote. Before she could hit the mute button, sound rattled around the room.

Kat held her breath when Alice stirred and let out a

fussy, mewling sound. The child raised her head, pushed up, and peered around, blinking sleepy-eyed.

Alice's gaze went straight to the couch where Ty had been sitting, then quickly traveled around the room and locked on Kat.

Kat set the remote down on the coffee table, edged toward Alice, and whispered, "Go back to sleep."

Alice rubbed her eyes, looked right at Kat, and said something that sounded like "Blah."

"My thoughts exactly."

Alice struggled to her feet, got her bearings, and shot toward the kitchen.

"Hey! Come back here." Kat went after her, but Alice beat her to the refrigerator and started banging on the door, yelling, "Ju! Ju! Ju!"

Kat knew enough baby-ese to understand.

"Hold on a minute. You have to move back." Kat put her hand on Alice's shoulder, lightly, just the slightest touch, so she could gently guide her away from the door.

She opened the refrigerator, found a bottle of apple juice. There were plastic sippy cups on the counter. She filled one with juice as Alice pressed against her leg chanting the juju chant and nodding her head.

Kat handed her the sippy cup, put the juice away, and headed for the living room, hoping Alice would follow. When she looked back, she saw that the baby hadn't budged.

Alice was in front of the sink, her delicate little fingers wrapped around the cup, her lower lip trembling.

"What? You've got your juice. Now come back to the living room. Stinko's in here." Kat cajoled, then she bartered, but Alice didn't budge.

The toddler's lower lip quivered a little more. One big alligator tear slipped down Alice's cheek. Then she held both arms out to Kat in a silent appeal.

"You're killing me, you know," Kat whispered.

"Up." The arms stayed up. The sippy cup swayed, threatening to dribble all over the floor. "Up."

Kat sighed, took a deep breath, and walked back over to Alice. "You're as stubborn as your grandpa."

"Up."

Kat leaned down and hooked her hands under Alice's arms and picked her up. The toddler triumphantly giggled and waved in glee as Kat settled her on her hip.

For a few seconds Kat didn't dare breathe, let alone move or think. Slowly her arms tightened around Alice. She swayed back and forth with her eyes closed, inhaling the sweet baby scent. The child was warm, her skin soft as pink satin ribbon, pale and perfect.

Alice stuck the lip of the sippy cup in her mouth and sucked down some juice. Finally content, she nestled her head in the hollow of Kat's shoulder. When Alice's curls brushed Kat's neck and cheek, Kat shuddered but held on tight.

She could hang on until Ty got back.

Surely he'll be home soon.

It wasn't Ty who arrived a few minutes later, but Sunny. When Kat heard a car pull up out front, she walked to the door in time to watch Sunny step out of a low-slung, red convertible Corvette and wave good-bye. The driver gunned the engine before he drove away.

Alice began to bob up and down in Kat's arms, reaching out for Sunny as soon as she came through the door.

"Where's Chandler?" Sunny took Alice and looked around.

Though the odor of beer and cigarette smoke clung to her, she was clear-eyed and steady on her feet.

"Out searching for you."

"Hi, French Fry. Mama's home. Did you have a good time tonight, baby?"

When Sunny rubbed noses with Alice and pretended to take a sip of juice, Kat grabbed her own sweater off a nearby chair and threw it around her shoulders.

Sunny finally looked up. There was no misunderstanding her expression.

"I can't believe he left her with you. You always act like she's got the cooties or something."

Nothing was further from the truth. Sunny would never believe it without an explanation, though, and Kat would rather be boiled in oil than open up.

Sunny walked over to the comforter on the floor, picked up Stinko, and handed the skunk to Alice.

"Ty had no idea where you were and he was worried."

"What's the big deal?"

"Other than the fact you're over three hours late? The polite thing would have been to call and let him know that you weren't coming right home."

"It's only ten-thirty—"

"It's ten fifty-five."

"What *is* this? One of your *private investigations*?" She bounced Alice up and down a couple of times and tried to shrug it off. "I met a guy. We had a couple of beers. So what?"

Kat took a deep breath and tried to remember where Sunny was coming from.

"So I care about Ty—" Kat immediately pressed her fingers to her lips but it was too late.

"I care about Ty."

She hadn't allowed herself to really care about a man for so long that the admission tasted as dangerous as razor blades on her tongue. She lowered her hands and her voice.

"Ty's welcomed you into his home. He's trying to help you get your life turned around."

"What makes you think my life needs turning around?"

"Look, Sunny, Ty was upset, and that upset me. Next time you're going to be late, you should call, at least to check on Alice and let him know when you'll be home."

Sunny's eyes narrowed. "You have no idea what I feel for Alice or . . ." her voice broke ". . . or what I'd do for her."

She turned her back and sat down on the comforter on the floor and started teasing the baby with the plush skunk.

"Want Stinko? You love your little Stinko, don't you, babe?"

Sunny looked up and caught Kat watching them.

"Give me an freaking break here, okay? You are not my mother. You are not a Chandler."

"My concern is for Ty."

"I'd appreciate it if you'd butt out of my life."

Kat held up both hands. "Fine. I'll be happy to." She grabbed her purse.

"I don't want him leaving you alone with Alice anymore. Ever."

Kat paused with her hand on the screen door. Unfortunately, her gaze was drawn to Alice, who was smiling and waving bye-bye.

"Don't worry. That's the last thing I want, too."

TWENTY

Ty cruised down Cabrillo, past shops and storefronts, to see if he could spot Sunny in Twilight. Most places were closed or closing. Foot traffic had dwindled to a few couples strolling along the sidewalk. He left his car in the parking lot off the Plaza and walked to Mermaid's, in the middle of the block.

When he came back out, he thought about calling Kat, then realized he'd left his cell phone on the coffee table. He'd almost reached the parking lot again when Kat pulled her car up next to the curb. He waited as she rolled down the passenger-side window.

She leaned across the center console toward him. The mellow sound of a CD playing Hawaiian guitar music filled the air.

"She's home, Ty."

He let go a sigh of relief and hunkered down on the curb beside her car.

"She just got back." Kat turned the stereo down.

"Did she say where she was?"

"She met someone and . . . forgot the time."

"What's wrong?"

"She'd prefer you didn't leave Alice with me anymore."

"Why not?"

She was quiet for a moment, as if going over how to explain. "She thinks I'm a little . . . hesitant around Alice." She shrugged. "I guess I am."

Kat killed the engine when he opened the door and got into the car. He glanced down the street, where the clerk at Sweeties was taking the chairs in off the sidewalk.

"She got fired today," he told her.

"Oh, Ty."

"I went by Mermaids. Earl was still inside tallying up receipts and told me Sunny left just before five, right after he fired her."

"What happened?"

He explained, and then wondered aloud, "How in the hell is she going to find another job in Twilight after pulling a stunt like that?"

"Someone else will be willing to take a chance on her. It'll work out."

"I hope so."

Kat touched his thigh, drew him back. "It's late, and I need to get back up the hill. Do you need a ride to your car?"

"I'm right over there." He nodded to the lot a few feet away.

He noticed she seemed edgy and unsure of herself. As if she'd lost her footing tonight. The more he thought about it, the more he realized that she *did* act uncertain around Alice, but unlike Sunny, he realized that Kat worked hard on not letting her feelings show.

He reached for her, kissed her, wished he could go home with her tonight, but he was just as anxious to settle things at home.

"I'm sorry about what happened. I'll talk to Sunny."

"I wish you wouldn't." She shrugged but didn't smile. "You've both got enough on your plates right now." Kat ran her hands around the steering wheel. When she finally spoke, he had to strain to hear her.

"I think she's trying, Ty, but it's got to be tough on someone so young. Things will work out or they won't. Just don't invest too much of yourself. Don't invest any more than you can stand to lose."

"I'm already way over my head." Tonight had shaken him and made him all too aware of how much a part of his life Sunny had already become.

"I'll follow you home," he offered.

"I'll be fine. You ought to get back."

He kissed her good-bye and stepped out of the car. After she pulled away from the curb, he watched until her taillights disappeared around the south end of the cove.

When he walked in the front door, the living room was empty, the house completely silent. Stinko was missing, but the comforter was still in the middle of the floor. The television was off.

He locked up, turned off all the lights, and headed upstairs. All was quiet in the room Sunny shared with Alice. He paused outside the door, listened for a second, then silently pushed the door open.

Sunny was in bed, sound asleep in a long tank top and pajama bottoms he'd loaned her, with the bedsheet tangled around her hips and legs. In sleep she looked years younger, as innocent and vulnerable as Alice. He had an urge to straighten the sheet, to make certain she was protected from the damp night air.

He was afraid to wake her, so he just looked, wishing he'd known her as a child, wishing he'd been there to kiss her boo-boos when she fell, to hold her when she cried, to tell her how proud he was of her every step of the way.

Would she have turned out any different? He didn't know, couldn't know, but he was no less determined to help her now.

When he'd walked into Mermaids looking for her earlier, the crowded store had given him claustrophobia. The place hadn't changed in years, nor had Earl Stanley. He was as out-of-date as vinyl records.

He wouldn't have lasted more than a couple hours in the cluttered little store and gave Sunny credit for making it as long as she had. But he'd have quit before he got fired for letting anyone get away with shoplifting.

He took another look at his daughter, wondered if he'd ever really know or understand her, then he turned toward the crib across the room.

Alice lay on her stomach just like her mother, but with her legs drawn up beneath her so that her rear end was sticking in the air. Stinko stood guard in one corner.

A mobile Sunny bought at Earl's dangled just out of reach. Mermaids with glistening silver scales spun in the faint breeze coming through the window.

Ty reached out, touched Alice's finely drawn brow with his fingertip, adjusted her blanket. As much as he wished his daughter had been spared this awesome responsibility at her age, there was no way he would wish away Alice. She'd already endeared herself to him.

He'd been given a chance to have not one, but two children. A chance to protect and guide them along their way. He wanted to be the kind of father he never had.

Now more than ever, he was determined to give it his all.

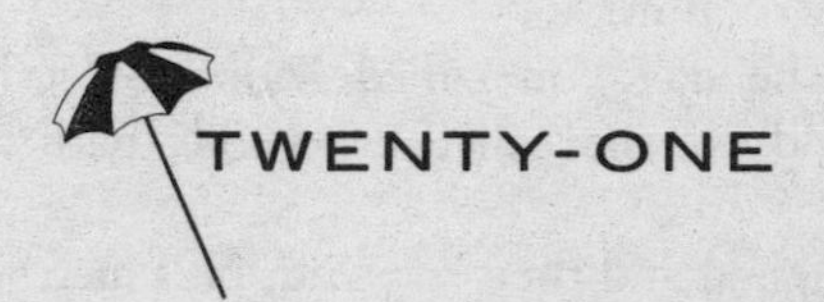

TWENTY-ONE

By the time Kat finally drifted off to sleep, it was well past two in the morning. She didn't wake up until the phone rang.

She sat bolt upright and stared at the clock on the bedside table, grabbed the phone, and heard her oldest sister, Sonya, say hello.

It was ten-thirty in the morning. Seven-thirty in Hawaii.

She was closer to Sonya than any of her other sisters.

"What's up? Everybody okay?" Kat sat cross-legged in the middle of the king-sized bed, shoved the pillows between her back and the headboard.

Every weekend a Vargas family event was held somewhere on the island. Birthdays, anniversaries, graduations, baby luaus, weddings. Something was always going on.

They were connected, close. After her accident, they'd all been there for her. Smothering her with love. The love, she understood. It was their pity that she couldn't take.

Until she decided to move to California, no one had ever left the *ohana,* the extended family, to move away.

She never forgot that it was *her* fault she wasn't there with them. *Her* fault. Not theirs. Not Justin's.

"Everybody's great," Sonya assured her.

"Dad and Mom?"

"Doin' good. Real good. How are you? How's the house-sitting going?"

"You heard, huh?"

"Sure. The day you called Mom to let her know where you'd be, she called everybody with the phone number."

They laughed and then Kat said, "It's nice here. Small town kine place. Like Kauai."

"Kauai's not so small anymore," Sonya reminded her.

"How are all the *keiki*?" She was always getting photos in the mail of all her brothers' and sisters' kids. She kept them in a basket in her apartment.

"Everybody's good. I just wanted to hear your voice."

She let Sonya relate all the comings and goings, news of potlucks and hula competitions, church gossip. Nani had a quilt on display at the Kauai Museum's contemporary quilt show in February. Their mom was taking ukulele lessons from Vern Kauanui at the senior center.

It was a relief and at the same time unsettling to know that life went on without her. As Sonya rambled, Kat's mind drifted to Ty. Adjusting to life with a normal teen who'd been raised with all the advantages of a strong family unit wasn't easy. In Sunny's case, he had no idea what she'd been through.

It hadn't been a cakewalk for Sonya to keep her kids out of trouble. Kat knew some of what her sister had gone through when the kids hit junior high. Somehow they'd all survived.

When Sonya stopped talking long enough for her to get a word in edgewise, Kat asked, "Hey, sis, how'd you get Wayne to come around that summer he gave you so much trouble?"

"Oh, boy. That nearly drove me crazy. He was running with a bunch of losers."

Kat could just imagine Sonya shaking her head and rolling her eyes. "So what did you do?"

"Same thing I always do. Let them know I'll be there for them no matter what, but that I won't put up with any humbug."

"That's it?"

"You kidding? That's *hard* to do. You know how hard it is to love somebody who is driving you crazy? How hard it is not to say something that's gonna make it worse? I never shut the door between us, but I never let them think they could get away with anything, either. So far, they always pull out of it."

"You're lucky, sis."

"I know. Thank God. What's up, Katrina? Why you asking this kine stuff? Something going on?"

Kat pulled her knees up to her chest and wrapped her arm around them. "A friend is going through some trouble with his daughter. She's nineteen."

Her sister became unusually quiet. So much so that Kat thought the connection might have been broken.

"Sonya? You there?"

"A *friend*?"

"Yes."

"A *he* friend?"

Kat sighed. Her sister knew her better than anyone. She'd hear a lie all the way across the Pacific.

"Yes, a he friend."

"Sounds like you're starting to live again," Sonya whispered.

Kat tightened her grip on the phone. "What?"

"You're finally starting to *care*. To feel. To *live*. I'm so glad, honey-girl."

Kat's gut wrenched. Caring was risky. Loving was downright terrifying.

"We've all been so worried about you. So worried for so long."

"I don't *want* anybody's pity, Sonya."

"Not pity. *Aloha*. We all love you. The way I loved my kids through their troubles. Tell your friend to love his daughter and to be there for her."

"He's doing that."

"Then hope for the best. Is there any reason to worry?"

"I keep telling myself there isn't, but I guess from all the things I've seen over the past few years, I have a hard time believing it could be this easy for him."

"You gotta trust, Kat. I know that's hard for you, but you gotta try."

Kat didn't reply, couldn't. Her sister knew her so well that sometimes there was no need for words. They'd all been there for her, her whole family had rallied when they brought her home from the hospital all broken. She had healed physically, but the sadness wouldn't leave. Memories were everywhere she looked. She had to get away, to leave the island to save her own sanity.

It was the hardest thing in the world for them to let her go—just as hard as it was for her to leave—but they understood.

Long after she and Sonya said good-bye, Kat stared out at the deep blue waters of the Pacific, thinking about everything her sister had said.

"You're starting to care. To feel. To live."

The last thing in the world she thought she'd ever want was to feel anything again.

Last night, holding Alice in her arms had been a sweet torture that brought tears to her eyes, but the experience hadn't broken her the way it would have a few years ago.

She was still breathing. Still alive.

Maybe she had grown a lot stronger.

Now the question was, how much was she willing to risk to find out how much stronger?

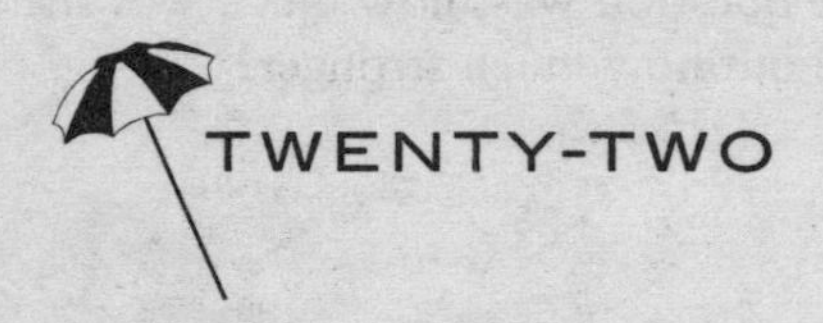

TWENTY-TWO

When Sunny awoke that morning, she went down to have breakfast while French Fry was still asleep. Though she had hoped to, there was no avoiding Ty.

The minute he heard her rustling around in the kitchen, he walked in from the patio with a cup of coffee and the newspaper in hand. He tossed the paper on the table.

She took one look at him and decided not to try to avoid what was coming.

"I'm sorry about last night. I didn't know there was going to be a hassle with me taking a little time to myself."

"From now on, just call and let me know when you're going to be late." He pulled out a chair and sat down while she made herself a bowl of Cocoa Puffs.

"I didn't know I had a curfew."

"It's just common courtesy, Sunny."

She wondered what he'd say if she told him that she'd grown up without a rule book.

Instead, she let it go and shrugged. "Fine. So I'll call next time."

"I went by Mermaids looking for you and talked to Earl last night."

She paused halfway to the table, uncertain of how he'd react to her getting fired.

"Earl the dweeb?"

"He told me he fired you. And why."

She walked to the table and set the cereal bowl down a little too hard. Milk slopped over the edge. She went to the counter, tore off a piece of paper toweling, daubed up the milk.

He was silent as he waited for her to sit down. She picked up her spoon, but all of a sudden, the chocolate puffs floating in nonfat milk didn't look very appetizing. Chandler leaned back in his chair, arms folded. She didn't look at him, concentrating on the Cocoa Puffs instead.

She expected a guy like him—a guy who probably didn't even fudge on his taxes—to blow up after what she'd done.

Maybe it was time to leave. Maybe she should just pack up French Fry and head back to L.A. before things got too bad down there. Maybe this whole idea was just plain dumb.

Then she thought of Alice, of what Jamie was getting into, and knew that she couldn't walk away from Twilight yet.

When Chandler spoke, he didn't even raise his voice.

"You made a rotten choice letting that kid go, Sunny."

She pushed the cereal away. "I wasn't going to bust somebody for five bucks."

"The money wasn't the point. The point is, the kid was stealing."

"Whatever. It was my decision." She couldn't believe how calm he was. Ty Chandler had just passed another test with flying colors. "You don't seem very upset."

"Like I said, you made a bad decision. Hopefully you'll think before something like this happens again."

His understanding tempted her to turn her back on everyone and everything she'd walked out on. For half a second she dared to wonder what he'd do if she told him everything. What if she laid it all out on the table? Would he be willing and able to help, or would he turn her in? What about the others?

It was too late for her to walk out on the commitments she had to the others anyway. Too late to turn back time for herself, but not for her baby.

"I'll have to find another job. Earl's place nearly drove me nuts anyway."

"I'll help you look."

"Thanks." She pulled the cereal bowl toward her again.

"Sunny?"

"What?"

"Kat told me you confronted her last night about watching Alice. Why?"

"She doesn't like French Fry. Or haven't you noticed?" She took a bite of cereal. It had already gone mushy. "Have you seen the way Kat looks at her? *When* she'll look at her, that is. Check it out sometime. You'll see."

She could tell she had him thinking. Still, he defended his little P.I. "Kat has a hard time trusting people."

"Trusting a baby?"

"She's afraid of her feelings. One thing I've learned over the past few days is that a baby can get to your heart faster than anything on earth and open up feelings you never knew you were capable of. Maybe that's why Kat's so wary around Alice."

"Maybe." *"A baby can get to your heart faster than anything on earth."*

So French Fry had definitely gotten to him already. Her relief was fleeting.

"Look, Kat's important to me, Sunny. I want you to try to understand her."

"Okay, I'll try, but you check it out. There's something definitely weird going on."

Upstairs, French Fry started crying. Sunny's appetite had left her anyway. She started to go to her daughter, but Chandler waved her back down.

"I'll get her. Finish your cereal."

The minute he walked out she got up and dumped the Cocoa Puffs down the sink. She didn't have to look at his tide calendar hanging near the back door to know that time was flying.

She heard the old stairs creak beneath Chandler's weight, then French Fry's shriek of delight. She closed her eyes and leaned against the sink.

God, I'm not ready yet.

The trouble was, she didn't know if she'd ever find the courage to leave.

Ron Johnson knew by the sound of Ty's voice that something was up. It wasn't until they were a couple miles out and had dropped anchor that Ty finally opened up.

"Sunny already lost her job and there isn't much hope of her finding another one." Then he quickly explained what happened at Mermaids and added, "Now she's not exactly employee of the month material."

"She made a dumb call, that's all."

"I would have fired her." Ty baited his hook, spun out the line.

R.J. watched gulls gather. The birds circled the boat as the bait disappeared below the water.

"Well, I'd probably have given her a stern talking to and another chance." He glanced over at Ty. "Would *you* hire her?"

"I can't answer that. She's my kid."

R.J. could tell that Ty was still blown away by the idea of having a daughter. He was pretty blown away himself.

"You're absolutely sure she's yours?"

Ty's response was immediate and sure. "Yes. No doubts at all. She looks like a combination of my grandmother and Amy."

They fished in silence. Ty stewed and Ron debated with himself before he stuck his neck out and came to a decision.

"One of my sunset-crew gals is quitting in a week. I could have her train Sunny, see if she can handle the mainsail when we come about, serve appetizers, help people aboard."

"If you'd hire her, I'd pay *you.*"

"Very funny. Does she get seasick?"

Ty shrugged. "Not if she takes after me."

"She'll have to ride the three o'clock shuttle to Gull Harbor."

"I could get her a car. I guess she can drive. I never asked."

"This is California. Everybody can drive. She'll need one sooner or later anyway." R.J. reeled in his lure, cast out again. "What did she do in L.A.?"

"She hasn't opened up about her life at all. I figure she will when she's ready."

"How's the little one?"

Ty didn't even have to answer. The look on his face said it all.

R.J. hoped he wasn't making a mistake that was going to cost him time and money, but he was willing to do anything to help Ty.

"Why don't you bring Sunny over to the dock tomorrow afternoon about four? We sail at five-thirty and get back just after sunset. I'll have Robin show her the ropes. Literally."

He laughed, of the opinion that life wasn't worth living if a man couldn't crack himself up once in a while. Then he ventured into new territory.

"Still seeing Kat?"

"You bet."

"Damn."

"Don't get any ideas, old buddy. She's mine."

"Sounds like this is getting pretty serious. I'm bummed. I was planning on snaking you and taking her for myself."

"Hey, no chance, pal. You remind her of someone who broke her heart anyway."

"And you've taken it upon yourself to mend it."

"It's on my list of things to do: Salvage teen mother, oversee care and feeding of a toddler, mend broken heart."

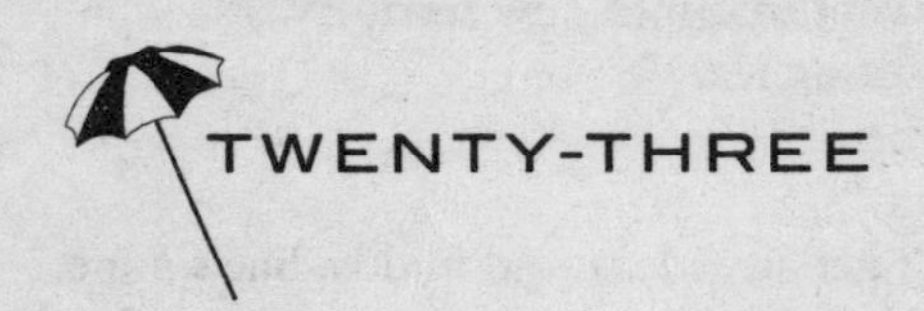

TWENTY-THREE

The drive to Gull Harbor hadn't taken Sunny more than twenty minutes, but it gave her a chance to get acquainted with the used car Ty had bought her. It was a Camry, a gutless wonder when it came to passing on the two-lane road. It wouldn't be a bad ride if she were middle-aged, or a soccer mom . . . or for driving to a job she'd probably despise as much as the last one.

Realizing she was almost two out of three was depressing as hell.

The Camry would never have been her first choice, but the gift had almost reduced her to tears. She was glad she kept it together in front of Ty, and more especially, in front of Kat Vargas, who'd gone to San Luis Obispo with him to drive the car back.

To please Chandler, she offered Kat a hasty apology for what she'd said the night she'd come home late, but she still wasn't comfortable with the way Kat acted around Alice.

She reached Gull Harbor, drove into the marina parking lot, and immediately saw the *Stargazer,* a forty-foot sailboat, moored at the far end of two rows of boat slips. It was right where Ty said it would be.

R.J. waved from the deck, shouted, "Ahoy! You must be Sunny," then walked to the ladder to welcome her aboard. She prayed she wasn't going to be seasick and toss her lunch on the deck.

She had imagined R.J. would be something like Ty, but he wasn't. R.J. was blond, heavier—not fat, just thicker—and an inch or so shorter. If the offbeat, sloppy way he was dressed—in an oversized faded T-shirt, shorts, and flip-flops—and his unhurried stride were any indication, he was a lot more laid-back than Chandler.

R.J. explained that for the rest of the week she'd be an apprentice to his current first mate and outlined her duties. Halfway through the tour of the open deck, he paused with his hand wrapped around a line, looked her straight in the eye, and warned, "Of course, if you make a wrong move when we come about, you could get knocked overboard, or worse, one of my paying customers might. I always turn around and pick them up, but you're on your own."

She blinked a couple of times, tried to read him, but couldn't.

"That was a joke, kid," he laughed.

"Oh, yeah?"

"You think you can handle it?"

"What? The stuff you just showed me? Piece of cake."

His gaze leveled on her eyes, unflinching. "That's what I thought. You have no idea, do you? But you're bound and determined to gut it out. You don't scare easily."

Scare easily? She never had time to get scared, never had the luxury. Back in L.A., she had to act and react in a heartbeat or she would wind up dead.

"No. I guess I don't."

"Good." He assessed her a couple of seconds longer than necessary.

"What?" She tossed her hair back, raised her chin a notch. "Why do you keep looking at me like that?"

"I'm trying to decide who you remind me of more, your great-grandma or your mom."

"You knew them?"

"Sure. Your dad and I have been best friends since grade school, and your mom, well, we all went to high school together."

"So, I guess in a place like this, her being pregnant was probably the talk of the town." Maybe now she'd find out that Chandler had known about her all along.

"Ty didn't know, if that's what you're fishing for."

He made her blush, but she didn't back off.

"Did she leave town first, or did he?"

"She went to L.A. and he went after her, but she refused to come back. He never knew about you, Sunny. Don't hold anything against him."

Hearing it again satisfied her, though it didn't salve the hurt. Chandler was turning out to be about as straight as a guy could get.

R.J. didn't comment on her shorts—Chandler had hinted that maybe they were too short for her to wear to work and maybe she had on a little too much makeup. He'd even suggested she ask Kat to give her makeup tips. *As if.*

R.J. gave her the once-over and obviously seemed to think she looked okay, because he didn't object. He had requested before she start that she buy some flat-soled tennis shoes to wear on deck, which she had done. Unlike Earl, R.J. treated her like an adult. She was both surprised and grateful.

"So, do you think Chandler is going to stick around or do you think he'll go back to Alaska?" She figured as long as R.J. was willing to talk, she'd ask him everything she hadn't felt comfortable asking Chandler yet.

R.J. shrugged as he walked around checking all the lines.

"He doesn't plan on going back unless the guy who bought his fishing camp goes belly-up."

"Did he make a lot of money?"

R.J. paused and looked at her. "Why don't you ask him?"

She shrugged. "I think he thinks of me as a kid."

"You are a kid."

That pissed her off, but he was smiling when he said it, so she let it go.

"He seems like a pretty squared-away guy." She leaned against the deck rail, shook out her hair. The breeze was blowing the heck out of it.

"Salt of the earth."

"What does that mean?"

"What you see with Ty Chandler is what you get."

As she watched him walk over to the ladder to help the first of the paying guests aboard, she found herself thinking that R.J. was a good-looking man. There was an edge to him and she liked the twinkle in his eye.

She closed her eyes and pictured Dodge's face, tried to remember the way things had been between them.

By the time the *Stargazer* reached open water, she'd grown used to the way the sailboat crested the swells and then dipped beneath the power of the wind. Kissed by sea spray, she fell instantly in love with sailing.

As they ventured up the coast toward Twilight, Ron introduced Robin Davis as his first mate and Sunny as the "rest of the crew," which brought a round of laughter from the tourists.

She blushed when he said, "Well, folks, tonight is Sunny's maiden voyage. But don't worry, if she causes an accident, there are ample life jackets aboard."

Everyone laughed and R.J. waited until they were listening again before he added, "The bad news is that the life jackets are bright orange and I recently read somewhere that sharks are attracted to orange."

As they sailed past Ty's cottage on the point, R.J. drew everyone's attention again.

"Sunny's going to be a natural sailor." He said it with a confidence she was just beginning to feel. "She comes from a long line of seafarers who settled the town of Twilight."

She stared at Chandler's house and listened as R.J. explained how it had been built by her great-great-great-great-grandfather, not of adobe, as was the style back then, but of wood, to resemble the homes back East.

Though the air off the water was cool and comfortable, she experienced a warm rush of pride when R.J. outlined the role the Chandlers played in establishing Twilight Cove.

She'd never had any notion of how deep her family ties ran. Her mother never spoke of her grandmothers or grandfathers, aunts or uncles or cousins, on either side.

Now here she was, out on the ocean, looking up at a house built by a Chandler 150 years ago, and the house was still standing. Someone who's blood flowed in her veins had a vision for a whole town.

Maybe that's why she was still standing, why she hadn't given up yet. She'd inherited DNA from someone who had made a real mark in the world.

And if Ty Chandler hadn't found her, she'd have never known about her history at all—hers *and* Alice's.

As she stood there in awe of the house, first mate Robin tapped her on the shoulder and whispered that it was time to pass around the appetizer tray. All she had to do was smile and keep a tight hold on the cocktail napkins so they wouldn't blow away. The guests were to help themselves.

Unfortunately there was a bit more to it. The guests

wanted to chat now that R.J. had built her up as somewhat of a town celebrity. She found herself having to be sociable and interact with strangers, and it wasn't as hard as she would have thought.

After a few minutes, she settled into it, imagining how, when they all got back to Iowa or Chicago—or wherever it was they were from—they could tell their friends about the town of Twilight Cove, California, and the great-great-great-great-granddaughter of one of its founders and how they met her on the sunset cruise.

Robin Davis helped her refill the tray, and once the appetizers were gone, Ron signaled to them that it was time to come about. She discovered scrambling along the damp deck was a bit more treacherous than she anticipated, but reminded herself she'd been in far more dangerous situations. In no time they had come about and were headed back to Gull Harbor.

R.J. watched the sun, timing the voyage so that they would reach the dock just as the sun was setting. Basically, her job was through.

Piece of cake, she thought. She wasn't making much more an hour than she had been at Mermaids, but she could stomach this job for now. In fact, if it weren't for the fact that she needed a lot more than she was getting paid, she might honestly come to love it.

Surreptitiously, she studied R.J. as he manned the wheel and continued to charm the dozen or so tourists aboard, pointing out various landmarks along the rugged coastline, regaling them with bits of history.

His voice filled with admiration when he told them of the Spanish explorers and conquistadors, of Vasco Nuñez de Balboa, the first to reach the Pacific Coast at Panama and name the vast ocean, and of Hernando Cortés, who christened California.

"California was the name of a wonderful island of

tall, bronzed Amazons ruled by their pagan Queen Califia. The island was filled with gold and precious stones but no other metals, so the women warriors carried spears of gold. Califia was more beautiful than all other women combined. She was valiant, courageous, and was said to have the bravest of hearts."

Sunny suddenly realized R.J. was smiling at her from across the open deck as he concluded, "Califia dreamed of being nobler than any other ruler. She wanted to accomplish great deeds, and she had the spirit it takes to win."

Something passed between them in that moment, an intensity that she tried hard to deny, but one she thought about long after the sun went down and the cruise ended.

She had no idea what the silent exchange had meant to R.J. Maybe nothing at all.

Maybe she'd only imagined the electricity that arced between them. For her it was almost visible, stark blue-white and crackling. But the look he'd given her was gone as fast as it had appeared.

Maybe she hadn't really seen it at all.

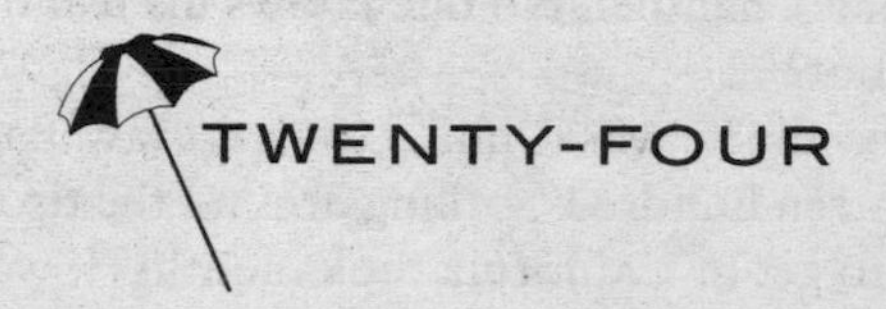

TWENTY-FOUR

"So, tell me about the guy who built this house."

Ty looked up from the battered old shoe box he'd found in a back closet. Sunny lingered in the doorway, her cheeks sunburned from her first full week working aboard the *Stargazer.*

"Why do you ask?" He was pleased with her sudden interest in Chandler history, though he couldn't help but wonder what inspired the question. He took her willingness to chat as a peace offering.

"R.J. points it out on the cruise and talks about the man who built it." She looked down at her hands, inspected her nails before she met his eyes. "He said the Chandlers were all seafaring men."

Ty nodded. "Come sit down." He indicated the chair beside him. "They were seafarers. Right up until my father. He decided he'd rather make a living peddling office supplies to accounts all over the western states."

One time he'd asked his father why he wasn't a fisherman like Granddad, and Thom Chandler claimed it was because he hated fish, boats, and anything to do with the ocean.

"Granddad Chandler thought my dad took after Grandma's side of the family. Except for her, they'd all been partial to money and comfort. Fishing, money, and comfort didn't go hand in hand unless you were a millionaire sports fisherman."

Ty fingered the edge of the faded shoe box. "The first Chandler in California jumped ship. He went by the name Elijah Chandler. No one knows his real name."

"Why not?"

"Supposedly he was running from the law. Back in the early eighteen hundreds, sailing around the tip of South America to get to California took months. It was a voyage to another world back then and a safe bet no one would ever track him down."

"What did he do wrong?"

"Nobody knows. He married a young Californio woman, which enabled him to buy land."

"And then he built this house." She gazed around the room. "So, how did you end up in Alaska?"

He pictured Amy the day she'd told him she wasn't ever going to leave River Ridge. She'd found what she'd been looking for. It was the day he realized she needed drugs more than she needed him.

He opened the box. "You asked if I had any pictures of your mom. I found these."

She held her breath as he pulled out a stack of pictures, school photos, yearbook mug shots.

"These are from our sophomore and junior years at Twilight High."

He noticed her hand was shaking when he handed them to her.

"I don't have any pictures of her." She stared at the photos in her hand. "Wow. She looks so different."

He'd looked at the photos earlier. In them, Amy was young and vibrant, smiling into the camera with clear-eyed innocence, as different from the way he remembered her the day she left as the sun from the moon.

"Here are some more. I didn't realize I had these." He handed her a few more. "They're from junior high."

Amy with braces and big hair. Sunny shook her head.

"I would never have believed it. She looks so young. Like a little girl. I wish . . ."

"What?"

"I wish she'd never left here." She stacked the photos, handed them back.

"Would you like to keep them?"

"No. No, you can put them back."

"I thought you might like to save them for Alice."

"You keep them for her."

"I tried to talk your mother into coming back to Twilight, but she was into . . . well, what she was into. I started a fishing camp for tourists using the skills I'd learned from R.J.'s dad and my granddad. I'm thinking about starting a fishing charter out of Gull Harbor."

She crossed her arms and leaned against the table. "You said R.J.'s dad and your grandpa taught you to fish and camp? What about your own dad?"

"He was usually out of town on business, so R.J.'s dad took me along on fishing trips, campouts, horseback rides. He taught both of us how to dismantle a boat engine and repair it. Granddad taught us to clean and fillet fish and bait hooks. My dad died when I was a freshman in high school."

All he'd ever learned from his own dad was how to wave good-bye.

Sunny was watching him closely, as if weighing the sincerity of his words, so he chose them carefully.

"I can relate to growing up without a father, believe it or not."

"You knew him. You lived with him," she countered.

"But sometimes, even though you live right under the same roof, that doesn't mean they'll be there for you.

My father wasn't here for me, for whatever reason. That's not the kind of father I want to be, Sunny." He met her eyes. She was so serious, so quiet, he wished he knew what she was thinking.

"You plan on ever going back to Alaska?"

"I hope not. That chapter of my life is over."

"Why'd you leave?"

"I came down here to be with your grandmother, Barbara, before she died." He suddenly remembered something his mother had left him, something that had come to him through her.

"I'll be right back. Wait here."

He asked Sunny to get him a Diet Dr Pepper while he ran upstairs, and by the time he'd found what he'd been looking for, she was waiting for him with two tall glasses of soda over ice.

When he held out a small, hand-carved wooden box, she looked at it, then at him. "What's this?"

"Open it."

Her fingers closed around the box. She laid it in one palm and traced the intricate oriental carving with her fingertip before she removed the lid and carefully set it aside on the coffee table.

The inside of the box was lined in midnight velvet, and nestled there was a pair of gold filigree earrings set with matching opals. The gemstones caught the sunlight streaming in through the window behind her. The light set off a rainbow of sparkling color.

"Those were your great-grandmother Chandler's. She would have wanted you to have them." He knew it was true. His grandmother had the biggest heart in the world. His mother would have taken one look at Sunny and said, "I told you so."

He thought of all the years his mother had kept Sunny's existence a secret, of everything they had all missed by not knowing one another. He couldn't bring those years back, but together they could make new memories.

"These will never make up for all the years we've missed." He wished she'd look up, wished that he could look into her eyes, to see if she cared, but she kept her head down as she fingered the opals.

"I can't believe you want me to have these," she whispered. "They look expensive."

"They're real gold. And they're very old. My grandfather gave them to my grandmother on their wedding day. They lived right here in this house."

She turned the box upside down and tipped the earrings into the palm of her hand. The rainbow colors in the opals shimmered in the light from the window.

"You can pass those on to Alice when she grows up." He tried to picture Alice at nineteen, wondered what the world would be like, what Sunny would become, and if the three of them would be close.

He shoved his hands into his pockets, waited for her to say something, doubted she knew what to say any more than he did.

He picked up the soda and took a long drink. Then, glass in hand, he told her, "I'm going back out to the garage to finish up those lures. Call me when you're ready to take off for work and I'll come get Alice. She ought to be up by then." He turned to leave.

"Chandler?" Her voice stopped him at the door. He watched her pour the earrings out of her palm and back into the box. "Thank you."

As Ty left the room, he realized this was the very first time that he'd ever really seen her genuinely smile.

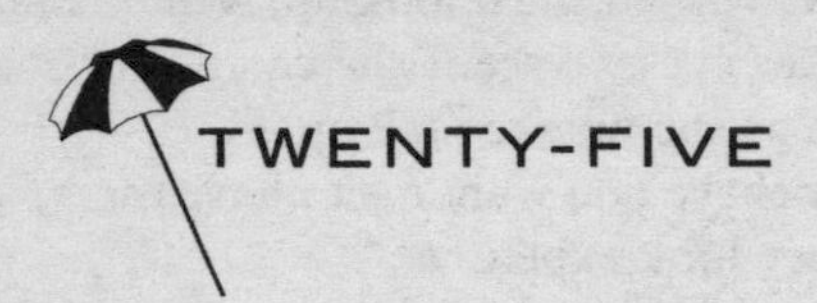

TWENTY-FIVE

Kat reached the top of Lover's Lane, paused high on the golden hillside overlooking the coastline, and stopped to enjoy the panoramic view.

She found herself looking forward to the quiet solitude of the long walks she'd been taking at dawn for the last few days. Walking along the winding road to the top of the hill was like a meditation.

She had expected time to crawl by in a place like Twilight Cove, thought that the days would be long and the hours empty compared to the pace of the city, but exactly the opposite proved true.

For the life of her, she didn't know where the weeks had gone, but looking back now, she realized that her time here had slipped through her fingers as quickly as dry sand.

Jake's plan to get her out of the city and her self-imposed isolation had succeeded all too well. A month ago, if he'd have asked her to imagine spending time walking on the beach, toasting the sunset with a glass of wine, watching old movies with someone special, she would have laughed and called him crazy.

Lately the thought of leaving made her ache in all the secret corners of her heart, places where she hadn't ached in a long time.

This morning, the breeze off the water blew across the land and the hilltop, bringing with it the taste and smell of the sea. Staring out at the blue water dappled with crests of whitecaps, she came to the realization that she needed to put time and space between herself and Ty, to get away, go back to the city, and see if the feelings they had for each other would survive.

"I wish you'd think about staying in Twilight."

"Anything's possible."

She heard his voice in her head and wished that she still had the ability to see life as something fresh and new, that she still woke up every morning believing in a world full of endless possibilities, but she wasn't the girl she used to be.

The Kat of old wouldn't have balked. If they'd met before Justin, she'd have given up everything for a chance at a future with Ty. She'd have packed up and moved to Twilight, started over if need be, to make the dream a reality.

But now? Now the stakes were too high. She'd worked hard and established her business in Long Beach. If she gave it all up and things didn't work out with Ty, she'd be right back where she started five years ago. Not only that, but to give her heart again only to have her trust betrayed—the loss would be too great.

She couldn't take that kind of chance anymore. Not if she wanted to survive.

Besides, Ty had never spoken of the future. He'd only asked her to stay beyond Jake's return. There was no denying he thought they were great together—she couldn't deny it, either, and although he made certain they spent time together every day, he was just as focused on working things out with Sunny, helping his daughter adjust to her life here—and that was as it should be.

His commitment to Sunny and Alice, to family, was one of the things she admired most about him, one of the things that made him so attractive to her.

He'd asked her to think about staying. She'd done that, but no matter how she looked at it, she continually came to the same conclusion. She had to go back.

Now she knew that the sooner she left, the better.

She started back down the hill, past the stand of eucalyptus trees, inhaled the fragrance the leaves gave off as they were crushed beneath her jogging shoes. The pungent scent would forever remind her of the weeks she'd spent on Lover's Lane.

After she climbed the low steps to Jake's porch and took the door key out from beneath a potted poinsettia, she let herself in and checked the phone for messages. There were none, so she decided to check in with Arnie Tate in Long Beach.

She'd made it a habit to talk to him every few days. The retired detective had a done a great job of taking care of the cases in progress after she left. He was thorough and enthusiastic, and as a new retiree, happy to have something to do.

She read her emails, shot off replies to her mom and two of her sisters before she called Ty to let him know she'd drive herself and meet him tonight in the parking lot at Gull Harbor.

Sunny had invited them both to the sunset cruise and Kat immediately accepted. She hadn't really seen the girl for more than a few minutes in passing since the night Sunny had been so upset about finding her alone with Alice.

After Sunny apologized, Kat was willing to move on. The truth was, she *was* hesitant around Alice, and Sunny had noticed.

Maybe it was the fact that she'd decided she had to

leave sooner rather than later, or perhaps because of who she was and what she'd seen after so many years on the job, but Kat still couldn't shake the idea that there was more to Sunny's move to Twilight than the girl had let on.

She'd tried to run a search on Dodge, but with only one name—and probably a nickname, at that—there wasn't much to go on. After a couple of hours of scanning through items about Dodge Ram trucks and vintage Duster models, she'd given up tracking down Alice's father on her own.

She'd placed a call to Fred Westberg, her contact at the L.A.P.D., only to be told that Fred was on a vacation to Catalina Island.

She wandered through the house feeling adrift and finally decided that she'd do what most women do when they get down—she'd go shopping for something new to wear to the cruise.

That evening, Kat followed the coast to Gull Harbor and parked near the brightly painted STARGAZER SUNSET CRUISES sign. When she didn't see Ty's car in the lot, she turned off the engine and sat there listening to the latest Iz Hawaiian CD that her youngest sister, Maile, had mailed her.

Spotting Sunny aboard the *Stargazer,* Kat turned off the CD and stepped out of the car, tugging on the hem of a new tank top that matched the hot-orange floral capri pants she picked up at a resort boutique in Twilight. The place was the size of a closet, but carried a fun selection of clothing.

She followed a young couple dressed in matching nautical red-white-and-blue striped T-shirts across the parking lot. Sunny, who was greeting guests and getting them settled, took her hand and helped her aboard. She surprised Kat with a warm smile.

"Welcome aboard the *Stargazer.* Captain Ron hopes you have a pleasant voyage."

"Thanks, Sunny."

The subtle changes in her were hard to miss. Sunny looked a little more wholesome. She was wearing less eye makeup and had on tennis shoes instead of platform sandals. Maybe it was the golden glow of her tanned skin, or the highlights in her hair, but she looked positively radiant.

The girl had definitely lost some of her edge.

Before Kat could say anything, Sunny glanced out into the parking lot and started waving.

"There they are!" She picked up a neon-pink, toddler-sized life vest.

Beside her, Kat watched Ty pull into the lot and park next to her own car. Alice was in the back, buckled into her car seat.

Kat's heart jumped involuntarily and an unexpected blush came to her cheeks when Ty stepped out of the car and waved. Just as quickly, the sinking sensation in the pit of her stomach hit her. Every minute they were together was doubly precious now.

This morning she'd made up her mind to tell him tonight that she was going back to Long Beach and let things cool off a bit, but her newfound resolve was having the opposite effect on her.

The more she thought about leaving, the more she wanted to stay, and aware that she was thinking with her heart and not her head, she was even more certain she'd made the right decision.

Ty carried Alice across the parking lot and in no time Sunny was welcoming them aboard, too. Though Sunny tried to act as if they were any other guests, she stepped out of character when Alice started to kick and shout, "Ma! Ma! Ma!"

"Hi, French Fry." Obviously pleased with the toddler's affectionate display, Sunny kissed Alice on the tip of her nose and then slipped the life vest on her and murmured, "We're going for a sail. You can watch Mommy work."

As another couple climbed aboard, Kat glanced toward the galley hatch and noticed that R.J. was watching Sunny interact with Ty and Alice. His expression was that of a man who was interested in far more than watching the pleasant exchange.

Intrigued, Kat focused on Sunny. Swift and sure, the girl's gaze soon met R.J.'s and she blushed before she turned around to help a couple in their late sixties come aboard.

Ty was too busy with Alice to notice his daughter's reaction to his best friend. There was definitely an attraction between them.

For the rest of the cruise, Kat tried to convince herself that she was mistaken, but all the signs were there.

Ty thought they couldn't have picked a better evening for a sail. The weather was hot and balmy, the bright robin's egg sky broken only by an occasional wisp of a cloud. Miles away, heat clouds were gathering on the horizon.

He'd taken a seat in the stern, and with Kat on one side of him and Alice stretched out on the flotation cushion beside him, he knew a sense of contentment he hadn't known in years.

The rise and fall of the sailboat as it plowed through the swells quickly lulled Alice to sleep. Automatically, he reached down and pulled up the hood of Alice's bright-yellow sweatshirt, never once taking his hand off her as the yacht pitched down the waves.

Kat nudged him and he smiled into her eyes.

"You're getting pretty good at this. Remember the day Sunny and I went shopping and left you home alone to baby-sit?"

"Do I ever. I was on the edge of panic. I'm still learning as I go, believe me." He reached down and adjusted Alice's life jacket without waking her. "I never dreamed my life would change this much—in a good way," he quickly added. Leaning close to Kat, he gave her a quick kiss. "Just like the day I met you."

A fleeting shadow darkened her expression before she turned away to watch the coastline pass by. She drew attention to his house when it came into view.

"You can't really see the other houses on the street from this angle. Your place looks lonely all by itself," she said.

"That's the way it must have looked when it was the first house on the point."

As they watched Sunny scramble along the deck toward the bow with a tray of sandwiches in her hand, they both started to speak at once.

"Sunny's doing a great job—" she began.

"It looks like she really—" he started.

"Go on," Kat laughed.

"She really enjoys this."

"I noticed that, too. She seems a bit settled."

"She's a real sailor. That's the Chandler in her." They watched Sunny negotiate the slippery deck. "I knew she would take to sailing if she gave it half a chance."

He looked so proud that Kat was truly happy she'd had a part in uniting him with his daughter. The pale-yellow shirt he wore set off his deeply tanned skin and dark hair to perfection, but as always, it was his smile and the sparkle in his eyes that made her heart leap.

"R.J.'s invited us to the Sail On Inn for dinner after we dock," he told her.

"That would be great."

He took her hand, needing to connect with her physically, needing to touch her. "Have you thought about staying?"

"Ty, I just . . . Of course I've thought about it."

"Good." He kissed her then, quick and sure, before he lowered his voice and leaned closer. "I don't want you to go."

"Can we talk about this later?" She glanced around, looking so panic-stricken that he suddenly didn't want to hear what she had to say. From the look on her face, her decision couldn't be in his favor.

He tried to shove his concerns to the back of his mind, to tell himself that he could change her mind. He concentrated on enjoying the sea spray off the water, the crack and billow of the sails, and the wind in his hair.

Halfway back up the coast as the sun was quickly lowering and staining the sky a bright tangerine, an older couple beside them started to chat.

At one point the woman smiled down at Alice, then turned to Kat and asked, "How old is your little girl?"

Ty watched Kat begin to answer, saw her struggle. She opened her mouth, but nothing came out. He squeezed her hand and answered for her.

"This is my granddaughter," he explained, unable to keep the pride out of his voice as he added, "First mate Sunny is her mother."

Then the woman went on to chat about her own granddaughter, her first, and to ask which sights they should definitely see while in the area. He watched Kat's face and could tell that her spirit was on the verge of capsizing.

He'd watched Kat since Sunny's comment and had noticed a hesitance where Alice was concerned. Tonight Kat had taken a seat on the other side of him, putting him between her and Alice. She never really fell into talking baby talk or tried to amuse Alice the way other people did. If Alice needed something, if she dropped Stinko or was about to trip or if he couldn't get to her in time, then Kat would step in, but she never made the first move toward the child if he was around.

Although Kat didn't outright avoid Alice, she kept their interaction to a minimum. He was becoming even more convinced that Kat didn't keep her distance out of dislike of Alice, but because interaction with the toddler was somehow painful for her.

She had turned to stare out across the water and he thought he saw tears in her eyes. There was so much he still didn't know about her, so much she kept buried inside. He wondered if he'd ever truly know her.

He turned his attention to his daughter, watched her move among the passengers and noticed that Sunny was far more animated whenever R.J. was near. She constantly referred to R.J. when anyone asked her a question. "*Captain Ron would know. Let me ask Captain Ron. Captain Ron says . . .*"

Ty began to find the way his daughter looked at R.J. unsettling. So unsettling that he found himself watching R.J., too. If his friend was aware of Sunny's admiration, it didn't show.

Right after the cruise, Ty started to ask Kat if she noticed anything, then decided he was being overprotective. But after a fresh-catch dinner at the Sail On Inn, he still couldn't shake the idea that Sunny was attracted to his best friend.

Before he made an ass of himself and mentioned it to Sunny, he decided to run it by Kat.

Alice grew tired and fussy, so R.J. volunteered to carry her out to the car for Sunny. Before Ty knew it, the three of them had said good night to Kat and him and were gone.

As they sat alone in the leather booth at the inn, he could tell that Kat wasn't in any rush tonight. Her mind seemed miles away as she finished her decaf.

She'd been subdued since the woman on the cruise had asked how old Alice was. Her expression had been closed and thoughtful all evening. In comparison, Sunny had been animated and more talkative than he'd ever seen her.

As he'd watched his lovely daughter interact with R.J., as well as keep Alice entertained, he'd marveled at the changes in her. His happiness was tempered by the idea that she might have a crush on R.J.

Kat shook him out of his revery.

"You were awfully quiet at dinner," she noted.

"You were, too. I guess it's that kind of a night."

"The cruise was great. Listen, Ty—"

"You know, to be honest, I was thinking about Sunny," he admitted.

She reached for his hand. "What about Sunny?"

"You don't think that maybe she's got a thing for R.J., do you? You don't think it's even possible, right?"

"Actually, I think she might be attracted to him."

"What are you saying?" He'd wanted her to deny it. She didn't even sound appalled by the notion.

"I think she might be infatuated with R.J."

"He's as old as I am."

"He's not exactly an old codger," Kat pointed out. "I think he's just as interested in her."

Ty reared back. "What in the hell makes you think that?"

She shrugged, as if the whole thing was no big deal. Then again, Sunny wasn't her daughter.

"I saw the way he looks at her when she isn't aware of it. She's a beautiful young woman, Ty."

"He's old enough to be her *father.*"

"But he's *not* her father. It's not that outrageous to think he might be attracted to her, too. If he were fifty-five and she were thirty-seven no one would think a thing of it."

"No, but when he was *twenty-five,* she was only seven!"

"This isn't the same thing and you know it."

"R.J.'d never do that to me."

"This isn't about you, it's about them."

"There *is* no them." A fierce protectiveness threatened to choke him.

From where they sat in the booth, he could see the *Stargazer* in its berth across the parking lot.

There were no lights on in the sailboat's cabin, but then, R.J. always turned in early and was up before dawn. Ty had an urge to march over and ask straight-out if R.J. had a thing for Sunny. But if the answer was yes, then what?

"Damn it," he muttered, frustrated as hell.

"Ty, this isn't the end of the world."

"I wanted you to tell me I was nuts. That there was nothing going on."

"Maybe there's absolutely nothing going on. Maybe we're both reading too much into this." Her expression was full of concern.

When he'd boarded the *Stargazer* tonight he realized that Sunny was the happiest he'd seen her lately, that she appeared to be settling in.

Now he couldn't help but wonder if her happiness stemmed from her new life here, or if it was because of R.J.

Claustrophobia was setting in. The smell of deep-fried shrimp and seafood, Kat's gradual withdrawal into silence, the idea of Sunny and R.J.—everything was getting to him at once. He needed to get out into the fresh air before he blew.

He noticed Kat's coffee cup was empty.

"Would you like another cup?" He hoped she didn't.

She took one look at his face and said, "No, thanks. I'm ready to go."

Outside, the breeze off the ocean had grown damp and heavy. The water slapped rhythmically against the hulls of the boats resting in their slips. He drank in the night air, tried to reason—instead of wrestle—with what they'd talked about. Sunny and R.J. He couldn't believe it. He simply didn't want to.

Thinking aloud he said, "I've got half a mind to go over there, wake him up, and ask him point-blank if he's lusting after my kid."

"Ty, if you do that, you *do* have half a mind. Let it go. Wait and see what happens. Besides, being with someone older might be good for Sunny after everything she's been through. She hasn't had much stability in her life."

"*I'm* giving her the stability she needs."

"You're her father. She's a grown woman. With a child. You don't want to do anything to alienate her, with things going so well. And you certainly don't want to jeopardize your friendship with R.J., do you?"

"Of course not. But you noticed something between them, too."

"If I were you, I'd be more concerned about her past coming back to haunt both of you."

"Great. Thanks. I needed that. Why in the hell would you bring that up?"

"I'm sorry, but I just don't think you should stir this up, Ty. Sunny's really trying and succeeding at this. She's a good mom. She's working. This has been a smooth transition for both of you. Why ruin that?"

"Then why the crack about her past coming back?"

"I was just trying to point out that there are bigger issues in Sunny's life than an attraction to R.J. Forget I said anything."

"Yeah, right." He glanced over at the *Stargazer* again.

She reached for him, took his hand in hers. "Ty, calm down. Sleep on it, okay?"

"What about you?"

"What about me? I told you that I don't think it's a big deal."

"Not Sunny and R.J. What about you and me? Are you staying in Twilight?"

"Let's not talk about this tonight, okay?"

"You've decided to leave?"

"Ty—"

"You're leaving when Jake gets back."

"I've got a business to run."

"You're running, period. You see something between R.J. and Sunny, but you don't see that *we're* good together—that we *belong* together!"

"You're yelling, Ty." She tried to let go of his hand but he held on and pulled her close.

Then he whispered against her lips, "Let me show you how great things are between us."

"You think sex is what successful relationships are made of?"

"I think the last few weeks have proved that we have a lot more going for us than sex. We enjoy the same things, old movies, pizza, being outdoors, jogging, fishing. I love being with you, Kat. There it is, plain and simple. I love having you in my life. Hell, I love—"

She pressed her fingertips to his lips. "Don't say it."

Frustrated, afraid of pushing her too far, he shoved his hand through his hair and watched in silent frustration as she reached into her purse and dug out her car keys.

He took her in his arms, expecting resistance, but there was none. He kissed her, hoping to communicate more than physical need, to let her know how much she meant to him.

When he drew back, he noticed that her eyes were bright with unshed tears. "What is it?"

"I'm leaving tomorrow, Ty."

"Jake's not back yet."

"I'm going to ask one of his neighbors to water the plants and pick up the mail."

"You're mind's all made up, isn't it? Are you ever coming back?"

"Of course."

He didn't know whether to believe her or not. The bottom line was that she was leaving Twilight. She was walking out on what they had.

"*Are* you coming back, or is this just an excuse to call it quits for good?"

"It's about taking a step back. About taking time to think without . . . without . . ."

He dragged her into his arms. This time she tried to hold back. Her protest was weak, a soft sigh that was lost when he covered her mouth with his. She might think she could walk away, but he wasn't going to let her go without giving her something to think about.

He kissed her until he felt her let go and flatten herself against him, until he heard her purse hit the ground and felt her arms slip around his neck. He kissed her until she was kissing him back with everything she had and more.

Then he let her go. Abruptly he stepped back and shoved his hands in his pockets because he was afraid he couldn't keep them off of her.

Breathing hard, he felt as if he was fighting a life-and-death struggle, and in a sense he was. He was fighting to save what they had as much as to save himself—for he was convinced he needed her as much as life itself.

"Think about that on the way to Long Beach. Think about that while you're running home."

"I'm not running," she whispered, her eyes huge in the glow of the streetlight, her lips swollen from their kiss.

"It sure as hell looks like it to me."

TWENTY-SIX

The next morning, Ty woke up pissed.

Kat was leaving Twilight. If she wanted to cool things off, fine. Let her see if she could walk away that easily. If so, then maybe they had no business being together in the first place.

Kat's leaving wasn't the only reason he was still upset. He hadn't had a chance to talk to Sunny yet. Last night when he got in, both she and Alice were sound asleep. Rather than wait for her to get up, he left a note saying that he had errands to run and that he'd be back shortly.

He drove straight to Gull Harbor.

R.J. was aboard the *Stargazer*, just as Ty expected, but he hadn't anticipated finding his friend conducting an early-morning tour for a half-dozen preteen, inner-city kids all wearing green and white D.A.R.E. T-shirts.

R.J. waved him aboard and introduced him to the boys, who were acting like any other kids that age—fidgety as hell. They couldn't keep from poking and swatting one another, but they settled down as soon as R.J. asked them a question.

"I'll walk down to the restaurant and wait until you're through," Ty offered.

"The tour is about over. Stay put. There's coffee in the galley."

Ty stayed on deck until the boys followed their group leader off the ship, then he let R.J. lead the way into the cabin.

He thought a shot of tequila might go down better given the circumstances, but accepted the coffee, added a spoonful of sugar, and settled back.

"How did you get hooked up with the D.A.R.E. program?"

R.J. sat down across from him after shoving a pile of mail and magazines out of the way. "Glenn Potter from A-1 Realty is president of the Twilight Chamber of Commerce this year. He hooked me up with the head of the summer program in San Luis Obispo. That's the third group through so far. We're looking to get a commercial charter boat to donate the time to take all of them out fishing before school starts."

Feeling about as low as a bottom-feeder, Ty decided to jump in and get the whole thing over with. He'd rehearsed what he was going to say, but he was convinced R.J. would assure him that he was way off the mark, then they'd laugh about it and move on.

He took a swig of coffee, set his mug down, and looked across the table at R.J. It was impossible to count all the hours and experiences they'd shared in their lifetime.

"Last night on the cruise, Kat and I couldn't help but notice that Sunny might have a crush on you." He let the statement hang there, waiting for R.J. to deny it. When R.J. didn't say anything, Ty prodded, "Does she?"

R.J. leaned back, stretched his arm along the back of the seat, and met Ty's gaze dead-on.

"I think so."

Ty almost choked on a mouthful of coffee. He sputtered and finally swallowed. "You mean it's true?"

"It hasn't gone anywhere, if that's what's worrying you." R.J. fell silent, leaving way too much unsaid.

"What are you saying?"

"There's something there, that's all."

"Something on her part, or yours?"

Ron leveled his stare, shrugged. "I guess both. She's beautiful. She's a smart kid, but she's just a kid."

"Exactly."

"Is that why you're here so bright and early?"

Shaken to the quick, Ty couldn't believe they were even having this conversation. "This is going nowhere, understand? I'm heading home to set her straight."

"About what? Nothing's happened. You're completely overreacting."

"Suddenly you know more about this than I do?"

"I'd say right up until Sunny came to town, we were dead even on who knew *less* about raising a kid. Now you think you've got the edge because you've got two of them living under your roof? If you go storming home and make something out of nothing, you'll be asking for trouble."

The acid from the strong coffee was eating its way through the lining of Ty's stomach. Reminded of what Kat said about R.J. being good for Sunny, he tried to calm down. He set the coffee mug aside.

"What about you, R.J.?"

"What *about* me?"

"You going to act on this attraction?"

"Give me a break. She's your kid, Ty. You're my best friend. I'm not about to jeopardize our friendship."

"Let's just say, if she weren't my kid, what would you do?"

"Hypothetical question. I have no idea."

"Is that supposed to reassure me?"

"Look, I'm trying to be straight with you. She's noticed me. I've noticed her. Maybe she's flirted, or maybe that's just the way she is. I've ignored it. She'll get bored. I'm too old for her anyway."

"Do I have your word you won't let this go anywhere?"

"Do you need it?"

R.J. watched Ty's car clear the parking lot before he pulled his mail out of one of the metal mailboxes lined up beside the marina entrance gate. He shuffled through the stack before he walked back to the slip.

In a couple of hours on the cruise, Ty and Kat had noticed what he himself had spent the last couple of weeks trying to ignore. He pictured Ty seated in the cabin a few minutes ago, his eyes shadowed with deep concern. It still smarted the man actually believed he would ever take advantage of Sunny.

Not that he blamed Ty for being uptight. He'd feel the same way if their positions were reversed. Not only was Sunny stunning, but her every move was downright seductive. A wardrobe that usually left little to the imagination didn't help, either.

Ty's question about how he would handle the flirtation if Sunny were just any other girl haunted him. He'd definitely never been attracted to anyone as young as Sunny, but the first time he looked into her eyes, he'd felt an instantaneous connection, one that was both deep and inexplicable. One that had nothing to do with age.

Sunny wasn't just another employee. She was Ty's daughter and Ty was his best friend. They'd been closer than brothers most of their lives. There was too much history, too many good years between them to throw it all away.

He hadn't lied when he said he hadn't acted on his feelings. Up to now, the only thing he'd offered Sunny was friendship. He listened to her, answered her questions, tried to disregard the looks she gave him.

But she was getting harder and harder to ignore.

That morning Kat packed up her things, intent on returning to Long Beach right away. She jogged up the hill to ask Jake's nearest neighbor if he would keep an eye on the place until the Montgomerys returned, and found him more than cooperative.

She tried to convince herself that she wasn't secretly hoping Ty would call while she tidied up, loaded the dishwasher, and put things in order so the maid would be able to clean when she came in.

She was almost out the door when Fred Westberg, her contact at the L.A.P.D., finally returned her call.

Phone in hand, she went into the office when he said that he had information on Jamie Hatcher. She started scribbling down notes as he talked.

"Hatcher's part of a street-racing gang. At the very least, we suspect he's into insurance scams, reporting auto parts as stolen, but we've never actually been able to make anything stick. We've been trying to nail them on grand theft auto."

She glanced down at the notes on the desk. "He's had a few 'exhibition of speed' tickets. Were those from street racing?"

"Yes. The cars these kids are into are so customized and modified that it takes quite a bankroll to fund them. They're into high-performance engines and racing tires, not to mention top-of-the-line car cosmetics and customizing. If Daddy doesn't have money, they fund their habits in a number of illegal ways."

"How?"

"Insurance fraud. Disreputable parts shops fill out bogus receipts for parts that haven't really been stolen at all. The phony claims are substantiated by the car owners and everybody makes money. Or they report their cars stolen. The cars are left stripped by the side of the road, receipts are padded way over what the car parts are actually worth.

"They put the cars back together with the new parts, sell the old ones. The sum of the parts are worth more than the whole." Fred always laughed at his own jokes. Kat waited until he got a grip and continued.

"Some gangs film porno videos. They also tape the races and show them, for a price, of course, on the Net. Some are into guns. Selling dope. Illegal betting. There are all kinds of ways to make fast money. These racers will do anything to support their habits."

Kat's heart sank. She thought of Ty and wondered what he'd do if Sunny had been caught up in any of the things Fred had described.

"You close to nabbing him?" She prayed the trail of evidence would never lead back to Sunny.

"I'd love to, but we're nowhere near yet. These kids are slick, but eventually we'll get them."

"Is he still driving the neon-yellow Civic?"

"Right. Why the interest, Vargas?"

"Just doing some follow-up work for a client. You have a name for Hatcher's crew?"

"Nothing. We've been planting bait vehicles around the Valley and Hollywood, but somehow they're able to sniff them out and steer clear. You stay out of trouble, you hear?"

"Thanks, Fred. By the way, how's your sister's kid doing?"

"Clean as a whistle."

"Good. Keep him that way."

"Right. Call anytime, Kat. I'll owe you forever for getting him out of that jam."

"That's what I like to hear. I love it when guys like you owe me. Bye, Fred."

Sunny noticed that Chandler returned from running his errands upset and silent. He acted strange all day, but she figured something was up between him and Kat—that maybe he hadn't gotten laid in a while or something.

Rather than stir up trouble, she steered clear of him after lunch and took Alice to the park before she left for work.

When she got to Gull Harbor and found R.J. in a shitty mood, too, she decided there must be something in the air.

The cruise that afternoon was at capacity, so R.J. should have been pleased, but he didn't act like it. He was nice enough to the customers all teachers from various parts of Nebraska. They'd come to San Luis Obispo to attend a behavioral modification seminar.

They asked all kinds of questions and heaped lots of cheery, positive reinforcement on her; how *great* that she had such a thrilling summer job; how *nice* that she could work outdoors. One woman wanted to know where she was going to attend college in the fall. Another volunteered to set her up with her son, a freshman at Stanford.

It was all she could do not to recoil. *As if.* It wasn't likely that any frat-house, beer-guzzling, Joe College type could ever really turn her on.

As the teachers disembarked and headed toward the parking lot, stopping now and again to pose for photos in front of the bright STARGAZER SUNSET CRUISES sign, she automatically started collecting the upholstered cushions to store them out of the damp night air.

Making a sudden turn with her arms full of bulky seat

cushions, she collided with R.J. and lost her footing. As she dropped the cushions and fought for balance, he grabbed her. Though she did go down on one knee, he kept her from sprawling on the deck.

She threw her head back to swing her tangled hair off her face. Their eyes met. Their gazes locked. Suddenly, there it was again. Hot white lightning crackled between them. She tried to deny it. Closed her eyes and called to mind Dodge's face. She forced herself to remember her plan, to focus on what really mattered, not this crazy, unwanted reaction to R.J.

His hand tightened on her arm as he brought her swiftly to her feet.

Her knees were shaking, her mouth suddenly dry. She opened it to say something, anything, but nothing came out.

"Are you all right?" he asked.

Finding her voice at last, she said, "Yes. Thank you."

"No problem." He looked pained, as if talking to her was a chore. As if he couldn't stand touching her, even slightly.

They were standing closer together than ever. His eyes were sky blue. He had a dimple in one cheek and a faint scar near the corner of his mouth she'd never noticed until now.

"You've been acting weird all night. Did I do something wrong?" she asked.

"No. Not at all."

"Good. I thought you were upset with me."

"Listen, Sunny . . ."

There was too much at stake for her to blow a good thing, but as she stared into his eyes, she found herself wondering if he was about to kiss her and what she would do if he did.

As if reading her mind, he slowly leaned closer. Innocently, their lips brushed. Her body began to hum, charged by a current of electricity. Then, as quickly as it had begun, R.J. ended it.

The same shock she was reeling from registered on his face.

"We can't do this, Sunny."

"I know," she whispered. "I *definitely* can't do this." It was exactly what she'd been telling herself, over and over, with every erratic beat of her heart.

"It was just a kiss." She tried to shrug it off, pretending there hadn't been more to it. She didn't want more. *Couldn't* have more.

"You're just a kid." He said the one thing that always pushed the wrong button.

"I'm nineteen. I'm somebody's *mother,* for God's sake."

"Your Ty's daughter."

"What does that have to do with it?"

"He's not just your dad. He's my best friend."

"And if he wasn't?"

Ron laughed.

"What's so funny?"

"That's *exactly* what he asked me this morning."

"What are you talking about?" she whispered.

He let out a long, slow sigh and shook his head. "I walked into that one. Ty drove over this morning. He wanted to know if there was something going on between us. He and Kat both noticed last night."

"Oh, that's just freaking great. What else did he say?"

"Go home, Sunny. You shouldn't get back late tonight."

"This isn't just about Chandler, is it?"

"No. It's about you. You're only a kid."

"You've never treated me that way before, like I was a kid."

"I don't intend to start now. But you and Ty are just getting to know each other. You've still got a lot to sort out."

If you only knew.

R.J. made it hard to focus. Hard to remember Dodge, how much she'd loved him and everything they once had. She combed through her memories, reminded herself why she'd come to Twilight and what she still had to do.

A thump against the hull made them both jump. R.J. hurried over to the ship's ladder. She followed him, half expecting to see Ty, boarding the ship like a pirate with a gleaming cutlass clenched between his teeth.

"Hel-lo?" One of the teachers from Nebraska was craning her neck to look up at them, one hand anchoring her floppy straw hat to her head. "*Yoo-hoo?* Captain Johnson?"

Sunny heard R.J. clear his throat before he asked what he could do for the woman.

"Everyone's gone but my friend and me, and I can't find my car keys. There's a purple puppy, like a Beanie Baby, on the key ring." She sounded frazzled and frustrated.

"Did you look through your purse?" Sunny stared at the woman's bulging straw bag with its countless pockets inside and out.

"I dumped it out and went through *everything*. May I come aboard and search?"

Sunny could tell R.J. was as relieved by the interruption as she. He flashed her a thoughtful look as the woman started up the ladder. Twenty minutes later they'd thoroughly covered the open decks, but found nothing.

"Looks like your keys are gone." He scanned the deck again. It was getting harder and harder to see as dusk settled over the harbor. "You didn't lock them in the car, did you?"

The woman shook her head. "No. I'm *sure* I took them out. I didn't see them hanging in the ignition, either."

"Hide-a-key?" R.J. sounded hopeful.

"I don't have one," she moaned. "My husband keeps saying he's going to get one made, but he never does. I have to get my car started. We have to check out of the hotel and be on the road tonight in order to make it back to Nebraska in time for my niece's wedding." The woman rubbed her plump hands together. Her friend fidgeted beside her, clucking and tsk-tsking.

R.J. called the nearest locksmith, but he couldn't get there until morning.

"You can leave the car in the lot until morning. It'll be fine," he told her.

"You don't understand. I *have* to leave tonight." The woman was becoming hysterical. "Can't you do anything? Isn't there any way to get the car started?"

Sunny touched Ron's shoulder. "Have you got a slim jim and a spare flathead screwdriver? And a hammer?"

He paused, nodded. "You thinking of hot-wiring? It's not as easy with a newer model. We'll need a key."

"Just get them."

R.J. disappeared into the cabin and was back in a few seconds. Sunny stayed with the frantic woman, whose friend, another teacher, had paced to the end of the dock and was standing beside the *Stargazer,* waiting.

The car was an early nineties Buick.

Piece of cake.

Sunny waited as R.J. fumbled with the slim jim for a couple of minutes.

"Let me," she offered, stepping up close beside him. He shot her a *yeah, right* look, but moved aside with a shrug. She slipped the slim jim into the door frame, and in less than a second had the lock popped and the door open.

She slid into the driver's seat, ran her hand over the floor mat in front, and then around the console, but didn't find the keys. As the car owner started to whine about missing the wedding, Sunny knocked the flathead screwdriver into the ignition and flipped her wrist. The engine started right up.

It had taken all of four seconds.

She stepped out of the car and wiped her hands on the back pockets of her denim shorts and nodded toward the idling Buick.

"You'll have to start it with the screwdriver until you get home and have the ignition fixed. Just don't lock the door."

The woman thanked Sunny profusely and began fumbling in her purse. "I can't tell you how grateful I am. I *told* Sam not to let our Auto Club membership lapse. It'll serve him right to have to replace the ignition."

Her companion was already belted into the passenger side. The car owner found her wallet, dug around inside, and thrust a crisp twenty-dollar bill at Sunny.

"Thank you *so* much, honey. I don't know what I'd have done."

Sunny glanced at R.J., afraid of questions. He was holding the slim jim, listening to the exchange, staring at her as if he'd never seen her before.

"No, thanks, ma'am. Keep your money," Sunny said.

"Well, if you're sure . . ." The twenty disappeared back into the wallet with lightning speed.

"No problem. Drive safe."

She stepped back as the woman drove away. It wasn't until the Buick cleared the parking lot that she finally turned to R.J. He was still staring intently.

"Where'd you learn to start a car like that?"

Darkness was gathering. The breeze off the water had picked up. She reached up to tug her hair off her face and shrugged.

"The Internet."

"Not bad for a girl." He looked around the deserted lot. "It's getting late. I'll walk you to your car."

"I don't have my purse."

He glanced back at the *Stargazer* riding dark and silent in her slip. "Run and get it. I'll wait here."

"Are you afraid of being alone with me now?"

"I'm not afraid of you at all, Sunny. Go get your purse."

Starting the car had her adrenaline pumping. She wished she'd kept her big mouth shut just now. She was on the verge of jeopardizing not only her job, but R.J.'s friendship—with her and with Chandler. She didn't need or want any heavy-duty attachments here.

Things were tough enough. She should have left long before now, but every time she looked at Alice and thought about what she was going to have to do, she felt like puking.

She tried backtracking. "Look, I'm sorry, R.J. I didn't mean to push it." She lowered her eyes so that he wouldn't see her tears, and suddenly the confusing truth rushed out. "When I look at you, I feel things I *can't* even think about."

But she *had* thought about him, late at night when she awoke in the little room in Chandler's house, when the sea breeze was lifting the curtains in their moonlight dance. She had no idea how to describe what she felt for R.J. She'd fallen in love before, but this was different.

What he inspired was a heat that dispelled the cold, dead nothingness that had taken up residence inside her, along with the constant worry and the weight of her responsibilities.

What she felt for R.J. was unique and tempting, while at the same time comfortable and familiar. As if they'd been in love before, in another place and time.

"I don't know what it is, but it's special. Don't you feel it?"

She knew she'd really blown it when he didn't answer right away. She wished he'd say something, anything, instead of letting her stand there like an idiot.

He stared across the lot, into the twilight glow beyond the streetlights, until he finally shook his head.

"No." He spoke softly at first, and then with more conviction, "No, Sunny, I don't."

Mortified, she ran to get her purse. When she got back, he was waiting for her beside her car. Whether or not he hung around to watch her drive out of the parking lot, she had no idea. She couldn't see through her tears.

With the night breeze at his back, R.J. headed for the bar at the Sail On Inn. He hoped they stocked a good supply of Crown Royal. He'd need it tonight. Sunny's confused admission still echoed through his mind.

"I don't know what it is, but it's special. Don't you feel it?"

He ordered a shot, knocked it back, then stared down at the empty glass.

More than you know, Sunny. More than you'll ever know.

TWENTY-SEVEN

After Kat spoke with Fred Westberg around noon, she couldn't resist turning on the computer. Surfing the Net somehow ate up the hours, so much so that she forgot to eat. She didn't look up until it was so late, she decided she'd postpone leaving until the next day.

Lost in a world of fast cars, auto theft, and new terminology, she quickly learned way more than she wanted to know about rival car gangs, domestic versus import racers, customizing and modifications for speed.

Big money bets went down on illegal drag races held in empty parking lots and deserted stretches of roads all over California. Checking the DMV for information, she found the number of people cited for engaging in the quasi-organized, illegal speed contests had steadily increased. Things had gotten so hot that the state of California had passed a law that made observing street racing illegal.

As Kat scanned articles from various news sources and bulletin boards on street racing websites, it was easy to see there was more to what was going on along dark, deserted byways and in dangerous chases through city streets and freeways than the riverbed drag racing of the old fifties' films.

DVDs and videos of the latest illegal races were for

sale on the websites, not to mention steamy porno shots of hot girls spread across hot cars. Thankfully, she hadn't seen any photos of Sunny on any of the racing websites.

News stories indicated drugs and guns as well as auto-parts scams were controlled by some of the gangs.

And street racing apparently appealed to young women as well as young men.

An equal opportunity pastime.

She started reading graphic news accounts detailing tragic accidents that had occurred all over the country as the result of street racing. The headlines, names, and ages of victims who had been disabled, badly burned, or killed reminded her so much of the accident she'd been in on Kauai that she had to turn away.

Twilight enveloped the landscape outside the office window. With her chin propped on her hand, Kat looked out into the gathering purple haze and watched the luminous orange glow fade from the sky.

Elijah Chandler, Ty's ancestor, had surely stepped ashore at this time of evening. It was easy to see how he'd been inspired to name the cove Twilight.

She stretched and tried to relieve the kink in her neck, and suddenly, the image of Sunny opening the hood of the Camry to check out the engine flashed through her mind.

How many nineteen-year-old girls were more concerned about the engine of a car than they were the outside? She knew it was a sexist thought, but how many girls would actually know what they were looking at under the hood?

Just then the phone rang, startling her. There wasn't a single light on in the house save the one Jake had set up on a timer in the corner of the living room. She flipped a switch on the office wall and dispelled the darkness.

"Hello?"

"Kat? This is Sunny."

"Oh. Sunny. Hi."

"Look, what I do with my life is none of your business."

"What are you talking about?" Kat glanced out the front window, suddenly wary. Sunny sounded as if she knew exactly what Kat had been doing all day.

"It's no business of yours what I do or who I do it with. R.J. told me that you and Chandler think we have something going on. I have a feeling this is more your doing than Chandler's."

Kat wasn't about to let herself be pushed around by a nineteen-year-old, even if she was Ty's daughter.

"Your dad thinks you're too young to get involved with someone that age."

"Don't blame this on Chandler. I'm telling you there's nothing going on between us."

"Actually, I told Ty that I thought someone like R.J. might be good for you."

"Yeah? Well, Chandler doesn't see it that way."

"Ty's doing the best he can, Sunny. He's just worried because he cares about you so much. You *and* Alice."

There was dead silence on the other end of the line, then Kat heard Sunny softly say, "I know he does."

"He loves you both."

"What do you know about love? You don't even let yourself fall in love."

"I—"

"Look, please just stay out of my life, okay?"

Kat thought of all the information Westberg had given her on Jamie Hatcher.

"Sunny, if you ever need to talk—"

"*As if* I'd ever tell you anything."

Curt, cold, final. Sunny hung up without another word.

Kat stared down at the phone. She had the information she needed to dig deeper into Sunny's friend Jamie Hatcher. Maybe even enough to find out what had happened to the late "Dodge."

And if Sunny had been part of an auto parts theft ring—or worse—Ty deserved to know, so that he could help her out of it. But she wanted to be absolutely certain first.

She walked out of the office and into the living room. It was too late to head south now, but she was packed and ready to go first thing in the morning.

The sooner she could get to L.A., the sooner she could start trailing Hatcher.

She chose one of the classic videos she'd brought along—Chuck Norris in *The Hitman*—and slipped it into the machine. Pushing play, she sat down and watched without really concentrating on the film. By the time the last kick was thrown, she'd convinced herself that if she discovered Sunny was into any of Hatcher's gang's illegal activities, there had to be something she could do to help her out.

Ty was stretched out on the couch watching a newsmagazine piece about another new strain of infection resistant to antibiotics when Sunny came barreling through the door. She closed it with something slightly less than a slam and tossed her purse on a chair.

With her fists on her hips, she planted herself between the sofa and the television. Her cheeks were bright pink, but from anger, not the sun.

"How *could* you?" Her eyes flashed, her lips were set in a tight line. She reminded him of Amy, of the heated, frequent arguments they'd had before she left town. He should have known it was the beginning of the end back then, but he'd deluded himself into thinking he could fix her. That he could save her.

For the first time since Sunny had shown up, he wondered if he'd fail with her the way he had with Amy.

"How could I *what*?"

"Talk to R.J. about me. Make him promise to stay away from me, like I'm some kid. You had no right to do that, Chandler. How do you think that makes me feel?"

Ty hadn't expected R.J. to tell Sunny about their conversation and couldn't figure out why he'd mentioned it to her in the first place, unless it was just to piss her off. He aimed the remote at the television, hit the power button, and the screen went black. He tossed the remote on the coffee table and sat up.

Sunny was livid. "I've already called and told your little powder puff private eye to keep her nose out of my life from now on. I'm not a child. *Alice* is a child. Look out for her, not me."

"You're the one standing in the middle of the room yelling. Why don't you sit down so we can discuss this?"

She lowered her voice but didn't sit. "There's nothing to discuss."

"R.J.'s too old for you."

"That's ridiculous. Besides, you don't know anything about me. Maybe Dodge was older than R.J. You don't know."

"I don't know much about you at all, Sunny. Only what you've been willing to share. And I don't care about the past. All I want is what's best for you and Alice now. R.J.'s too old for you."

The sight of her eyes so huge and bright and full of tears nearly broke his heart. He forced himself to calm down.

Seconds passed as they exchanged stares.

He didn't want to argue. What he really wanted was the power to turn back time, to have been there to watch her grow up, to guide her, help her pick out her school clothes, teach her to cross the street alone, to ride a bike, and put Band-Aids on her cuts and scrapes.

He wanted to have helped her make all the little decisions before she was faced with the really big ones. Maybe by now he'd have earned her trust. Maybe by now she'd have grown to realize he was only thinking of her and of her future.

He didn't want to be controlling and manipulative like his mom, or a nonentity like his dad. He wanted to be there for Sunny and Alice, wanted the best for them.

He wondered how anyone ever successfully raised children, saw them safely through their teens, sent them off to college, or helped them get established.

Did some parents really have all the answers, or were they just luckier than others?

She was still tense and silent. Ty took a step toward her, tried to hug her.

"Listen, Sunny, I don't know how to be a dad any more than you know how to be a daughter—"

She shrugged him off. "I just want some space. I don't like people snooping around in my life or talking about me behind my back. I don't see why this is such a big deal. R.J.'s your friend. He's a good guy." Sunny rolled her head back and forth to ease the tension in her neck, then let go a tired sigh. "Better than you know."

"When Alice is your age, maybe you'll understand," Ty said.

"Yeah? Well, hopefully I'll remember to cut her some slack."

He hoped he was around to see it. For now he kept his

opinions to himself. His argument wasn't with Sunny, it was with R.J. for telling her that he'd been by to see him.

He had to back off, or risk losing her.

"Why don't you go on up to bed?" he suggested.

"I'm gonna take a shower first." She turned to walk through the kitchen on her way to the outdoor shower, then paused to linger in the doorway.

"Kat's not in love with you, you know. She's never going to love you."

His stomach already felt like he was getting an ulcer. "What makes you say that?"

"She told me that day we went shopping. She said she doesn't ever let herself fall in love. So if you're falling for her, you're just wasting your time."

He couldn't even respond. She didn't need to know her warning came too late.

He'd already fallen in love with Kat Vargas and he had no idea how to deal with her any more than he did Sunny.

All he knew for certain was that he wasn't ever going to give up either of them without a fight.

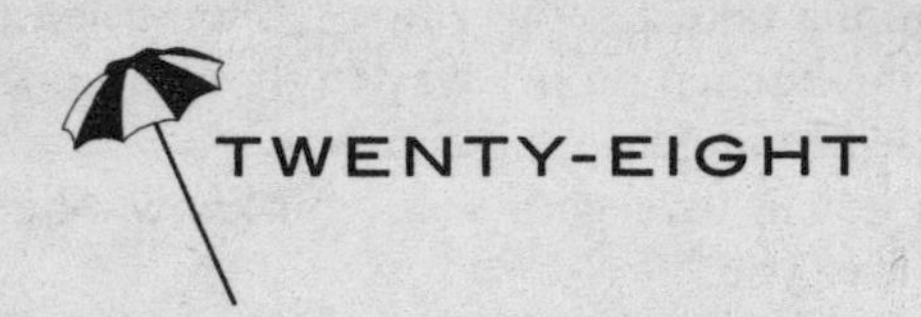

TWENTY-EIGHT

When things get tough, the tough go fishing.

Ty hadn't seen the phrase on a bumper sticker yet, but he thought it would sell as he spent the entire day on his boat making a halfhearted attempt not to think about Kat or worry any more about Sunny and R.J.

It was Sunny's day off but he left her and Alice home so he could be alone when he took the boat out. It was a wasted effort, because the fish weren't biting and he couldn't stop thinking about Kat, Sunny, or R.J.

By late afternoon, driven by a tropical storm off the coast of Baja, the swells slowly built to a point where he decided it was best to head in.

Hoping to run into R.J. at the marina, he stopped by the *Stargazer* and then hung out at the inn, nursing a beer and snacking on popcorn as he watched ESPN, but R.J. never showed. He tried to reach him by cell, but his own cell wasn't working, and when he finally broke down and decided to call Kat, he couldn't reach her, either.

By the time he'd had dinner, battened down the boat, and headed home, it was ten-thirty. He pulled into the driveway, parked behind Sunny's Camry, and walked up the flagstone path. The house was dark as pitch.

He let himself in and fumbled for the light switch.

He'd been looking forward to seeing the girls before they went to bed and was sorry they were already asleep. He headed up to their room anyway.

The door was open wide, and even in the dim light, he could tell that both beds were empty.

"Sunny?" He flipped the light switch, squinted against the glare of the overhead lamp, then walked across the hall to his own room. It was empty, too.

He called their names as he walked through the house, turning on the lights. Since the Camry was in the driveway, he decided they must be out back.

The night air, unusually warm, held the heat of the day. With the remnants of Hurricane Felicia moving up the coast, the air felt heavier than normal.

The clouds parted for a second and the back patio was suddenly awash in moonlight that glittered with a milky patina across the smooth surfaces of leaves and blossoms in the garden. He headed for the edge of the bluff and scanned the beach below. The tide was in, raging high and angry.

Phosphorescent waves foamed neon green against the rocks at the base of the stairs.

He shouted for Sunny, but his voice was drowned out by the sound of crashing waves and the wind off the ocean. If the girls had been on the stairs, he'd have seen them. There was no way anyone was on the beach with the tide this high.

Back inside, he looked for a note, though Sunny had never left one before. With a pang, he realized he wouldn't even recognize her handwriting if he saw it.

He walked to the window, looked outside again to make certain her car actually was there or if he'd just imagined it. She'd parked the Camry close to the garage doors. His worry mounted, drove him to check inside the garage, but they weren't there. Back in the house, he went through every room again, taking stock.

Alice's toys were in the basket in the living room, her play comforter, neatly folded, was lying across the upholstered footstool near the time-worn leather easy chair.

Upstairs in their room, Sunny's clothes were still in the closet. Alice's things were folded in the drawers of her bureau. Sunny always kept the wooden earring box on the dresser, but it was gone.

He didn't see anywhere the oversized plastic purse she'd carried the day she showed up.

He had no idea what she'd been planning besides a trip to the beach. She'd been thoughtful and quiet after their argument, but she'd seemed fine that morning.

Since he hadn't been able to reach R.J. all day, he decided that maybe the two of them were off somewhere with Alice.

It was 10:45 when he dialed R.J.'s number from his house line. Again, he got no response, but he left another message.

Ty rubbed the back of his neck, paced over to the front window, and stared out at the deserted point. Then he walked back to the phone. Automatically, he dialed Jake's number to call Kat, then it hit him that she was gone. He was about to click off when she unexpectedly answered.

"I thought you'd left." Relief rolled through him. *She changed her mind.* "Did I wake you?"

"Me? Are you kidding? I was still up."

"Are you staying?"

"I was all set to leave yesterday but work got in the way, and by the time I was done, it was too late to leave. When I got up this morning, I discovered the hot water heater had flooded the pantry last night, so this morning

I had to have a plumber come out, and then it took all day for him to bring a new one over from San Luis Obispo."

She drifted into a silence that echoed over the line and made him more aware of the emptiness around him. It was hard for him to even tell her what was up.

"Sunny and Alice are gone."

"What do you mean, *gone*?"

"I was out fishing all day and got home a few minutes ago. The house is empty. They're not here."

He could just see her mulling over what he said and coming up with a way to rationalize Sunny's absence.

"Maybe she took Alice into town for some ice cream. I saw a poster the other day announcing a band concert at the Plaza tonight."

"Her car's still in the driveway and the stroller is in the garage."

"Have you tried calling R.J.? Maybe she's with him."

"I couldn't get ahold of him. I left a message. I'm sorry she called you about my talking to R.J." When Sunny told him that she'd talked to Kat, he'd thought that she'd reached her by cell phone. He'd had no idea Kat was still at Jake's.

"Was she upset enough to leave, do you think?"

His anxiety hadn't diminished, but he was relieved he had Kat to talk to.

"I thought we'd smoothed things over. She was kind of quiet this morning when I left to go fishing, but she seemed okay. She had the day off and said she was going to take Alice to the beach in Twilight."

"Just sit tight. Maybe you'll hear from R.J., or maybe she'll just come strolling in in a few minutes, like she did before."

"I wouldn't even care if she *is* with him right now. At this point I'd be happy knowing where they are."

"I'm coming over."

"It's too late." It was a halfhearted attempt at a protest. He wanted nothing more than to have her here beside him instead of back in Long Beach. Now that the rest of his world had turned upside down, he needed to know that she wasn't going anywhere, but it was late and the weather wasn't looking good. He didn't want her out on the streets.

"You're right. She'll probably be home in a few minutes." He walked over to the picture window and stared out into the night. "I'll call you in the morning."

"No. I'll be right there."

Within minutes Kat pulled up outside his house.

The warm, tropical air on her skin reminded her of hurricane weather. As she crossed the yard, she rubbed the scar on the back of her hand. Not even the memory of the shooting was as terrifying or as threatening as the idea that she had fallen in love with Ty Chandler.

She had to be there for him. Had to help in any way she could. She was not about to let him wait alone and wonder where Sunny was.

The place was lit up like a lighthouse, inside and out. The porch light illuminated Sunny's car in the driveway.

Ty was at the front window, a dark silhouette against the light. He was on the cell phone when he opened the door and waved her in.

She realized he was talking to R.J. when she heard him say, "I thought she might be with you."

She glanced around the living room. Everything was in its place. She pointed to the ceiling to let him know she was going to run upstairs. He nodded, listening to R.J.

On the second floor, things looked perfectly normal. By the time she came down, Ty was off the phone.

"R.J. was in San Luis Obispo all day. He has no idea where she is," he said. "She didn't take her clothes or Alice's. She didn't take anything."

"She didn't bring anything with her, either," she reminded him. "Is Stinko missing?"

Ty glanced around the room. "I haven't seen him."

"Does she have any money?"

"Just what she's saved from her job." He shook his head, frowning. "And my grandmother's opal earrings."

Worry was etched on his rugged features. Kat walked over to him, tried to slip her arm around his waist.

"Ty, listen—"

He shrugged her off.

"*Don't*. This is all my fault." His expression was hard with anger, but she understood him perfectly. He hurt too badly to be touched right now.

He didn't want her sympathy. He was taking the blame for running Sunny off, and losing the battle to keep his feelings in check.

"I should have listened to you and not made such an issue out of this thing with R.J.," he told her.

"I know you're worried sick, but Sunny has a good head on her shoulders. She's street smart and she would never let anything happen to Alice. She'll be fine."

She ached for him. Wished she could say or do something to ease his pain. What she *could* do was track Sunny down again if the girl didn't show up tonight—but this time she wasn't working for Ty and she didn't intend to tell him anything until she knew where Sunny was and exactly what was going on.

If the girl was in over her head with Jamie Hatcher and the others, then Kat would do everything she could to get Sunny out if it.

"Damn it," Ty mumbled. His shoulders were rigid, his features set as stone.

Kat went into the kitchen to get a diet soda. He paced and stewed.

All the windows were open wide, but the heat in the house had intensified. The air was close and still. The calm before the storm. Ty followed her, leaned against the doorjamb.

"If you're still planning on driving to Long Beach early in the morning, you should go."

It was impossible to miss the anger in his tone. She knew he was upset with Sunny's disappearance right now and that he was focusing his impatience and frustration on her because she was here. He needed to lash out at someone.

"Is that your *not*-so-subtle way of asking me if I'm still planning to leave tomorrow?"

"I guess it is." His gaze was intense, his shoulders rigid. She tried to hide her conflicted emotions, afraid the new, raw cracks in the Kevlar lining of her heart would show.

"You didn't have to come over," he reminded her.

"I know that, just as I know that you're upset right now, so I'm going to ignore your tone. I'll leave when I'm good and ready." She headed for the refrigerator. "You want a Diet Pepsi?"

"I need a beer." He walked over to the fridge, reached around her, and grabbed a cold Pacifico. She took out a diet soda just before he shut the door—too hard.

He opened the beer, took a long swig. "This is the pits, you know?"

"Ty, I know how much this hurts—"

He turned on her. "And *how* would you know? You've never lost a child. Besides, you won't let yourself get close enough to anyone to know *what* hurt feels like."

The air rushed out of her as hard as if he'd sucker

punched her. She fought to take a breath and wound up leaning against the counter for support.

Unwittingly, he had nearly brought her to her knees, but somehow she found the will to stand up straight and head for the door. She heard him set the beer bottle down hard on the countertop, heard his footsteps as he crossed the room behind her.

She picked up her pace, rushed through the house. A sudden wash of tears made it almost impossible to see. She bumped into the coffee table, winced, kept going.

"Kat, wait."

He caught up just as she reached for her purse.

"*Leave me alone.*"

With a hand on her shoulder, he forced her to turn. His gaze searched her face, her eyes.

"You're crying." He made it sound like an impossibility, even as he reached out to thumb her tears off her cheeks.

"You think I don't have feelings? You think I don't know *exactly* what you're going through?" She choked on the words she hadn't been able to say to anyone for years. "I lost a baby, Ty. In the accident. The whole thing was *my fault*. I was pregnant that night I got behind the wheel. I was upset, hysterical, and I wasn't thinking of anything but confronting Justin.

"He'd come back to Kauai and moved out of our apartment while I was at work. He didn't even have the nerve to face me. I knew he had to be at his parents' place on the north shore. I grabbed my keys and headed out during a terrible storm—"

"You weren't responsible. You said the truck hit you head-on."

"But I shouldn't have been driving at all. I was a mess. Maybe if I'd seen the truck sooner, if I'd been thinking straight, I might have been able to swerve off the road in time. But I wasn't thinking and . . . and my baby died. I was five months pregnant." She let go a deep, shuddering sigh and whispered, "I killed my little girl."

He tried to take her into his arms, but she shoved him aside.

"That's why I try to keep from feeling anything. That's how I was able to survive. Then Sunny showed up with Alice, and every time I looked at them, it all came back. I didn't have to imagine. Every time I looked at either of them, especially Alice, I could see what I lost, past *and* future. I would never know my little girl as a toddler. I'll never know her as a teenager.

"Watching them, being near them, it's hard, Ty. So hard."

Her last words came out on a whisper before she turned and walked out the door. He followed her down the walk, called her name. When she ignored him, he grabbed her arm. She tried to twist out of his hold.

"Please, Kat. Stop."

"Don't do this, Ty. Just let me go."

"You shouldn't be driving."

That stopped her in her tracks. She balled her hands into fists, took a deep, shuddering breath, and forced herself to center, to calm down. He was standing over her, close, so close she could feel his warmth. It would have been so easy to melt into his arms, to give in, but she held strong.

"Don't worry." A bitter laugh escaped her. "I'll be careful. I've already made that mistake once." She walked to her car but didn't open the door until she was a lot calmer and thinking somewhat clearly.

"I'm all right." She knew when she was back in control. She'd had years of practice. Her hands were barely trembling as she reached for the door handle.

"Stay with me tonight. Please. Just until the rain

passes." His hands were on her shoulders again. This time she didn't try to shrug him off.

"Stay, Kat," he urged.

"You've got enough to worry about. I'm all right."

"Damn it, Kat. Don't look at me that way. I'm so sorry. I had no idea—"

"I know that."

She wanted nothing more than to stay with him tonight. To sit beside him, wait for Sunny, but she'd come too close to losing herself again.

Besides, if Sunny didn't show up tonight, if she was gone, then Kat knew she just might have enough information to find out where Sunny was and why she'd left. She could do more for Ty down south than she could here.

"When are you coming back?" His jaw was set. His eyes were as troubled as the sky now filled with low-lying storm clouds.

"I don't know." A fine mist had begun to fall since they'd come outside. It was cold in comparison to the sultry air and gave her chicken skin. A shiver slipped down her spine.

He let his hands fall away from her shoulders and stepped back. She opened the car door, got inside, and buckled up.

She drove off slowly, without looking back.

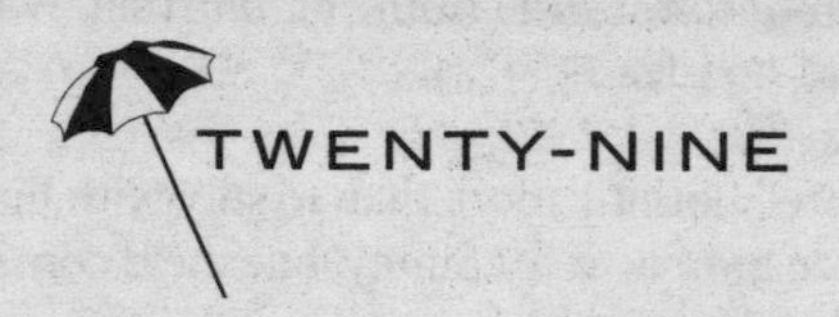

TWENTY-NINE

Preparing for foul weather, R.J. secured the lines and climbed back aboard the *Stargazer.* His tension was building with the storm, but the sky, at least, could open up and let go. He couldn't.

Once he was in the salon with the hatch battened down, he called Ty back.

Chandler answered on the first ring. "Sunny?"

"It's R.J. Sunny didn't show up yet?"

"No. She was pretty upset with me for talking to you about her yesterday. Why in the hell did you tell her?"

R.J. knew Ty was worried sick, he could hear it in his voice, but after watching Sunny break into the Buick last night, he was pretty damn sure she knew how to take care of herself—no matter where she was.

Girls that lived the life Sunny had lived and looked like Sunny looked never got into trouble. They caused it, carried it with them, left it behind in their wake.

"It just came out. Look, I have to be honest with you. . . ."

"Go on," Ty prompted.

"We argued last night. And we kissed."

"What do you mean *kissed*?"

R.J. closed his eyes, leaned his head back against the bulkhead. Every time he turned around today he found himself recalling the innocent exchange. It was nothing more than a brush of their lips, the merest touch—and yet he couldn't forget it.

"It just happened, that's all. It wasn't anything passionate. I told her it didn't mean anything."

"*Did* it?"

R.J. knew, in that split second, he could choose the truth or he could choose to salvage thirty years of friendship.

He chose their friendship.

"It didn't mean a thing."

There was another stretch of intense silence before Ty responded.

"Was she angry enough to leave?"

"I have no idea. I didn't think so, or I wouldn't have sent her home."

"I've got to hang up."

"Look, call me when she gets back."

"Call me if you hear from her." Ty hung up first.

It was almost midnight. Clouds obscured the sky, hanging so low they hugged the black water. R.J. knew he wasn't going to get much sleep tonight, not with the boat riding the angry swells that swept through the small boat harbor.

It was a lot easier to convince himself the storm would keep him awake than to admit that he would be worrying about Sunny and Alice and the irreparable damage he might have done to his friendship with Ty Chandler.

As Kat drove back through Twilight, most of the shops along Cabrillo Road were closed. Foot traffic had thinned to a few couples lingering in the moonlit park or strolling along the walk overlooking the cove.

Her tears had dried by the time she slowed her car to a crawl along the deserted main strip.

She tried to focus—not on Ty and what had just happened, but on finding Sunny. Taking refuge in her work had always served her well. She fell back on it now.

A CLOSED sign was hanging on the door at Selma's diner, but there was still light streaming out of the kitchen.

Whipping the wheel to the right, Kat drew the car up to the curb and parked. She walked up to the diner door, leaned toward the glass, and started knocking. Within a few seconds, Selma Gibbs came strolling out of the kitchen, hastily running a hand over her hair, then tucking in the hem of a knit tank top that would have looked great on someone twenty years younger.

Selma waved, opened the door, and ushered her in. Kat realized there was a lot to be said for small towns where a shopkeeper recognized you and opened up no matter how late.

"The kitchen's closed, but if you want something cold, a salad or sandwich, I can have Joe rustle it up." Selma's lipstick looked like it had just taken a beating. Obviously Joe had been rustling up more than a sandwich.

"I'm just here for a little information," Kat replied.

Selma's interest was suddenly piqued. She lowered her voice to a gravelly whisper. "Are you working a case?"

"Ty's daughter, Sunny, isn't home yet and he's concerned. Was she in here tonight?"

Selma shook her head. "I still can't believe Ty Chandler has a kid. Why, I'd just come to town when he was a quarterback at Twilight High. What a good-looker that kid was—"

"So, have you seen Sunny, Selma?"

"Actually, she came in late this afternoon. Waited on her myself. Let's see . . . she ordered a grilled chicken salad, and some fish sticks and toasted cheese for French

Fry. Who'd of ever thought to name a child French Fry?"

"Exactly when was Sunny here? Do you know?"

"About four-thirty. Maybe a bit later."

"Was she alone? Except for French Fry?"

Selma nodded. "Yes. A couple stopped by the table to talk to her. An older couple. Complimented her on French Fry's good behavior. First time I ever saw Sunny smile like that."

"You didn't happen to see her with a guy with dreadlocks, did you?" She went on to describe Jamie Hatcher.

"Is that a bunch of hair all matted together? If so, I didn't see anyone like that."

Joe—middle-aged, with quite a belly beneath his spattered white apron—walked through the darkened diner and stood so close to Selma their shoulders touched. He smiled down into Selma's eyes and Kat found herself tempted to dare to want the same thing for herself.

"You know Ty's kid? Sunny?" Selma asked Joe.

Joe nodded. "I saw her when I went out to empty the trash."

Kat rubbed the back of her left hand, tried not to wince as she practiced curling her fingers into a fist. "In the parking lot out back?"

"Yeah. She was talking to some guy with a shaved head. Not completely bald. Stubble. You know the look."

"Could you hear what they were saying?" It may have been Jamie, maybe not.

"I wasn't paying attention. She was standing next to her car. Her little one was getting fussy. Sunny looked ready to leave, but the guy just kept talking."

"You didn't actually see her leave?"

"No. You think she's all right?"

Kat had no idea, but the man's dark eyes so expressed

his obvious concern that she wished she could put his mind at ease.

"I hope so."

Kat thanked them and walked out. Maybe Sunny had left town on her own. Or maybe she'd talked someone into giving her a ride back to Southern California. She would have known it would be easy to trace the Camry, and she might not have wanted to risk being found.

The question was, had she gone back to Hatcher and the others, or had she taken off for parts unknown? And if so, why? Had she been that upset with Ty and R.J.?

There was only one way to find out, and that was to look for Hatcher and see if he would lead her to Sunny.

THIRTY

In the wee hours of the morning, with her palms locked in a death grip on the wheel, Kat turned onto the 101 off-ramp and into a well-lit Carl's Junior parking lot. She rested her forehead on the backs of her hands and took long, cleansing breaths.

The windshield wipers swished and clicked, swished and clicked rhythmically, cutting the stillness of the night. She killed the motor and sat there, staring through the rain on the windshield into the glaring emptiness of the fast-food restaurant.

The streets were slick, deserted, and shimmering beneath the haunting amber glow of streetlights. Normal people were home in bed, not out on the road alone in the middle of a storm.

Beyond the plate-glass window fronting Carl's, two lone employees stood at attention at their posts. She sighed, longing for the taste of hot coffee, even bad hot coffee, but she couldn't bring herself to move.

The constant rain, the sultry weather, were all too reminiscent of the day of the accident on Kauai.

Kat shuddered, stared at the lights distorted by the rain smearing her windshield, and let her mind drift.

* * *

After hearing from Justin, she stops leaving messages. Somehow she struggles through the week, fights to stay sane, to carry on as usual.

Pretty hard when you're five months' pregnant, your fiancé is cheating on you, and everybody knows it.

Without telling her, he switches to an earlier flight and arrives home while she's at work. By the time she gets home, he's already been by the apartment. His half of the closet is empty. The dresser drawers hang open. She stares around in shock, realizing what he's done.

Coward. Shit-for-brains.

They're having a baby. Doesn't that mean anything? Doesn't she mean more to him than some silicone-enhanced 8x10 glossy trying to pass as a real woman?

She grabs her car keys and tears out of the apartment, headed for his parents' estate near Po'ipu, certain that's where he's gone.

A couple of blocks from the condo, she turns left onto the bypass road that winds its way through the cane fields, but she's forgotten that it's June, that school is out and the annual caravans of teens are cruising the island. She's forgotten that reckless young drivers, kids naive and foolish enough to believe they are immortal, play chicken on the bypass road.

Even in the rain.

The windshield wipers' monotonous song brought her back.

She laid her hand over her abdomen. The emptiness was always there. She'd lost her baby girl that night. Her body had slowly recovered, but not her spirit.

Riddled with guilt, she'd tried to go on with her life on Kauai, but in the end she had to leave Kauai behind to survive.

She'd run fast and far—from all the sorrow in her

family's eyes, from their worried glances and hushed whispers.

It was much easier not to open up to anyone. Not to love or be loved, not to risk all that pain spilling out again. Better to wall up her heart than to take a chance on being hurt, knowing next time she might not survive.

Before Twilight Cove, before Ty Chandler, she'd given up on love. It was the one thing she feared most. Loving too much. Losing control. Losing everything again.

But now, because of the shooting in Seal Beach, because of the things Jake said, but most of all because of Ty Chandler, she had to decide whether or not she was strong enough, brave enough, foolish enough, to let herself love again.

THIRTY-ONE

Dawn crawled across the hazy L.A. skyline, tinted miles of glass in the high-rise windows a bright, Day-Glo pink. Traffic on the 101 was nearly at a standstill when Kat exited the Franklin off-ramp in Hollywood. She stopped long enough to grab another cup of coffee and a breakfast burrito before she threaded her way through the busy streets to Sunny's old apartment.

The shady side street was relatively quiet. There was no one in the courtyard garden, no sign of life. One porch light was still on, faded to almost nothing under the early-morning sun.

She pulled over a few yards away and parked on the opposite side of the street, where she could watch the apartment door. Reaching for her cell phone, she checked her voice mail. Two missed calls from Ty, one from Arnie Tate, and a message from a Mitch Carson.

She tried to place Mitch, then slowly the memory of a heavyset stockbroker with brown hair and hazel eyes came back to her. She'd met him at the gym, had dinner with him, and had gone back to his swanky redevelopment loft in downtown Long Beach for a one-nighter. That was her old life—running from any meaningful relationship, trying to become the exact opposite of the starry-eyed, naive virgin she'd been before Justin.

Mitch said he wanted to take her out to dinner again. She knew what he really wanted.

She played the message twice, and before she could change her mind, called and left Mitch a voice mail, telling him she'd meet him at the bar at Kelly's Restaurant in Naples at six.

What better way to stop thinking about Ty than to go out with someone else? Wasn't that what Jake had advised? Get out more?

She didn't remember much about Mitch Carson. She'd thought at the time he seemed like an okay guy. She'd never really given him a chance.

Kelly's was an institution—crowded, dark, and smoky, with deep burgundy leather booths and rich prime rib. At least she had a hearty meal to look forward to.

She polished off the burrito and coffee and waited. Two hours later, she recognized the old woman who walked out of an apartment in a ratty chenille robe and worn slippers to pick up her morning *Times*. The woman shuffled back inside, and for a good thirty minutes more nothing happened.

Kat glanced at her watch. It was almost eight in the morning. She holstered her gun beneath a light-brown blazer that complemented her khaki pants, then she stepped out of the car and headed across the street.

She knocked on the door, waited, listened, knocked again. There was no response, no muffled sounds behind the door. She headed for the apartment across the courtyard. As she passed the old woman's window, the draperies shifted. She caught a glimpse of the woman's face staring back.

Kat waved, and the drape fell back into place. She rang the manager's bell.

A lanky, dark-haired man with a lock of hair falling

over tortoiseshell glasses blinked and rubbed his hand across the night's growth of stubble on his chin.

"We got nothing available," he informed her, looking her up and down.

"I'm not looking for an apartment. My name's Kat Vargas. I'd like a little information." She pulled her wallet out of her blazer pocket, flashed her library card, and shoved it back in her pocket. It usually worked like a charm, and did this time, too.

He didn't ask her to step in. "Yeah? Go ahead."

"Your name?"

"Charles Gomez."

"Mr. Gomez, I'm looking for someone who lives in number nine."

"Aren't we all? They're behind on the rent."

"You know where they hang out?"

"No. The best time to catch them home is early morning."

"It is early," she reminded him.

He yawned. "Nah. I meant three or four in the morning. They leave when it gets dark, come back in the early morning hours. They didn't come home last night. I've been watching for them. They owe somebody else?"

"May I see their rental agreement?"

His lip curled slightly, but he nodded. "Yeah. Let me get it."

She waited on the porch, kept an eye on Sunny's apartment, while the neighbor lady kept an eye on her. Sparrows flitted in the branches of a crepe myrtle in the garden. An old orange tree loaded with blossoms attracted bees. The air was almost clear after the rain.

"Here it is."

She turned, took the application, and quickly scanned it for a place of employment. The form was dismally lacking in information, the apartment originally rented to Dodge Radisson and Jamie Hatcher. Finally she had Dodge's last name. Sunny Simone wasn't listed, nor was anyone else.

"Do you know Dodge Radisson?"

"I haven't seen him around for months. Over half a year at least."

"What about the pretty girl who was living here? You see her yesterday?"

"Long, reddish hair? With the kid? She hasn't been around lately, either. Probably got fed up with that little turd Hatcher. He's a bastard."

"In what way?"

"Thinks he's hot shit with that car of his."

"Neon-yellow Civic?"

"Yeah."

She glanced down at the form again. Noted both Hatcher and Radisson had listed an address in the Valley as their place of employment. California driver's licence numbers were listed. No Social Security numbers. She pulled out a small spiral notebook and quickly copied down all the numbers, handed the form back to the manager, pocketed the notebook and pen.

"Thanks."

"They in trouble?" He appeared hopeful. "I've been wishing they'd move."

"I'm only looking for the girl."

"Good luck. If you see them, tell them the rent's overdue."

Before she could thank him, he closed the door and disappeared inside.

She went down the walk, past the birdbath and broken statue. Where the saint's head should have been, a plain brown sparrow perched atop St. Francis's empty cowl collar.

Just before she reached the curb, a late-model Mitsubishi Eclipse whipped into the open space in front of the apartment building. Kat realized she'd been surfing car sites on the Net too long when she mentally started to tick off the car's features at a glance: electric-blue pearl finish, alloy wheels, and Yokohama Parada tires. She couldn't hazard a guess as to how much muscle might be under the hood or how much money the young man who stepped out and hit the power lock had spent on his ride.

"You looking for Jamie?" She hoped that her looks-younger-than-she-really-is gene was working overtime this morning.

Five-ten, brown hair, with a clean-shaven full face, he frowned, more hesitant than wary, from beneath the brim of a navy ball cap. He might have a fully loaded car, but the kid's expression was fairly blank.

"Yeah. Is he here?" His glance strayed to Jamie's apartment door.

She shook her head. "No one's here. I thought maybe I'd find him at the warehouse. Is he still using the one over in Van Nuys?" She named the address listed on the rental application.

He shrugged. No help at all.

"I've got an insurance check for him," she improvised. "You have any other idea where he might be?"

"Probably at the new place."

"He *really* needs this check and I promised to hand-deliver it." She pulled out her spiral notebook, acted as if she was flipping to an address. Her heart was knocking a mile a minute, amped on excitement, too much coffee, or both.

Moments like this, she loved her job, but she'd never had so much riding on it before. The high was better than drugs. "Are you planning on going over there?"

"Naw. I just stopped by 'cause I was close."

"Exactly where is the new place again?" She held her breath, waited. The new warehouse could be anywhere in Southern California, but she was betting the kids wouldn't have gone too far afield.

He gave her another location not far from the one on the rental application.

"Great." She flashed him a flirty smile and tucked her hair behind her ear. "That's a great car."

"Thanks. Tell Jamie to call Brian."

"Sure." She didn't look back until she was almost across the street. Then she glanced over her shoulder and caught him staring at her butt. She waved, and he raised his chin in acknowledgment before his eyes dropped to her rear again.

Boys will be boys.

Once inside the car, she adjusted the rearview mirror. Sunglasses hid her bloodshot, tired eyes. She was reaching for her L.A. County Thomas Guide directory of street maps as the blue Mitsubishi squealed away from the curb.

She punched in Fred's number at the L.A.P.D. before starting the car. He still owed her. Maybe it was time they made a deal.

"Westberg."

"Fred, it's Kat. If I can hand you Jamie Hatcher, will you help me out with someone close who'll testify against him?"

"I can't make you a promise like that without any hard information. *How* close?"

"Real close."

"Can you give me *anything*?"

"I'm helping a nineteen-year-old without any priors. The daughter of a friend of mine. Have a heart. She's a mom, Fred."

There was silence on the other end of the line, silence colored by Fred's need to nail Jamie Hatcher.

"Fred?"

"Call me when you've got something concrete and I'll contact the D.A. And don't do anything stupid, Vargas. You're not Wonder Woman."

"Me? No way." She glanced at the scar on her left hand, closed her eyes remembering her argument with Ty last night.

"When have you ever known me to do anything stupid, Fred?"

He was still laughing when she ended the call.

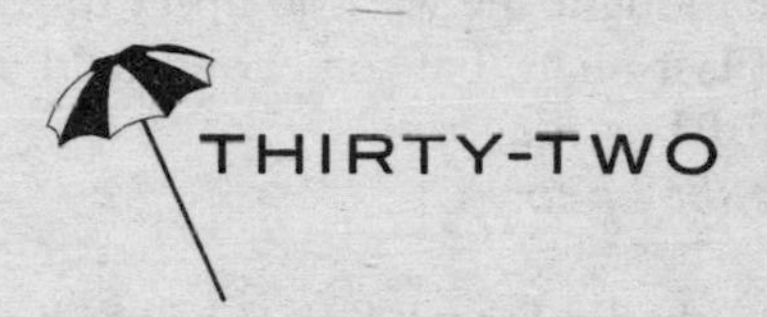

THIRTY-TWO

The harsh ring jolted Ty out of a deep sleep, dragged him up from the depths of the too soft sofa cushions, and sent him scrambling to find the phone before the answering machine picked up.

He stubbed his toe on the footstool on his way through the living room, knocked the phone onto the kitchen floor, grabbed it, and cursed as he hit the talk button.

"Hello?" Without thinking, he shouted into the receiver.

"Geez. Ty? It's Selma down at the diner."

Not Sunny. Not Kat.

The air rushed out of him as he sat down heavily on a kitchen chair. It was still drizzling outside, adding a gray pall of gloom to the morning.

"Hi, Selma. What's up?"

"I worried all night. Did Sunny ever get home?"

Elbow on the table, he rested his forehead on his palm and stared down at the scarred pine that had seen generations of meals, games, gatherings.

"How did you know she was gone?"

"Kat came by last night asking if we'd seen her. Joe sure wishes he'd paid more attention when he saw Sunny talking to that kid."

"Kat came by?" Ty straightened. "What kid?"

"The one with the baseball cap. The one I told Kat about."

"The one I told Kat about."

He'd have thought she was too upset to go anywhere after she left last night, but somehow she'd managed to shift into her P.I. mode.

What was she up to?

"Ty?"

"What exactly did Joe tell Kat, Selma? I haven't heard from her yet today."

"Joe saw Sunny out back, in the parking lot, after she and the baby were here yesterday afternoon. Fish sticks and toasted cheese. Nobody orders toasted cheese much anymore, 'cept kids, but Joe makes one that melts in your mouth—"

"Selma, about the guy with Sunny . . ."

"Oh, yeah." She muffled the mouthpiece, conferred with Joe. Seconds later, she was back.

"Shaved head. Almost six feet. Not heavy, not skinny. Medium build, I guess. That's the kind of stuff she wanted to know. P.I. stuff. I still can't believe that cute little thing is a private eye. In the old days, we called them private dicks. I guess that doesn't apply now that women are liberated. Some days I wish somebody'd come along and liberate me. Hand me a couple of million for this place and I'd be long gone."

He heard Joe banging pots in the kitchen, thanked Selma for the call, hung up, and immediately dialed R.J.

"I still haven't seen her." R.J. sounded as worn-out as Ty felt.

"I'm going down to L.A." The decision felt right the minute Ty made it.

"You think she's there?"

"I don't know. I'm going after Kat."

"What's up?"

What's up? Last night he'd hurt Kat deeply and yet she'd gone searching for Sunny. Now they were both gone.

"I think she's looking for Sunny. Would you mind coming over here and hanging around in case Sunny shows up? I'll leave the door open."

"I'm on my way."

"If Sunny comes back—"

"I'll call you ASAP."

Last night she made $2,500 in sixty seconds.

Sunny couldn't help but wonder what Chandler would think if he'd seen all that money change hands.

She'd have had to work for R.J. for months before she cleared even close to that amount.

There was no keeping it, though. Jamie had borrowed money from a guy who didn't like to wait to be repaid, so by the time they were clear, there was all of three hundred dollars left.

Jamie had shocked the hell out of her when he came strolling up to her in the parking lot at Selma's. Without making a scene, he'd let her know that he would do whatever it took to get her back to Hollywood. She knew by now things were getting tough back in L.A. and he wouldn't stop at anything.

He tried to coerce her into taking the Camry, but she refused. He took Alice in his car and followed her to Chandler's, where she left the Camry behind.

If it hadn't been for Callie, he might never have found her. But one night, while Callie was watching an old *Twilight Zone* episode, she remembered Chandler said he was from a town called Twilight Cove. It was only because Jamie had threatened to throw her out on the street that Callie finally told him where to look.

One of the neighbors told Butch that the landlord had marshals looking to serve them with an eviction notice, so Jamie moved them all to a motel, promising that after tonight, they'd have enough to cover the back rent and plenty to spare for a while.

The television mounted on the wall in the sparse motel room sounded tinny. The noise ricocheted off the bare walls and linoleum floor. The place used to be a Motel 6, but after it fell below chain standards, it became just another dive along Sepulveda Boulevard.

Alice and Callie were on the bed, the baby sound asleep, with her fingers wound around Stinko's tail. Callie was glued to Jerry Springer's latest exposé on transvestites in tutus. When the television audience started chanting, "Jerry! Jerry!" Sunny had to get outside or lose it.

She grabbed the cheap plastic ice bucket off the scarred Formica dresser and opened the door. Butch was outside running a polish rag over the already dust-free silver S2000 Honda parked in front of the motel room. She opened the door and held up the ice bucket, and with a nod indicated the alcove not far away, where the ice and soda machines stood in plain sight.

He hooked the rag into his back pocket and fell into step beside her. Jamie left him there to insure that she'd still be around when he came to pick her up tonight.

"You know I'm not going anywhere, Butch. Not with French Fry inside."

"Jamie told me to keep an eye on you."

"And you always do what Jamie says."

Butch nodded, his eyes shadowed. "Yeah, now that Dodge is gone, I do."

"Now that Dodge is gone."

There wasn't one of them, except Jamie, who didn't wish Dodge was still around.

She fell silent. Butch waited while she shoved the ice bucket beneath the spout and watched the perfectly matched cubes clatter into the beige plastic bucket.

When she turned around, he was still there, still watching.

"You think it's right, what he's making me do tonight? You think it's right for him to have me and French Fry watched like this? Dodge would be furious."

Butch held up both hands. "Hey, look, this ain't my idea, okay? I just do what I'm told. Just like you used to—until you took off. Things have been real tough on us the past few weeks, Sunny. On me, and Leaf, and Callie. All the bills have been pilin' up. Jamie's got a lot of pressure on him. You shoulda thought about that before you walked out."

Trouble was, she *had* thought of it. She knew they'd suffer for it when she left, knew things would be tight without her pulling in the big money, but she had to think of Alice, too. She had wanted to see her little girl settled and safe before she came back to pick up where she left off.

If there had been any other way out, she'd have taken it, but for the life of her, she hadn't come up with one. She should have walked out, left Alice with Chandler sooner. He'd have kept her baby safe and raised her right. But every time she had looked at French Fry, her heart would break and she'd tell herself that she needed one more day. One more day and then she could leave her behind.

Now it was too late. Jamie was using Alice to keep her around. As if there wasn't enough reason to stay as it was.

Kat left Hatcher's apartment and staked out the warehouse in an industrial section of the San Fernando Valley. Jamie's car was in front of the building, so she'd parked beneath the shade of a slim magnolia across the lot and waited until she saw him walk out.

He was wearing a black billed cap and a frown, his dreadlocks gone, his hair shaved in a close buzz cut. He was alone. She tailed him back to the Hollywood apartment, where she waited a good thirty minutes before she knocked at the front door.

Jamie answered, looking rumpled and exhausted. "She's not here. You can come in and see for yourself if you want."

"No thanks."

Behind him, the living room was empty, the television off, the drapes drawn.

"Have you seen her lately?"

"No." He braced his hand on the edge of the door and stared back. "What are you doing here? What's up?"

"Her dad's worried about her, that's all. I was on my way to Long Beach and told him I'd stop by and see if she was around."

"I haven't seen her for weeks. I figured she was with him."

"If you do see her, tell her to call him. She has the number."

"Right. *If* I see her."

Liar.

A hard-eyed stare dared her to challenge him, but his eyes couldn't lie. Even if Sunny wasn't in the apartment, she was around somewhere and Jamie knew where.

Kat thanked him and walked away, doubting he'd be going anywhere soon. She felt as beat as he looked, so she decided to head home to Long Beach and come back later, hopefully before Jamie was on the move again.

Back at her apartment, she went through all the mail

that hadn't made it through first-class forwarding to Twilight. Ninety-nine percent of it was bulk junk that she tossed. She screened the phone messages, and when she woke up after having fallen asleep with her head on her desk, she forced herself to take a nap for a couple of hours, then took a shower.

She'd been tight as an overwound clock all day and regretted setting up a date with Mitch but forced herself to keep it. She didn't even try to kid herself. She was going just to prove that Ty Chandler, Sunny, Alice, even Twilight with its small-town, homey atmosphere hadn't really gotten to her.

Kelly's Restaurant was one dimly lit room with a crowded bar where the rich and not-so-famous mixed with the older yacht club crowd.

Mitch Carson hadn't changed a bit in the two years since she'd last seen him. His favorite topic of discussion was still himself. From the moment she sat down, he talked about his job, his new Beemer, all the money he'd made in spite of the bad market, and his goal to buy a condo on Ka'anapali Beach.

She nodded, half listening, making the appropriate responses, silently planning what she was going to do after she left him.

Tuning out Mitch's endless stream of one-sided conversation, she played with the stem of her wineglass, determined not to have more than one drink. She'd need all her wits about her when she drove back to the Valley later.

Her enthusiasm for being out with Mitch had dwindled completely away before the Caesar salad arrived. Somehow she'd made it through the main course, but she knew she couldn't sit through dessert.

"So, what have you been up to?" He had moved

closer when she wasn't paying attention. His nearness startled her.

The fact that he'd finally asked a personal question astounded her.

"The usual."

"Working on a hot case?" He spread his hand over her thigh, rubbed his thumb against her black silk trousers.

Hot? A flash point ignited the memory of her and Ty in the backseat of his car. Compared to Ty, Mitch didn't know hot from cold.

She shook her head. "Nothing hot. Not at the moment."

"I'm glad we could hook up again." His smile was rehearsed, as wide as it was false. She was sure it worked for the clients and partners down at the brokerage, but it wasn't doing a thing for her tonight. She found herself wondering how she ever thought him attractive enough to sleep with before.

He leaned close, skimming his fingers over the back of her hand.

"Why don't we go to my place and you can tell me all about your not-so-hot case . . . in detail."

She drew her hand out from beneath his, grabbed her purse, and slid across the banquette seat. "I just remembered I have another engagement."

"You're joking, right?" Mitch was out of the booth, tossing bills on the table. "You're not leaving now."

He trailed her to the door.

"Kat, wait a minute." He grabbed her wrist.

She stepped up so close to him that she got a good look at the pores on his nose. "Let go of me, Mitch, or so help me, I'll have you on the ground before you can take another breath."

"What the hell is wrong with you?" Instantly, he let go, but she could see he wasn't happy about it.

She smiled, feeling better than she had in a long, long time.

"I guess you could say I just woke up."

By the time Ty finally pulled up outside Kat's apartment it was around 6:25 and he was brain dead. After reaching the metropolitan area, he had sat in gridlock for nearly two hours before he finally got to Long Beach.

He parked, pulled out a small overnight bag, and headed up the drive to Kat's small duplex. The owner of the larger cottage in front was watering the garden between the two wood-frame structures.

He figured Kat wasn't home when he didn't see her car but he knocked twice anyway before he dug her hide-a-key out of the dirt beneath a half-dead geranium plant in a pot on the front porch.

As he swung the door open, he called her name. It wouldn't do to startle a woman who owned a gun.

The living room looked as if a hurricane had hit. She'd dumped her overnight bag on the floor, tossed mail at the small can beside her desk, but most of it littered the floor.

In the compact bathroom off the kitchen, he saw a few drops of water left on the glass shower door. The heady jasmine scent of her perfume lingered on the air.

He helped himself to a diet soda, and back in the living room again, he checked the desk, looking for a note, a calendar, anything that might give him a clue as to where she'd gone.

A calendar did lay open on top of the desk, but the dates after she'd left for Twilight were all blank.

A side desk drawer gapped open, and as he stood there wondering where she might be, he caught a glimpse of what appeared to be a child's wooden building block sticking out from beneath a stack of papers.

Nudging the pages off, he found himself staring at a frame bordered with wooden baby blocks, chubby teddy bears, and bunny rabbits.

He picked it up, held it right-side up, then upside down, trying to figure out the black-and-white Polaroid inside, until he noticed a digital date and time printed out in the corner. He saw Kat's name and that of a medical group on Kauai and suddenly realized he was looking at a sonogram image.

He checked the date again. Almost five and a half years ago.

He sat down heavily on the pine folding chair near Kat's desk, held the photo between his knees, and stared at it. Absently, he rubbed his thumb back and forth across a teddy bear seated on a wooden block.

She's kept her baby girl's shadowed image all this time.

He remembered everything she'd said last night about Sunny and Alice and the daughter she'd lost, and vowed that he'd give her the child she craved. Hell, he'd give her a houseful.

Reverently, he replaced the photo beneath the stack of papers and left the drawer open, just as he'd found it.

It was almost eight when Kat turned the corner off Fifth Street, still congratulating herself for walking out on Mitch, until she noticed Ty's Land Cruiser parked in front of her place.

Her heart started hammering, her hands tightened on the steering wheel. She kept right on driving, trying to convince herself that she really hadn't experienced a sudden burst of joy when she realized he was there.

She didn't stop until she'd circled the block and

parked where she could still see his car, but where hers wouldn't be visible from inside the apartment.

She sat in the gathering darkness, knowing Ty was a little less than a block away, wanting to go to him in the worst way. She knew if she saw him that she'd have to lie about where she was going tonight and run the risk of him finding out what she was up to. She couldn't go home to change before she drove up to the Valley to stake out Hatcher's place again.

Luckily, she had on black slacks and she always kept an old black sweatshirt and running shoes in the car in case of an emergency.

They'd have to do.

THIRTY-THREE

Sunny's palms were sweating. She was on the streets again, this time racing the law, not time. The red Ferrari would be easy to spot, though she was driving it fast enough to outrun almost anything else on the road. They'd stolen three cars tonight. *Boosted* three cars, she amended.

She had tried to reason with Jamie, but he wouldn't take no for an answer. She argued that racing was easier, reminded him she'd made $2,500 last night, but he was convinced the new connection with the car ring would set them up faster and add to the cash they needed. He didn't have to remind her their need for so much cash was all her fault.

She was never scared racing, but her stomach had hurt all day, right up until she got the Ferrari started. Her heart rate didn't slow until she put the car into gear and was a couple of miles away from the crowded, upscale residential area where she'd picked it up—right where their contact said it would be.

There was a big party going on in one of the mansions along the winding hillside drive where the Ferrari had been parked. Party-goers celebrated inside the house, too busy snorting coke to worry about whether or not their cars were getting ripped off right under their runny noses.

She'd memorized every turn in the route to the warehouse, and the closer she got, the more her confidence came flooding back.

She blew through a red light at a deserted intersection, slid around a corner, and shot into the industrial park where the guys were waiting.

New moon. It was dark as pitch behind the corrugated-metal garage warehouse, uncomfortable as hell atop the shipping container parked beside the back wall.

As she climbed and crouched on a container with a great view into the warehouse through one of the high, open windows, Kat was thankful she'd kept up her workout routine in Twilight. The place was a chop shop, well supplied with automotive tools and a lift. Car exhaust mingled with the odors of grease and gasoline. Heavy rock music pumped from a boom box on a workbench, competing with the scratchy sound of a police scanner.

Jamie Hatcher paced in front of the closed garage door, pausing to listen to the scanner and check his watch every few seconds. From her vantage point, Kat had already seen him open the huge garage door twice to let in two cars, a Porsche Boxster and a Mercedes, one right after the other.

As soon as they were inside, the young drivers jumped out of the cars, slammed the doors. Then the men jubilantly high-fived each other.

The metal warehouse was cavernous; the echo of music, the scanner, and their words bounced off the metal walls, but the sound of their voices carried over the other noise.

"Sunny'll be here, Jamie." The slim Hispanic kid who'd driven in earlier walked over to a stained and rusty refrigerator in one corner of the room and helped himself to a beer. He wasn't one of the guys she'd seen at Hatcher's that first time with Ty.

"So where is she?" Hatcher paced to the door and back.

"Nothing on the scanner." The youngest of the three, a lanky blond in baggy jeans and an oversized T-shirt leaned casually against the silver Porsche he'd driven in. He accepted the beer the other driver handed him and took a long swig, intent on the scanner broadcast.

Twisting away from the window, Kat pulled her cell phone out of her pocket and hit Fred Westberg's number. She prayed he'd answer, thankful when he caught it on the second ring.

She spoke in a near-whisper, though it was impossible for the men inside to hear her over the noise in the warehouse.

"Fred, it's Kat."

"Shoot."

"Jamie Hatcher has two stolen cars in his possession right now and I think he's waiting for more."

"Where?"

"I need a deal first, Frank."

"I told you I'd do everything I can."

"Not good enough."

"You want me to put my job on the line?"

"Nothing less."

She heard him sigh. Tension ratcheted up the knot in her stomach, feeding a rush until he finally agreed. She had no finalized plan for getting Sunny out of this if Fred and the cops didn't show up.

"Okay. Where are you?"

"Nothing goes on the scanner, Fred. They're listening in."

"Got it."

She gave him the address. Before he hung up, he warned, "Stay safe, Vargas."

"Right."

As she shoved her cell phone into her pocket, a car horn sounded one sharp hit and she heard a powerful engine amplified by modified pipes. Turning, she grabbed the bottom of the window frame, pulled herself up, and watched Jamie Hatcher hit the garage door button.

A low, sleek red Ferrari purred into the garage. As the door shut behind it, the driver pulled up alongside the other two cars. The door opened and Sunny stepped out. She tore a black knit stocking cap off her head and tossed it on a nearby workbench. Then she threw the keys at Jamie. He caught them in midair.

"Okay, I delivered. Now I'm out." Sunny glared at him, shoving her hair off her face.

"Are you crazy?"

"You said just one time and that was it."

"So I lied."

"Damn it, Jamie, if Dodge was here—"

"He's not here. I'm running things now."

"Yeah? You're running things right into the ground and all of us into jail. The money we made off parts scams and racing was enough. We don't need to steal cars."

"It wasn't enough and you know it. Thanks to you there's never enough." He crossed the floor, headed toward Sunny.

Even from afar, Kat felt the tension and anger in Jamie's every move as he bore down on Sunny.

But Sunny didn't back down. "I want to go to Alice."

"So you can disappear again?"

"I was coming back, just as soon as I had Alice settled."

He took a menacing step closer. They were nose to nose and still Sunny wasn't willing to give an inch.

"*Were you*, Sunny?"

She nodded. "Yes. Yes, I was." There was such a wistful sadness in her voice that Kat believed her.

"I don't think you would have ever left the kid, but we'll never know for sure now, will we?"

"You *knew* I'd come back. You know why I can't leave yet. Why screw everything up like this?" She shook her head, held out a hand in appeal. "Just let me take Alice to my dad's. I *promise* I'll come back and race every night if I have to. We don't have to do this, Jamie."

My dad.

Kat had never heard Sunny refer to Ty as anything but Chandler. She was stunned to hear Sunny had shown up in Twilight looking for a safe haven for her daughter.

Knowing the girl had been willing to give up Alice in order to keep her out of harm's way made Kat ache for her. Her heart went out to her and made her even more determined to help.

In the cavernous room below, Sunny and Jamie's argument quickly escalated into a shouting match.

"You think I'm stupid enough to let you walk out of here with the kid? As long as I've got her, I've got you. Get over thinking you have a say anymore. I'm running things."

Sunny's face mirrored her disgust. "You aren't *capable* of running this crew. That's why you still need me so bad."

"Just as much as you need us," he shot back.

Kat's hands tightened on the sill when Jamie lashed out and slapped Sunny across the cheek. The girl reeled, but didn't fall. She reached out and slapped him back hard enough to rock him on his feet. Then without a word, she turned and walked across the garage.

"Where are you going, bitch?" Hatcher yelled.

Sunny didn't look back. "Out to cool off, you prick. Don't worry, I can't *walk* back to Hollywood."

The air outside the warehouse was thick with the heavy, greasy smell of a dirty cooking grill. The odor from the twenty-four-hour hamburger and taco stand a block away drifted on the night air. The 101 Freeway was so close that the constant hum of tires against the pavement sounded like the ocean's roar, but only if Sunny closed her eyes, imagined real hard, and didn't inhale.

She opened them and glanced around. Cloaked in darkness, she fought her tears, wondering whether Chandler had given her a second thought after he discovered she'd left. Surely he missed Alice by now.

She reached into the pocket of her jeans and touched the earrings she'd hidden there. She'd fast-handed them and kept them out of sight when Jamie followed her upstairs to gather up some diapers. She didn't want to part with them, but if she got away somehow, she could pawn them and get a one-way ticket out of L.A.

As she fingered the opals, she pictured the old house on the point, Ty and R.J., and even the great-grandmother she had never known.

Tears stung her eyes and she cursed. Blinking hard, she looked up at the night sky. No stars here. Too much light, too much smog and overcast. The glow of streetlights glistened off razor wire wrapped around the fence behind the salvage shop next door. Twenty-first-century starlight. Shining, deadly bands of sharpened steel.

She closed her eyes, pictured Alice's sweet angel face, the way her baby's smile reflected Dodge's.

Why did you have to crash that night?

If he were still here, there'd be no worries. She

wouldn't have to make life-or-death decisions. It was too much for her. Way too much.

Now Jamie was using Alice as a pawn.

I'll never get out.

She took a deep breath, wishing she didn't have to go back inside, when she heard the soft scrape of a step against the paved parking lot. Jamie had followed her.

Her heartbeat accelerated. Away from the others, there was no telling what he'd do.

Before she could turn around, someone grabbed her from behind. A gloved hand covered her mouth.

Her first reaction was to struggle, but she couldn't break the intense hold.

"Sunny!" It was a woman's voice in her ear, not Jamie's. The low warning came with a shake. Sunny felt the softness of a woman's body against her back. She fought harder.

"I can get you out of this if you'll hold still and *listen.*"

Sunny thought she recognized Kat's voice and tried to glance over her shoulder, but she was pinned tight. She tried nodding okay. Anything to get Kat to ease up.

"You won't call out?"

She shook her head no and Kat slowly uncovered her mouth but didn't let her go.

"The police are on the way," Kat whispered.

"No!"

The hand was back across her mouth, hurting her bruised cheek. Kat whispered against her ear, "All you have to do is testify against them and you'll be okay. You'll be out of it."

Sunny struggled. The woman had no idea what was at stake here. She didn't understand. Sunny tried to wriggle free.

"I can get you out of this."

As if Kat somehow knew. As if God actually answered prayers.

Fat chance.

"Where's Alice?" Kat whispered, and eased her hand away from Sunny's lips.

"At a motel on Sepulveda. Callie and Butch are with her."

"Then let's go get her. Before the police get here. Before all this comes down."

Sunny glanced at the warehouse a few feet away. If Jamie found out about the police, if he had time to get a call off to Butch, no telling where Butch would take Alice, or what might happen.

Sunny nodded. Her heart was beating so hard it was ringing in her ears. She thought for a second that she might faint. If Kat was here, then Chandler couldn't be far behind. Maybe he was waiting in the car. Surely they'd both come after her, just like that first time. Kat and her dad.

He does care.

He'd cared enough to find them again. Maybe this time it would all work out. Maybe things would be just fine.

She glanced back at the warehouse. Acid Folk Display was rocking on the boom box. The police scanner hummed steadily beneath the heavy folk-rock. Her stomach knotted. She had to take a deep breath before she could get a word out.

Kat's hand was still wrapped around her arm.

"Let's go," Sunny whispered. "Now."

Let's go before I change my mind.

THIRTY-FOUR

Nothing Sunny had ever done, not racing, not meeting Ty Chandler for the first time, or walking into the E.R. the night Dodge crashed—not even stealing the Ferrari tonight—unnerved her as much as the idea that Alice's safety depended entirely on her playing her part.

"You know what to do." Kat wasn't asking. She made it sound as if she had faith in her, as if she was sure there would be no problem.

They waited for the police in Kat's car in the motel parking lot, directly across from the room where Butch was guarding Alice.

Though Sunny hadn't taken her eyes off the door, she could feel Kat staring at her profile through the darkness.

"Why isn't Chandler here?" She couldn't stop shaking.

"He doesn't know I'm here. I wasn't sure I'd find you, so I didn't tell him."

"Is he pissed?"

"He's worried sick."

Sunny swallowed the tears choking her, rubbed her eyes, and wondered what was happening to Jamie and the others.

On the drive over from the warehouse, they'd passed

a convoy of police black-and-whites headed in the opposite direction. No flashing lights, no sirens.

Kat told her that she'd alerted her contact at L.A.P.D. to the fact that Jamie had a scanner on. As she drove, she explained the situation. All Sunny had to do was testify in court and provide the D.A. with information about the insurance scams and anything she knew about the auto theft.

"All you have to do . . ."

Kat made it sound so easy. Just get up there on the stand, and in exchange for her freedom betray everyone she knew—anyone who ever meant anything to her. Rat on the only family she'd ever had, for the chance to see her daughter grow up. For a life with Alice.

"As soon as the police get here, you'll be going in," Kat reminded her. She'd been talking to someone named Fred on her cell phone, working out the details. "Leave the door unlocked when you walk in. Leave it open if you can."

"Butch will ask about Jamie."

Kat nodded. "Right. You know what to say. Give the police time to get in position. Stay calm, stay cool. Just get in, grab Alice, and get out."

She was to tell Butch she was going out to the soda machine. She'd have Alice in her arms. She didn't have a car, so he wouldn't have to worry about her taking off on foot. The only catch was that she was supposed to have come back with Jamie.

"What if he doesn't let me out?" Her palms were sweating. She wiped them on the knees of her jeans. Getting behind the wheel of a car and hitting over a hundred miles an hour was a thousand times easier than this.

"You just keep that door open and be ready to run with Alice."

Kat's contact had told her the raid at the warehouse had gone off fast and easy. No one had been hurt. They'd taken Jamie and the others by complete surprise. Sunny had begged Kat to get Alice out without police help, but Kat refused. She was adamant about having backup.

The longer they sat, the more the jitters took over, until Sunny thought she was going to crawl out of her skin.

Visions of film shoot-outs flashed through her mind, one worse than another. She wanted Alice out of the motel room *before* the police arrived, before Butch caught on to what was going down and did something desperate.

All they needed was for him to look out the door and notice anything he thought was suspicious in the parking lot. Who knew what he'd do?

Sunny took a deep breath, and on impulse, without a word of warning, hit the door handle and jumped out.

"Sunny!" Kat hissed.

Sunny took long strides to quickly eat up the parking lot, until she was almost jogging. She'd intended to knock, but ended up pounding on the motel room door. The sound echoed the frantic beat of her heart.

It was Callie, not Butch, who cracked the door open. Sunny prayed Kat wasn't right behind her. She couldn't risk turning around to find out.

"It's me," Sunny whispered, then added a bit louder, "let me in."

Callie opened the door barely enough for her to slip in. The television was blaring, tuned to *CSI: Crime Scene Investigation*. Marg Helgenberger was watching someone dissect a cadaver. Across the room, French Fry was wide-awake, balanced on Butch's knee. As soon as she saw Sunny, she started clapping and laughing.

Sunny knew the guys loved French Fry, but Butch, like the rest of them, was totally loyal to Jamie. They'd been raised at River Ridge, taught not to question leadership. They shared and shared alike.

Butch, more than any of the others, was a follower. He never questioned Jamie, just as he'd never questioned Dodge.

Sunny stepped inside, immediately started talking, and pushed the door almost shut. As Sunny crossed the room toward Butch and French Fry, Callie walked back to the bed and flopped down on her stomach to watch television.

"So, how's my little French Fry?" Sunny reached for Alice, who mirrored her, laughing joyously.

It wasn't until Butch handed Alice over that Sunny noticed the gun lying on the Formica phone table beside him. She forced herself to look into Butch's eyes and casually smiled. She *had* to convince him nothing was wrong.

"Where's Jamie?" He glanced at the door.

"He got hung up. I talked him into sending me back in a cab." It was a lame excuse, but the only one she and Kat could come up with.

"Alone?" Butch was the least likely of any of the guys to jump to conclusions. Leaf was always as nervous and twitchie as Jamie was suspicious. She was lucky she was dealing with Butch.

"Sure." She shrugged it off as no big deal and nuzzled Alice's neck, inhaled the clean baby powder scent, closed her eyes, and promised herself everything would be all right. That they'd make it out alive.

"He said he'd call me when you two started back." Butch slowly pushed away from the chair and stood up, his thick forehead furrowed into deep lines. He swung his head toward the door. Sunny held her breath.

"He changed his mind when they had trouble with the Mercedes. The ignition is touchy." Her arms tightened around Alice and she turned toward the door. "I'm thirsty. I'm going down to the soda machine."

"Hang on. I have to give him a call."

"I'm thirsty, Butch. I'll be right back. Want a Pepsi? How about you, Callie?" She started walking.

She felt Butch's hand on her shoulder. Nothing forceful or threatening, just a gesture meant to make her wait. She glanced over her shoulder, saw him reach for his front pocket, for his cell phone. He let her go.

"Tell Jamie to hurry back. I'm hungry. Ask him if we can all go get something to eat." Sunny turned around again. She took three steps toward the door.

A couple more feet and we'll be outside.

A few more inches and we'll be outside.

She couldn't think of anything but getting Alice out.

"Hang on, wouldja? He's not answering." Butch sounded more frustrated than angry.

When Sunny's hand hit the doorknob, she didn't look back.

Kat crouched to the right of the door with her .380 in her hands, barrel pointed at the ground. With the television blaring, she barely heard what Sunny was saying, but snippets of the conversation sounded like the girl was sticking to the scenario they'd rehearsed in the car. If only she'd waited for the police.

Suddenly Kat heard a thick male voice say, "Hang on, wouldja?"

The door whipped open. Sunny and Alice stepped into view. Sunny's eyes were wide and wild, huge pools of fear in a face as pale as moonlight.

Kat's heartbeats tripled. She caught a glimpse of the number on the motel door, the same as in Seal Beach.

Not a very good sign.

"Damn it," the man inside yelled. "Get back in here, Sunny."

Alice recognized Kat and squealed with delight. Kat's heart contracted. Sunny nearly tripped. Her face registered alarm. Kat flicked her head toward the dark parking lot, indicating that Sunny should take off.

"He's got a gun," Sunny whispered before she started running toward the street.

"Shit," Kat mumbled. She expected the man inside to run out firing. She took a deep breath, and with her weapon in position, realized she could see most of the room reflected in a mirror on a wall inside.

The tall, heavyset youth across the room was reaching for a gun on a phone table. She took another deep breath and stepped into the open doorway.

"Leave it. Raise your hands or I'll shoot." She trained her weapon on him, held it steady. Foolishly, he grabbed the gun and turned.

They fired simultaneously. A magnified explosion and an unbridled scream filled the small room.

Sunny heard the gunshots, heard Callie's hysterical nonstop screams, put her head down, and kept running. If she'd been alone, she'd have gone back, but not with Alice in her arms. There was no way she would ever put her baby's life in Jamie's hands again, no matter what that decision meant for the future.

She hadn't reached the end of the driveway when an unmarked police unit turned into the lot. A black-and-white pulled up to the curb outside the motel office. Inside, the night manager was staring out the window, with a phone to his ear.

A tall, rumpled, tired-eyed detective, probably overworked and underpaid, stepped out of the unmarked car and flashed his badge, distracted by Callie's screams.

"Kat—" Sunny began.

He didn't bother to question her. He signaled to one of the uniformed officers to stay with her, pulled his weapon, and bolted toward the room with the light and screams streaming out. His partner and a uniform were hot on his heels.

Sunny was quaking so hard she was afraid she'd drop Alice. The patrol officer escorted her to the police car, moving her swiftly along. He put her in the backseat without taking his eyes off the motel room, then radioed for backup.

Sunny stared through the window, watching the silhouettes of the two detectives as they shifted around inside the motel room. Finally one of them came jogging back to the car, radio in hand.

He was calling for ambulances. Two gunshot victims were down.

By one-thirty in the morning, Ty had convinced himself Kat wasn't out looking for Sunny, but that she was out with someone.

The hint of her perfume lingered in the bathroom when he'd first come back. Her makeup kit was dumped out on the vanity in the bathroom.

Who wears perfume and makeup to a stakeout?

He had no hold on her. They'd made no promises. She'd been straight with him from the very beginning. Last night he'd found out why she was so terrified to let go and fall in love.

After the way it all happened last night, he felt like a heel.

He wanted to see her, to talk to her about what she'd

told him, help her in any way he could. He knew damn well she cared about him, and about the girls.

Why else would she have stopped by Selma's after what happened to ask about Sunny?

He called home every hour on the hour but R.J. still hadn't heard from Sunny. He paced to the living room window and stared out into the night. The quiet residential street was dark and deserted. The lights in the main house in front of her duplex bungalow had gone out a long time ago.

Worried and frustrated, he snapped off the muted television. There was nothing on this late but old reruns and bad infomercials, and he didn't need any diet supplements or miracle wrinkle creams.

What he really needed was to get the hell out of here and get a room someplace. After what happened last night in Twilight, Kat probably never wanted to see him again anyway. It would be better if she didn't come back and find him here.

Then he thought about the framed sonogram in the drawer and about everything she had said about the loss of her child and how it still affected her.

There was a world of hurt inside Kat, and he wanted a chance to love her, to prove to her that not all men were like Justin Parker. To prove to her that when he gave his heart, he wanted it to be for keeps.

His overnight bag was still in the car. There wasn't anything to clear out except himself.

He was about to walk out the front door when his cell phone rang, shattering the silence, startling him. Hoping it was R.J., he slipped it out, fumbled flipping it open. He didn't recognize the caller's number.

"Hello?"

At first all he heard in response was a choking sound, then a quick indrawn breath.

"Chan . . . Chandler?" It was Sunny. Crying into the phone.

His gut tightened and sent his heart to his throat. "Where are you? Is Alice all right? Are *you* all right?"

"Kat . . . Kat's been shot. Can you come down here?"

"What do you mean *shot*? Where are you? How's Alice?"

"Alice is okay. Don't worry. Just come to Van Nuys. The hospital, on Sepulveda."

"I'll be right there."

"I didn't know . . . who else to call. I'm sorry. I'm so sorry."

"How is Kat? What happened?"

"I don't know. They won't let me see her."

There was no time to waste talking.

"I'm on the way."

THIRTY-FIVE

The overhead lights in the hospital corridor were painfully bright, stark and raw as the sanitized white walls and linoleum floor.

Sunny leaned against the wall outside Kat's room, arms crossed, empty to her soul. Child Protective Services had taken Alice, screaming and kicking, pulled her baby from her arms in the hospital waiting area on the first floor.

Down the hall, Kat's friend, Detective Fred Westberg, spoke with two plainclothes officers. Every so often one of them would glance at her, catch her eye, and turn away, as if she were no more than a speck on the wall.

She wiped another tear from her cheek, hating to let anyone see her cry, but no matter how hard she tried, she couldn't seem to stop. Not since they'd taken Alice.

She wanted Alice back, she wanted Dodge back, she wanted everything to be all right, but nothing would ever be the same again.

She couldn't get the shooting out of her head. The scene in the motel parking lot played itself over and over like a bad rerun.

The police had been all over the place within minutes. Ambulances arrived, sirens blaring, lights flashing. A crowd had gathered on the sidewalk outside the motel.

Curious Looky Lous stared into the patrol car at her and Alice. Mobile television crews were there in an instant.

Worse yet, the patrolman guarding them wouldn't tell her anything. She had no idea if Kat and Butch were still alive. If it hadn't been for Kat's detective friend taking her into his custody, letting her call Ty, she would have already been booked at County.

Detective Westberg explained that Alice would have to be placed in protective custody. No amount of pleading helped. He was already bending the rules by bringing her along with him to the hospital to wait for her dad to show up.

She hadn't informed Westberg that Chandler lived three hours away.

She shivered and shoved away from the wall as she heard the bell ring at the bank of elevators. When Chandler stepped out she was shocked.

She fought for breath, tried to move, but her throat was choked with tears. His long strides ate up the distance between them. Her breath hitched when she saw the worry in his eyes.

When he was a yard away, he opened his arms, and she rushed into them, felt them close around her as he held her tight and rocked back and forth. She broke down and cried like Alice, cried like a baby in her father's arms.

She had been responsible for her mom as long as she could remember, almost as if she were the grown-up, not Amy. For years she'd taken care of herself. Dodge had tried to keep everything going, to find ways to provide for all of them, but then he was gone and everything fell on her and Jamie.

She had Alice to protect and care for—

"Sunny? Sunny, shh." Ty was rubbing her back, patting her, comforting her the way he did Alice.

If I have to go to jail for what I've done, then he'll be there for Alice. He'll raise her right.

She wished she could hide her face against his shirt-front forever and pretend she was a child with her whole life ahead of her, wished she could start over with Ty there to hold her hand and guide her steps, the way he did for Alice.

"Sunny, what happened? Where's Alice? Where's Kat? They wouldn't give me any information downstairs."

She stepped back, wiped her face with both hands, finally met his eyes. He rested his hand on her shoulder, as if afraid to break the connection, as if he hated to let go.

She asked, "How did you get here so *fast*?"

She thought he'd been in Twilight.

"I was already at Kat's place in Long Beach, waiting for her to come home. What in the hell happened?"

She could see how afraid he was for Kat. He was practically holding his breath, expecting the worst.

Sunny glanced toward Kat's room. "They won't let me see her. She . . . she was wounded. A . . . a head wound."

Ty's hand tightened on her shoulder as he looked past her. Sunny turned, saw the bald detective walking toward them.

"Mr. Chandler?" The man extended his hand, gave Ty a quick once-over. "I'm Detective Fred Westberg of the L.A.P.D. I'm also a friend of Kat Vargas's."

"How is she?"

"Still unconscious. A bullet grazed her temple, but according to the doctors, it didn't do any critical damage. They're concerned about her being out this long, though. It's a waiting game at this point."

"I need to see her. Now."

"Does she have any family we can contact? I tried to

get ahold of Jake Montgomery, but I haven't been able to reach him."

"All of her family is in Hawaii. Jake Montgomery is in New Mexico on vacation." He looked at Sunny, included her. "We're all she's got."

The detective didn't look impressed, but he seemed to weigh Chandler's concern as he shoved his hands into his baggy trousers.

"Go on in." Then Westberg nodded at Sunny. "She waits out here."

"She's my daughter."

"I gathered."

"Where's my granddaughter?"

"With Child Protective Services until they can find suitable care."

Sunny watched her father's expression darken. "*I'm* suitable care. How soon can I pick her up?"

"She's in good hands. As soon as they can run a background check on you, you'll probably be allowed temporary guardianship."

"Why was she taken from my daughter?"

"Your granddaughter was caught in the middle of a very dangerous situation tonight. Your daughter is in my custody. And Kat's in there alone. I don't want her to wake up by herself. If you aren't going in—"

"What about my daughter? Will you release her to me?"

Sunny bit her lips to stop them from trembling. Chandler wasn't going to walk away.

Only Dodge had ever cared as much.

Then she remembered what Kat had done for her, and started crying again.

"Right now, your daughter is my responsibility," Detective Westberg told Chandler. "She's in a heap of trouble, and if it wasn't for Kat, she'd be behind bars. I gave

Kat my word I'd do everything I can to help the kid out of this jam, so long as she cooperates and testifies about her friends."

Westberg hesitated. He glanced down the hall. The plainclothes men were gone. The uniformed officer who'd accompanied them here was sitting on a chair beside the door to Kat's room.

The detective let go a weary sigh. "How about I see that Sunny gets something to eat down in the cafeteria for now? I'll check back in thirty minutes."

Sunny wanted to protest, to stay with Chandler. She knew how badly he wanted to see Kat, but he was waiting for her cue.

She glanced up at Detective Westberg. The man was Kat's friend, and he had agreed to try to get her out of the mess she was in. It wouldn't help to piss him off.

She nodded to Chandler. "It's okay. I'll see you later."

She thought he'd rush into Kat's room, but when she and the detective reached the elevators, she glanced back down the hall. Chandler was still there, watching her.

Kat hears the sounds first, smells the antiseptic hospital smell. She's in Queen's Hospital, air-vacced earlier from Kauai to Honolulu.

She opens her eyes and her little brother Zachy is there. He lives on Oahu, works as a sound manager for the Don Ho show at the Hilton Rainbow Lagoon.

"Hey, sis." His eyes are red, but he smiles.

"Hey, Zachy." He is the second youngest and takes after Pop the most. With his huge brown eyes and curly lashes, he's been all the Vargas girls' real-life doll since his infancy. They spoil him rotten. Zachy has never faced anything like this alone.

He looks so nervous and frightened for her that she is

sorry he's ended up in the wrong place at the wrong time.

He's trying hard to keep it together. It's his duty to represent the family until reinforcements arrive.

It takes a moment before she notices the emptiness inside.

Her mouth is dry, but she manages to speak.

"The baby?"

Zachy looks everywhere but at her. "Mom and Pop are taking the first plane from Kauai."

"Zachy . . ." She knows, but has to hear him say it so it's real.

"The doctors say it's a miracle you're alive. Your pelvis is cracked. Your car is totaled."

She wants to scream Screw the car! *She wants to grab him, shake him so that he will say the words she knows are coming.*

"What about the baby?" *She sees the immeasurable pity in his eyes.*

"She's gone, sis. The baby's gone." An alligator tear starts down his smooth brown cheek, spikes the end of his lower lashes.

"Where did they take her?"

He tries to hold her. She struggles in his arms. What she needs he can't give. She needs to touch, to hold her little girl, to prove to herself that the baby has been more than a dream.

She fights him, tries to break free.

"Kat! Kat, it's okay. You're okay. Wake up."

Sound filtered through the darkness. Someone was calling her name. She struggled, tried to move her head, to open her eyes. Finally, there was light behind her eyelids. She tried to blink.

"Kat. Open your eyes."

I'm trying.

Didn't he know her head hurt like a son of a bitch?

Finally, she opened her eyes, but the world was out of focus. Someone was holding her hand.

Zachy?

"Zachy?"

"No, Kat. It's Ty."

Panicked, she blinked. Her eyes slowly focused. A television was hanging on the wall beyond the foot of the bed. Beside her, a rolling tray with a green plastic water jug and cup. An I.V. bag and line.

Her heart started pounding. Somewhere behind her a beeping sound intensified with her heartbeat.

"Kat?"

Ty, not Zachy, was holding her tight, not enough to hurt, but enough to keep her from hurting herself. He was on the bed, sitting beside her, watching her closely.

"Ty? How long have I been out? How did you get here?"

"A couple of hours, I think. I was already in town. At your place."

"At your place."

Slowly it all started coming back. She remembered seeing his car parked outside her house, remembered leaving without talking to him. She went to the Valley, trailing Hatcher. Had to find Sunny. Help her get away.

"Sunny?" Frantically, she tried to sit up. "Where's Sunny? Is she all right? Where's Alice? Don't let them hurt Alice."

He slipped his arms out from around her but held on to her hand. "Sunny's downstairs in the cafeteria with your friend Westberg. Child Protective Services has Alice. How do you feel?"

"Okay, except for my head. How should I feel?"

"The doctors say you'll be just fine." His expression

spoke volumes. He wanted details. "You're lucky you have your head."

"Did Fred tell you what happened?"

"No time. I wanted to be with you." He leaned over and kissed her gently on the cheek. "Why didn't you tell me you were searching for Sunny?"

"I wasn't sure I'd find her. I didn't know if she had even come back down here."

"You went and got yourself shot. Again."

She shrugged, and then winced, and tried to smile. "I guess I'm a slow learner."

"Maybe you should give this up." He rubbed her hand. "Detective Westberg said something about Sunny having to testify in order to stay out of jail."

Kat started to nod, winced at the pain, and held her head perfectly still.

"She's going to have to testify against her pals from River Ridge. If she doesn't, there's not much we can do for her. They were into street racing, insurance fraud. Tonight they graduated into grand theft auto."

"Shit." He rubbed his eyes, shook his head. "Sunny was part of it?"

"She was their best driver, so she says, and I don't doubt her."

"Is that why she left Twilight? To steal cars?"

"Actually, she intended to come back all along, but she was planning on leaving Alice behind with you."

"With me?"

"She went to Twilight hoping you'd provide a stable home for Alice. For some reason, she feels obligated to these guys and she can't walk away. She wanted Alice out of it, but Jamie Hatcher found her before she could leave town on her own. He forced her to come back and was holding Alice as leverage, to make certain Sunny danced to his tune. He was arrested tonight, along with the rest of them."

"Good. Then he's where I can't get my hands on him."

"I think I shot one of them." Her memory came to her in bits and pieces, putting itself together like a patchwork quilt.

"I'm glad."

"I'm not." She closed her eyes, tried to remember everything. Only bits and pieces came back. A heavyset youth whipping around with a gun in his hand. Both of them firing. The sound of a girl screaming. Scalding pain.

"Oh, Ty . . ." She closed her eyes. "Did I kill him?" She knew she was in the wrong business when she realized she couldn't live with herself if she had.

"I don't know, but I'll find out."

Afraid he was going to walk out, she tightened her grip on his hand. "Don't leave me yet. I need you."

He smiled and leaned over to gently press a kiss upon her lips. "You must be hurt a lot worse than the doctor thinks if you'll finally admit you need me."

As she lay there looking up into his eyes, she realized she *did* need him, far more than she'd been willing to admit. She watched him study the bandage on the side of her head.

"Why didn't you let the police handle things, Kat?"

"I wanted to make sure Sunny would cooperate first. If I'd turned this over to the police, she'd be in jail right now."

She pieced together everything that had happened, how she and Sunny had planned everything out, how they waited for the police, until Sunny panicked and ran into the motel.

"At that point, I wasn't sure if she was going to go

along with the plan or if she'd get scared, grab Alice, and disappear."

One look at Ty's anguished expression kept her from giving him all the details. What mattered was that Alice was safe, that Sunny was with Fred Westberg, and that things might eventually work out for Ty's daughter.

"I wanted to find your daughter for you," she said, trying to smile through her pain.

"I should have been with you."

"Oh, sure. We'd probably have ended up in a double room in this place."

"Why'd you do it, Kat?"

She felt as if she was standing on the edge of a deep, dark pool, ready to dive, not knowing if there were rocks below the surface. She took a deep breath and plunged in.

"I know I can never, ever bring my little girl back, but I could try to save yours. I've seen how much you care, how much Sunny and Alice mean to you. I wanted to give them back to you. I had to try."

THIRTY-SIX

The nurse finally convinced Ty that Kat would sleep for hours. He left his cell-phone number at the nurses' station and took the elevator down to the cafeteria, where he found Sunny and Detective Westberg in a back booth, staring at each other in silent regard over mugs of coffee.

There was only a handful of staff members in the huge room permeated with the smell of coffee and toast. Ty's stomach rumbled, reminding him he hadn't eaten since three in the afternoon. He walked over to the booth and nodded to the detective.

Westberg looked a lot like Yogi Bear in a rumpled tweed sports coat, tie, and khakis, but what the man lacked in style, he made up for in concern.

"How's Kat?"

"She came to and she's sleeping naturally now. The prognosis is great."

"Thank God." The detective glanced over at Sunny. She hadn't yet acknowledged Ty's presence. Instead, she concentrated on the tabletop. "I spoke to the D.A.'s office. I'm putting your daughter in your hands until eight in the morning. I'm sure I don't have to tell you what it'll mean if she skips."

"Don't worry. She's not going anywhere." Ty couldn't

be a hundred percent certain of anything anymore, except that he wasn't about to let Sunny out of his sight.

The two men shook hands after a weary Westberg gave him instructions as to where they were to show up in the morning, then he walked away without a word to Sunny.

Ty slid into the seat that Westberg just vacated. He leaned forward, wishing he knew what to say. Six weeks ago if anyone told him he'd be in this situation right now, he'd have called them crazy.

Sunny looked forlorn and isolated, with her hands clenched, fingers laced together. She leaned forward, elbows on the table, her eyes red and swollen from crying.

The void of so many lost years yawned between them. He felt totally inept.

"How are you doing, Sunny?"

Her head snapped up. Her face was streaked with dark smears of mascara and liner, her lashes damp.

"How do you *think* I'm doing, Chandler? I'm one step away from jail, my kid's locked up in Child Protective Services, and my whole life just crumbled around me. I'm just fricking fine."

"We'll have Alice back tomorrow."

"You have no clue how things really work, do you?" She stared back at him in disbelief. "You think they're just going to hand her over to you? It may take weeks."

"I don't intend to let it take that long. I'll bribe someone if I have to." He'd hire a lawyer, talk to a judge. Whatever it took.

"Yeah? Well, good luck."

She was older than her years, with no reason to trust the system. For the first time he saw all the raw hopelessness in her eyes and read in them everything she'd suffered. He wished he could shoulder her pain.

"How did you get into this, Sunny?"

She shrugged. "Do you really care?"

"Of course I care. I wouldn't be here if I didn't."

One corner of her lips tilted. "Yeah, right. You're here because of Kat." She leaned back against the booth seat and wiped her eyes with the cuff of her sleeve.

He lowered his voice but kept his tone firm.

"Yes, but I'm also here for you. I want to hear your side of this, Sunny."

As she stared at her hands again, another tear plopped on the table.

"It's a long story." She wiped her nose on her sleeve.

He handed her a napkin from the chrome dispenser on the table. "Let me get a cup of coffee, and then you can tell me everything."

Sunny watched him walk over to the counter, grab two ceramic mugs, and fill them with coffee. He bought two bagels and cream cheese, and when he got back pushed a plate at her.

"Eat," he told her. "And talk."

Eating was impossible. Talking sounded easier. She had no idea where to start, so she started at the beginning.

"Five years ago, we all found each other again, all the River Ridge kids, just the way we'd been trained to. We left messages at the Outreach Mission in Hollywood—Dodge, Leaf, Jamie, Butch, a few others. Leaf brought Callie. She was a runaway.

"We did some panhandling. The guys did odd jobs. They'd all been taught trades. Dodge was a natural with car engines. He could get anything to run. He got a job at a high-performance auto parts shop and came into contact with a lot of street racers. He started going to the races, checking things out. Pretty soon he bought an old Honda, fixed it up, started racing. Before long he was winning everything.

"He taught me to drive when I was fifteen and took me to races with him. I loved it. In a few months, I was better than Dodge. I had no fear. He always worried about crashing. He was only in it for the money. Me? I was in it for the rush. I get high racing.

"One thing led to another and pretty soon we were making more money racing a couple nights a week than at anything else. Leaf was into tech stuff, burning CDs, filming the races, and selling copies on the Net.

"The automotive guys Dodge worked for approached us about an insurance scam. They wanted us to get guys to report their cars as stolen, and strip the parts. They sold the parts and ordered more with the insurance money they collected. Everyone got a percentage; the shop marked up the appraisals and got a cut of that, too. Eventually the cars were 'found' and the parts replaced."

Sunny waited for him to react. Chandler hadn't interrupted once, nor had he said a single word the whole time she'd been talking. His expression was blank. If he was judging her, he didn't let it show. He wiped his hands on a paper napkin and pushed it aside.

"Did you think it would last forever? That you wouldn't get caught?"

She shrugged and answered truthfully. "In the beginning, we never thought about it much. We lived day to day. After a while we got a better apartment, bought more high-tech computer equipment, had better cars. Life was great. I was bringing in more money racing than Dodge. He was running the insurance scams at quite a few shops.

"Dodge and I got married after I had Alice, but we never told the other guys. We just went down to the courthouse and did it. Everyone would have asked a lot of questions. We were taught the River Ridge group was all the family we needed—but Dodge and I wanted more for Alice. We wanted her to be part of a real family, with both a mom and a dad. The kind we never had, you know? Like the kids on TV."

"But then Dodge was killed," he said.

She glanced down at the table, avoiding the intensity of his gaze. "The night he crashed, he was winning big. He was so far ahead of the other car that the spectators had no idea he was so close to the finish line. Some idiot pulled away from the curb, right in front of Dodge. . . ."

She'd been waiting at the finish line. She'd never forget the sound, like a banshee's scream, metal tearing across metal, sparks flying above the pavement as the force of Dodge's car dragged the other one down the street.

Until that night, she had no idea that blood actually had a scent. She could still smell the blood and grease, the blood mixed with oil on the asphalt.

"Dodge died, and you became the main breadwinner."

She drew a long, shuddering breath. Ty's attention hadn't wavered. It was almost three in the morning but he was wide awake.

Time and time again over the last few weeks, he'd told her he was trying to be a father to her, but she had no idea how he was going to react to what she was about to tell him.

She had nowhere else to turn.

She threaded her fingers together in her lap. "Actually, Dodge didn't die that night. Dodge is still alive. He's in a convalescent home in the Valley. On life support. He never woke up after the race."

He was stunned. His face revealed his shock. Finally, he asked, "Is there any hope of recovery?"

It was the question everyone had been asking her for months. She and Jamie argued day after day about Dodge. It was always the same fight.

"We can't do this forever, Sunny. The doctors say he's never going to get better."

"I'm not giving up hope. I can't."

"You're crazy. He's gone already. He's brain-dead. Let him go."

"He's not dead. *His heart is still beating."*

"Because machines are keeping him alive. He might as well be dead. This is sick. Get over it. Move on."

Now, bone-tired, she sighed, watched her hand shake as she reached for the coffee mug, hated the show of weakness. She had to be strong. She had to keep it together so they'd give Alice back, if not to her, then to Chandler.

She took a sip of coffee before she finally answered.

"The doctors say there's no hope. That he's brain-dead. I'm his wife. They left it up to me to . . . to . . ."

"End life support," he finished for her.

She pressed her lips together, jammed a fist against them until she had herself somewhat under control.

"None of us has any insurance. Alice is covered by the state, but Dodge, he . . . I wanted him in a good place. His hospital bills are unbelievable. I couldn't walk away from racing or there wouldn't be enough. Jamie took over running the insurance scam. Butch and Leaf work the website and races. So does Callie, when she isn't baby-sitting for me. But after the accident, there was never enough. So Jamie got hooked up with this car guy. . . ."

"What kind of car guy?"

"He calls himself an exporter. He was going to pay us

to boost cars every so often. Our trial run was last night."

"Boost?"

"Steal. Heist. That's what really got me scared for Alice. When Jamie was planning this, all I could think was, what would happen to her if we got busted? And I knew. I knew she'd end up in foster care, just like I did after the Feds busted River Ridge. I didn't know what I was going to do, until you showed up. It was like a miracle.

"I decided to slip up to Twilight, check out the situation. If you were for real, then I hoped you'd want Alice, too. If you were an okay guy, I planned on leaving her there, where she'd be safe. I walked out of the apartment, took the bus, and left the guys without telling them where I was going.

"You turned out to be perfect. All those books you bought about how to raise kids. All that time you spent helping me find a job, talking about me going back to school. The way you took to Alice, baby-sitting and all that. Getting to know her. You're being so great only made it worse.

"I kept telling myself to go back to L.A., but I just . . . I couldn't leave her."

"I take it Jamie came after you?"

"One night Callie was watching *Twilight Zone* and suddenly remembered the name of the town, but she couldn't remember your name. The place is so damn small that Jamie found me within an hour of driving into Twilight.

"He was running out of cash and said they needed me, that I had to get back in the scene right away. He followed me back to your house. He wanted me to bring the Camry to L.A. and let them strip it for parts, but I told him to go screw himself. When we got back to

L.A., he had Butch watch every move I made. Alice was guarded twenty-four–seven to make sure I didn't skip out again.

"I tried to convince him I hadn't really left them for good, that I couldn't because of Dodge. I keep hoping there might be a chance, you know? Some miracle that his brain will heal itself and Alice can grow up with her dad around."

Even through her tears, she was aware that Ty had pushed away his coffee mug. When he abruptly stood, she was afraid he'd heard enough. Who could blame him?

She wiped her tears on the back of her sleeve, and noticed that he hadn't walked away. He was sliding into the booth beside her. Before she knew it, he wrapped his arm around her, and all the tension and fear she'd carried around for so long started to crumble. She began sobbing into her hands.

She had no idea how long she sat there crying. She wasn't aware of the passage of time, only that she wasn't alone anymore. Her dad was holding her. Her dad was patting her shoulder, murmuring that things would be all right.

She wanted to believe him so badly that she cried even harder.

Finally, when she was spent, he picked up a napkin, put his hand beneath her chin, and tilted her face up so he could wipe her eyes.

For Sunny's sake, Ty wanted to wish it all away, to magically transport her back to her childhood and let her start her whole life over, this time with him there watching out for her.

She'd survived heartache and burdens that would have crushed many adults, and yet she had gone on. She had shouldered the responsibilities, along with the pain, and had fought to hold on to her child.

His heart ached for her. Now he was in deep, uncharted water. He had no clue what to do or say to Sunny. There was only one thing he knew for certain—he'd never abandon her.

Not when she needed him most.

"I'll do everything I can to get Alice back right away. Things are going to be tough for a while, but I'll be with you every step of the way."

"Really?" She snuffled against the cuff of her sweater, then looked at him through swollen eyes.

She didn't trust him enough to know that he meant every damn word, and that hurt.

"Really. As long as you truly do want to turn things around and you testify against the others. I know how hard that'll be on you."

"I'm *not* changing my mind."

"I know what's ahead of you won't be easy, Sunny. None of it. I'll be the first to admit I don't have a clue what I'm doing, but I'm trying. R.J.'s dad was like a father to me. So was my grandpa. They're the ones I'm trying to emulate, the men I looked up to as a kid."

"You're doing okay," she sniffed. "I haven't exactly had much practice being a daughter, either."

He wanted a real father-daughter relationship, the kind that inspired the lines of sappy greeting cards and put tears in a man's eyes when he walked his little girl down the aisle.

He wanted a bond between them that would never be broken, the kind of closeness he'd always envied R.J. and his father—hours spent together, shared hobbies, laughter, joy, and even tears.

And he wanted Kat in their lives to make his world complete.

Because of Kat, they would have a second chance. Over and over he silently thanked her for risking her life to save Sunny and Alice's future, for giving him back his girls.

She might not be able to admit she loved him yet, but now he knew for certain that she did. Tonight was a new beginning. Tonight they'd all started down a new road together.

One step at a time, he told himself. *One step at a time.*

"Thanks, Chandler," Sunny whispered.

He tightened his arm around her shoulder. "Hey, that's what dads are for."

THIRTY-SEVEN

Three days later, Kat was dressed and sitting on her hospital bed waiting for Ty to pick her up. Fred Westberg walked in as her doctor walked out with the release order.

The detective paced to the bank of windows overlooking the city, gazed out, and jingled the change in his pocket.

"You sure you don't need a ride home?" His bedside manner was in need of polishing. He looked like he'd rather be anywhere else.

"Positive. Ty's on the way."

"You sure you're okay?"

"Don't I look it?" One side of her face was bruised and swollen, the graze stitched closed and covered with a small bandage.

They'd shaved her head, but only on the injured side, so she looked like a split personality—one half punk rocker.

"How's the kid I shot?" Her gaze dropped to her hand where the puckered scar remained.

"He lost two fingers. You shot the gun out of his hand."

"I was hoping—"

"He would have killed you if you'd been a fraction of

a second later. This way he's not up for murder and you're still here. Two fingers are a small price to pay."

She looked at her left hand and thought, *Some scars show, others don't, but they're with you forever.*

"The girl surprised me." It was the first time he'd mentioned Sunny. "She gave a full deposition and seems more than willing to testify and name names. She's out on bail, in her dad's custody." He stopped jingling coins, moved to the foot of the bed. "He's a good guy, Vargas. I can see why you fell for him."

It was bad enough she'd decided not to fight it anymore. Could the whole world tell?

"Who says I've fallen for him?"

"Me."

She walked over to where a small overnight bag occupied the only chair in the room. Ty and Sunny had gone to her apartment and packed a few of the basic necessities for her. She pretended to look through the bag while she gathered her thoughts.

"Maybe I have." She looked over at Fred again. "When I figure it out, you'll be the first to know."

He snorted. "Sure. Whatever."

She wished he'd stop smirking. He looked like he'd just solved the Black Dahlia murder.

"Well, I'll be seeing you, Vargas." He headed for the door.

She hurried after him. He stopped short, turned to face her. Kat took his hand.

"Thanks, Fred. Now *I* owe *you*. Big-time."

"Nah. Let's just say we're even. I still want to hear from you now and then, though."

"You bet."

He was gone, but a few seconds later there was a quick knock on the door and Ty walked in with an orchid lei in his hand and a smile on his face.

His dimples, coupled with the shine in his deep blue eyes, were nearly her undoing as he slipped the lei over her head and kissed her on both cheeks.

She cradled the lei in her hands, let her fingertips caress the blossoms, seeing them through a blur of tears.

A lei was so much a part of life in Hawaii that no milestone ever passed without gifting someone with one. The strands of flowers were an outward expression of love that she always treasured.

"Where did you get this?" she whispered.

"I have my sources."

"You have no idea what this means to me." She couldn't resist raising her lips for a kiss, anxious to taste him, eager for the thrill.

He didn't disappoint her.

When the kiss ended, he walked over to get her bag. "You ready to go?"

"More than ready."

He paused with the overnight bag in his hand and stared out at the cityscape beyond the window.

"What's wrong?" She moved up behind him.

He turned, set the bag down.

"I was hoping you'd agree to a detour, but only if you're up to it."

"I feel great. In fact, I'm up for just about anything."

"Don't tempt me," he said, but he didn't smile.

"What's up?"

"After a lot of soul-searching, Sunny's come to a decision about Dodge." He'd already told her about Sunny's husband's situation, about how he and Sunny had talked long into the night about Dodge, her life with Jamie and the others, the coming trials. "She's been through so much that I think it's better that she doesn't wait. I notified the convalescent hospital, and the doctor is a hundred percent behind her decision."

"What can I do?"

"Sunny wanted me to ask if you would watch Alice while we're there. If you don't want to, we'll understand completely."

"Of course I'll watch her."

"The counselor said there's a private garden where you can wait."

"Are you sure Sunny doesn't mind?"

"It was her idea. She's starting over, Kat. She's grateful for what you did for her—for all of us. I know it's asking a lot on your first day out of here, but we could use your help, if you're up to it."

How could she refuse? "Of course. Let's go."

There was a fountain in a shaded corner of the small garden courtyard behind the long-term care nursing facility. Birdsong added notes to the lilting splash of water. Sparrows and finches darted around the shiny leaves of well-trimmed ficus trees. A hummingbird sought sweet nectar, stabbing at blossoms on a vibrant hibiscus.

Alone with Alice, Kat watched Ty and Sunny walk through the hospital's double glass doors and disappear inside. She couldn't imagine what they were facing. She focused on the child playing in the garden beside her.

Alice smiled over her shoulder, reminding Kat of Sunny. If anyone deserved a break, it was Ty's daughter.

Alice toddled from bench to bench before she leaned against the lowest tier of the shallow fountain. She draped herself across the colorful tiles as Kat watched from the shade of a weeping pepper tree.

Alice was barely tall enough to stretch over the wide edge of the pool and touch the water. Slapping the surface, she giggled at first, then began to squeal with delight when flying droplets splashed her face.

Kat let her play a few more seconds before she went over and sat on the edge of the small pool.

"What are you up to, silly girl?" At the sound of Kat's voice, the child immediately stopped shrieking and smiled up at her.

"I'll bet that smile gets you plenty of mileage with your grandpa, doesn't it?"

Alice tugged on Kat's linen pants, leaving behind wet handprints. Kat obliged by settling her on her lap. She touched Alice's baby-fine strawberry blond hair, then ran her fingers over the soft skin of her dimpled elbow. She straightened the hem of Alice's bright pink sundress, then rubbed the toes of her scuffed tennis shoes with yellow ducks parading on them.

Kat tried to imagine what her own daughter might have looked like. She would be almost five now. Starting kindergarten in the fall. A bittersweet ache welled up in Kat and so did tears, but the pain failed to crush her.

Opening up to Ty had helped. Like the scar on her hand, her heart would always carry a reminder of her loss. She might never be as strong as she was before, but she would survive.

Alice hid her face behind both little hands and then peeked out at her.

" 'Eh, Alice." She spoke softly, in lilting pidgin. "You one lucky girl."

Ty would become more father than grandfather to Alice. Though the toddler would never know her birth father's love, she would have Ty's in abundance.

He's a great father.

There would still be road bumps along the way, but he was so confident and committed. Sunny was committed, too. They were a family now. Adversity had made them stronger, brought them together.

At thirty-seven, he still had plenty of time to have more children.

With that realization a swift sadness settled over her, but instead of fighting, she accepted it. For the first time in weeks, her indecision was behind her and she knew what to do.

She kissed Alice on the top of her head and noted the time. It was 2:45. She closed her eyes and said a silent prayer for Sunny and Ty, then she gave Alice a squeeze and set her on her feet.

Alice blissfully started splashing water again.

The first thing Sunny noticed whenever she walked into Dodge's hospital room was the utilitarian black-and-white clock on the wall and the way the red second hand continuously swept past the bold numerals.

It was odd seeing a clock in this room where time never moved for Dodge. She hated to think that his essence—that vibrant, charismatic part of him that made him the leader, the Dodge she'd loved for as long as she could remember—would be forever trapped in this sterile place.

She hoped his soul had checked out the night of his accident, that his spirit had followed her and Alice around ever since, watching over them.

She crossed the room, careful not to make a sound as she moved to his bedside. These last few moments, these final sweeps of the red second hand were meant for her and Dodge to be alone, but before she'd stepped through the door, she'd asked Chandler to join her. She wanted him near, hoping Dodge would sense that she and Alice weren't alone anymore.

Unlike Jamie, her dad hadn't begged off to wait in the hall. He was right behind her—here for her sake alone.

He hadn't tried to push her into making a decision

about Dodge, the way Jamie had since the accident. Over the past couple of days Chandler had been nothing but supportive—patient with both her and Alice, working within the system, getting her released into his custody, getting Alice back.

In regard to Dodge and his condition, all Chandler ever said was, "It's up to you. We'll find a way, no matter what you decide."

He'd never once mentioned how much it would cost to keep Dodge alive. Nor had he ridiculed her for hanging on to hopeless hope. Chandler never tried to tell her what was good for her or for Dodge. It was his silent acceptance and his patience more than anything that helped her come to a decision.

Right after Dodge's accident, she'd been overwhelmed with grief and mired in confusion. Even though he was on life support, the doctors had expected his heart to stop a few days after his brain flatlined, but when his heart kept beating, she took it as a sign that she shouldn't give up.

His body had stubbornly lasted far longer than the doctors predicted. She was convinced Dodge was hanging on for her and Alice, and didn't have the will to dash all hope.

Now, seeing him again for the first time in weeks, emaciated, slowly slipping away, she knew what she had to do, what she should have done eight months ago. The doctor in charge, the nurses who'd been taking care of him were all waiting down the hall.

Dodge lay suspended in time, still as death beneath the sheets. The respirator moved his lungs in a steady rhythm. Monitors blipped and beeped beside the bed with steady uniform beats of a heart that once loved her and Alice more than anything.

She stared at his placid, peaceful face, at the beautiful features she'd known since childhood.

They were five and running through the Angeles Crest pines, chasing each other down narrow footpaths that crisscrossed between the cabins.

They were six, playing hide-and-seek with the other kids at River Ridge. The huge dining hall scented with wood smoke, incense, and pot. Years later they decided contact highs probably accounted for the blissful early years of their childhoods.

They were eight, lying on the cool linoleum floor tiles, staring up at the fuzzy black-and-white television in her mom's cabin, watching *The Brady Bunch* reruns, glimpsing a suburban world as foreign to them as Tasmania.

Instead of attending public school they'd been trained by the "counselors" in how to hot-wire cars and pick pockets, shoplift, handle firearms.

She was eleven when the Feds busted River Ridge and the kids were carted off to different foster homes.

"You know what to do," Dodge told her the day they were separated. "We'll find each other again, Sunny. I'll find you. I promise."

She hadn't seen him again until she ran away from the foster home at fourteen. He'd kept his promise. He hung out around the mission until she'd been able to panhandle enough bus fare to get to Hollywood.

From the moment they were reunited, their childhood love intensified into an exploration of bodies and senses, and from their love came Alice.

She leaned close to the bed as she reached for his lifeless hand, found it chilled as the air around them. The room was constantly cold. He was so thin she could feel even the smallest bones beneath his flesh.

"Hi, baby," she whispered. "I'm sorry I haven't been

here for a while. I found a place for Alice. A place for me, too. A place where we'll both be all right."

Before she could go on, she had to stop, draw a breath, and will herself not to crumple. She was shaking so hard she could barely stand.

"You know I love you, Dodge. You know I said I'd do anything for you. I don't ever want to let you go, but I've got to, 'cause this isn't good for any of us anymore, not for you, or me, or Alice. We've . . . we've all got to let go and move on."

A tear trickled down her cheek. Captivated, she watched it roll off her hand and onto the stiff, starched bedsheet. She clung to Dodge's lifeless fingers and let her tears flow.

A heartbeat later, she felt Chandler's hand on her shoulder, warm and solid. He didn't say a word. He simply stood beside her, offering his strength the way he had in the hospital cafeteria, in the custody hearing, before the deposition.

With her dad's hand on her shoulder, she was able to let go of Dodge and step back.

"Are you ready?" Chandler's voice was thick with emotion. She looked up, surprised to see his eyes glistening with unshed tears and knew those tears weren't for Dodge, but for her.

"Yes." She wanted to be brave for him, to make him proud. "I'm ready."

"I'll go get the doctor."

When he started to walk away, the room began to spin.

"Dad? Wait."

He stopped, rushed to her side, quickly led her to an empty chair, and made her sit with her head down.

She hung her head between her knees and the room slowly stopped spinning.

Sunny was staring at his Nikes. "Is it all right if I call you Dad?"

There was a moment's hesitation before he answered. When he finally did, she could barely hear him.

"Of course it's okay." He cleared his throat. "It's more than okay, honey."

She nodded, finally able to stand on her own, growing more sure of herself and where she was going than she'd been in a long, long time.

"I'm okay now," she told him. "You can get the doctor."

Ty stepped out of the hospital, thankful for the sunshine streaming down onto the center of the courtyard patio. The heat of the afternoon was a relief after the chill inside. He inhaled deeply, filled his lungs with much-needed fresh air after the smell of long-term illnesses clinging to the hospital halls.

Kat was across the patio, playing peekaboo with Alice. He paused to admire them. Kat had her head close to Alice's as they sat in a shaft of sunlight beside the sparkling fountain.

It was a glimpse at a soft side of Kat that he'd rarely seen, the one she was always so careful to hide. She laughed with Alice, and the joyful sound filled the sorrow in his heart with light. Kat reached for the child and tickled her, then the two of them started blowing raspberries at each other.

Alice spotted him first and started toddling across the courtyard as fast as her little legs could go. Then he heard the door behind him close, turned, and watched Sunny walk out of the hospital and call to Alice. She knelt down and opened her arms to her daughter, and Alice barreled right past him, into Sunny's arms.

Ty caught Kat watching Alice with undisguised longing and thought of the photo hidden in her desk drawer.

Their eyes met and their gazes held. There was such a deep, abiding loneliness in her eyes that he ached for her and wondered if his love would ever be enough.

He longed to hold her, but there would be time for that once he got her home.

She deserved all the happiness in the world. He was determined to be the one to give her another child to change her life and keep her smiling. To keep her safe and close and to watch over her the way he intended to watch over Sunny and Alice.

He made sure Sunny was all right alone before he joined Kat beside the fountain. When he reached her side, she didn't attempt to make small talk, nor did she try to assure him that Dodge was in a better place. She simply took his hand, squeezed it, and tried to smile.

"It's so peaceful here." Her gaze drifted over to Sunny and Alice. "I'll have to thank Sunny for trusting me with her."

Alice started fussing and tugging Sunny toward the garden gate. Sunny looked back at them apologetically.

"I'll wait by the car, Dad." She used the word *dad* easily, as if she'd done it all her life.

Kat squeezed his hand again, and he looked down into her upturned face, into her dark, soulful eyes, wishing she would smile.

"Oh, Ty. She just called you Dad." Her gaze swept his face and he could tell that she, above all people, understood exactly what he was feeling.

He would have answered, but he couldn't. Not with his heart in his throat.

THIRTY-EIGHT

They were about to leave the garden when Kat took his hand and said, "Ty, wait."

He turned expectantly. "What's up?"

"I've decided not to go back to Twilight."

"Are you all right? Are you dizzy?"

She shook her head. "It's nothing like that."

"Then what is it?"

"I . . . I've changed my mind. I can't go back with you."

"It's no problem. Sunny will follow us in your car. She promised not to go over eighty."

She wished she could smile.

"That was a joke, Kat."

"I know." She dropped her gaze.

She heard Alice outside the garden wall, fussing, and knew he had to go.

"Look at me, Kat." He cupped her chin in his hand and forced her to meet his eyes. His gaze was full of concern, and something greater. She recognized the love in them and felt like an impostor.

"What's going on?"

"Jake will be home in a few days. There's really no reason for me to go all the way back." It was hard to believe over five weeks had come and gone since the day she'd wondered how she was going to deal with the peace and quiet of Twilight Cove.

"No reason? I'll give you one good reason—me. I want to take care of you. Soon you'll be a hundred percent again."

She knew as long as she lived she'd never be one hundred percent again, but that's the way life goes. She'd made a decision and she was going to stick to it.

"I can't go back, Ty."

"You mean you *won't* go back. I love you, Kat. I want you in my life. I want to marry you."

"Oh, Ty."

He started to go down on one knee. "I wasn't planning on doing this today, but you leave me no choice."

She grabbed his arm and glanced around the garden. "Don't, Ty!" Then she lowered her voice and begged, "Please, don't."

"Will you marry me, Kat?"

"No."

"What do you mean, no?" He stared at her in disbelief.

"No, I won't marry you."

"Why not? I know you love me."

"You deserve the family you've always wanted."

"So do you. I want to have it with you."

"I can't—" She shook her head, choking on the words, unable to say anything.

"Don't tell me you *can't*. You love me enough to have put your life on the line for Sunny. I'm even willing to hang in there until you're absolutely sure. I'd stake everything I've got on us making it work."

"Ty, please don't—"

"Don't what? Don't love you? Don't want us to be together? I know that terrifies you. I know falling in love is probably the only thing that you're afraid of in the entire world, but I'll never hurt you, Kat. Ever."

"I'm so sorry," she whispered.

His mouth tightened. "What happened?"

She looked away. "I saw your face when Sunny called you Dad. I know how much you treasure Alice. You've turned your life upside down for them."

"Don't you think I can love you as much as I love them?"

She started to reach for him, then realized it would only make things worse. She was afraid to touch him, afraid her resolve would crumble.

"Whenever I think with my heart, I end up in a mess, but right now I'm thinking with my head, and it's telling me we'll both be better off if I walk away."

"I think that wound is affecting your mind. Why in the hell won't you give us a chance? The other night, when you opened up to me, I thought we were finally getting somewhere. Five minutes ago, I thought you were going home with us."

She had to clear her throat before she could go on. "I can't have any more children, Ty. Ever since the accident. I . . . my uterus was ruptured. When I lost the baby, they took everything."

He stared into her eyes for so long that she wanted to gather what was left of her soul and walk away. Then he took her face between his hands and made her look into his eyes.

"So you can't have kids. So what?"

"So you just admitted you want a big family."

"I have Sunny. I have Alice. I want you to be one of us. Yes, I want a family—one with you in it."

"Right now you think that's enough, but what's to

keep you from regretting it later? What if you wake up one day and realize you want more children of your own? What happens when Sunny gets married and Alice goes to live with her? How will you feel about me in a few years, after you realize what you've given up?"

The silence between them was so thick it was almost deafening. It drowned out the sound of the fountain and the birds. Her cell phone went off in her pocket, reminding her that she still had her business. She could bury herself in it again.

She ignored the phone, wished Ty would say something, anything, and stop this gut-twisting free fall.

"You want to end this, fine, but when you get home and you're all alone again, just remember it wasn't *me* who broke your heart on Kauai. And that *I'm* not the one making an issue about you not being able to have children."

Before she could move, right there in the middle of the hospital garden, he pulled her into his arms. There was no gentleness in his kiss this time. None at all.

She understood he was a man fighting for what he wanted, fighting to hold on. It was clear in the desperate way he kissed her, in how his grip tightened around her upper arms.

A heady dizziness came over her. It might have come from nearly having her head blown off seventy-two hours ago—but she suspected it was because of the way he was kissing her.

Breaking his hold would have been simple, but even a black belt was defenseless against her own heart.

He kissed her until Sunny called through the gate.

"Dad?"

Kat quickly backed away. Ty ran his hand through his hair, took a deep breath, exhaled.

"In a minute," he called back.

Sunny looked at Kat through the wrought-iron gate and blushed. "Alice is throwing a fit. We really ought to get her something to eat."

"We'll be right there," he promised.

"I'm taking a cab home, Ty. There's no sense in you driving an hour out of your way to take me back to Long Beach."

"You've already got this all worked out, haven't you? What *you* want. What you think *I* want. I guess there's nothing left to say but good-bye, is there, Kat?"

"I'm sorry, Ty."

"Hey, don't feel sorry for me. You're sorry enough for yourself. How long do you think it'll be before you atone for what happened? The fact is, you must not think that you deserve to be happy, otherwise you'd take a chance."

She *did* want to be happy, but more than that, she wanted him to be happy. She wasn't changing her mind and she wasn't going to argue anymore. As stubborn as he was, she knew this could go on and on.

Somewhere close by, a dog barked. Dappled sunlight streamed through palm fronds. Their shadows lined the walk. Ty's hair glistened where the afternoon sunlight touched it.

He was staring at her so hard that her cheeks burned with embarrassment. Her lips had been bruised by his kiss. She could taste him still.

"Your heart will be safe with me, Kat. Love will take care of the rest." He stared deep into her eyes, as if fighting to connect with her very soul.

Her eyes stung, betraying her. When his image blurred, she turned away, refusing to let him see her cry.

"I'm not strong enough to find out, Ty. I can't risk another broken heart." It was a weak excuse at best, but it worked.

Ty started to walk away, but before he left, he paused at the gate long enough to stop and say, "Then you're not the woman I thought you were."

THIRTY-NINE

A week later Sunny carried Alice through the parking lot of the marina at Gull Harbor, trying to ignore her jitters as she strolled along the dock toward the *Stargazer.*

R.J. was easy to spot silhouetted against a crisp blue sky, tall and rugged on the open deck. His hair, long enough to reach his collar, was ruffled by the wind.

He was a man who didn't care about convention or appearances, yet with his sun-streaked hair and soulful eyes, he was striking enough to turn a woman's head, no matter her age.

Alice had been fussy all morning. By the time they reached the *Stargazer,* she was fighting to get down. R.J. spotted them and walked to the port side. He waved.

"Ahoy!" Sunny called out. "Can we come aboard?"

Even though she was wearing sunglasses, she had to squint against the bright light, and shaded her eyes with her hand when she tipped her head back to look up at him.

He leaned down the ladder to take Alice from her. The toddler stopped whining the minute R.J. set her on his hip. Sunny grabbed the rails and followed. As soon as her feet hit the deck, she felt as if she'd just reached the finish line of a long-distance race.

She loved the sway of the boat beneath her feet, the

rhythmic slap of water against the hull. She took a deep breath of air seasoned with the salty tang of the sea and let her gaze wander to the horizon, where clear blue sky met sparkling water.

She studied the eroded face of the sandstone cliffs that sheltered the harbor, a host of stately Mexican fan palms swaying in the onshore breeze. A fishing boat with full bait tanks motored by, headed toward open water. A noisy flock of gulls circled and dove into its wake.

Despite the upheaval in her life, despite her recent loss and the abrupt break from everyone connected with her past and the pending trials in Los Angeles, standing there on the open deck of the *Stargazer* she knew a surprising sense of peace.

Maybe I'll make a good Chandler, after all.

R.J. recognized her need for silent communion with the sea. He left her standing alone as he walked to the bow with Alice and pointed out a seal sunning itself on a buoy. Sunny walked along the deck until she reached his side. Alice was engaging him in deep conversation—all toddler gibberish. He responded with an explanation of why seals sun themselves. It was worthy of the Discovery Channel.

Sunny couldn't help but smile, for the moment content to watch and listen. When Alice reached for R.J.'s sunglasses, he didn't pull away or tell her no. Instead, he slipped them off and handed them to her for inspection.

It wasn't until he turned around that Sunny saw the uncertainty on his face. After the way she acted the last time they'd been together, she couldn't blame him.

"How's Kat doing?" he asked.

She knew Ty had told him everything about her life in L.A. and about what had happened. There were no secrets left to hide.

"Kat's doing fine. She's back in Long Beach working full-time."

"How's Ty handling that?"

She shrugged. "He pretends he's okay and that he doesn't miss her." Glancing at Alice, she noticed that her daughter had dropped her head on R.J.'s shoulder and was sucking on the frame of his sunglasses. "They don't really talk. I call her once in a while."

"How are you doing?" he asked.

She stared at the Keds she'd bought when she started working for him. They weren't pristine white anymore.

When she looked up, she thought about how natural he was around French Fry. Her daughter had fallen asleep against his shoulder.

"I'm doing okay. I came by to apologize."

"Look, Sunny—"

She thrust her hand out like a traffic cop, effectively silencing him. "Let me finish first, okay? I was scared when I first got here, scared the guys in L.A. would track me down before I was sure this was a good place for Alice. My feelings were all over the map."

"You'd been through a lot."

"I was pretty screwed up, but you were always honest with me. You didn't try to fix me overnight." She shrugged. "You went out on a limb to hire me and I almost came between you and Dad and I'm sorry."

"Things were as much my fault as yours. You know that, don't you?"

She nodded. "Maybe. Yeah, I guess." She was thankful that she was wearing sunglasses, hoping he couldn't hear her uncertainty.

"It was just a kiss, Sunny. Just a kiss."

"Yeah. That's all it was," she said softly—not quite sure at all.

"What are you going to do now?"

She walked over to the rail, watched the chocolate-brown seal rouse itself, clumsily shift its bulk around until it slipped back into the sea. Once in its element, it immediately became graceful, a shimmering dark streak cutting through the water.

"We . . . my dad and I . . . were hoping you'd go with us to spread my . . . Dodge's ashes."

"I'd be honored." There was no hesitation. She could tell he meant it sincerely.

"I've decided to get my high school diploma, then go to junior college part-time next spring, after the trials are over." She wished she hadn't blown things with him. Nervousness had her talking a mile a minute. "I know you've had to hire someone else, but I was wondering if there's a chance I could work some of the cruises for you again. Part-time, maybe? If you ever need somebody. Probably not, though, huh?"

He gently shifted Alice without waking her and leaned against the hull of the cabin. "I hired someone, but on the condition that if you came back, the job would be yours again. I'd already okayed it with your dad, of course."

It was an odd feeling, this buoyant, fragile contentment, but one she wouldn't mind getting used to. She hadn't had much experience with dreams ever actually becoming reality, not until Ty Chandler walked into her life. Ty, and Kat, and R.J.

"Really?"

"I had a feeling you'd be back, Sunny."

"What made you so sure?"

"You're a Chandler, aren't you? They always find a safe harbor in Twilight Cove."

FORTY

KAUAI, HAWAII
DECEMBER . . .

Two weeks before Christmas, Kat stepped off the plane in Honolulu and Hawaii embraced her. The air was thick with humidity, spiced with the heady mixture of plumeria and ginger, sensual as plush velvet against her skin.

She took the WikiWiki shuttle to the Interisland Terminal and caught the connecting twenty-five-minute flight to Kauai. Mixed feelings of elation and dread unsettled her nerves as she anticipated being with her family again.

She'd expected Sonya or one of her kids to pick her up at the airport in Lihue. What she hadn't expected was the whole family to turn out dressed in bright aloha shirts and long floral-print muumuus, looking like escapees from a Hilo Hattie clothing factory tour.

As soon as she wheeled her carry-on out of the baggage claim area, everyone from Mom and Pop to all the nieces and nephews nearly toppled her with hugs and kisses and then buried her up to her chin in leis—all kinds of leis—from *mokihana* and maile grown high in the mountains, to Anahola plumeria, Vanda orchids, ti, white ginger, and *puakinikini.*

As they ushered her to the car, everyone talking and laughing at once, she felt like a float in the Rose Parade. The leis quickly grew hot and heavy, but they were so much a part of the island homecoming ritual that she didn't dare remove any of them until they reached her parents' place in Kapa'a.

She quickly changed into shorts, a tank top, and rubber thongs—or slippers, as everyone called them here—but it was impossible to slip into her old life. The carefree young woman she'd been while growing up here was long gone.

She might look the same, but she was no longer the Kat they once knew, the sister/daughter they remembered. The trouble was, she was no longer that *other* Kat, either, the hard-hearted mainland P.I. she'd been for a while.

No matter how hard she tried, the emotional armor she'd forged no longer fit.

She'd fought the changes, but she'd lost. She had plenty of new clients to keep her busy and a new partner who didn't mind her taking time off now and then. The world was full of cheating spouses, embezzlers, fraudulent workers' comp cases. There were court papers to serve. Missing persons to track down. Business was great.

On the mainland she'd tried not to let anyone see the changes or the confusion in her, but she was with her family now. There was no hiding anything from family.

She had hoped the island would help her settle into a middle ground and find the answers she was looking for. She was no longer the wounded young woman who had lost her first love and her baby, nor was she the bitter workaholic. She'd opened her heart and taken a chance, walked away from Ty for his sake, and ached ever since.

Jake's plan to have her stop and take a look at her life had given her a glimpse of what she was missing, what she would always be missing. Now her days and nights were filled with thoughts of Ty and his life in Twilight Cove.

On Kauai she jogged along familiar beaches and trails, well-known and unchanged. Everything was so much the same that it was unsettling to realize only she had changed.

But it was easy to delight in the moist air and liquid sunshine, the trade winds, the beauty of the clouds hugging the mountaintops, the misty rainbows of morning that brought tears to her eyes.

She shopped for Christmas presents for everyone, laughed aloud one afternoon in the middle of Wal-Mart as "White Christmas" played over the loudspeaker while tourists in tank tops and thongs chose souvenir trinkets to take home. It was mid-December, eighty-three degrees, and sunny. Plastic snowflakes dangling from the fluorescent overhead lights were the only signs of a white Christmas Kauai was ever going to see.

When the crowded cab of her dad's rusting Nissan pickup was so stuffed full of packages she could barely wedge herself in, she drove over to Sonya's house near Kukui Grove Center. Of all her sisters, she was still closest to Sonya.

Her sister ushered her in, handed her a can of Diet Pepsi without asking if she wanted one, and they walked out onto the lanai that looked over the ridge behind the house.

The outdoor room was full of comfortable furniture upholstered in a hodgepodge of island floral patterns, rattan love seats, ottomans, tables. Sonya's family spent most of their time out here, all but her oldest boy, Kyle Kailani, who was always surfing the Net.

"So how's it, Kat? You getting used to being home?"

Kat took a long sip of soda and thought before she answered. "In some ways it's like I never left, you know?"

"How would I know? I've never been any farther than the big island."

"You can come to California to visit me anytime."

Sonya nodded. "I know, but with all the kids' activities and the running around I do, one day slides into the next, and pretty soon another year is gone."

Sonya kicked back, put her feet up on a rattan footstool. Sonya never hurried. She had time for everyone and everything.

"So, how's your love life?" she asked.

Kat set the can down on the end table beside the love seat.

"Did mom tell you to ask?"

"No."

"I can almost *hear* her thinking sometimes. I know she wonders, but she won't ask me herself."

"Hey, we're not trying to butt in. We just want to see you happy."

"So she *did* ask you to find out."

"Maybe, but I'm really asking for *me*. We all still feel real bad, you know, about what happened."

"You weren't the one driving."

They fell silent. Sonya's husband, Reggie, was into birds, and just now noisy java sparrows and crimson-feathered cardinals were vying for space on a feeder hanging from a guava tree near the lanai.

Kat let go a sigh. "Would you have married Reggie if he was sterile?" She could see the blunt question took Sonya by surprise.

"I love all my kids, you know," Sonya said softly.

"I know. It was a dumb question."

"Believe me, there are days I'd like to send you a couple of them, though. I guess I never thought about it."

"So?"

Her sister rolled her eyes. "Hmm. Would I marry Reggie if he couldn't give me kids?" Absently, she started to twist her wedding ring around her finger. "Of course. We'd work it out."

"What do you mean, work it out?"

"We could always *hanai* some kids."

Hanai didn't have anything to do with a formal adoption, but it was an old Hawaiian system that worked. Children were raised by those who loved them best, those who cared for and nurtured them when their own families could not.

Sonya suddenly straightened in her chair. "So who's the guy? And don't look at me like I'm crazy. Why else would you be asking?"

Kat gave in. "I met him last summer when I was house-sitting for Jake and Carly."

"Ah. The *he* friend. Does he love you?"

"He wants to."

"What's the problem?"

"He loves kids. He's got a daughter who's twenty and a granddaughter. But he's still young enough to have more children of his own."

"What does he say about you not being able to have kids?"

"That he doesn't care."

Sonya leaned toward Kat, studying her. Her sister reminded her of their mom in the way she weighed Kat's expression and mood before she sat back again.

"So then . . . what's the problem?"

"What if he wakes up one day and realizes what he's missed? What if he's sorry?"

"What if you wake up one day and your life is over and you never gave this a chance. Would you regret it?"

"I already do."

"Then, sis, why not let him love you?" She slapped her knee and laughed as if Kat were crazy for thinking twice. "Why you make everyt'ing so hard?"

"Why you make everyt'ing so hard?"

An hour later Kat was running along the cane haul road toward Kealia Beach. Sonya had made it sound so incredibly easy.

"Let him love you."

She hadn't talked to Ty since that day at the hospital. At first she thought he'd try to call and she was determined to be polite but firm.

But he never called once. He hadn't tried to communicate with her at all.

She'd spoken to Sunny a few times, asked after Alice. Learned Ty was doing fine and that he'd been back and forth to Alaska a few times. The new owner of Kamp Kodiak wanted him to sign another, more lucrative contract and hold his hand long-distance.

Fred Westberg had let her know when Jamie Hatcher's trial would start. Street racing was all over the news and the case had a high profile. The courtroom was so packed she was able to slip in late and leave early without Ty seeing her. Sunny had been too nervous to notice her at all. Kat had been proud of her for showing so much courage. She hadn't broken down once on the stand, and she'd made a credible witness.

Kat waited for a break in the traffic before she jogged across the highway, then she walked down to the cemetery spread out on the hillside overlooking the ocean. In the winter, whales migrated along the coast on this side of the island. They hadn't yet arrived.

She entered St. Catherine's Cemetery, and though she hadn't been to her daughter's tiny grave since the burial, she walked unerringly to the site. Someone had trimmed away the weeds. There was a small, wilted bouquet of ginger in a jar beside the headstone. Her mom's doing, no doubt.

Kat stood there buffeted by the heavy trade winds, tasting the mist off the water. The grass was sparse, struggling to grow though beaten down by the wind and the sun. Where ground around the graves was bare, the dirt was the color of rust.

The small headstone was engraved with only two words. *Baby Vargas*.

Sitting by the grave, she thought back to the days shortly after the accident.

Justin moved to L.A. and never called, though when she came home from the hospital, his parents dropped by the apartment with flowers. They told her how sorry they were that things ended so badly. She almost felt sorry for them, but then, they seemed to do it so well that they were probably used to apologizing for him.

After the burial, the family gathered around and did what all families do where there is really nothing they *can* do—they tried to feed her.

The backyard was full of people. Two barbeques were smoking, covered with chicken, ribs, and fish, a table was laden with food—as if trying to drown the hurt in calories, as if enough potato macaroni salad and lomilomi salmon could ease the pain.

As if anything could help.

She was lucky, they all said. One of the kids in the pickup had died. She was lucky she came out of it alive.

Virtually unharmed . . .

All she'd seen after the accident was the pity in her family's eyes. Not their sympathy or love. Only the pity.

She felt it whenever Mom touched her.

Heard it in all that her sisters didn't say. In the way they stopped bragging about their kids around her.

More than anything, she hated the outpouring of pity, knowing that whenever they looked at her now they weren't really seeing Katrina No'ilani Vargas. They were seeing a daughter, a sister, a woman who would never again know the sweet, special joy of carrying a baby beneath her heart or watching her children grow.

She thought it would be harder, standing here at her baby's grave again, but instead of the sorrow she expected to feel, the quiet solitude gave her a sense of peace.

She sat down on a patch of grass near the headstone and watched the waves roll in along Kealia Beach. It might have been minutes, it may even have been hours. She had no idea how long she sat, but when she finally leaned over and touched the headstone warmed by the sun, when she finally whispered good-bye, she was able to smile through her tears.

Jogging along, carefully avoiding potholes and rocks in the red dirt, Kat came to the end of the cane haul road and started walking through the deep, soft sand along the beach. The surf was rough, agitated as water in a washing machine, blown out of shape by the wind. The surfers weren't interested.

The parking lot along the highway was nearly empty. A few tourists were sprinkled here and there on the beach, braving the stiff onshore breeze for the sake of a tan to show off back home in snow country after the holidays.

She kept thinking of what Sonya had said, but she

needed convincing. She needed a sign—something to help her decide what to do.

Pausing to catch her breath, she planted her hands on her hips, watched the waves batter the shore, and finally, out of frustration, yelled, "Come on, already! Somebody up there help me out!"

The sea and the trade winds off the water swallowed the sound of her voice.

If the god Maui could pull the sun across the heavens, if Laka, goddess of hula, could pass on the hula and sacred dances and chants to the ancient ones, then surely *somebody* up there could take pity on her and show her the way.

The waves rolled in. The sun warmed the land and fried the tourists, but there was no sign, no answer. No sudden clap of thunder, no cloudburst. Not even a misty rainbow.

Stretching, Kat bent over and touched her fingers to her toes, and noticed something glinting in the hot sand. Kneeling down, she brushed the sand away to reveal a piece of white beach glass. Once clear, it was heavily frosted, its jagged edges worn smooth from tumbling and tossing in the surf.

It was the biggest, most perfect piece of beach glass she'd ever seen. As she held it in her palm, she thought back to the day she'd given Ty the pieces she'd found on the beach near his home. Later, they'd made love in his outdoor shower and then Sunny had shown up at his door with Alice.

"This means you thought of me at least seven times."

Clear as a bell, she heard Ty's voice. She heard it over the sound of the wind and the waves. She closed her hand around the beach glass and started running back up the beach, back toward Kapa'a.

FORTY-ONE

TWILIGHT COVE
CHRISTMAS DAY . . .

Christmas carols were playing on the CD player at the old Chandler house high on the point. Ty enjoyed carols right after Thanksgiving, but he was glad the big day was finally here and he wouldn't have to listen to one more rum-pa-pum-pum until next year.

True to form, the cold front they'd suffered for three weeks had moved on. The Santa Ana winds were blowing a heat wave through the canyons and passes, temperatures had been steadily on the rise all week long.

It was ninety-five degrees in the shade and even hotter inside—prime weather for the Rose Parade next week, the kind of weather that brought all the "snowbirds" flocking to retire in California.

The turkey was done to perfection, soaked in brine and barbequed the way his grandpa Chandler had taught him. Before he carved the bird, he opened the refrigerator, looking for the bottle of salad dressing Sunny had bought at the Twilight Farmer's Market. The dressing was low fat, low salt, and he was sure low flavor, but he opened her contribution anyway and set it on the counter next to the salad.

When she walked into the kitchen in a peach sundress and pretty, low-heeled sandals, he marveled again at how very beautiful she was.

"You look great," he told her. "Very beach."

With a smile, she pulled back her hair and he noticed that she was wearing his grandmother's opal earrings. She'd never worn them before. Memories of the night she'd disappeared hit him hard.

"What's wrong, Dad? I thought you'd be pleased."

"I was thinking about the day you left. I looked around, saw that those earrings and Stinko were gone, and I was afraid you'd left for good. I thought maybe you sold them. "

"How come you never asked?"

"I gave them to you. What you do with them isn't up to me." They'd come a long way, he and his girl. He gave her a hug, let his arms communicate what he was afraid words could not. "I'm really glad you kept them."

"I would have only sold them if I'd had to. I took them to remember you by."

He was moved as much by her words as the tears he saw in her eyes. "Hey," he warned, "don't you dare. It's Christmas."

Sunny sniffed. "Did you call Kat?"

He wished she hadn't asked. She'd been bugging him about it all day. It was one of the few Christmas gifts she'd asked for—that he call Kat so she could personally wish her a Merry Christmas. He knew that behind her request was the secret hope that he and Kat might get back together again. His daughter had turned out to be as stubborn as any Chandler before her.

"She didn't answer." It still hurt too much to talk about Kat, so he handed her the salad dressing and abruptly changed the subject. "Shake this up, please. Is everybody doing all right outside?"

"The last time I looked, R.J. was pushing Alice's new kiddie lawn mower around the yard."

Nothing serious was going on between R.J. and Sunny—he had both their words on it—but he wouldn't take bets about the future. Both Sunny and Alice worshipped the ground R.J. walked on. That was apparent whenever they looked at him.

Ty was starting to think Kat had been right. Aside from their age difference, he really couldn't think of a reason to object. Who better to trust his daughter to than his best friend?

Sunny was tossing the salad and Ty had just pulled baked sweet potatoes out of the oven when the doorbell rang.

Expecting another FedEx driver with a last-minute delivery, he wiped his hands on a dish towel as he walked through the house. He'd already signed for six packages of smoked salmon from friends in Alaska.

He whipped the door open and felt like he'd been kicked in the gut as he found himself face-to-face with Kat.

Her hair was styled in a short, artfully mussed cut that gave her an elfin look. Her skin glowed with a deep golden tan that brought out the freckles across the bridge of her nose.

At first glance he thought she'd changed her makeup, but then realized she was simply radiant, glowing from within. The shadows that once lingered in her eyes were gone.

He wanted to touch her, to prove to himself that he wasn't dreaming, that she was really there. She'd come to him just the way he'd wished she would during the countless sleepless nights he'd lain awake, wishing things had ended differently, regretting everything he'd said, everything he had done that last time they'd been together.

Seeing her now, he thought he might be dreaming this impossible, miraculous moment. He wanted to take her in his arms, carry her upstairs, lock her away from the world, and keep her for himself forever.

But now that she was here, he couldn't move or speak, even though his mind was racing.

Move, idiot. Take her in your arms and never let her go.

Tell her how much you love her.

When he didn't immediately say anything, she started to blush. Her hand fluttered at the neckline of her knit top as she grew flustered.

Suddenly, they both spoke at once.

"I should have called—" she began.

"I'm glad you're here—" he said.

Afraid she was going to turn tail and run, he reached out and took her hand.

"You look great, Kat. Really, really great."

"I just flew in from Kauai," she said softly, her eyes searching his face.

"Come in." He drew her into the room, prayed no one would interrupt. Not yet. He wanted her all to himself. He didn't want anything to ruin the moment.

"I came to give you something. Something from Kauai." She took a deep breath and reached into the pocket of her khaki slacks, then held out her hand.

He extended his, and she dropped a silver dollar–sized piece of white beach glass into his palm. Speechless, he stared at it for a moment, realizing that the simple gift meant more than she could know, which made him smile.

She'd been a couple of thousand miles away and she'd been thinking of him. He felt a surge of hope—more hope than he'd even dared to wish for. Even more than hope, it was a promise of things to come.

"This is unbelievable." He couldn't stop staring at the beach glass in his palm. "You have no idea."

"It's just a piece of glass," she whispered, awed by his reaction. Kat studied his every move, holding her breath, hoping she wasn't too late. Praying she hadn't waited too long to follow her heart.

Last night she'd left her family shortly after their Christmas Eve celebration and flew standby on the red-eye out of Lihue in order to be here now.

A few hours ago it seemed imperative she see him immediately, that she be with him for Christmas. Last night, waiting in line with the handful of passengers who'd opted to fly on Christmas Eve, she felt as if she were standing on the edge of a deep, dark pool, ready to dive in with no hint of what dangers lurked beneath the surface of the water.

She wasn't afraid anymore. All she knew was that she had to take the plunge or she would regret it for the rest of her life.

Now, with her hand in Ty's, her heart was racing and her cheeks were on fire. The rest of her life would be determined in the next few minutes and she wanted them to be perfect, but she had no idea what to say or do next.

Watching Ty stare down at the piece of glass in his hand, a fragment that had once been part of someone's rubbish, she thought she must have been crazy to think it was the perfect Christmas offering.

Right now, miles and hours away from the glistening sands of Kauai, a hunk of beach glass seemed like a paltry, foolish gift.

Tell him. Tell him why you're here.

She was tongue-tied just looking at him. She felt the

warmth of his hand, the strength tempered by gentleness in his touch.

He was a thousand times more handsome than she'd remembered. Tall, dark, handsome—and more than that, he was a good man, a solid, caring man. The kind of man who gave his word and kept it. A man who valued family above all else.

She'd walked away from all he'd offered once, but then she'd been afraid. Her fear was gone now. It was a thing of the past. She wasn't running away this time.

The only way she would leave was if he sent her away.

Ty, this crazy house, a quiet life in Twilight Cove, they were all she wanted.

So tell him.

"Ty, I—"

"Wait. I have something for you, too." He drew her arm through his and led her through the living room without further explanation.

Department store boxes and tissue paper were strewn all over the floor, along with gift bags and tags and enough toys to fill a Portacrib.

A huge Christmas tree was crammed into the corner of the room, the pine needles dry, branches drooping from the heat. A popcorn chain and another made of red and green construction paper was looped through the branches, surrounded by old ornaments and new, many of them nautical. A mermaid tree topper with wide gauze angel wings that were covered with glitter perched on the highest point of the trunk.

He stopped before the Christmas tree and carefully reached up into the branches. There, amid the homemade paper chains, the popcorn, snowmen, Santas, sand dollars, and starfish, a small box wrapped in gold foil paper dangled from a shiny red ribbon.

Kat watched as Ty carefully slipped the ribbon off the

tree branch and handed her the box. She stared at a small gift tag with her name carefully printed on it, cradled it in the palm of her hand.

"Dad?"

Kat recognized Sunny's voice calling him from the kitchen.

"I'll be there in a minute."

Kat started to protest, to tell him to go to Sunny, to get on with their celebration. This was a day for family. She should have known that they would be sharing Christmas. He wasn't alone now.

But Ty gently shushed her by placing his fingertips against her lips, and then he whispered, "Come with me."

Stealing through the living room, he drew her out the front door. The heat and sunshine hit them full-on. He closed the door silently behind them and then, hand in hand, he led her through the front garden and across the lane to a wooden bench with a view that stretched all the way to Twilight. The town looked even smaller than it was, set against the backdrop of the rolling hills and the ocean that stretched to the horizon and beyond.

The bench was perched on the side of the point in front of the house, out of sight of the patio in back.

"Sit down, Kat." He waited until she acted settled—no small feat with her pulse hammering through her veins—before he slid onto the bench beside her. "You can open it now," he urged.

Her hands were shaking as she slipped off the ribbon, then the gold foil paper. He took them from her, balled them up, and shoved them into his pocket. Kat held her breath as she lifted the lid and saw a velvet jewelry box tucked inside the outer one.

Her heart skipped a beat. She looked up into his dark

blue eyes and hoped what she saw in them was her future.

"Ty, what have you done?"

"Maybe you'd better open it before you say anything." His smile was as mysterious as it was tempting.

Slowly she lifted the hinged lid on the black velvet box, and there, nestled inside, was a piece of frosted white beach glass in the shape of a heart. It had been set with a gold loop and threaded onto a gold chain.

The minute she saw it, her eyes misted with tears and she knew exactly why he had reacted the way he did when she'd given him his gift.

"It's beautiful, Ty. It's perfect."

He held out his hand, and there, lying on his palm, was the beach glass she'd given him. Before she could say another word, he put his hand beneath her chin and kissed her, slowly, thoroughly. His lips were warm, gentle, eloquently saying all that he hadn't been able to voice.

More than the blazing heat of the stifling afternoon had elevated her temperature as he tucked her against his heart and deepened the kiss. They fit together naturally, but there was an urgency now, a need to be filled because they'd been apart.

She was blinded by his touch, his kiss. She wrapped her arms around his neck, held the necklace tight in one hand while she let the fingers of her free hand slip through his hair.

He wanted her. She could taste it on his kiss, feel it in his touch. She moaned, frustrated, fully aware that they were out in broad daylight where anyone could see them, but if the soul-stirring kiss lasted any longer, she was afraid she was going to throw caution and good sense to the wind and rip his clothes off him.

Somehow she mustered the will to draw back and catch her breath.

Without saying a word, he took her hand, opened her fingers and picked up the necklace. Then he slipped it around her neck and fastened it, smoothing it down against her skin below the hollow of her throat.

"I'd say our gifts prove we're meant for each other, Kat."

She had been moved by his gift, his kiss, but touched the most by his steadfastness.

"Once upon a time you told me that my heart would be safe with you, no matter what," she said.

"I meant every word. I still do. I love you."

"That's all I wanted for Christmas—to hear you say it. That's why I had to come back here today. I had to find out if you still love me, the way I love you. I had to ask you to give me another chance."

"Telling you exactly how much I love you is going to take a while." He tried to look serious, but couldn't hide his smile.

"How long?"

"A lifetime, for sure. Are you interested in sticking around that long?"

"Of course." With the beach glass warm against her skin, she wrapped her arms around his neck again and said softly against his lips, "Maybe you should get started right now. What do you think?"

He glanced over her shoulder, toward the house, and gave her a quick kiss. "There's nothing I want more, but I'm afraid we've got company."

She turned in his arms and saw Sunny walking down the garden path. Sunny wasn't alone.

"Is that R.J.?" Kat watched as he waved at them from across the sandy lane.

"He's here for Christmas dinner."

"So, everything is all right?"

"More than all right. Sunny is working for him a couple of days a week again."

Sunny waved, too. Kat waved back and watched as Callie appeared at the front door and then started down the walk carrying Alice. Callie was still thin, but not painfully so. Alice looked as if she'd grown a couple of inches. She was frantically bouncing up and down, shouting "Key! Key!" and waving a spoon around.

"I barbequed turkey," Ty sighed, then smiled into her eyes. "I'm afraid I won't be able to welcome you home the way I'd like, at least not for a few hours. A whole lot has happened since we saw each other last." Then he laughed and shook his head. "Maybe you shouldn't agree to *anything* before you've spent a few days here. There's no privacy and definitely not enough bathrooms anymore."

"Callie's living here, too?"

"What's one more?" He shrugged and tried to pretend he was put out, but he couldn't hide his contentment. He was gathering the houseful of kids he'd always wanted, *hanai* style.

Sunny ran across the road. Kat stood up to greet her, and without hesitation, the girl threw her arms around Kat's neck and gave her a big hug.

"What a great surprise!" Sunny turned her megawatt smile on Ty. "Isn't it, Dad? Isn't this a great surprise? You're staying, aren't you, Kat?"

Ty gave Kat no chance to decline. "She's staying."

By now R.J. and Callie had reached the bench. Alice was still yelling, "Key! Key!" when Callie handed her over to R.J. Alice promptly began hitting him on the head with the spoon.

"There's going to be a mutiny if we don't eat soon,"

R.J. grumbled, but there was a definite twinkle in his eye when he added, "Glad to see you, Kat. Welcome back."

"Just give us another minute alone, would you?" Ty found Kat's hand again and threaded his fingers through hers. "Start carving the turkey and passing out samples," he suggested to R.J. "We'll be right there."

"Don't blow it, Dad." Sunny winked and quickly herded them all back to the house. Ty draped his arm around Kat and she leaned into him, watching them go.

"Are you sure this is what you want, Kat?" His voice was low, his breath tickled her ear as he pressed his lips against her temple.

She turned in his arms and laid her hand against his chest, felt his heart beating strong and true beneath it.

"There's no place else on earth I'd rather be than in your arms, and in your life."

"You know this is forever? I'll never let you go now."

"As if I'd *want* to go anywhere."

"No more guns? No more stakeouts?"

"We'll talk about that later, okay?"

"Kat—"

"Shut up and kiss me, Chandler. I've missed you so much."

There, on the bluff above the Pacific, as the waves rolled in and crashed over the rocks below, gulls circled overhead, the sun beat down, and the Santa Ana winds blew through the canyons toward the sea, he kissed her, and she knew she'd finally come home.

Read on for a sneak peek
at the compelling conclusion
to the Twilight Cove trilogy,

HEARTBREAK HOTEL . . .

Available in hardcover from
Ballantine Books.

After dark, the lobby of the Heartbreak Hotel seemed to expand, like the walls of a carnival fun house. At night, the persistent pounding of the waves against the shoreline filled the rooms like the amplified beat of a solitary heart. Except for an occasional passing car, there was no competition for the echo of the waves.

Loneliness also filled the rooms in the evenings. Tracy Potter didn't notice it as much during the day, when she was running in all directions. But at night, after the workmen left, the sun had set, and she and her nine-year-old son, Matthew, were tucked in bed, she would struggle with an ache so deep, so raw, that it took everything she had to convince herself that circumstances change—that life was bound to take a turn for the better.

She still found it hard to believe that in a couple more weeks, her husband, Glenn, would have been gone six months.

Gone.

The word made it sound as if he had just stepped out to meet a client and would be back any minute.

Her footsteps echoed against the scuffed hardwood floors of the wide open lobby, falling silent whenever she paused to pick up a sticky wad of used masking tape or carefully sidestep a pile of drop cloths that the workmen had left on the floor.

Six months ago, if anyone had told her that she'd be a widow at thirty-three, or that she'd be renovating the Heartbreak Hotel, let alone living in it, she would have laughed and called them crazy.

A few days after Glenn's death, when his accountant, David Sylvester, informed her that Glenn had been deep in debt, she thought he'd been joking. But David had been dead serious and the joke was on her.

It was a morning she'd never forget, sitting there in David's office, listening as he outlined the bleak details.

"There's no easy way to put it, Tracy. You're broke. As far as I can tell, there's enough left in your joint checking account to pay expenses for the next six months, if you're careful and if you're lucky."

She knew things had been tough. She'd confronted Glenn about the mounting bills. She'd wanted to go back to work, gladly offering to renew her real estate license. She would have done anything to help keep them from going under, but he'd been adamant. He wanted Matt to have a full-time mom. There were listings about to close. Things were tight just now. Things were going to change soon.

Still she'd worried, and with good reason. What the accountant told her after Glenn's death made that quite clear.

"Glenn refinanced the Canyon Club house to the limit," David explained. "There's no equity left. Your credit cards are maxed out, too. In fact, he made your last two house payments with his American Express card. And unfortunately, he was underinsured. You'll be able to cover the funeral expenses and, if there's anything left, I'd advise you to pay off your car, and Chelsea's."

Luckily, hers was free and clear.

Chelsea's wasn't. Chelsea was Glenn's daughter by his first marriage. Nineteen now. A freshman at the University of Southern California. Tracy had sat in stunned silence, thinking of Chelsea, of the hefty tuition Glenn had been paying. What now?

"Sell the house," David had advised. "Get the bank off your back before they foreclose."

The luxurious house had been Glenn's dream, part of an upscale development he'd spearheaded. Cabrillo Canyon Club was a gated community of sixty high-end homes scattered around a golf course designed by Rex Burrell, one of the West Coast's premiere course designers. They were well built but overpriced, even in a good market. The homes all sold eventually, but not overnight.

"There is one bit of good news, I guess," David had quickly added, as if aware that she was quickly slipping into a self-induced coma. Anything to escape.

"And *that* would be?"

"That the IRS and the banks can't touch your inheritance from your grandparents. It's not much, but it'll help. And there's that old hotel on the coast road. Glenn put the title in Matt's name, with you as trustee."

"Matt? When? Why?" Matt was only nine. What had Glenn been thinking?

At first she couldn't even remember the place and then it had come to her. The Heartbreak Hotel. Perched on the coast off the old Route One. Glenn had purchased the derelict nineteenth-century hotel a handful of years ago, planning to tear it down and replace it with elegant condos. The project was quickly bogged down in California Coastal Commission hearings. After the Twilight

Cove Historical Society and the Central Coast Preservation League entered into the fray, he had tabled the project idea altogether, too busy to spend time and money fighting them all.

She had left David's office that morning determined to sell the white elephant. But prospective buyers couldn't walk away fast enough once they learned that the hotel was to be registered as a historic landmark—thanks to the Twilight Cove Historical Preservation Society—and that the Coastal Commission had deemed the prime ocean-front land beneath the hotel off limits to any new development.

She'd looked into renewing her real estate license, then realized that it might be months before her first escrow closed, if and when she got a quick listing and actually sold something.

Forced to do the only thing she could under the circumstances, she'd taken a leap of faith, relied on her ability to see things the way they could be, not the way they were, and had used her inheritance from Grandma and Grandpa Melton to clean up the Heartbreak.

Now darkness was quickly gathering as she walked over to a bank of wall switches behind the desk, flipped on the lights, and surveyed the progress. Though the place would never be a five star hotel, it was finally coming along.

Six guest rooms were already completely finished. There were three left to paint and furnish. The painting was nearly finished in the lobby. The adjacent sitting room was no longer as dingy and derelict as it had been the day she took her first hard look around.

Even she, a consummate optimist, had been hard pressed to envision possibilities for the place. If Matt hadn't been with her the first time she walked around, she'd have been tempted to break down and bawl her eyes out.

Old wallpaper had to be stripped. Thankfully, the hardwood floors were still solid, but needed refinishing. An army of termites had taken up residence in the walls. She'd handled the damage with spot repair and fumigation. Basic cosmetic renovations and a race to open for the coming tourist season would never have been her first choice, but she'd seen no quicker way out of her financial crisis.

Walking away from their home at Cabrillo Canyon Club, selling off almost everything, including the designer furnishings hand chosen for the house, hadn't hurt anything but her pride. But then, she'd never really felt as attached to the country club house as Glenn. It had been his dream to live in an impressive showplace—one that left no doubt as to his success.

It wasn't like her to look back, so counting on the future to bring change, she glanced out the wide bay window that curved around the entire front wall. It was gloomy out tonight. Not a single star brightened the heavy sky.

She was heading for the sunroom and the small kitchen area off the lobby to see if the freshly painted cabinets had dried yet, when she heard the deep throated rumble of a motorcycle on the coast road. When the sound abruptly stopped, she froze.

Alone in the empty room, she was suddenly all too aware of how vulnerable and alone she and Matt were, living out on the deserted stretch of road. It was one thing to have considered running the Heartbreak all by herself, but the cold, stark reality of it chilled her blood. She held her breath, hoping to hear the motorcycle start up again.

* * *

He couldn't have conjured up a better place to stop.

Poised in isolation on a remote stretch of road bypassed by the main highway, the huge two-story wooden hulk had been visible from a quarter mile away. Reminding him of the Bates Motel in *Psycho*, it rose stark and ominous against the night sky. The place beckoned him, compelled him to slow down as he neared.

Complete with a widow's walk, the old hotel clung to the bluff above the Pacific. It might have been abandoned, except for the neon sign out front that blazed EAR EAK HOT L in hot pink. Below that, in aqua letters, glowed the word VACANCY.

Once he saw the place at close range, there was no way he could ride on. No way he could leave.

Perfect.

He rolled the bike beneath the eave of the building where it would be out of a slow drizzle that was making a halfhearted attempt to turn itself into rain. Quickly he unsnapped the saddlebags, pulled off his helmet, clamped it beneath his arm, and ran splayed fingers through his short hair, forcing it to spike up in front. Taking a deep breath, he headed around the corner of the building along a path nearly covered by weeds.

Hoping like hell that whoever was manning the front desk wouldn't recognize him, Wade cleared the worn treads in the front steps and stared at the oval etched-glass window in the front door. He gave in to an overpowering need to step inside.

Tracy knew all along that she would be obliged to greet late arrivals and that she'd be vulnerable every time she opened the door to a stranger. Thankfully, she'd been a firm believer in the innate goodness of people all her life, but the minute she heard footsteps thudding on the porch outside and then an insistent knocking, Tracy found herself slipping her cell phone out of her pocket. Clutching it in her hand, she crossed the lobby. Through the window set in the front door, she saw the silhouette of a man.

He stood beneath the golden glow of the porch light—tall, not thin, not heavy. Solid, with wide shoulders beneath a black leather jacket that glistened with moisture. His deep-set dark eyes stared back.

While he waited for her to open the door, he wiped his face with the back of his hand and she realized it must be raining. She stepped closer to the window in the door and noted the shiny black helmet beneath his arm and motorcycle saddlebags dangling from his left hand.

"We're not open for business." She raised her voice so that he could hear her through the oval pane.

He leaned closer. He was smooth-shaven and his clothes appeared to be clean.

"Your sign says vacancy." His voice was low, but she easily heard him through the window and suddenly realized that she must have accidentally hit the switch for the neon sign when she turned the lights on.

"We're not open yet," she told him again, damning the sign. Fixing the sign hadn't made it to the top of her to-do list yet, and she didn't have the money. So many letters were burned out, that the first time Matt saw it lit up he asked who would want to stay at a place called Ear Ache Hot L and she'd collapsed into gales of laughter.

"Come on, lady. Give a guy a break. It's raining." He shifted his weight and the helmet, and reached into his pocket.

Before she could react, he pulled out a wad of bills and

flapped them back and forth, then pressed them against the window.

"I've got cash. I just need one room for one night."

Tracy sucked on her upper lip and frowned.

He was a good head and shoulders taller than her. Stronger, obviously.

Wet. Possibly tired.

He had the money, he needed a room, and she had an abundance of those—not to mention a bank account in need of an injection.

"It's one-twenty-five a night." She quoted what she thought was an outrageous fee for a room in a place still being renovated.

He leaned closer to the oval pane. "I'll take it."

She'd always thought you could tell a lot about a person by their eyes. Though this man's appeared to be open and honest, there was something else in them she recognized; something she'd seen looking back at her from the mirror lately—a deep, abiding sadness that no amount of positive pep talks could erase.

That underlying sadness moved her more than the fact that there were day laborers to pay tomorrow and additional paint to buy, not to mention extra bedding and linens on order. At the rate she was going, she'd have very little money left to fall back on if the Heartbreak didn't immediately take off.

She wasn't exactly desperate. Not yet anyway. Besides, *desperate* wasn't a word she ever used. It conjured up hopelessness and despair. She certainly wasn't hopeless or desperate. She was still determined to start over, to make something of the Heartbreak.

And she could certainly use the extra cash.

She was going to have to act like an innkeeper sooner or later. Why not start tonight?

She pasted on a big smile, opened the door, and indicated the torn-up lobby with a flourish and a little too much exuberance.

"Welcome to the Heartbreak Hotel. You're our first official guest."

2

Wed

13th

5:00

— Nobon
CPL
2.2000